"Deliciously real, modern, hot, and funny, Lorelei James delivers a book that will make you smile, swoon, and sigh."　　—*New York Times* bestselling author Katy Evans

PRAISE FOR THE NOVELS
OF LORELEI JAMES

"Filled with unforgettable characters, fiery passions, and an all-encompassing love story, it's a must read."
　　　　　　　—Tara Sue Me, *New York Times* bestselling author
of *The Exhibitionist*

"Her sexy cowboys are to die for!"
　　　　　　　—Maya Banks, *New York Times* bestselling author
of *Darkest Before Dawn*

"Sweet, seductive, and romantic . . . an emotional ride filled with joy, angst, laughs, and a wonderful happily-ever-after."
　　　　　　　—Jaci Burton, *New York Times* bestselling author
of *Love After All*

"[James] never forgets to bolster the story with plenty of emotional power."　　　　　　　—*Publishers Weekly*

"[A] fascinating read."　　　　　　　—*RT Book Reviews*

What You Need

THE NEED YOU SERIES

LORELEI JAMES

A SIGNET BOOK

SIGNET
Published by New American Library,
an imprint of Penguin Random House LLC
375 Hudson Street, New York, New York 10014

This book is an original publication of New American Library.

First Printing, January 2016

For more information about Penguin Random House, visit penguin.com.

ISBN 978-0-451-47755-2

Printed in the United States of America
10 9 8 7 6 5 4 3 2

Designed by Kelly Lipovich.

Penguin
Random
House

Prologue

BRADY

The first time I saw her, I nearly walked into a wall.

Not the behavior expected from the CFO of a multi-billion-dollar corporation.

And not the behavior I wanted the willowy blonde with the killer legs to witness. I'd suffered through too many years of being the gangly, bumbling, tongue-tied twerp to even approach her. Even now, when supposedly I was one of the most eligible bachelors in the Twin Cities, I erred on the side of acting aloof.

So as far as she knew, I hadn't taken notice of her at all.

But I had. Had I *ever*.

We'd crossed paths maybe . . . half a dozen times since I'd first set eyes on her in the lobby of Lund Industries.

Ten months later I still didn't know her name.

I didn't even know which department she worked in.

It was information I could've easily accessed, given my

last name was on the letterhead of the company that employed her. But in my mind, that might be misconstrued as borderline stalking behavior. I wasn't opposed to using my position to take shortcuts, but with her somehow that seemed like cheating.

But I did know a couple of things about her.

She was brusque, especially around upper-level management.

She had a husky laugh that she shared only with her coworkers.

A laugh I'd heard thirty seconds ago.

So the mystery blonde worked on this floor, in my department.

Interesting.

Before I headed toward her cubicle, I made damn sure I knew where all the walls were, because nothing was going to trip me up this time.

One

—

LENNOX

"**W**hat's *he* doing in our department?"

I glanced up from my computer, knowing even before I saw the suit at the end of the hallway who garnered the reverent tone from my coworker Sydney. I had the same reverence for the man; however, I did a much better job at masking it.

"Oh hell, here he comes. How do I look?" she whispered.

"You know the only thing that matters to him is if you look busy."

Sydney smoothed her hair. "Lennox, lighten up. And ignore me while I busily and silently compose sonnets to that man's everything, because he is the total package."

I laughed—longer than I usually did. "Go for it, Syd. I'll just be over here, you know, doing my *job* while you're waxing poetic about him." I returned my focus to spell-checking my notes from this morning's meeting. I knew I had a misspelled or misused word, but I couldn't find the damn thing.

"Wait. He's stopping to talk to Penny," Sydney informed me.

I felt a slight sneer form on my lips. Of *course* he's stopping to talk to Perky Penny—she hadn't earned that nickname from her disposition. Even I couldn't keep my eyes off her pert parts—which she kept properly covered in deference to the dress code at Lund Industries. But I knew that given the chance, she'd proudly display them as if she worked at Hooters.

Wouldn't you?

Nope. Been there, done that.

Sydney muttered and I ignored her, hell-bent on finding the mistake. I leaned closer to the computer monitor, as if that would help. *Ah, there it is.* I highlighted the word in question. Had he meant to say disperse? Or disburse? And was there enough difference in the definitions to warrant a call for clarification?

Without checking the dictionary app on my computer, I said, "Sydney. You were an English major. What's the difference between *disperse* and *disburse*?"

"*Disburse* means to pay out money. *Disperse* means to go in different directions," a deep male voice answered.

I lifted my gaze to see none other than Brady Lund himself, the CFO of Lund Industries, looming over my desk.

Outwardly I maintained my cool even as I felt my neck heating beneath the lace blouse I wore. I picked up a pen and ignored the urge to give the man a once-over, because I already knew what I'd find: Mr. Freakin' Perfect. Brady Lund was always impeccably dressed, showcasing his long, lean body in an insanely expensive suit. He was always immaculately coiffed—his angular face smoothly shaven, his thick dark hair artfully tousled, giving the appearance of boyish charm.

As if a shark could be charming.

My coworkers and I had speculated endlessly about whether the CFO plucked his dark eyebrows to give his piercing blue eyes a more visceral punch. And whether he practiced raising his left eyebrow so mockingly. For that reason alone I avoided meeting his gaze.

Okay, that was not the only reason. I didn't make eye contact because the man defined hot, smart and sexy.

But he also defined smug—half the time. I wanted to ask if he job-shared with an evil twin, but I doubted he'd laugh since he had no sense of humor, from what I'd heard.

Aware that he awaited my response, I said, "Thank you for the clarification, Mr. Lund."

"I shouldn't have to clarify that since you've worked here for—what, ten months? Financial terms should be familiar to you by now."

He was chastising me? First thing? My mouth opened before my brain screamed, *STOP*. "I've been employed here for almost a year, actually. And, sir, I'll remind you that just because the office temps department is located on the sixth floor—one of the five floors that are the providence of the financial department—we floaters don't specifically work *only* for the Finance department at Lund Industries. We also float between Human Resources, Marketing, Development and Acquisitions, as well as Legal."

"Explain what you mean by *floaters*."

"You had absolutely no idea that our small department exists, let alone what we do, did you?" I said tartly.

I heard Sydney suck in a sharp breath next to me. "What she means is that since as CFO you have an executive assistant and don't normally utilize the services of the office temps—also known as *floaters*—you wouldn't personally be aware of the breadth of our responsibilities," Sydney inserted diplomatically. "Our department is supervised by Personnel."

"Indeed. Then, please, enlighten me on which department you're transcribing that document for?"

"Marketing."

"Mind if I take a look?" Then he sidestepped my desk and sidled in behind me.

My body went rigid as he literally looked over my shoulder. I wasn't as disturbed by the thought he might see something I had done wrong as I was by his close proximity. His *very close* proximity, since I could feel the heat of his body and was treated to a whiff of his subtle cologne.

He put his hand over mine on the mouse and murmured, "Pardon," as he completely invaded my space. I didn't move because it'd be my luck if I shifted my arm and elbowed the CFO in the groin.

Three clicks and two huffed breaths later, he retreated. "I apologize. I understand your confusion. Marcus in Marketing misused the word. It should be *disburse*. Nice catch."

"That's my job."

"Since it's a formal request, Marcus will have to correct it before you can pass it on to Legal. If you'll give me the original paperwork, I'd be happy to drop it off in Marcus's office on my way to my meeting."

"Thank you, sir, for the offer. But company protocol requires me to deliver the paperwork directly to Marcus—Mr. Benito."

His shoes were so silent I didn't hear him move. One second he was behind me; the next he stood in front of me. "A real stickler for the rules, aren't you?"

"Yes, sir." I finally met his gaze. "With all due respect, how do I know this isn't some sort of performance review pretest?"

His lack of a smile indicated he wasn't amused.

But I didn't back down; I needed this job. It was the first job I'd ever had where I wasn't slinging drinks or scrubbing toilets. Besides, the CFO—of all people—should be aware of the rules.

"Bravo, Miss Greene—sorry, that's an assumption on my part. Or is it Mrs. Greene?"

"No, sir. Ms. Greene is fine. But I prefer to be called Lennox."

Then Mr. Freakishly Perfect bestowed the mother lode of smiles; his lush lips curved up, his dimples popped out and the lines by his eyes crinkled. "Well, Lennox, please see that Marcus—Mr. Benito—is aware of his error before day's end, because I *will* follow up on this."

"Yes, sir."

He nodded and started down the hallway.

I clenched my teeth to keep my jaw from dropping. Not just from the weird interlude, but because the man looked as good from the back as he did from the front.

"Holy shit." Sydney breathed after she was sure he'd gone. "What was that?"

"No idea."

"Lennox. He knows your name."

"Of course he knows my name. It's right here on my desk." Working as a floater meant my nameplate went everywhere with me, but on the days I was at my desk I usually didn't bother putting it out.

Aren't you glad you bothered today?

"Come on. He was fishing for information on whether you were single."

I groaned, hating that Sydney wouldn't let this go. "So, now he knows . . ."

"Maybe he'll ask you out," she said with a drawn-out sigh.

"Maybe you should put some of that creative thinking into your report," I retorted, and got back to work.

BRADY

"Jenna. Could you come in when you have a free moment?"

I didn't wait for my admin to answer. I just poked the intercom button off and spun around in my chair. Not even the forty-fourth-floor view of downtown Minneapolis held my interest.

Restlessness had dogged me the past several months. I kept waiting for it to abate, for something to occur that required my full focus. But nothing had happened either professionally or personally. I just continued to drift along, waiting for . . . what, exactly?

Your life to begin?

Jenna knocked twice and walked in. Why she bothered to knock escaped me; there was no pause between the knock and her entrance. One time when I asked her why she knocked first, she said her Midwestern upbringing was too ingrained to just barge in. I warned her that someday she might barge in and find me in a delicate situation. She'd retorted that if I actually took the time to do something bad, raunchy or out of character, she deserved to be the first person to witness it.

"You rang, sir?"

Sir. Jenna refused to call me Brady. It was "sir," or "boss" or "Mr. Lund." She'd been my admin for two years and I spent more time with her than anyone else in my life. When

I was newly minted in my position as CFO, I'd equated her using my first name as a sign of our professional intimacy, whereas she saw using it as a sign of disrespect since she had fifteen years on me agewise.

"Yes. Forgive my ignorance, but how closely do you work with the office temps—the floaters?"

She sat in the high-back leather chair across from my desk. "Not often. If you've got a large presentation that requires assembling reams of paperwork, I'll ask for assistance. But they're usually spread so thin down there it's just easier to get Patrice to help out."

Patrice. She was my admin's secretary, which gave Patrice the false impression that she was somehow *my* undersecretary. And Patrice had made no bones about how much she'd like to be under me.

"Why do you ask?"

Because there's this prim blonde I'm hot for who intrigues the hell out of me. "I ended up down on the sixth floor and publicly showed my ignorance about what the term floater means as well as what the office temp job entails."

Jenna's eyes widened. "I imagine that went over well with their department."

"Not so much."

"What were you doing down by Personnel? Are you looking for a new secretary, boss?"

"I'll get you any secretary you want if you'll send Patrice packing," I said dryly.

"No deal. She's still afraid of me. Once she loses that fear, she'll slack off and I'll replace her."

"So that's how it works with you and your minion. I wondered."

"Back to the floaters. Did you find them lazing about or something?"

"No. And can't someone come up with a better term for their department than *floaters*?"

"If you want to be technical, sir, in the past that group of employees used to be called the 'secretarial pool.' They're permanent office workers who temporarily float to any department where additional help is needed, hence the term floaters."

"I still don't like it. Anyway . . . am I really that out of touch with this company that I didn't know about the existence of an entire group of employees?"

"First of all, boss, the number of employees working for Lund Industries in the Twin Cities is over five thousand—fifteen hundred employees work in this building alone. You don't know the minutiae of the dockworkers' jobs any more than you do the floaters in the office temp department. That doesn't make you out of touch. It makes the managers in those departments effective, because they're not coming to you with personnel problems."

"You should've gone into diplomacy."

"It's my job to remind you of yours—you cannot do it all and know it all, sir, though you are determined to try." She smirked. "There are some people in this company who claim the floating crew of office workers concept is outdated and they're proposing Lund do away with that department altogether and outsource temporary help when needed."

"From your tone, I take it you don't agree?"

Jenna pointed at my computer. "We have an IT department. They go to whatever department they're needed in. I don't see how the office temps are any different. Like with IT, it's important to keep hiring new secretarial workers because they're trained with the most recent technology."

"You've given this more than just a passing thought."

She shrugged. "My executive assistant title means 'secretary with more responsibilities at a higher wage,' so the office workers, floaters, secretaries—whatever you prefer to call them—are my sisters in arms. I get defensive when their abilities or importance is questioned."

Usually Jenna was so even-keeled. Her brittle attitude alarmed me, so I needed to keep a closer eye on the situation with her *sisters in arms*, regardless of whether it was my job. "Where'd you hear these rumors about disbanding the temp workers?" I held up my hand. "Forget I asked. I know you won't reveal your source. But I would ask, if you do hear anything else, to let me know so I can make sure Personnel handles it fairly." I disliked Anita Mohr, the head of Personnel. Human Resources fielded more issues involving her than all other employees in this building. But she was my uncle Archer's pet, so she had a weird immunity.

"Will do." Jenna stood. "That was all you needed to talk to me about, sir?"

"Yes."

"Then I'll remind you there's a meeting at three in the boardroom." She paused after opening the door. "And Maggie seemed really excited that your father has some kind of big opportunity for you."

I gave Jenna an arch look. "As my admin, the least you could do—"

"Huh-uh, boss. You're on your own with the craziness that is the Lund Board of Directors. Buzz me if you need anything else."

I glanced at my watch. Even for a Friday, it was too early to start drinking.

———

Maggie, who'd been my father's secretary for the past twenty years, was in deep conversation with my mother when I entered the anteroom to the boardroom. They both looked up and looked guilty as hell.

My eyes narrowed. "Who's in your crosshairs now?"

"It should be you," my mother cooed. "You are, as they say here, treading on thin water."

I knew better than to roll my eyes. My mother defined over-the-top, but any show of disrespect resulted in threats yelled in Swedish. Selka Jensen had come to the United States from Sweden over three and a half decades ago to work as a fashion model. She met my dad, fell in love and abandoned the land of lingonberries and Ikea. So it made zero sense that she still spoke with an accent that sounded like Zsa Zsa Gabor doing an impersonation of Natasha from the *Rocky and Bullwinkle* cartoons. And she mixed up idioms—on purpose, I suspected—so she could remind people she wasn't *from around here*. But she was a fiercely loving mother, a tireless supporter of community causes and devoted to my father above all else. It was a little freaky anytime I caught them making out like horny teenagers— thirty-five years of marriage hadn't cooled their ardor. They'd provided the blueprint for what a marriage should be, which was a blessing and a curse. A curse mostly because Mom constantly reminded me of my single status.

"You mean *skating on thin ice*?" I corrected.

"Yah." She bussed my cheek and then playfully tapped it. "My smart, handsome, successful son. Why is there no woman coming around to put smile on this gorgeous face, mmm? What good is all of this"—she gestured to the front of my body—"if you have no one to share it with?"

"I asked myself that exact same question."

"And?"

"And I came up with a reason. Eighty of them, actually."

She frowned. "You joke."

"No. I work eighty-plus hours a week."

"Mom, stop harassing him," my brother Walker said from the doorway. "Uncle M wants to get the meeting started."

"Fine. But I haven't forgotten where we are in this discussion," she said as she sauntered past me.

I focused on Maggie. "Tell me about this opportunity my father is going to present to me."

Maggie laughed. "I like me job, boy-o. I've no desire to get on the boss's bad side."

Hearing my mother's accent always brought out Miss Maggie's brogue. I wasn't opposed to playing dirty to learn the truth of the "opportunity" about to be heaped upon me.

She wagged her finger in my face. "Save whatever charmin' words be spillin' from that silver tongue of yours, lad. I've been immune to the Lund charm for nigh on two decades."

I set my palms flat on her desk and leaned in. "I've not got the charm gene, Miss Maggie, and you damn well know it. As a businessman I prefer to use incentives instead of flattery."

"And what kind of *incentive* would you be flatterin' me with, Mr. Lund?"

"A bottle of Midleton whiskey, distilled in County Cork. A rare bottle, lass. One wee nip and you'll swear Saint Peter himself came down and poured the heavenly spirit into your soul."

Maggie whapped me on the arm. "No charm, my arse, Brady Lund. Although your attempt at a puttin' an Irish lilt in that Yankee voice is laughable, I'll admit you've piqued my interest."

I grinned.

"But offer me something else. Your *da* gave me a bottle of Midleton for my birthday, so you'll have to do better on the bribery."

"A ticket to the Super Bowl when the Vikings finally make it in this century."

She snorted. "Oh, that's a pie-in-the-sky dream, with the lousy way those lads have been playin'. That's one favor I'd never be collectin' on, yeah?"

"Point for Miss Maggie." I threw a look at the conference room door. "What'll it take?"

"I don't need you to buy me anything, Brady Lund." She cocked her head. "But you could be doin' me a wee favor. Tit for tat, eh?"

"Name it."

"My young niece Siobhan is visitin' from Ireland. It'd be lovely if you could take her to dinner and a nightclub. Give her the true American experience. She's been stuck with me all week."

Shah-von. That had a sexy ring to it. "When?"

"Tomorrow night, since she's leavin' for California on Monday."

"Deal. Now what's the opportunity?"

Maggie leaned across the desk. "The boss man's given in to your ma's badgering about you getting out in the community more to represent the Lund name and he's givin' you the first choice of one of her pet projects. 'Choice' bein' the operative word, because you don't got one, but you—as the oldest—do get to choose first."

Great. "What are they?"

"First, an entire weekend helping her with the annual art sale, fund-raiser and ball for the Minnesota Arts Foundation. Seems that'd be the easy one, yeah? Not so, lad. She's plannin' on holdin' a bachelor auction as a fund-raiser, and she means to put you or your brothers or your cousins up on the podium for sale!"

"I'll pass on that one. What are my other options?"

"Being a runway model for a charity fashion show put on by Dayton's and the Minneapolis Art Institute."

I could just see them giving me nothing but a strategically placed canvas to wear. "Pass. Next?"

"Participating in activities for at-risk youth for the Lund Cares Community Outreach program. That one will give you more leeway, but since the commitment is for Saturdays when you're always buried in work, no one will ever be expectin' you to pick it."

My eyes narrowed. "This isn't some reverse psychology thing you and Mom cooked up?"

"So suspicious, but I can't say as I blame ya. God love yer ma, but she's got some barmy ideas."

I kissed her cheek. "Thank you. You're the best. What time should I pick up Siobhan?"

Her eyes danced. "Can ya send a car service for her? She'd get a right kick outta that."

That actually worked better for me, not having to make small talk at the door. And not letting Maggie witness first-hand how little charm I actually possessed when it came to chatting up women I didn't know. "Absolutely. Say . . . seven?"

"Perfect." Maggie gave me a push. "Get in there. Good luck."

Two

LENNOX

Friday night I slipped on my pajamas, made myself a mug of Lemon Zinger tea and cracked open my bookkeeping program on my laptop. I downloaded two weeks' worth of banking transactions—expenses and income—getting a giddy sense of satisfaction at seeing my once meager bank account growing, as well as my retirement fund. The fact I even had a retirement fund was still something to celebrate as proof that I had a real job with benefits and everything.

One more year and I would have enough money for a down payment for my own place. But for now I had a pretty sweet gig, living in a house instead of a cramped apartment.

Since my roommate, Kiley, had warned me she wouldn't be home tonight, I curled up on the couch in the living room and watched TV. After living on the road for almost a decade and then spending the next two years in school, I finally had time to catch up on all the TV shows I'd heard people talking about. Lately I'd been obsessed with *Dexter*, mostly because I'd met a lot of psychopaths, but none of them had that slightly warped moral compass—they'd all been just plain crazy.

My phone rang and I glanced at the caller ID. A number I didn't recognize showed on the screen. I was too curious to ignore it. "Hello?"

"Lenni, baby girl, how are you?"

I tensed up at hearing her fake cooing tone. I was twenty-eight—not eight. Not that she'd been much of a mother to me at that age either. "I'm fine. This is another new number."

"I was getting pissed that I hadn't heard from you in so long and I realized I'd forgotten to give you my new number."

We both knew I wouldn't have called her even if I'd had the number. But I could feign interest in her screwed-up existence for five minutes. "So what's up?"

"Me 'n' Billy Ray moved again."

Meaning: They faced eviction by skipping town in the middle of the night. "Where'd you end up?"

"Billy Ray's cousin promised him a job in Saint Augustine. That didn't pan out 'cause his cousin is a drunk. He got a lead on a job in Boca, so that's where we are now."

Last time I talked to her—eight or nine months ago—they were in Houston. I thought maybe she'd found a place to settle, but I should've known better. In the thirteen years since I'd left home, she'd flitted from man to man. Billy Ray had lasted the longest, at two years.

"It's expensive to live in Florida. Things have been really tight."

Was she seriously hitting me up for money? "Moving as often as you guys do costs a ton of money. Have you been able to find a job?"

"Billy Ray don't want me workin'—you know that. He

says it's his job to take care of me. I told him I could get hired at Hooters—god knows I've still got the kind of rack that'd earn me some big tips, and I'm still hot, for a forty-six-year-old broad."

My mother had been stunningly gorgeous in her younger years and refused to acknowledge that time hadn't been kind. In her head, and when she looked in the mirror, she saw what she wanted to. But that had always been the case with her. "Billy Ray wouldn't have a problem with your boobs being the focus of all that attention?"

"Nah. I know he'd be proud that his woman could still flaunt it." She paused and sighed heavily. "But it's hard. All this moving and him starting at the bottom every place he gets a job. And we've been living where there's such god-forsaken humidity that I've actually missed the snow and the cold."

Please. No. This couldn't possibly be a hint she wanted to return to Minnesota.

Then she leveled the boom. "So since I don't got a job, Billy Ray couldn't really complain if I packed up my car and went home to visit my baby girl. You have a couch your old mom could crash on, don't you?"

"Actually, no, I don't. The woman I'm renting from was very explicit about overnight guests—regardless if it's a boyfriend or a relative."

A harsh laugh exploded in my ear. "You just couldn't wait to say that, could you? Tell me that I'm not welcome to stay with you. Are you afraid that your bigwig friends at the bigwig job you bragged about will think less of you since your poor backwards mama ain't edjucated?"

Here we go. "First of all, you didn't ask to sleep at my desk. You asked to crash at my place, which is not the same thing. Secondly, trouble follows you. I don't need you making trouble for me at the first decent place I've lived since you were married to Rick. And trust me, I've rented some real shitholes over the years and you sure didn't ask to stay with me then."

Silence.

For a fraction of a second I felt guilty. But then she opened her mouth. "So you're turning your back on me, you bratty little bitch?"

Aw. I love you too.

"You're gonna throw Rick in my face at every turn? It's been thirteen years. You need to get over it."

"You need to understand I'll never get over it. You can't change the past and I won't ever forget it." My chest was heaving and I patted my back pockets for my pack of cigarettes, even though I'd quit smoking four years ago. That's what one five-minute phone call with her did.

"How many times have I said I was sorry?" She practically wailed.

"That's the thing. You've *never* said it. You've said everything from you're not perfect to you had regrets, but not once have you said you were sorry for upending my life. Not once."

"You're just another person who doesn't listen to me, Lennox. I've said it before." She sniffled. "You just didn't hear me."

Maybe she thought she'd said it in one of her drugged-up or drunk states, but I wouldn't forget something like that. Especially since she'd been more prone to shouting at me.

"That's why I left Rick. Because he didn't listen to me either. He didn't see me. I was just part of the furniture. Adam made me feel beautiful and worthy."

Just the mention of Adam's name caused me to shudder.

"You'll see," she said sharply. "It's hard for beautiful women like us, used to having every man look at us and want us, to have those men start looking elsewhere. After you cross into your thirties, the need for male approval consumes you to the point you don't act rationally."

That's you, not me—and it'll never be me. I couldn't even take the fact she'd called me beautiful as a compliment, because she said things like that only when she wanted something. "I doubt it. But whatever. Look, I brought work home with me"—such a lie—"and I need to get back to it. Take care." I hung up.

Then I got up and snagged a beer out of the fridge. I twisted off the cap and took a sip as I stared out the kitchen window that looked into the backyard.

I don't know what I expected to see, since it was completely dark outside. After the conversation with my mother I felt the darkness pulling me in.

What sucked about my family situation was that it hadn't always sucked. At age eighteen my mom and her best friend, Maxie, got jobs traveling with one of the big rock bands of the day, selling T-shirts and other stuff at the merchandise stand during the concerts. Mom began sleeping with a roadie—not the members of the band, as she'd planned. When the tour ended, she found out she was pregnant. My father took off. Six months later she gave birth to me.

Yeah, I understood she'd been just nineteen years old and a single mother. In a show of solidarity, Maxie stayed in the Twin Cities with her. They lived together—not that I remember any of that—until Mom married Rick when I was three.

Rick was a rock-solid, dependable guy and a decent provider. We lived in Burnsville, in a tiny house Rick had inherited from his grandmother. I'd had a lonely childhood—even being her only child hadn't made me interesting to my mother. She did her own thing and that usually didn't include me. After a while, her activities didn't include Rick either. The year I turned thirteen, my mom—who'd asked me to start calling her Lisa—scored a job as a cocktail waitress at a bar twenty miles from where we lived. Since Rick was a delivery-man for a grocery supply company, he was gone by five A.M. Some nights she didn't roll in until he'd left for work.

That was when everything fell apart. Mom and Rick started fighting. He accused her of sleeping around. She accused him of trying to turn her into a boring old woman. I still remember the nasty stuff they shouted at each other as I cowered in my single bed in the room next to theirs. Rick pleaded for her to go to counseling so they could save their marriage, but Mom refused. She was done with him.

One day I came home from school to find she'd packed all of our things in the back of her minivan. I remembered thinking it was sad, how few possessions she wanted to keep. She said we were going to stay with a friend until she'd sorted a few things out.

We lived with Maxie for a month. By month two, Mom informed me she'd fallen in love with Adam, a regular at the bar where she worked, and we moved into Adam's shitty trailer.

For the first six months, Mom sent me to stay with Rick on the weekends because she wanted to act like an unen-cumbered single woman. Although I'd lived with Rick most of my life, I'd never been allowed to call him Dad. He'd never really acted like my father; like my mom, he mostly ignored me, but at least he wasn't mean.

Adam defined low-class redneck trailer trash. He lived

in filth, half the time without electricity, and he kept my mother drunk or high so she could sexually service him whenever he demanded it. When I'd had enough, I informed Mom I was going to live with Rick permanently. So in my first rebellious move, I took the bus over to our old house, figuring there was little she could do.

Wrong.

She called Rick and threatened him with child abduction charges, which she could've made stick. Rick took me back to Adam's run-down trailer and I was devastated when he admitted that he legally had no claim on me because my mother had refused to let him adopt me. He was done with her and now he was done with me too.

What sliced me the deepest was my mother's childish reasoning about why she kept me from him; she was afraid I'd love Rick more than her. She hadn't been far off, because my resentment grew into hatred. She didn't give a shit about me and she couldn't stand to think that someone else did.

My life had gone from tolerable to horrible. I'd always been a straight-A student, but the change to the new school sent my grades spiraling. I started hanging out with the tough crowd—kids like me with a shitty home life. I clicked with a girl my age named Taylar, whose older brother, Travis, was in a band. The siblings were on their own after a bad family situation, which was why they let me crash with them most nights. I wasn't a leech, so on Friday and Saturday nights when the band had a gig at one of the local bars, Taylar and I did grunt work—hauling trash out, hauling ice in for the bartenders, cleaning bathrooms—and we were paid cash under the table.

I was in heaven.

I was also only fifteen.

During that time I rarely thought about my mom. So I hadn't realized I hadn't been to Adam's place in over three months, until the day my mother showed up at school looking for me.

The instant I saw the mean glint in her eye, I knew I'd have to lie about my whereabouts; she'd go after Taylar and Travis just as she'd gone after Rick. And luckily, a few times when my friends had been out of town, I'd stayed at a homeless shelter for runaway teens, so they had me on record.

So, on one hand, I was happy that the principal chewed my mom's ass for waiting so long to find out where I'd been. On the other hand, the obvious disconnect between me and my mom meant we were assigned a social worker. My schoolwork wasn't an issue. Neither was truancy. Since we qualified as low income, I got two free meals a day at school, so I didn't miss a day, because it was the only time I ate. I also didn't skip class, because the last thing I wanted was the school calling my mother and asking where I was.

The social worker warned us she'd make surprise checks, leaving me no choice but to be where my mom was—at least during the school week. I hated every second of being trapped in the cramped tin shoe box known as Adam's trailer.

But the worst part of living there was the creepy way Adam watched me. If I knew my mother wasn't there, I wouldn't go inside by myself. As soon as six o'clock Friday night rolled around, I lit out. Back to working in whatever bar Travis's band had scored a gig in. Back to crashing with Taylar and Travis.

That went on for the rest of the school year. When summer vacation rolled around, my social worker was reassigned and I was freed. Taylar and I found part-time jobs in the janitorial department at a nursing home. Since we worked only Monday through Thursday, we could still travel with the band on the weekends.

On the night of my sixteenth birthday I crossed three milestones. Travis popped my cherry. I got a tattoo. And I smoked pot for the first time.

It was the best summer of my life.

A talent management company had taken notice of Travis's band and had booked them on a six-month cross-country tour. Taylar's boyfriend was the band's drummer; she decided to drop out of school to travel with the band. They asked me to come along, but I had it in my head I needed to finish high school. Since Travis and Taylar weren't re-upping the lease on their apartment, I had only one place to go: back to the crappy reality I'd tried to avoid.

So it was no surprise that when I showed up at Adam's trailer two days prior to the start of my junior year, my mother was livid. Not because I'd been gone for three months, but because I'd come back.

Adam, the asshole, had actually acted decent for a change. I wouldn't say I'd misjudged him, but I wasn't afraid to be alone around him.

Mistake number one.

I'd been back only three weeks when Adam made a move on me. I told him when my mother found out she'd leave his sorry ass for good, and he attacked me. I got away with a split lip and bruises on my arms from where he'd tried to hold me down. I'd kneed him in the balls. When he howled in pain and released me, I ran out of the trailer. I hopped a bus to where my mom worked.

But the transit system was slower than Adam's car and he'd gotten there first. He told her I came on to him—and it hadn't been the first time. He claimed to be tired of me always taunting him about having a young piece of ass like mine instead of an old wrinkled one like hers. Of me trying to hurt my mother by using him to make her jealous. So when I kissed him, he grabbed me by the upper arms to push me away, and in a desperate move I grabbed his balls.

I watched my mother sweep her hand down Adam's arm in a show of support as she glared at me. Then she launched into a verbal attack so vicious I lost the ability to breathe. I'd never been so mortified as I was in that moment hearing what my mother really thought of me—in front of a bar full of people. Her parting shot was she'd beat the hell out of me if I didn't get out of her sight for good.

I didn't cry. I didn't react at all besides getting out of the bar. I figured I was safe for a few hours—likely they'd be celebrating about what a stand-up guy Adam was for spurning the advances of a horny sixteen-year-old girl—so I took a bus back to the trailer. I packed the few things I owned, called Taylar and hit the ATM for some traveling money. Then I hopped a Greyhound bound for Kansas City and joined the band. I stayed with Travis for only two years and spent the next seven years . . . wandering.

The neighbor's dog started barking, pulling me out of the memories I tried so hard to keep buried.

I owed my mother nothing, especially not a place to sleep, and definitely not a second thought. I drained my beer and turned on the TV.

Three

BRADY

Saturday night I waited outside the restaurant to meet Siobhan.

I'd worked all day. One of the perks of being CFO was my executive office had a private bathroom as well as a dressing room, where I kept several changes of clothes. I'd never voluntarily admit how many nights I've spent sleeping there after working until close to dawn the next day. Most people didn't know I'd been there all night; they just assumed I'd gotten in early.

I forced myself not to pace as I waited. I'd worn a blazer, not in an effort to impress but because October in Minnesota meant the weather could change from balmy to frigid in as little as an hour. What I had on wasn't club wear by any stretch, but I'd never grasped the need for a different look when hitting the bars.

My cousin Nolan constantly harassed me about dressing

like a stuffy old man. The pushy jackass had even brought his personal shopper into my office to stage an intervention. The guy seemed nice enough, if more enthusiastic about men's fashion and grooming than I was accustomed to. Plus, his personal clothing choices set off my warning bells. No fucking way was I ever wearing skinny jeans. Or a neon yellow shirt that would stop traffic on Hennepin Avenue. Or a fedora.

Nolan had given up on me. He'd sworn I'd have to beg him for help when I finally came to my senses.

As if that'd happen.

The black Lincoln Town Car pulled up to the curb and I pasted a smile on my face. The driver came around the back to open the door and a redhead stepped out.

A young redhead. Christ, the girl—and yes, I mean girl—looked barely legal. Then it occurred to me I'd never clarified why Maggie's niece was here. A horrid thought crossed my mind. What if this girl was a high school foreign exchange student?

Upon closer examination, I decided Siobhan was college aged. But it made no sense why Maggie had chosen me to be her niece's companion. I was easily a dozen years older than this girl. I had two younger brothers who were better suited.

You agreed to do this because you just had to know what opportunity your dad was springing on you. Maybe if you weren't such a control freak, you'd just go with the flow once in a while. Then you wouldn't be in the situation of having to card your fucking date.

I offered my hand. "Siobhan? I'm Brady Lund."

She sized me up. "Well, Mags din't tell me to expect an older gent."

Great.

"But I'm happy to meet you, Brady Lund, if for no other reason than to get out of me aunt's flat."

"Shall we go in?"

Siobhan glanced up at the marquee. "Fancy place, eh?"

"No, just a good steakhouse."

"Mags didn't tell you I'm vegetarian?"

I froze. "No, she didn't."

"No offense, but you'd better be comin' up with another place to chow down. Meat is murder and all that."

"Of course."

"I'll get the car back here." She let loose a piercing whistle that rivaled an air horn for loudness. When that didn't work, she stepped into the street and started waving her arms. She'd dressed like a street urchin in a skirt over leggings, heeled boots, a ruffled blouse and a long cardigan. I felt as if I'd stepped into a Dickens novel.

Right then, I should've gone with my gut instinct and called off the evening. Instead, I pulled her out of the street and said, "I have the car service number, so there's no need for that."

She rolled her eyes. "Whatever."

I took out my phone and typed "vegetarian restaurants Uptown Minneapolis" into the search engine. "There are five places around here. Would you like to choose?"

"Are any of them within walkin' distance to Steel Balls, the club I wanna hit after?"

Steel Balls? "I have no idea. And what makes you think that going to that club is on the agenda tonight?"

"*Agenda?* Dude. You are uptight. This club is right hard to get into, but I thought a guy with your connections—"

"My connections?"

"Business bigwig, flush with a lot o' the green."

"Well, you thought wrong." I scrolled through the restaurant list. "There's sushi or Indian a block either way."

"Sushi."

I hit the walk option on the map and spent our short stroll staring at the cursor blinking on the map image, half hoping I'd trip off the curb. Surely an ambulance call was a valid reason for ending a date.

I held the door open for her.

"Now this is more like it."

The restaurant had a small sushi bar in the middle of the room and tables scattered throughout.

The hostess appeared. "Two for dinner?"

"Yeah, and put us close to the bar, will ya?" Siobhan said.

She stated that as if it would be a drunken free-for-all.

Like hell.

After we were seated, I said, "No bullshit, Siobhan. How old are you?"

"Twenty-one. Why?"

She was lying; I was sure of it. "Because if you order a drink, they *will* card you. America isn't like Ireland."

"Hey. What's that supposed to mean?"

"Like you don't know Irish bars don't really give a damn if you're only fifteen. As long as you have money and don't act like a pain in the arse, they'll serve you."

"Been to Ireland, have ya?"

"Twice."

That surprised her.

The waitress came by to take our drink orders. I opted for a Leinenkugel Red Lager.

"That's sounds good. I'll have the same—but bring me two. Bein' from Ireland, one gets tired of drinkin' Guinness. Although you Yanks serve it way too cold." She winked at the waitress.

The Asian waitress smiled. "Yes, these Yanks try and improve on everything, don't they?"

Then the two of them launched into a discussion about all the foreign things Americans had gotten wrong.

When I took out my phone, the waitress got the hint to skedaddle and fill our drink order.

"That was rude," Siobhan said.

I tucked my phone in my pocket. "Not as rude as your comment about Americans and their misuse of the word football."

She smirked. "Got your back up, eh?"

"Since my brother plays for the Vikings? Yes."

"One of the more hapless teams in American football, I've heard."

Enough. "How about you don't malign a true sport that you don't understand and I won't have a hard go at your beloved footie, eh?"

Her eyes flared with anger. "You're more than a bit of a puss face."

"I don't know what that means. But I can't imagine it was a compliment."

"'Twasn't. Least you aren't completely daft. Ah, perfect timing," she said to the waitress as she dropped off the beers.

Siobhan gulped her first beer and leaned back in her chair, daring me to say anything.

I clamped my teeth together. The little brat wasn't getting the best of me.

I hoped the service was fast, because I couldn't wait for this to be over.

She probably feels the same. Story of your dating life, isn't it?

LENNOX

Of all the sushi joints in town . . . Brady Lund had wandered into mine.

Well, not mine as in I owned it, but mine as in my roommate, Kiley, and I splurged every other week and had a girls' night out at the Sake Palace. Since we'd been coming here so long we were considered regulars—and I didn't like that he was on my turf.

With a date.

I checked out the redhead sitting across from him at his cozy table for two. Not at all the type of woman I imagined Brady Lund would go for.

Woman? She's, like, twelve. Maybe he's babysitting.

I snorted. That'd be the day.

Kiley glanced up. "What's so funny?"

"Nothing."

"Then why the self-amused snort?"

I hated that she knew my tells. I leaned in. "Don't look—" I put my hand on her shoulder to keep her from whipping her head around. "Seriously, *don't* look, but the CFO of Lund Industries is here with a date."

"Where?"

"Back and to your right."

Kiley shrugged her shoulder to dislodge my hand. "I hate it when you do that. I can be discreet."

I bit back another snort.

"This is the clueless dude who didn't know about the temp department?"

"Yes."

"The one who is so freakin' gorgeous that you could orgasm just from looking at him?"

"Kiley! Shut up! I never said that."

She poked her chopsticks at me. "But you've thought about it and it's all over your face whenever you talk about him."

I snatched up a piece of pickled ginger and popped it into my mouth.

"So, since I can't look, give me a play-by-play on what's going on."

"They just got their drinks. I can't believe Jailbait is old enough to drink."

Kiley choked on her sake. "Jailbait?"

"She looks really young."

"Maybe it's his niece."

I shook my head. "Neither of his brothers nor his sister is married."

"Scary that you know how many siblings he has, Lennox."

"I work for Lund Industries, so I know about the entire family because that's part of my job," I retorted. "His sister, Annika, is in the PR division of Lund, his brother Walker does something in construction, and his other brother, Jensen, plays for the Vikings."

Kiley's eyes widened. "No shit? Jens 'The Rocket' Lund is his brother?"

"I didn't know you were a football fan."

"I wasn't until he started playing. Man. Have you *seen* The Rocket's ass in his football pants? It really emphasizes his *Tight End* position. He shoulda got the Heisman for that alone."

I barely resisted smacking myself in the forehead. But then I saw Jailbait lean back in her chair, with her arms crossed over her chest. Mr. CFO ran his hand through his hair. Neither of them looked like they were having a good time.

Why that caused a spark of happiness made no sense.

Jailbait stood, grabbed her beer and headed to the sushi station.

"Hello?" Kiley snapped her finger in front of my face.

"Sorry." I refocused on my friend. "Before I got distracted by the orgasm generator"—I grinned at her—"you were telling me about your newest project."

"I was telling you about it because I need your help." Kiley set down her chopsticks, serious face in place. "One of the centers my kids attend got closed down because of drug activity. While I'm glad the cops are following through with their promise to get rid of the troublemakers, it feels like these kids are being punished. So if they've got nowhere to go on Saturday, and nothing productive to do, what do you think will happen to them?"

My roommate was passionate about "her" kids and the work she did with them. That was part of the reason I adored her, since it took a special person to see the potential in kids who couldn't count on family to raise them. "They become even more at risk."

"Exactly. A couple of them have already been in juvenile more than once."

"How can I help?"

"Once we nail down a place to have an activity outside of their neighborhood, I'd love it if you'd hang out with them. If they give you shit, you can share your success story."

Success story. Oh, it was a helluva story, all right. I was still working on the success part. "You let me know when and where."

Kiley squeezed my hand. "You're such an awesome person, Lennox. I'm so glad you answered my Craigslist ad."

"Me too." My last year of school my roommate had flaked out on me and decided spontaneously to move to Iowa with her boyfriend. Since the apartment was in her name and the lease was up, I'd been pretty much screwed. Even though the place had been a total dive, it'd still cost more money each month than I could swing alone. And I would've had to go through an entire approval process to take over the lease, in addition to forking over first and last month's rent. So I'd had no choice but to look for a new living arrangement.

I'd always gotten a kick out of reading the *City Pages* ads for roommates, but those "Must love craft beer and quinoa" roommate ads were less funny when I needed a place to stay. On a whim I checked Craigslist and saw Kiley's ad for a roommate to share a house. The private bathroom and second-floor sitting area trumped the requirement for snow shoveling and summer yard maintenance. I'd shown up in the area known as Dinkytown and fallen in love with the older house.

The first month Kiley and I were respectful of each other's spaces. She'd bought the house after her sister assured her that she'd pay half the mortgage—then she'd left her high and dry. Making the mortgage payment on her own had proven difficult since she was just starting out as a social worker. But our polite distance around each other changed the night she'd come home from work a complete mess after one of the kids in her program had been killed in a drug deal gone bad. Problem was, the kid wasn't buying or selling drugs; he'd been walking his little sister home from the playground because they lived in a dangerous area, and he ended up with a bullet to the chest when a gun accidentally went off.

That night she and I downed a bottle of wine, swapped life stories and then started hanging out regularly. What I loved most about Kiley was that she didn't need a man to validate her. So many women my age felt like failures if they didn't have a boyfriend, whereas Kiley and I were open to a relationship if the right guy came along, but we were both focused on our careers. I loved that we were beyond the pressure of heading out to the meat market bars every weekend in hopes of a hookup.

"What's the hottie CFO up to now?" Kiley prompted, pulling me out of my ruminations.

I glanced over at the sushi bar. Lund and his date were chowing down on sushi as if they had somewhere else to be. They weren't talking—at all. "Looks like they're ignoring each other."

"I think you should go over and say hello."

My pulse jumped. "What? Why would I do that?"

"Because it'd be fun to see if he's embarrassed about the age of his date."

"You're evil."

She shrugged. "Maybe he'll try and explain her."

"Maybe I don't care."

"Uh-huh. You don't care and that's why your gaze keeps darting over there every five seconds."

When she phrased it that way, I felt a little pathetic.

"Think of it this way: You're approaching him first, so the control of the situation is yours. If he admits he saw you in here but didn't acknowledge you in any way, then you know he's a tool. If he genuinely seems surprised—"

"Then he'll think I want something from him, when I don't."

Kiley sighed. "You are using skewed logic. But whatever. You're too chicken to do it anyway."

I watched as Jailbait got up and headed to the ladies' room. She'd just given me a chance to casually swing by and say hello. I pushed my chair back and stood.

"Thatta girl!" Kiley said. "Go get 'im, tiger."

Lund was the tiger. He'd probably eat me alive.

So in a total chickenshit move, when I was within four feet of him, I cut around the side of the sushi bar and headed for the bathroom.

I swore I heard Kiley clucking behind me.

I used the facilities, and when I stepped out of the stall, I froze.

Jailbait stood in front of the mirror, affixing piercings to her face. She now sported a nose piercing, two nose rings, as well as snakebite piercings in her lip. I continued to watch as she shed her skirt, revealing skintight leggings. Beneath the blouse was a Sex Pistols T-shirt, strategically ripped and then held together with a row of safety pins.

At that point, I was helpless to look away. I washed my hands, trying to discreetly watch her apply thick black eyeliner to her eyelids and then outline her lips.

"What're you lookin' at, eh?"

She had an accent I couldn't place. British? Irish? Scottish? And because the "What're you lookin' at?" question annoyed me, I didn't temper my answer. "Your outfit. Wondering if you're going to an eighties costume party. Or if I somehow missed the fashion update that punk style from that era was back in style."

For a moment anger sparked in her eyes. Then she grinned. "Ballsy one, ain't ya?"

I shrugged.

"Punk never went out of style where I'm from."

"Where's that?"

"Great Britain—specifically I was born in Ireland and went to uni in London."

"Ah."

She pulled a long studded belt out of her bag and wrapped

it around her hips and waist. Then she attached studded bracelets to each wrist. "Look, you seem like an okay lass, so could I get you to do me a wee favor?"

"What?" I said cautiously.

"There's a man sitting out there. Can't miss him, right stodgy as hell. If you look closely enough, you might see a stick up his arse."

"What about him?"

"Tell him I left, yeah?"

"Wait. Is he your date?"

"Hard to believe, ain't it? Him 'n' me on a bloody date."

Hard to believe indeed. "Why are you ditching him?"

She snorted. "Because I don't like old dudes."

My eyes narrowed at her. "How old are you?"

"Twenty-one. Can you believe the arsehole asked to see me ID? After the bloody waitress didn't card me? What kind of bastard does that?"

A smart one. "Why'd you agree to go out with him if you think he's too old for you?"

"My auntie set up the date—though now I know why she was very careful not to call it a date, eh? But I can see why he agreed to go out with me. I bet the poor bugger never gets his pole waxed. I might've given him a ride because he is right nice to look at, but he's such a cold wanker."

Wow. Harsh assessment of Brady Lund. But how could she have come to such a fast judgment about him when they'd spent less than an hour together?

"Anyway. Tell him I bailed, yeah? And I'll find me own way back to Auntie's." With that, she sailed out of the bathroom.

I followed her and watched her yell at the kitchen workers before she bolted out the back door.

Freakin' awesome.

But there was no way I could tell the CFO of a multibillion-dollar company that his blind date had dumped him.

I carefully kept out of his line of sight as I returned to the table. When I told Kiley what'd happened in the bathroom, she had no problem switching seats with me. So I didn't see when he'd left. I only know he was gone when I turned around.

BRADY

Sunday afternoon I got that familiar buzz of excitement when I entered the stadium. Vikings home games had always been fun, even before Jensen started playing pro ball. I was damn proud of my youngest brother for getting to live his dream.

I swiped my access pass in the key card machine in the elevator and slumped against the wall with my eyes closed.

Last night's events pushed to the forefront of my mind, no matter how hard I'd tried to forget them.

After Siobhan had slammed her first two beers, she hadn't turned into a sweet and charming Irish lass. She proceeded to tell me everything that was wrong with me.

I had a superior air that made me a wanker.

My clothing style made me a wanker.

Even my hairstyle made me a wanker.

All the time she was lecturing me about the evils of money and my sense of entitlement, she ordered the five most expensive sushi pieces on the menu.

Then she ditched me.

Her ditching me didn't affect me as much as her assumptions. After I'd demanded proof of her age, she'd guessed mine to be a full decade older than my thirty-two years. I'd looked at her at one point and wondered what I'd done to piss Maggie off so badly that she'd sic this horrible creature on me.

At first, I hadn't noticed she'd left. I had another beer, ate more sushi and checked e-mail on my phone. So when I looked at my watch, it surprised me to see thirty minutes had passed by.

I knew it made me a jerk to feel relieved that she'd left. I was just glad that no one I knew had been around to witness the debacle. I'd lived through public humiliations from various women throughout the years and it never got any easier.

Still, I wasn't a total dick. I'd called Maggie to let her know that Siobhan would make it back there on her own steam.

Maggie had let out a litany of curse words—then she'd apologized profusely. So I'd felt entitled to ask what she'd been thinking, setting us up in the first place. Maggie finally admitted she'd picked me because I was safe, gentlemanly and solid—meaning as bland as oatmeal—and not only would I not take advantage of her niece, chances were slim Siobhan would be attracted to me.

I'd come away from that conversation feeling worse than before.

Some men are confident in their attractiveness to the opposite sex. I've never been that guy. I was the shy, dorky kid in junior high. It was even worse for me in high school. I stayed in that awkward stage—a long-necked beanpole with acne and glasses—until the last month of my junior year, when Jessica Lewis started talking to me. Being a clueless dumbass, I had the foolish hope that Jessica, a girl who was moderately popular and more cute than pretty, had seen beyond my wimpy, skinny, zitty outer shell. And she had seen beyond it all right—she was looking at dollar signs. Jessica wanted to go to prom in style, and who better to take her than a Lund? She insisted on eating dinner that night at the exclusive club my parents belonged to. She insisted on taking a limo to the dance.

But once we got to the dance, she refused to dance with me. She said the prom was lame and if I wanted to get with her at all, I'd invite her and some of her friends to my big fancy lake house that I'd bragged about. Hormones overcame common sense. We left the dance; she didn't even hold my hand. The limo dropped us and eight of her closest friends off on the road in front of the lake house—a guesthouse in the Lund Compound—that was still closed against the endless Minnesota winter. But I had a key. No sooner had I opened the place up than two dozen more people appeared. Booze flowed freely after they found the liquor cabinet.

And the whole time I heard these people, who I'd gone to school with for three years, asking who the house belonged to and the response was always the same: that weird rich kid.

That weird rich kid who wasn't even memorable enough to have a name.

So I was at my first high school party, in my own house, and I was still persona non grata.

Not cool to cry in front of anyone at age seventeen, so I went outside. But that proved to be an even bigger mistake. Someone had opened the window in the bedroom, presumably thinking blowing pot smoke through the screen would somehow mask it. It didn't. The pot smoke and their voices drifted to where I sat alone on the back deck.

"Jessica, stop hogging the joint! You never take that many hits."

"I'm fine. It's a special occasion. It's prom!"

"You might not say that when you're out of it and your boyfriend takes advantage of you and starts feeling you up."

"Eww, Carly—he is *not* my boyfriend and that is too sick to even think about!" Jessica declared.

"What? That's probably the only way he'll get anything. You'd have to be passed out."

Jessica laughed. "Or maybe be totally stoned."

Everyone laughed.

I thought my cheeks couldn't burn any hotter, but they did.

Someone asked, "So that weird rich kid is your boyfriend?"

"Hell no."

"But you went to prom with him," Carly pointed out.

"So? Doesn't mean I'm gonna do anything *else* with him. Yuck. I don't even like him. But I knew since he'd never had a girlfriend and he's rich that he'd go all out for prom to try and make me think he was cool."

"So, are you gonna be his girlfriend now?" some dude said and made kissing noises.

"Fuck off, Tyler. No. Gross. I can't imagine rubbing against his zitty face if he kissed me."

"Hey, he's rich. Maybe he can get plastic surgery to fix his face."

More laughter.

I'd had enough. I cut through the grounds and ran the half mile to my house. Once I was in the sanctity of my room, I ditched the tux. Then I dialed 911 and reported a break-in on the Lund property.

I finished out the last two weeks of school at home. I changed to an all-boys prep school for my senior year.

So over the years I'd learned to be more cautious, but

rejection still had the power to send me spiraling back to that awful night.

"Mr. Brady!"

The doors to the box were open and our regular security guy manned the door. "Burt. Are we over capacity in the suite yet?"

"Not even close. Miss Annika didn't arrive with her usual entourage today. And I believe Mr. Archer isn't here because his wife is feeling poorly."

I walked into the private box. Game day meant the Lund jerseys came out. No one in the family was exempt from wearing them. Not only were we a supportive bunch; we were suspicious too.

My mother was the first one to greet me. And by her somber look and long hug, I knew Maggie had filled my parents in on last night's events. I didn't blame her; Siobhan hadn't considered that her actions might put her aunt's job in jeopardy. Not that it would—my dad wouldn't survive a day without Maggie running his daily affairs—but it'd been a poor decision on Siobhan's part, especially after Maggie had gone out of her way for the thankless girl.

"Brady," my uncle Monte boomed. "Come and meet some associates from Texas."

Warily, I eyed their Texans jerseys. At least they weren't Cowboys fans. We exchanged pleasantries and Monte let me drift away because I could tell he was in business mode.

I snagged a beer and wandered over to the window, watching as the stadium filled in with a sea of purple and gold.

Only a few minutes passed before my brother Walker stood next to me. "Oddsmakers are saying this game will be too close to call."

"It'll be interesting to see if Jensen plays."

"Second half, I'm betting."

"Did you talk to him this morning?"

"Briefly. He said they're confident they'll win this one."

I snorted. "PR. He always says that. Their record of one and three doesn't back up that statement."

"No shit."

An arm snaked around my waist. Another one snaked around Walker as our sister, Annika, inserted herself between us. "Hey, thing one. Hey, thing two."

"Hey, brat. What's up? Where are all your hangers-on?"

"Why is everyone saying that? I don't always surround myself with a million people."

Walker and I exchanged a look over her blond head and we both laughed. "Right."

"Can't a girl just spend quality time with her family without being grilled about it?"

"In this family? No."

She faced us, putting her back to the window.

Our little sister took after Mom—she was undeniably gorgeous. Annika had done some modeling in the Twin Cities, mostly to appease our mother. For being raised the daughter of a fashionista, Annika didn't always present a flawless appearance. Oh, she could. When she was on, the girl was on fire. But when she wasn't running PR for Lund Industries, she took the term "dressing down" farther than our flannel-shirt-and-faded-jeans-loving brother, Walker, did.

Walker said, "Want a beer, sis?"

"Sure. Leinie Bock if there are any left."

"Brady?"

"Sure." I kept my focus on Annika, because something clearly troubled her.

After Walker left, I said, "What's on your mind?"

"I'm tired of Mom harassing me."

"What's she harassing you about?"

"You name it, I've screwed it up somehow. That's why I didn't bring anyone today. With the rate she's been going the last week, she'd tear into me in front of my friends."

"You know Mom wouldn't do that." My gaze searched her face. She looked more tired than usual. "What's this really about?"

She shot a look over to where our parents stood. "Not here. It actually has to do with work. Can we go to lunch next week?"

"Sure, but since it's your idea, you're buying."

That got me a quick smile. "Deal. I also pick the place."

That meant I'd be eating quinoa salad or quiche or some girlie shit. "On second thought . . ."

Walker returned with beer.

"Three minutes to kickoff," Dad announced.

We took our seats.

At the end of the first quarter the Vikings were up three to zero. Jensen hadn't played.

A wild second quarter put the Vikings ahead seventeen to ten.

My cousin Nolan finally appeared at the start of the second half with a skinny blonde. But since Jensen played the third quarter, I paid attention to the game, ignoring Nolan when he motioned me over.

When the fourth quarter started and the Texans had possession, Nolan approached me where I stood at the bar by myself. "Brady. Got a second?"

I faced him. "Sure." I angled my head toward the blonde. "You got her to wear a jersey? I'm impressed."

"Just had to show her firsthand how much fun it was for both of us when I put it on her." He grinned. "She's something, huh?"

"Yeah. Where'd you meet her?"

"Out and about."

His standard response. For once, I didn't give him shit about it.

Nolan leaned in. "Look, I'm going to do something that I swore I never would."

"That's a short list, cuz," I said before taking a sip of my cocktail. "What are you going to do?"

"Offer you my help."

"With what?"

"With showing you how to cut loose, find some loose chicks, and demonstrating how to have a life outside of work. It's time. Actually, it's past time."

I wasn't expecting that at all. Then I knew. My face heated. "Goddamn Selka said something to you about what happened to me last night, didn't she?"

He nodded. "I thought maybe you'd come to me long before this. But you haven't and your mom is worried, Brady."

Fucking awesome.

"I'm worried too. So are your brothers and Ash. It's been going on for too long. Now you're working seven days a week."

I raised a brow. "I'm here at the game, aren't I?"

Nolan poked me in the chest. "Because Selka would skin you alive if you weren't. And you'd be talking business if we didn't have the 'no work talk' rule at family things. It just reminds me that you weren't always all about work all the time. It changed—you changed—when you set your sights on the CFO position." He swirled the ice cubes around in his glass as he studied me. "But you were—what, twenty-eight?—when you started down that path."

Wrong. I'd made that decision at age eighteen after a

particularly nasty conversation with Grandpa Lund. "Around thereabouts."

"You're thirty-two. You've been CFO two years. I don't gotta tell you what a bang-up job you're doing. You hear that every damn day from your dad, my dad and Uncle Monte. But that doesn't mean you should work even harder. That means you should take the time to enjoy the station you've reached at your young age." He pointed at our cousin Ash. "Between us, Ash had this same kind of crisis situation two years into his stint as COO too."

"It's not a crisis situation," I said with an edge. "And this has nothing to do with a woman. He was messed up during that time about Veronica." My cousin's ex had been a real piece of work. No one had been sorry to see the ass end of her except for Ash.

"But it's a woman—a blind date who ditched you—that has you here looking like a pathetic bum and drinking. But I suppose that's better than you working." Nolan plucked the half-finished drink from my hand and passed it to the bartender. "I'm done watching you wallow. Your life is about to change, my friend. Friday night you, me, Walker and Ash are going out."

I opened my mouth.

Nolan shook his head. "You don't get to know where we're going. You don't get to know what we're doing. And you *will* spend time with Andres, my personal shopper, this week so it doesn't look like we're taking a homeless guy out on the town."

I tempered my *The fuck I look like a homeless guy* response to "Fine" after I caught sight of my reflection in the glass. Hell, I did look like a bum. Had I even combed my hair? I hadn't shaved and I still wore the sweat-soaked shorts and ratty running shoes I'd put on first thing this morning.

"Whoa. No arguments? No conditions?"

I saw my mother watching us very closely. Dammit, I was an adult and didn't need Mommy meddling in my life. I'd pretend to go along with this "Brady needs a life intervention" thing while I followed my own agenda—not that I had an agenda; I just knew whatever I did would be the polar opposite of what she wanted. The smile I offered her had her eyes narrowing with suspicion.

"Brady?" Nolan prompted.

I faced my cousin and sighed. "Would you listen even if I demanded conditions?"

"Nope." Nolan grinned again. "This is gonna be so much fun."

Four

LENNOX

Monday mornings were the worst. Everyone needed something right away. Everything was crucial. As much as I wanted advancement in this company, I planned to work toward something more than what my boss, Lola, did—coordinating schedules.

I spent the morning entering new templates for interoffice memos, which I considered ridiculous busywork. But Personnel wanted each department to have a uniquely colored memo so they could tell at a glance which department the correspondence was coming from. Just an easier way for Anita—aka Attila—to avoid those e-mails she didn't want to deal with.

I'd brought my lunch and ate with my coworker Sydney in the break room. She'd had a date this weekend with a guy she'd connected with through an online dating service. So I had to hear all the pros and cons about whether she should agree to a second date. What she told me about the man didn't trip any warning bells, but I knew the guy wouldn't trip my trigger either.

"Lennox, you should totally join the service," Sydney said for the hundredth time. "I bet you'd have hundreds of guys signing up to take you out."

"Syd, I'm happy that this is working out for you, but I'm just not the type to let a computer pick a match for me."

"That's what it does. It finds your type. It really works!"

"So I've heard, but I still have a problem meeting a guy who could've totally lied about who he is, just to get a hookup."

"You make it sound like an escort service."

I wiped my mouth. "No, with an escort service you know exactly what you've paid for going into it. With online dating? Not so much."

"You are impossible," Sydney complained.

"Wrong. I'm practical."

"So very glad to hear that, Lennox."

Thankfully, all I did was gasp with surprise at Brady Lund's interruption. But he had scared me enough that I threw my bag of chips all over the table. My face flamed.

"Didn't mean to frighten you."

Yes, you did. "Then maybe you shouldn't sneak up behind people." Crap. Had I really said that to him? What was wrong with me? Why was I always as prickly as a cactus around him?

He chuckled.

I looked up at him. Mistake. Few men wore a suit as well as Mr. Perfect. My thoughts rolled back to how he'd dressed for his date on Saturday night. If I were dating him, I wouldn't want him in casual attire. I'd want the hot-looking suit-and-tie-wearing guy.

When he continued to stare at me, I said, "Was there something you needed, Mr. Lund?"

"Yes. You'll be assisting my admin today in the conference room since her secretary is out sick." He held up his hand before I opened my mouth. "I know protocol, Lennox. I cleared this with your supervisor."

"And Lola sent the CFO of Lund Industries as the errand boy to tell me?" *Dammit, mouth, do* not *engage before brain.*

"No. I came in here to get my lunch."

Now I really felt like an idiot. A sassy idiot. This was a large employee break room; it served the whole building—the entire company. Sometimes we even had catered lunches in here. But in the last year I'd never seen the CFO step foot in here, let alone admit that he brown-bagged it once in a while.

"I'm sorry. I just assumed—"

"That I don't eat lunch?" He flashed his teeth in a predatory smile. "Or that I prefer raw meat tossed in my office rather than swimming around looking for chum?"

I couldn't help but smile. Of course he was aware of his reputation as a shark. And it was really hard for me not to make a crack about sushi.

He walked over to the fridge—and I told myself not to gawk, but my greedy side ogled him: the way his suit pants rippled as he walked and how broad his shoulders looked in that perfectly cut suit jacket when he bent over.

Sydney kicked me under the table so I was innocently picking up my chips when he turned around. And I might've peeked at what he had in his lunch—a takeout deli salad.

Which he apologized for. "I was supposed to meet my sister for lunch, but she had some crisis in PR so she's placating me with this." He sighed. "I'd really hoped for something more substantial."

"Me too, but the lunch fairies are stingy today," Sydney said.

She always knew what to say.

But the CFO paid no attention to her. He zeroed in on me. "You know where my office is?"

"Yes, sir."

"Good. Jenna will see you up there in an hour." Then he strode off.

I crunched a chip.

"Lennox." Sydney leaned forward and whispered, "I think he likes you."

"Don't be ridiculous. I always say the wrong thing around him."

"I'll bet he asked for you specifically to assist his admin."

"Unlikely."

"I'm going to ask Lola if he requested you."

I grabbed her arm. "Don't you dare. I don't want Lola to think I've got a crush on him. And that's exactly what she'd think if I ask her if he was asking about me."

"But it wouldn't be *you* asking her. It'd be me."

"Same difference."

"Fine," she huffed out. "But you have to tell me if he sticks around to flirt with you while you're working."

"He's a busy man. I doubt he'll even be there."

So I could admit some disappointment when the hottie CFO with the killer smile and dreamy blue eyes was out of the office for the afternoon.

Jenna, his admin, was great, though—everything I aspired to be. I marveled at her ability to do twenty-seven things at once while she answered her headset every thirty seconds.

At one point she took the headset off and tossed it on the table. "Calls can go to voice mail for a bit so we can get this done."

WHAT YOU NEED 53

We worked in silence for a while. Then I said, "It's pretty cool that you've got a secretary."

"I haven't always had one. When Mr. Lund became CFO, there was so much paperwork that no one had looked at in decades, but we still needed to archive it. It was a full-time job just sorting that out, so he had to rely on Anita to do the day-to-day secretarial stuff for him for a few months."

I bit my tongue to keep from blurting out a question about Attila.

"Meanwhile," Jenna continued, "an incoming CFO has twice as much work as a CEO because they have to justify spending across the board. Although this is a family business, no one cut him any slack. Not that he would've stood for it if they'd tried it. He is the most single-minded man I've ever met." She peered at me over the top of her glasses. "And my husband is an engineer, so I don't say that lightly."

I grinned. In addition to being a whirling dervish, Jenna had a great sense of humor.

I definitely wanted to be her when I grew up.

Friday afternoon I was back on the forty-fourth floor helping Jenna compile more packets.

I must've sighed loudly because I heard a deep male chuckle behind me. I whirled around and saw Mr. Lund lounging in the doorway, looking as if he'd just stepped off the cover of *GQ*. Looking at me with a sexy smile and a twinkle in his eyes. My heart rate sped up so fast I felt the throbbing pulse in my eyeballs.

Mr. Lund sauntered forward, his gait loose and measured. His hands were tucked into his pants pockets. "Is everything all right, Lennox?"

How was it fair that he seemed hotter looking every time

I saw him? And why were my reactions to him either tongue-tied or snappish? I could do this. Be normal around the smartest, sexiest man in the company.

"Everything is fine except for the fact you tend to sneak up on me and scare the crap out of me every time we cross paths."

He seemed to be measuring me in the resulting silence.

Drop your pen and hide under the desk, you idiot. I rather loudly stacked a pile of papers. "I'm sorry, Mr. Lund. Did you need Jenna? She went to track down missing covers."

"No. I don't need her for anything specific. I was just wandering, trying to clear my head, and noticed the door was open." He sat on the edge of the conference table, close enough that I caught the scent of his cologne. He angled his head toward the stack of reports. "I'll bet you're wondering why we don't outsource a project like this to a printing shop."

I moved in closer to him as I assembled the second-to-last row. "Actually, I'm not wondering that, because if Lund started outsourcing projects such as this one, I'd likely be out of a job I happen to really like." I blushed. Add "gushing like an idiot about his family's company" to my list of reactions around the superfine CFO.

"It always makes me happy to hear employees like working at LI."

LI—company lingo for Lund Industries—sounded weird coming from Lund himself.

He gestured to the stack of finished reports. "The reason LI doesn't outsource these types of projects is due to the sensitive nature of the financial information. We trust our own people more than outsiders."

"And if the information is leaked, you have a paper trail to follow."

"Exactly."

I looked up at him. We were less than a foot apart. His eyes were a blue deep enough to drown in. It took me a moment to regain my train of thought, but what came out wasn't what I'd intended to ask. "Did you request me to be assigned to this project?"

His gaze briefly dipped to my mouth before he refocused on my eyes. "And if I say yes?"

"I would say thank you for the opportunity to prove my loyalty."

"That's why Jenna requested you. You've already proved it."

I frowned. "When?"

"Last week. She thought it was hilarious that you wouldn't give me the erroneous report for Marcus because it would've broken company protocol."

My cheeks burned. "You told her about that?"

He grinned. "Yes. It's not often I'm told no."

"I imagine it is a rarity for a man like you, especially coming from someone like me, who's beneath you." I could've kicked myself for my stupid phrasing. "I mean under you." Dammit. That wasn't any better.

"I don't purposely surround myself with yes-men and -women, but it certainly turns out that way. So your honesty and honest reactions are refreshing."

Yep. He knew the right thing to say too. "Is it hard knowing who to trust?"

He shrugged. "Does it make me sound like a controlling dick if I admit I test people from time to time?"

It seemed he wanted to talk, so I supposed I could oblige him. Oh, who the hell was I kidding? We were having an actual conversation for once where I wasn't making an idiot out of myself. "For example?"

"I mentioned a few months ago that it'd be beneficial to add aquatics to our employee fitness center."

"Like adding a swimming pool?"

"Yes. I touted the health benefits of swimming versus high-impact exercise."

"I hope they told you that you were crazy."

He cocked his head. "Why?"

"Why?" I snorted. "Because, first of all, the fitness center isn't on the ground floor. I imagine the price of putting in a pool—even a lap pool—would be cost prohibitive because of the added structural support systems needed to hold that much water. Plus, there would be maintenance issues, as well as chemical storage issues. Not to mention insurance issues. And I can't believe a fitness pool would get that much use in a business environment. I mean, can you imagine seeing your supervisor in a skimpy polka-dot bikini or a Speedo? Employees would avoid it for that reason alone. Or what if Bob from Accounting whistled at Susie from PR? Would that qualify as sexual harassment if it happened over the lunch hour?"

A startled look crossed his face.

Crap. I'd become a babbling idiot again.

Then he smiled at me as if I'd passed some kind of test. "Those were my thoughts exactly."

Whew. "So what did the members of your team say when you brought it up?"

"At first, no one said a word. Then, let's say . . . Bob"— he smirked—"agreed it was a damn fine idea and he'd take the lead on getting the project under way."

I groaned. "Did you dress him down in front of everyone for being an ass-kisser?"

His eyes narrowed. "My reputation is that bad?"

"Mr. Lund. Surely you're aware of the terror you invoke merely by walking into a department," I said dryly.

"Didn't appear to hold true for you, Lennox." That sexy smile danced on his lips and I found it impossible to look away from his mouth.

"Wrong. You can't tell I'm quaking in my stilettos?"

He blinked as if he didn't believe me.

I held out my hand, showing him how badly it shook. "See?"

He took my hand and squeezed it. "You must be a helluva poker player, because I never would've guessed. You're always so . . . I can't place my finger on it, which is probably why I keep finding reasons to talk to you and try to figure it out."

The way he was looking at me—not like a CFO passing the time with a secretarial worker, but a man wanting to spend time with a woman he was attracted to—utterly addled my brain.

Jenna hustled into the room. "There you are," she said in an exasperated tone.

Feeling guilty, I immediately dropped his hand and spun around to face her.

But she wasn't talking to me. "You cannot hide in here." She handed Mr. Lund a file folder. "They're waiting for you in Mr. Nolan's office. He told me to make sure you brought that."

His mouth flattened into a grim line. Then he looked up at me. The frown bloomed into a charmingly sheepish smile.

My belly jumped.

"Thanks for the enlightening conversation, Lennox. I hope we can do it again sometime"—he shot Jenna a dark look—"without interruptions."

"Me too, Mr. Lund." One hank of his dark hair fell over his eye as he studied the paperwork in the folder, and I had the urge to smooth the hair back into place. After he disappeared through the door, I glanced up and realized I'd just been ogling Jenna's boss—right in front of her.

She didn't wear a look of censure, just a knowing smirk. "Yes, he always looks that good. It's annoying really. Just once I'd like for him to show up at work in stained sweatpants with his hair uncombed and facial scruff."

"Even then I bet he'd look amazing."

Jenna chuckled. "Good point. Luckily, Mr. Lund is somewhat . . . unaware of his attributes. That makes him a little more human."

"After talking to him a few times, I see that he isn't nearly the big bad I thought he was." At least not in the same way I had before.

"Big bad. You kids and your weird phrases. I never understand half of them." She pointed to the stacks of paper. "Let's wrap this up so you can finish the day in your own department. I'm sure you've got big plans for the weekend."

"Not really."

Jenna studied me. "Seriously? You're—what, twenty-five?"

"Twenty-eight, actually."

"I'm just surprised you won't be out hitting the clubs and partaking of the Twin Cities nightlife."

"I lived it up plenty in my misspent youth," I admitted. "My idea of a perfect weekend is staying in."

"You sound just like him."

I didn't have to ask who "him" was, but it intrigued me that the CFO of one of the Twin Cities' richest families wasn't out at charity events every weekend. I imagined him soaking in a bubble bath, a lowball glass of Scotch in his hand. Then, when he unfolded himself from the deep water—because I knew he wasn't the type who could sit idle for very long—the bubbles slipped down his gleaming naked torso, revealing—

"Lennox?" Jenna prompted. "Are you okay?"

Not really. Just ignore me while I have explicit sexual fantasies about your boss. "Yes, you just got me to thinking about the weekend."

"Well, whatever put that dreamy look on your face, I hope it figures into your plans."

Not in a million years. But I smiled and said, "One can hope."

Five

—

BRADY

"I look like I'm trying too hard to be cool and hip," I complained to Nolan Friday night as I entered my living room, wearing dark jeans and a black shirt with the cuffs rolled back. I wasn't ready to go with the unshaven look—I'd scraped the scuff off my face after work—but following my shower I went with the current "I don't give a damn about my hair" trend and did nothing, letting it dry naturally.

Nolan gave me a head-to-loafer inspection. "Damn, cuz. You are one ugly fucker. You'll probably sit in the corner as me 'n' Walker and Ash score."

"Asshole. Who's driving?"

"Car service."

"Smart." Tempting to ask where we were going, but I decided to just go with it, since I was basically being railroaded into this night out. "You want something to drink before we leave?"

"Whatcha got that's new?"

"A small-batch whiskey distilled in Wisconsin."

"I'll take that." Nolan parked on one of the barstools as I ducked behind the bar.

I snagged two lowball glasses and filled them halfway with ice. Then I pulled out the small bottle and poured three fingers in each glass. We touched glasses without an official toast and drank.

After Nolan drank, he picked up the bottle. "Pretty good stuff. Where'd you hear about it?"

"I've got a buddy who's a pharmaceutical rep and it's his mission in life to find the best handcrafted small-batch whiskies. His wife isn't a drinker, so he brings me a bottle and we can discuss all the geeky stuff about notes and hints and aftertaste that few people care about."

"Wait. You have friends?"

"Piss off. I actually manage to get laid too." Although it'd been a while.

"Hey, I'm trying to keep you from turning into a hermit that hides in his lair." Nolan looked around. "Freakin' sweet lair. I still can't believe you got the jump on me with this place."

It'd taken two years to refurbish the run-down warehouse I'd bought for a song a few years back. Now the top level was my living space. The main floor was the ultimate man cave—half of it was a garage that stored my collection of cars. The other side had a home gym, a half court, a regulation boxing ring, a weight room, and a separate area for cardio. Most of the gyms in the Twin Cities weren't as big as this. But my schedule was so crazy that I had to create a place that fit my needs.

We walked through the fitness area and Nolan said, "You still training with Nate?"

"Only twice a week. His hours are different now that he and his partner have adopted a kid. He goes on about how blissfully happy they are and I ought to try it."

"He sounds like my mother," Nolan said. "Oh, and thank you for passing on the bachelor auction. Dude, you might hate being listed as one of the most eligible bachelors in the Twin Cities, but I eat that shit up."

"I know."

"Cheer up. Next time the auction rolls around, you'll be a new man. No more the serious brooding type. Chicks like it when you actually smile at them. I've made it my goal in life to perfect my panty-dropping smile."

"There's a goal worth having," I said dryly. For some reason my thoughts zoomed to the genuine smiles I'd eked out of Lennox Greene this week. In those unguarded moments, when her hazel eyes had shown humor and her lips had curved, she'd gone from pretty to stunning.

From a distance she seemed like a woman who was confident in herself and was happy enough to smile frequently. But the second she was around me, she defined uptight—I was uptight enough to recognize the signs. I didn't buy her argument that her standoffish attitude was because I scared her. She'd actually stood up to me when others wouldn't have. But an unpredictable and prickly woman was not my type, no matter how stunning she was. Or how quickly she made me laugh when so few could these days.

"Brady? Where are you, man? And why do you look so pissed off?"

I glanced up at my cousin. "Just thinking about this woman I met recently."

"No thinking about any specific woman. Tonight all women are on the menu. Tonight you are stepping out of your comfort zone, my friend."

I'd never been a player—although after I grew out of my awkward stage, I'd never had a problem finding women to share my bed. Even before I'd become CFO, my work came first. I had no idea why—or how—I was supposed to change that. I doubted one night in a bar and new clothes would do it. This all seemed pointless.

Nolan got in my face. "Leave your job, your worries, your baggage right here. You are not going to puss out. This is the tough-love part, Brady."

"Got it."

"Time to get your head in the game." Then my younger cousin slapped me on the cheeks—like he was my godfather taking me to a whorehouse to lose my virginity—and I half expected him to tack on, *Capisce*?

Thankfully he didn't.

The car pulled up.

Here we go.

LENNOX

Another Friday night and I had the house to myself. I looked forward to my ritual of balancing my accounts and unwinding with bad TV.

Again.

I was debating where to order a pizza from when my cell phone rang. I picked it up and saw Maxie on the caller ID.

It couldn't be a coincidence that Maxie was calling a week after I'd talked to my mother. I answered with a short "Hello?"

"Is this the high-and-mighty Lenni Greene who's forgotten all of her old friends since she's working in some big fancy office building?"

I grinned. "You're hilarious. I thought you'd lost my number."

"Oh, sugar, I've got *your* number. I've had it for a long damn time. It's *you* who seems to have forgotten where you came from."

Guilt swamped me. I hadn't stepped foot in Maxie's place for almost a year. "I've been busy with the new job."

"I figured. But you ain't workin' right now, are ya?"

I started to say, "No, but I have a community service thing to do early in the morning," but, as usual, Maxie beat me to the punch.

"So there's no excuse for you not to haul your buns down here. Pronto." She dropped her voice. "I already told everyone you were gonna be here tonight, so don't you make a liar outta me, girlie, after all I've done for you."

Unlike my mother, she knew exactly what buttons to push. "Fine. Gimme two hours and I'll be there."

"Two hours?" She hooted. "You'd better look like hot shit and a side of taco chips when you stroll in and not like you just got outta court."

That got my back up. The last time I'd seen the crew at Maxie's, I'd been wearing an interview suit. Long sleeves, tight skirt, high heels. They'd razzed me endlessly about it. When they'd gone a little too far, accusing me of not being one of them, I'd felt a little cocky. I *wasn't* one of them anymore. I'd changed from being Lenni, the smart-mouthed cocktail server, to Lennox, the newest office temp at Lund Industries.

"Lenni?" she prompted. "Did you hang up on me?"

"You wish. See you in a few, Maxie."

Since I had to drive, I skipped making myself a strong cocktail and headed straight for the back of my closet, where I kept clothing that wasn't office attire.

As I tossed out miniskirts and leather pants, I took a moment to remind myself that I'd always hated the nickname Lenni—and I wasn't Lenni anymore. I'd been giddy when everyone at work called me by my real name, Lennox. I'd once asked my mother where she'd gotten the name, and she claimed she'd seen it in a magazine ad for dishes, thinking it'd be cool to name me after fine china. But she wasn't the brightest crayon in the box, even when she was sober, so she misspelled my name on the birth certificate.

Although Kiley knew about my past—some of it anyway—I was happy my counselor roomie wasn't home to assess my transformation. She'd probably have some choice words about why I felt the need to keep the two sides of myself separate since they were both part of what made me who I am.

I stripped, got in the shower and afterward slathered lotion on my legs to make it easier to get my leather pants on. I piled my hair on top of my head in a messy bun. I always wore my hair down at work because of the tattoo on the back of my neck. That's also why I always wore long-sleeved shirts. Although sporting ink was more acceptable and tattoos didn't necessarily carry the stigma that they once did, Lund Industries was a conservative company with a dress code. And I'd spent enough years being prejudged because of my tattoos that I'd welcomed the chance to cover them up and start fresh. I knew Maxie and the others wouldn't understand, so just for one night I'd let my ink show. I'd be the wild child I'd left behind.

It confused me why I looked forward to it so much.

Maxie's Hideaway—regulars referred to it as Maxie's Pad—was an old-school dive: dark and smoky. A huge mirrored bar spanned the length of the room. The other half of the space was tables and a performance area. Sometimes bands played there. Sometimes comedians showed up and tested out a new set. Maxie's had the occasional burlesque show. She broke out the karaoke machine once in a while. We'd even had line dancing and hip-hop classes. Maxie's defined "anything goes."

Because Maxie had a three-pack-a-day habit, when the government banned smoking, she'd basically flipped them the bird and said she'd rather pay the fines than lose her core customers. That'd worked for a while. Until the city hired some pencil-pushing, by-the-book doorknob that'd bypassed the fines, closed the place down, and tossed Maxie in jail.

The desk jockey with an overinflated ego didn't understand about how the real world worked. Less than twenty-four hours later, Maxie was out of jail, with an apology from her councilman. Then Maxie's Hideaway had been legally declared a cigar bar, so smoking wasn't regulated.

This had all happened before I worked there, but the story was the stuff of legends. That was another thing I loved about the people who hung out there. They had stories to tell. They'd lived hard lives, but they'd taken such joy in being able to brag that they'd come out all right.

On the drive over I pumped myself up by listening to classic seventies rock, because that was what I'd hear tonight. No matter where I was or how old I got, CCR, Zeppelin, the Stones and the Eagles would always take me back to Maxie's.

It was early when I parked my ancient Corolla in the lot. That was one thing I hadn't changed: I still drove the same car. It ran like a champ, so I saw no need to sink money into a car payment when I didn't have to. Anticipation hummed through me. Friday night at Maxie's. The regulars would be sitting at the bar swapping "My boss was a dick this week" stories as they poured their hard-earned money down their throats.

When I walked in, I made an entrance. I slammed the door until it hit the wall behind it. Everyone turned around and looked, just as I'd wanted.

"What's a girl gotta do to get a drink around here?"

No fewer than five guys rushed me. Boz, a burly biker from the Wastrels motorcycle club. DJ, who used to host a morning show on KXRX. Fatso, a rail-thin guy who worked as a mechanic. Dickie, who was almost short enough to be considered a midget and worked at the same body shop as Fatso. Pistol, who managed a gun range.

Hugo, the bartender who'd been tending bar here even before it was Maxie's, waited behind the bar for his hug. "Lenni, girl, how you doin'?"

Before I could answer, Pistol said, "We thought you forgot about us."

Dickie chimed in with, "You still drinkin' beer, or you switch to champagne now that you're workin' bankers' hours?"

Hugo shushed them all. "Let her catch her breath, assholes."

"Thanks, Hugo."

"You got it, doll—Maxie's missed you. She's gonna act like a tough old bitch, but the truth is—"

"She's got a heart as soft as a Moon Pie."

"What's an old broad gotta do to get a hug around here?" Maxie said behind me.

I didn't hold back when I saw her. I squealed and nearly knocked her over.

She must've been prepared, because she didn't have a lit cigarette between her fingers the way she usually did. "Lord, girl, I thought I wouldn't recognize you." She eased back and checked me out, a smile kicking up one corner of her mouth. "But you're still my same Lenni." She hollered at Hugo. "Where's her beer? Make it two, one for each hand."

And just like that, it was as if I'd never left.

Six

—

BRADY

"Damn, Walker. Are you sure we won't get stabbed in there?"

My brother looked at me and shrugged. "When was the last time you used your medical insurance?"

Hardly reassuring.

"Quit being a pussy," Nolan said to me. "See the rougher edges of our city."

The insult combined with a dare should've sent me through the door first. But I let Walker and Nolan lead the way; I'm nothing if not cautious. I looked over my shoulder at Ash just to make sure he wasn't about to bail and cool his loafers in the car.

"Get going. The sooner I don't have my back to the door, the better."

"We should've brought Jensen with us," I grumbled. "He's a bigger target and he can run faster."

"Hell, they'd all want his autograph and they'd ignore us completely."

"Exactly. It'd give us a chance to get away."

Ash laughed.

We were finally in this "great dive bar" Walker loved. I watched as he got a chin dip of acknowledgment from the heavily bearded bartender. No one else paid attention to us, or at least if they were sizing us up they did it discreetly as we headed to a table in the back. I didn't look around until we all had seats.

The bar back was enormous. Bottles lined the wall from the counter level to the crown molding around the tin ceiling. Bar signs—some vintage, some new, all neon—were hung on the walls above the tables and in some places were attached to the pillars covered in more elaborately carved molding. The tables and chairs were relics, backless chrome barstools with Naugahyde seats and heavy wooden tables, the tops scarred from years of use.

A dark-haired cocktail waitress paused at the edge of our table. "What'll it be, boys? And remember—we don't take American Express."

Sure, we didn't look out of place in here.

"A pitcher of—what kind of Leinie are you pouring this week?" Walker asked.

The cocktail waitress took an interest in Walker. "Honey Weiss."

"What the hell happened to the Red you served last week?"

"Uh, the customers drank it all."

Walker stared at her and smoothed a hand over his beard. "We'll take a pitcher of MGD."

"Four glasses?" she asked.

"Yeah."

"Coming right up."

Nolan leaned in. "MGD? Dude. That tastes like horse piss."

"I'll refrain from asking when you've sipped horse piss," Ash said with a smirk.

"Ha-fucking-ha."

"This is the kind of place where you drink the cheap American stuff," Walker said. He looked at Nolan and mimicked, "Dude. You order wine and I'm throwing the first punch."

"Bring it. I've been training at an MMA gym. I'll knock you on your ass."

Typical. Walker and Nolan fought more than I ever did with Walker—you'd think they were brothers instead of cousins.

The jukebox kicked on. Classic rock drifted to us. Not loud enough to be annoying—the benefit of sitting in the back of the bar.

"So, how'd you find this place?" Nolan asked Walker.

"A buddy who works for me brought me here."

"See any action?" Ash asked.

"Not really. It's not that kind of a place. It's an old-school neighborhood bar." He grinned. "Before the neighborhood went to hell."

I saw movement up by the bar. A couple of women dancing together. Nothing too dirty, but the night was still young. I set my elbows on the table and caught my brother looking at me. "What?"

"What happened that's brought about this radical need for human companionship?" Walker asked.

"He needs the ritual," Nolan said.

Before I could ask what the hell *that* meant, the waitress was back, setting the beer and the mugs in the center of the table. "Anything else?"

Nolan said, "Do you have an extra napkin I can write on?"

"Ooh, lemme guess . . . you're writing down your phone number for me?"

"Sorry, sweetheart, but we're working on dry-rub barbecue recipes," Nolan lied smoothly. "Our other buddy is going to Kansas City to compete in the annual men's barbecue challenge. He's kind of a dick, so secretive about his special recipe, that we're trying to figure out the ingredients."

I choked on my beer.

"Sure thing. But if he wants to win in Kansas City, he'd be better off with a thick, sweet sauce rather than a dry rub. They like it wet down there."

The sexy way she'd said that and the knowing curve of her lips indicated she hadn't been fooled by Nolan's on-the-fly lie. At all.

Nolan grinned at her. "But we do have to make a list, so if you've got any kind of paper around, we'd be grateful for it."

"I'll see what I can do, slick."

Ash held his fist up for a bump, which I met. Perfect nickname for our cousin. Ash had already started pouring. He slid the first glass to me. "You need the ritual, man. At first it pissed me off that my friends and family butted into my life." Ash slid a mug to Walker. "But it turns out they were right. I needed to change."

"Hence the ritual was born," Nolan said.

"Jensen was here for it, when you were in Ireland," Walker said.

Ireland reminded me of Siobhan and why these guys thought I needed this. "I was thinking we'd get hammered and find me a random hookup, not that I'd have to do some dumb ritual," I said, downing half my beer in one gulp.

"I've been there, Brady. I didn't want to do this dumbass ritual either. I didn't believe it'd amount to anything." Ash pointed a cigar at me. "But something will come out of this night that will make your life better. Trust me."

"How will I know what it is?"

He grinned. "That's the thing. You won't know. So you've gotta be open to everything."

I mumbled, "That sounds like a recipe for a night in the drunk tank with a maxed-out credit card."

The waitress dropped off two sheets of paper and a pen.

"Thanks, doll."

"Now, as Ash is refilling our mugs, let's get down to it." Nolan looked at me and held out a cigar.

I tried to decline the stogie, but Nolan shook his head and said, "Take it."

Evidently lung cancer was part of my new persona.

I ripped off the cellophane. A rich, earthy scent drifted out and I lifted the cigar to my nose and inhaled.

"Attaboy," Nolan said. He held out the cigar clipper and snipped off the end. Then he snapped open a Zippo lighter and sparked the tip. I drew in several puffs. It'd been so many years since I'd smoked, I'd forgotten how calming that first hit of sweet smoke was.

Nolan lit cigars all around—Walker was the only one who didn't light up.

For a few moments we enjoyed our cigars and the icy-cold beer as we soaked in our surroundings. I would've been content to stay like that for a while longer, but Nolan apparently had a schedule to keep.

"It's time."

I groaned.

"You have a choice," Nolan said. "You can either write the list yourself or read it out loud to all of us."

"So either way you'll all . . . know," I said with a tinge of horror.

Walker clapped me on the back. "Only way to do this. Rip off the fucking Band-Aid, rub some dirt in it and get back in the game."

"Jesus, Walker. It's almost like you're channeling Jensen," Ash complained.

My youngest brother did love his sports analogies.

I pointed at Ash. "You've done this before. You get to play secretary." Secretary made me think of Lennox Greene.

Yeah, I'd be up for anything and everything anywhere with her.

Pervert. She works for you.

Technically, she didn't work for *me* specifically.

That's the beer talking, man. She's exactly the type of woman you don't *need to get involved with. A beautiful, by-the-book, buttoned-up blonde.*

Nolan snapped his fingers in my face. "Focus."

"Christ. All right."

Ash tapped his pen on the paper. "Here's the deal. You have to list two things to change in your life immediately. One thing to stop doing, one thing to start doing."

That wasn't as bad as I'd thought.

Nolan ordered two rounds of shots.

I didn't pay much attention to what he'd ordered—I was too busy mentally compiling my list, because god forbid I failed at this.

Nolan slid a shot toward me. "We drink this first."

"What is it?"

"Vanilla vodka."

I made a face. "Why?"

"As a reminder that you're done living a vanilla life," Ash said.

Of all the stupid— Okay, maybe it wasn't stupid. Maybe it made sense. I raised my glass. "Bring on the rainbow of flavors." I knocked back the booze. Shuddered. That was some nasty stuff.

My cousins and brother all wore the same look of distaste after their empty shot glasses hit the table.

"All right, man. *Now* you can start the list. Tell us one thing you aren't gonna do anymore."

First one was easy. "No more eighty- or ninety-hour workweeks."

They looked at one another and nodded. Then Ash jotted it down.

"Next thing?" Nolan prompted.

This one was trickier. I studied my empty shot glass. "I'll do something new, daring and out of the norm every week." My cheeks burned with embarrassment, because I should not have had to make a fucking pact with them about changing my life and then announce it to the free world.

Nolan shook his head. "Specifics, man. With something that vague, you could claim that ordering orange sesame chicken instead of orange sesame beef qualifies as daring."

Walker and Ash nodded agreement. My brother said, "This is us, B. You know we've got your back unless you decide your 'new' thing is torturing small animals."

"Or if your 'daring' thing is taking up professional ice dancing," Ash said.

"Or if your 'out of the norm' thing is donning fetish wear on casual Fridays," Nolan tossed in.

Bunch of freakin' comedians. But I knew they were trying to find that balance point between sappy and helpful. So in turn I tried to find the halfway point between the full truth and a partial lie. "It won't come as a surprise to any of you that I fear failure"—no way was I confessing why I feared failure—"but I'm tired of using that as an excuse. From here on out, I'll take steps to actually have a personal life outside of work and family. I'll really put myself out there. And any failure just means I actually tried to make a change."

Ash wrote that down on the second piece of paper.

And I felt good about what I'd said—even if I'd spoken somewhat disingenuously. I puffed on the cigar. "Now what?"

"Now it's time for the ritual."

"I thought that *was* the ritual."

Walker shook his head.

Great.

I got a little worried when Walker put his palms together in prayer position, his unlit stogie dangling from the corner of his mouth. "Dearly beloved. We are gathered here today—"

"What the fuck does a Prince song have to do with the damn ritual?" I snapped.

"Nothing. We're just fucking with you to see if we could get you to dance on the bar singing 'Let's Go Crazy.'"

"Bunch of jackasses," I muttered.

Nolan passed out the next shot. He raised his shot glass and paused while we all did the same.

"To having the balls to admit your life needs a change and taking that first step. *Skål.*"

We repeated, "*Skål,*" touched glasses and knocked back the drink.

Somehow I managed not to choke on the cinnamon-flavored whiskey.

Nolan grinned. "From vanilla to fire. Variety is the spice of life."

Ash held up the two pieces of paper. He slid the one in his right hand across the table. "This is the one you look at every day as a reminder."

"And the other one?"

"This one you never want to see again. Crumple it up and torch it."

Moving my cigar to my left hand, I crushed the paper in my fist. Then I dropped it in the big metal ashtray and held the smoldering end of the cigar to the corner of the list. It caught fire immediately.

I watched the flames consume the paper, turning it into black flakes of nothing.

"Last thing," Nolan said. "You gotta pay this forward like Ash did. Time's gonna come when Walker, Jensen or I ask for redirection."

I noticed he didn't say "if," but "when." I raised my glass in agreement.

The conversation tapered off from the serious topics to other things. Football and hockey, mostly. The music had gotten louder. More people had shown up at the bar. I looked around and wondered what had drawn my brother to this place. Normally he preferred sports bars.

You sure? In the two years since you took the CFO position, how many times have you gone out and hit the bars with Walker?

Not once.

Walker and Nolan were debating the outcome of Sunday's Vikings game. I looked at Ash. He had his phone out and was typing furiously, his brow furrowed.

Ash had taken over as COO of Lund Industries two years before I'd been offered the CFO position. Although my bachelor's degrees in accounting and economics, plus my dual master's degrees in finance and business administration, played a huge part in getting the CFO position, I also knew that Ash had gone to bat for me. Especially when the two dissenters on the board of directors had gotten pissy, claiming I was too young for such responsibility—despite the fact I'd been working in the family business since age eighteen.

Ash glanced up at me, flashed a sheepish grin and set his phone down. "Not providing you with a very good example of how to leave work at the office, am I?"

"Was that work related?"

"Actually . . . no. Dallas is bitching via text because the players have private rooms and the cheerleaders have to share."

"I forgot to look at the schedule this week. Who is U of M playing?"

"Hawkeyes." He shook his head. "Sometimes my little sister forgets that she's lucky the cheerleaders get to travel with the team during the regular season, and not just cheer at home like most collegiate cheerleaders." Ash took a drink of his beer. "But you don't care about Dallas's cheer dramas. What's up? You're looking at me like you've got a specific question."

I'd planned to ask about a wrinkle we were having with the rising costs of raw material for the packaged-food division, but I found myself blurting out, "How'd you learn to do it?"

"What? Feel like I'm giving my all to the company and still manage to have a life?"

I nodded.

He studied me for a moment. "It's a weird story. Remember Max Miner?"

"The snowboarder? X Games world champ, Olympic medalist? Ended up paralyzed?"

"Yeah. Him. Right around the time you moved up to CFO, and I broke it off with Veronica, I went to hear him speak. The program started out listing all of Max's accomplishments, video clips of him from the time he was a young kid. His obsession with snowboarding. His wins. Then it talked about his accident. The challenges he faced during his recovery. I was waiting for the 'You can do anything even in a wheelchair' motivational portion to start, but it turned out that wasn't the focus." Ash fiddled with the bar napkin beneath his beer mug. "When he rolled out in his wheelchair, he said, 'Name two things in your life'—besides your job and your family, which counted as one thing—'that are important to you.' Then his assistant started walking through the audience, randomly picking people to stand up and share what gave them joy. What motivated, inspired and fulfilled them."

"No pressure."

"No kidding. So I sat there, panicked I'd be put on the spot, because I realized I had nothing."

I would've had that same panicked feeling—because I had nothing but those two things in my life either.

"It hit home for me, especially when Max said if we couldn't name two things, then we were emotionally crippled." Ash looked at me. "I realized he was right. While I still define myself by what I do as COO, I also have found other things that matter to me."

"Such as?"

Ash shook his head. "Tell you what. When you come up with your two things, I'll tell you mine."

"Fair enough."

Nolan leaned over. "Finish your beers. We're heading out."

I pushed away from the table. "I gotta hit the can first."

I wound my way to the front and noticed a crowd had gathered around the bar. Chants of *"Do it, do it!"* erupted into applause and whistles when two women jumped up on the bar. The brunette was familiar because she was our waitress. So it didn't make sense why the blond woman seemed familiar too. She spun around in a sexy move that would've done any stripper proud.

When she looked over her shoulder—her tattooed shoulder—my jaw nearly hit the floor.

The hot-bodied blonde with the skimpy clothes, body art and killer dancing skills was none other than Lennox Greene.

I about swallowed my tongue.

The music started. I skirted the crowd and moved to the end of the bar. Now I had a better view of those long legs encased in leather, her halter top that billowed out in the front, providing a teasing glimpse of the curve of her breast.

So much for my idea that she was too buttoned up.

When she raised her arms above her head, her shirt rode up, revealing the piercing in her belly button. Jesus. I wanted to wrap my lips around that hoop and tug on it with my teeth.

Lennox appeared to be as mesmerized by the music as I was mesmerized by her.

No way was I leaving now.

As far as signs went? This was a damn good one.

Seven

LENNOX

I was having a great time.

Maybe too good a time, I realized when I looked down and saw dollar bills littering the bar top I was dancing on.

Shasta bent at the waist and wiggled her ass as she scooped up the bills.

I let her have them all. For me, dancing on the bar wasn't about shaking my ass for a little cash, but a reminder I didn't *have* to. This was fun. I didn't have to worry about scoring extra tips so I could make my rent this month.

There was considerable freedom in that.

The musical selections on the jukebox weren't the bump-and-grind sexy tunes played in nightclubs—no Timberlake or Timbaland—so we had to make do with "Mustang Sally" or "American Woman." When "Sweet Emotion" started, Shasta and I looked at each other and grinned. At one time we'd had an actual routine worked up for this song. Just for kicks, I tried to remember the moves as the regulars shouted, *"Do it, do it!"*

Shasta was game and jumped right in. We slowly twisted our bodies down to the bar top during the long "sweet" chorus, and then we rolled back up during the equally long "emotion" portion of the chorus, ending with a hair flip, a full spin and a foot stomp when the guitar part started.

An even bigger crowd gathered, and Shasta and I let their catcalls and wolf whistles pump us up even more.

By the time we reached the last section of the song, I was sweating and that last shot of tequila hit me. I made it through the shimmy down fine. I made it through the roll up fine. I made it through the hair flip fine. But when I started to spin, I overrotated and lost my balance. I had a split second to decide whether to save face and fall behind the bar, or take my chances, fall forward and hope someone caught me.

I hit a warm body with a loud *"Uhf."*

Patrons cheered.

Even beneath my hair, which had come loose and masked most of my face, I could see male hands patting the back of my savior. I was jostled as we moved through the crowd.

Then my rescuer, who had an amazingly hard chest and incredibly muscled arms—I guessed that part since he was lugging me around like a sack of grain—lowered me onto a bench seat.

I brushed my hair from my face and got my first good look at the man who'd caught me.

No.

No, no, no, no, no. This wasn't happening to me! "Mr. Lund?"

"Given the circumstances of my lifesaving heroic action, don't you think you should call me Brady?"

I knew my mouth hung open and I probably started drooling because Brady Lund—aka Mr. Perfect—looked even better than usual, dressed down in jeans and a tight black shirt that molded to his upper body. His hair was slightly mussed and I had the urge to sift my fingers through it and mess it up even more.

That last shot of tequila? Bad idea.

But Brady—*Call him Mr. Lund, dumbass, to keep this professional!*—was far too busy looking me over to notice me doing the same thing to him. He reached out and traced the tattoo on my right biceps with one rough fingertip.

That gentle touch sobered me up faster than a punch to the arm.

"This is cool, Lennox," he said huskily, not taking his eyes off my ink. "Why didn't I know you had a tattoo?"

"Because I cover all of them up at work."

Brady's gaze snapped to mine. "You have more than one?"

I nodded.

"Show me." He gave me a slow, wicked grin. "Unless they're on a place on your body that requires you to strip down."

"Mr. Lund—"

"Brady," he corrected.

"Fine. Brady. I don't want to talk about my tattoos—that's why I keep them hidden beneath my clothes during working hours."

"Why?"

"Because three companies declined to hire me prior to getting the job offer at Lund Industries," I said testily.

He seemed taken aback by that. "Because of your tattoos? You know this for sure?"

"Yes, because I'd done the 'honest' thing and let my ink

show during the interview process. I'm not ashamed of my tattoos. But it's obviously a red flag for some companies."

"That's a little archaic. Tats are everywhere."

"Not a big hiring point for an office worker who's just starting out in corporate America. You know that LI has a dress code, right?"

He shrugged. "I never thought about it."

"Exactly. *You* don't have to. I do." I touched his forearm and was momentarily sidetracked by the sinewy muscles beneath the skin-warmed cotton. "Please don't tell my supervisor." Or, worse, Attila.

"I wouldn't do that." Once again he dragged his fingers over the swirls of ink on my arm. "How you choose to express yourself in your off time . . . has no effect on how well you do your job when you're on the clock."

Relief swept through me. "Thank you."

Then his intense blue eyes snared me. "Tell me another place you're inked."

"Even if it's X-rated?"

"Especially if it's X-rated," he shot back in a husky tone.

This man was so sexy. Without even trying.

Or maybe he *was* trying. Maybe I was just that hard up for a man that I'd consider flirting with my boss.

Technically, he's not your boss. He's "a" boss. And there aren't "no fraternization" rules at Lund Industries—the company is too big.

Justification much?

"Lennox?"

My belly tightened at the way he murmured my name. I looked away from where those surprisingly rough fingertips stroked my arm, then into his eyes. "What?"

"You were going to reveal another tattoo?"

"You'll have to get closer for this one."

Brady's eyes gleamed and a half smirk kicked up one corner of his mouth. He scooted in and slid his arm along the back of the booth. His hard thigh connected with the outside of my leg. His breath drifted over the ball of my shoulder. "Ready."

I wasn't ready. His nearness was doing crazy things to me. My hands shook when I angled my neck, giving him a close-up of the birds that started between my shoulder blades. The tiny birds followed the arc of my spine, up my neck and ended at my hairline.

More of his hot breath drifted over my bare skin and gooseflesh rippled down my back.

"The detail is incredible," he said, way too close to my skin. "Do you mind if I touch it?"

Please touch it first with your mouth, then with your tongue, and then sink your teeth into the curve where my shoulder meets my neck. And then start all over again.

I managed, "Uh, no."

I wasn't expecting the tender sweep of his thumb over each individual bird and I bit back a moan. It'd been so long since I'd been touched in any manner, let alone touched with this sort of . . . awe.

When he kept lightly caressing my skin, I must've held my breath, because he whispered, "Breathe."

I forced in a lungful of smoky air. "You're very thorough."

"You shouldn't be surprised," he said offhandedly as he continued to stroke and torment me. "Do you mind that I'm so fascinated by your ink?"

"No. Half the time I forget the tats are even there."

"I'd remind you every day," he said softly.

"What?" I had to have misheard him.

"This bird at the top. It doesn't look like a blackbird."

"It's a starling."

Brady swept his thumb across it. "There's symbolism here that I'm not getting, isn't there?"

"Yes."

"Will you tell me about it?"

"Maybe someday."

He was so close his soft chuckle vibrated against my skin. "Fair enough."

I had to have imagined a whisper-light brush of his full lips across the base of my neck. But my body reacted anyway.

"Thank you for showing me."

"You're welcome." I let my hair fall down across my back and faced forward. Brady was right there, inches away. "What?"

"You are so goddamned gorgeous, Lennox."

Goddamned gorgeous. Two words I never imagined would be directed at me. From Brady Lund. I swallowed, trying to do something about the sudden dryness in my mouth.

"Would you let me take you out?"

"Out? Like on a date?"

"No, take you out and shoot you." He laughed when my eyes widened. "Yes, I meant take you out on a date."

"Why me?"

He touched my cheek. "I'd planned to ask you out before Jenna interrupted us."

"You did?"

"Yes." He frowned. "You couldn't tell that's what I was working up to?"

"No! I told you that you make me nervous, remember? I showed you how bad my hands were shaking."

"That floors me," he murmured. "Especially now, seeing that you're rocking awesome tats beneath the prim-and-proper clothing you wear from nine to five."

"So it's my wild side that fascinates you?"

"Everything about you fascinates me—and it has since the first time I saw you ten months ago."

I struggled with how to respond. I'd worked hard to leave the girl who danced on the bar behind, but that girl was the one who'd prompted this gorgeous, sexy man to approach me and admit he'd known I worked for LI for months.

"But seeing you dancing on the bar clinched it."

"Clinched what?"

"My determination to get you to go out on a date with me. I suspect you would've shot me down if I'd asked you out during office hours. Wouldn't you have?"

I nodded.

"So seeing you here? I'm taking it as a sign that we're supposed to try at least one date."

"What the hell happened to you?" a male voice demanded.

A male voice I recognized. Crap. That was Ash Lund, another one of the big bosses. I turned, ducking my head as if looking for something in my purse—not that I even had my purse with me.

"I'm rescuing damsels in distress," Brady said coolly. "Why?"

"Time to go. Nolan and Walker are out front waiting."

Nolan Lund was here too? Perfect. What were the odds he saw my bar-top antics?

"Give me a few minutes and I'll be right there." He didn't offer to introduce us—another point in his favor.

"All right."

A beat passed and Brady said, "Stop hiding. He's gone."

That was a little terse. I looked up. "Of course you're here with the COO of Lund Industries as well as the son of the CEO of Lund Industries."

Annoyance flashed in his eyes. "No, I'm here with my cousins and my brother. I never asked who you were here with."

"No one."

"Really? You just show up at a bar like this by yourself?"

Now I was annoyed by his skepticism. "*A bar like this?* I'm sure it's vastly different from the upscale places you're used to patronizing, Mr. Lund. But don't worry—I've had enough experiences in 'a bar like this' to know exactly how to take care of myself."

"Don't patronize me. You know nothing about me or the places I frequent. For all you know, I could be a regular here."

It took about five seconds before I laughed. "You? Right. You couldn't convince me of that even if I didn't have insider's knowledge that you are most certainly *not* a regular."

He quirked a brow that managed to be sexy, imperious and irritating. "You know that . . . how?"

"I worked here as a cocktail waitress for years, and trust me, I would've remembered servicing a man like you." Wait. That wasn't what I'd meant to say.

Brady gifted me with a grin so hot I was surprised my hair hadn't caught fire. "Fair warning, dancing queen. I'll expect you to explain that statement in full detail on our date."

He'd gone beyond asking, apparently. And apparently I'd lost control of my vocal cords.

Then he stood.

As he turned to walk away, I said, "Mr. Lund."

He faced me. "Brady."

"Brady. Thanks for saving me from an ass-buster off the bar."

"My pleasure, Lennox. I'll be in touch. Soon."

I watched him cut a path through the bar until the door opened and he disappeared outside.

What were the odds? And what the hell had just happened?

Maybe he is drunk and he won't remember this conversation come Monday.

Unlikely. He couldn't have caught my tumble off the bar if he'd been too impaired.

Maxie wandered over, cigarette dangling from her lip as she carried two mugs of beer. She sat across from me and slid one of the mugs over.

"You're bringing me a beer?" I joked. "It's not my birthday."

She rolled her eyes. Then she set her cigarette in the ashtray. "So you're rusty on your bar-dancin' skills."

"Too much tequila and excitement is always dangerous for me."

"Never used to be."

I wouldn't give her the argument she wanted.

"The dude who caught you." She sipped her beer. "You know him?"

"No," I lied. "But he wanted to get to know me."

"You looked pretty cozy over here."

"I figured it'd be rude to tell him to take a hike after he'd saved me from a trip to the emergency room." I took a drink. "Why?"

"No reason." Maxie picked up her cigarette and drew in deeply. Then she slowly exhaled. "Used to be you wouldn't give a man like that a second glance."

"I used to wear blue eye shadow too, Maxie. People change."

"It's not your blue eye shadow that I take issue with, Lenni. It's the fact you're forgetting your blue-collar roots."

I'd known this would come to a head; I just didn't want to say the wrong thing. Although she was my mother's friend, she'd looked out for me—especially when my mother hadn't. "You cannot have it both ways. None of the regulars who hang around were ever good enough for me. And if other guys come into the bar and I notice them, then you say I'm acting like I'm too good for the regulars?"

She grinned. "Exactly."

"No wonder I'm still single."

"Ain't nothin' wrong with bein' single. Been happily single my whole life."

"Wrong. You've been married to this bar."

"Always been too damn smart for your own good."

I smiled and used that as a chance to change the subject.

And a reason to forget about my run-in with Brady Lund.

Eight

LENNOX

The next morning I knocked on Kiley's door at eight A.M. I usually slept in on Saturdays, so I'd used my alarm for the first time on a weekend in well over a year. I hadn't stayed at Maxie's very long after she alternately grilled me and guilted me. I stuck around long enough to switch to Coke and make sure I was totally sober before I climbed behind the wheel of my car.

"What?" Kiley said from inside her room.

"Coffee's on."

"Be right there."

Five minutes later Kiley strolled into the kitchen. "You're an angel." She filled a mug, dumped powdered creamer in it and looked at me over the rim. "You were out late last night."

"The woman who runs the bar I used to work at called and nagged me for forgetting my old friends. So I drove down there and hung out for a while." Although I'd never taken Kiley to Maxie's place, she knew about the years I'd worked there. "What did you do last night?"

"Paperwork. And then more paperwork. I'm half afraid that none of my kids will show up today, and half afraid they'll all show up."

"Where are we going today?"

"Southside, baby." She swallowed another gulp of coffee. "There's a playground that's seen better days, but it has a basketball court, which is all the guys care about. There's some nasty graffiti spray painted on the abandoned brick building. I've gotten permission from the owners to fix it."

"How're you gonna do that?"

Kiley smirked. "You mean, how are *we* gonna do that? I'll give you the options the same time I tell the kids." She gave my outfit a slow perusal. "You don't care if you get paint on those clothes?"

"Yes, I care if I get paint on these clothes. I'll have to change." I pointed at her. "And no yelling at me to hurry up, because I didn't know this was a painting party."

"No yelling. But there is one thing I want to ask you."

"What?"

"Can you let your tats show today? And put your piercings in?"

Okay. That was a weird request. "Can I ask why?"

"These kids are borderline cases. And since I've met with them, I know they feel . . . marginalized or ostracized. Sometimes by where they live, or their parents' actions or inactions, a lot of them think there's no life for them beyond what they can see. I want to show them they can retain their individuality, but still fit into a more mainstream life."

I didn't know what to say. I had a regular job, but at that job I had to hide those things that made me stand out. So would it be more hypocritical to put the piercings in and show the tats, or to say no and then not tell these kids that I willingly cover up a part of myself five days a week in order to fit into a world I never thought I'd belong in? "Kiley. I don't know. That seems—"

"Dishonest? Maybe a little. But it's not like you never wear them anymore."

"It's rare. And I did let most of the holes close up." Out of pure laziness—not that I'd tell her that. I found I slept better without the piercings in my nipples, my nose and my ears. I'd never gone for gauges, though at one time I'd been tempted to try it just because few women had them.

Kiley shoved me. "One piercing. Crappy clothes. Get moving."

"And to think I woke up early for this."

She laughed and drank the last of my coffee.

On the way to the meeting spot, I said, "So it's just you and me today?"

"There's one other person coming. I don't know him."

"You didn't grill him? You're just assuming this guy isn't some kind of perv preying on kids?"

"You're more suspicious than I am, Lennox. This guy is from a charitable foundation run by a bunch of rich women who feel guilty for being rich, so they round up their other guilt-ridden pals a few times a year and force them to volunteer." Kiley pulled off the freeway. "That wasn't meant to come off snotty sounding. I'm grateful for these foundations because there's no way we can do this without them. This foundation in particular sends qualified people that don't come off as entitled. My kids would crucify them for that. And there is nothing nastier than a sixteen-year-old with a chip on his or her shoulder. Nothing."

I knew that.

"You never said how long this lasts."

"Depends on how many kids show up. If it's over fifteen, I usually take them to lunch after we finish the community service project."

"And if it's less than ten kids?" I prompted her.

"I packed lunch and we'll be out of here by one."

She pulled into the deserted parking lot. I didn't see any teenagers loitering. My gut clenched. I hoped for Kiley's sake some of the kids made an appearance. She'd put so much thought, effort and money from her own pocket into this project that it would crush her if it didn't succeed.

Kiley opened the back of her SUV. "Grab a bin."

The plastic bins were heavy, but we each lugged one to the picnic table near the graffitied wall. We walked back to her car and saw a skinny black kid leaning against the car.

"DeMarius—happy to see you here! Grab a box."

The kid, probably around fifteen, gave me a once-over. "This another rich do-gooder they saddled you with, Kiki?"

It was interesting to me that the kids called her Kiki. Even more interesting was that this kid thought I could pass for rich.

Kiley rolled her eyes. "Lennox is my roommate. I'd be ticked off if she was secretly rich, because the woman has been late on the rent more than one time."

Not true, but I saw how quickly the kid relaxed and how fast his grin popped up.

"That's cool."

"But there's supposed to be a volunteer showing up today, so I'm gonna ask you don't pull attitude, okay?"

"No promises," he said as he hefted the bin and headed toward the picnic table.

Kiley pointed to the case of water and the cooler. "Let's load the water on top of the cooler and each take a handle."

After we dropped the cooler off, I noticed two more kids had shown up. A short Hispanic girl and a rail-thin redhead who stood at least six feet tall.

"Hey, Kiki," the redhead said. "I brought my basketball."

"Great. I see that you talked fiery Maria into coming today." Kiley addressed her in Spanish and the girl responded, adding a flurry of hand gestures.

"I don't wanna play ball with girls," DeMarius complained.

"You might not have a choice if it's just the five of us."

Whoa. I had not signed on to participate in some athletic contest. I was not the sporty kind. At all.

"Check out your girl Lennox's face," DeMarius said with a laugh.

Kiley looked at me. "What?"

"I'm fine shaking up spray cans and such, but you are *not* getting me on that court, K."

"DeMan is such a ball hog you wouldn't get to play much anyway," the redhead said.

"Red. You're just pissed 'cause you're tall and you oughta be good at playing ball but you suck it up bad on the court."

I was seriously screwed if these kids all had nicknames as well as real names. Three was about my limit to keep straight.

"We'll see if your moves are better, DeMan, because I stuffed you last time." Another kid had joined us, except he didn't look like a kid. He had a full beard and was built like he spent his time in a gym, not in high school.

"Juice," Kiley said with a smile. "Glad you're here."

"Well, if this is all who shows up, I ain't staying long."

Kiley shrugged. "Suit yourself. It's not a requirement for you to be here."

"I thought Jonesie would drag his sorry ass along with you, since he's livin' with you and shit," DeMan said.

"My old man is a dickhead. He said Jonesie had to pay rent if he stayed there. So Jonesie's been crashing somewhere else."

That caught Kiley's attention. "Did he go home?"

"I doubt it. His stepdad getting outta jail is what made him crash with me."

Even as I was trying to place the ages of these kids, four more showed up: a chubby white boy, a lanky black boy with a younger black girl who looked to be his sister, and another man/boy with dreadlocks who I guessed to be part Native American.

"Seems you got your wish, DeMan. There are enough people to play three on three."

The kids all started talking at once and their level of energy hit me. It had been a lifetime for me since I'd been around teens—I'd preferred the company of adults even when I'd been a teen myself.

Kiley clapped her hands. "Before we do anything, this is Lennox. She's my roommate and she's here to help out."

"Roommate?" Dreadlocks said with a snicker and elbowed Juice.

"Or is she your girlfriend?" Juice asked. "Because I'm gonna be pissed if I've been usin' my best moves on you, Kiki, and you play for the other team."

The group laughed.

Before Kiley—I had to remember to call her Kiki—answered, the group's attention zoomed in on something behind me. Kiki and I turned at the same time.

Her "Holy shit" summed it up perfectly.

Brady Lund stood fifty feet away.

Nine

LENNOX

No freaking way.

"Isn't that . . . the guy who got ditched at the sushi joint?" Kiley asked.

"Yes."

"And he's your boss?"

"Technically . . . no."

"Then why is he here if he's not tracking your ass down to finish some paperwork or some damn thing?" she demanded.

Good question. Why *was* he here? A thought occurred to me. "What's the name of the organization sending a volunteer?" I asked Kiley.

"LCCO. Why?"

I groaned. I'd seen that name on interoffice memos. "That stands for Lund Cares Community Outreach. That's Brady Lund. CFO of Lund Industries."

"You're kidding me, right? Why is a CFO wasting time doing community service?" She paused. "Not that it's a waste of time, but damn, Lennox. We never get the bigwigs to help out. It's usually the bigwigs' wives or lackeys or employees on probation."

I knew that. So I was equally confused. "Did you list my name as a volunteer?"

"No."

So there was no way Brady knew I'd be here. This was just one of those weird coincidences.

Wasn't it?

Or fate, some ridiculously romantic voice trilled inside my head.

I mentally snarled at it to piss off.

"Come on." Kiley nudged me with her shoulder. "Follow my lead, even if it doesn't make any sense."

Right. Last time she said that? I ended up hungover and could barely say the word "kamikaze" without barfing.

As we approached him, Brady wore that sexy smile and never took his eyes off me.

My stomach had no reason to turn somersaults.

"Mr. Lund," my roommate said when we were ten feet away. "I need you to give Lennox a big hug like you haven't seen her in weeks. I'll explain afterward."

Brady didn't miss a beat. He actually closed the last few feet between us and gathered me into his arms. "Good morning, dancing queen."

His hard chest was warm and solid against my cheek. And did he have to smell so good? I wrapped my arms around his waist.

"Here's the breakdown, Mr. Lund. I'm Kiley Kinslie and I work in the Hennepin County Outreach program. I had no idea the LCCO would send their best and brightest to volunteer. While I'm grateful for it, there are two things we need to address ASAP."

"Go on."

"First, since you and Lennox know each other, and I don't need my boys drooling over her, let's go with the story that you two are in a relationship and that's why you're here volunteering. Second, if these kids find out you're Richie Rich, it'll be twice as hard to get them to accept you."

"Sounds logical and that works for me. How do you know Lennox?"

"We're roommates," I said. I tipped my head back to look at him, but couldn't quite make my arms release him. "And I don't see how this will work."

"What part?"

"Any of it. You're . . ." *All that and a bag of supersized chips, baby.* "You. You scream da man."

"Seriously? As in *da man* keeping them down?"

I blushed. Back to insulting him at every turn. *Way to go.*

"I'm not a total dumbass, Lennox. I didn't drive my 7-series BMW here and I'm hardly dressed like a corporate executive."

True. He wore loose nylon athletic shorts, a T-shirt and a warm-up jacket. His jaw was covered in dark scruff. In my mind he still managed to look powerful. But I couldn't admit that, so I went with the other issue. "These kids are street-smart, Mr. Lund. None of them will believe we're involved."

"By all means, Miss Greene. Let's test that theory."

The next thing I knew, his hands were on my hips and he lowered his face to my neck. He settled his warm lips on the pulse point of my throat and then glided his mouth up and down before he eased back to look at me.

I swayed against him, my fingers digging into his biceps.

Kiley laughed. "Yeah, they'll believe it. Let's get back.

Remember, no last names. Also remember, they're kids, so giving us—and each other—shit is their way. Roll with it but always err on the side of less is more. If you find yourselves in a situation out of your comfort zone, let me know."

No way would I admit that I was already out of my comfort zone.

Without waiting for our response, Kiley walked off.

Brady kept his hand in the small of my back as we followed her. He put his mouth on my ear. "Don't mess up and call me Mr. Lund, Lennox."

"Why are you here? Office gossip indicates that you work six—sometimes seven—days a week."

"I'm here because volunteering for causes is what Lunds do, according to my mother. And it was either this or humiliate myself at a bachelor auction."

"Why would you humiliate yourself? You'd probably raise thousands of dollars."

He chuckled. "You flatter me. I'm the nerdy bean counter, too analytical for most women's taste, and I'm also a workaholic, so, statistically speaking, I wouldn't be the top draw."

I stopped, forcing him to stop too. "Are you serious or is this some self-deprecating attempt to get me to say something else complimentary about you?"

"I'm serious." In a nervous, fidgety movement, he adjusted the Vikings baseball cap on his head. "I prefer to work behind the scenes rather than in the spotlight."

That didn't surprise me. His family name was synonymous with power in the Twin Cities, and he maintained a lower profile than any of his siblings and cousins. But this show of uncertainty did surprise me. The man defined confident.

Didn't he?

Brady curled his hand around the side of my face, his gaze firmly on the left side of my mouth. Then his thumb slid over to stroke my bottom lip. "This lip ring . . . Christ, do you have any idea how much I want to suck on it?"

The sexy way he growled that sent slow, delicious heat unfurling in my belly.

"Before the end of the day, Lennox, I'll know what that metal feels like on my tongue."

A tingle shot from his gentle stroking motion on my mouth straight between my thighs.

"Come on, you two—let's get a jump on this," Kiley shouted.

One of the kids said something and they all laughed.

Brady smiled. "Let's do this thang."

That phrase sounded all sorts of wrong coming from him, but it charmed me.

We stopped outside the half circle where Kiley held court.

"Intros. Everyone, this is Brady. He's a volunteer. He's also attached to Lennox, so they're both off-limits."

A chorus of boos broke out.

Kiley pointed to each kid and introduced them. DeMarius "DeMan," Willa aka Red, Feisty Maria, Juice. The chubby white kid's name was Owen, dreadlocks had the un-PC name Tonto, the skinny black kid's name was Quay, and his sister was Needra.

"Who's doin' what?" Tonto demanded. "I came to play ball and we ain't got enough for one team."

"Who all wants to play ball?" Kiley asked.

Tonto, Juice, DeMan, Quay, Red and Brady's hands all shot up.

"Six total. Play three on three," Kiki suggested.

"She's a damn girl," DeMan complained about Red.

"A girl who can outshoot you," she shot back.

"Prove it."

Kiley signaled for time-out. She looked at Brady. "You're team captain one." Then she looked at DeMan. "You're team captain two. You were here first, so you pick first."

"Juice."

They high-fived.

Brady pointed at Red. "You."

She seemed surprised, but pleased.

DeMan picked Tonto, which left Quay on Brady's team.

"We'll leave you to it. When you're done, come over to the wall."

The rest of us followed Kiley to the picnic table. She pointed at the brick building. "While dirty words have their place, it's not on the side of a building. We're gonna fix that today. So I see two options. One, we paint over the entire side, or we redo the words and incorporate them into some kind of design."

"The last option," Owen said. "It won't be hard to turn the *C* into an *O*. Then we can fill it in with whatever we want."

"Everyone in agreement?" Kiki asked the others.

"Owen should be in charge. He's a great artist," Maria said.

Owen blushed.

Since I was about as artistic as I am athletic, I volunteered to shake up the paint cans and act as the all-around gofer. Which also meant I could watch the basketball game.

After Brady took off his jacket, revealing muscled arms and a broad chest with pectorals so defined I could actually see the outline of them through his cotton T-shirt, I wished he'd been playing on the skins team.

And he played with a balance of aggressiveness and

teamwork. I'd wondered if he'd be overly competitive, not only because these kids were younger than him, but also because his brother was a professional athlete. So I had to admit his sense of fair play intrigued me.

One time he caught me watching him and he stole the ball and sank a jump shot. The way he moved that lean body was almost as compelling as the cocky grin he aimed in my direction.

"You've been holding out on me, roomie," Kiley said behind me.

"I haven't. I ran into him last night at Maxie's, which was almost as bizarre as him being the corporate volunteer. I've worked at Lund for almost a year and before last week I could count on one hand the number of times I've seen him. Now it's like he's everywhere."

"The universe is telling you something."

I turned to face her. "Telling me what?"

She shrugged. "Don't know yet. But there is a reason you two keep ending up at the same places—outside of work."

A shout brought us back to the wall to help out.

The next time I happened to glance over at the game, the players had switched it up and Brady *was* playing for the skins team.

And I froze in place, seeing the musculature rippling in his back as he jumped to block, but Red shot over him and the ball dropped neatly through the hoop.

That must've been the game ender. Both teams high- and low-fived as they walked off the court toward the picnic table.

After Brady plucked his shirt off the ground and used it to mop his face and neck, his gaze connected with mine.

It took every ounce of willpower I had not to let my focus drop to the dark hair covering his chest, or fall lower to what

I assumed were killer abs, or become mesmerized by the way his biceps flexed as he walked closer, holding his T-shirt.

Eyes on his face, eyes on his face—crap, my eyes did their own thing and dipped down to his neck and across those wide shoulders and down over his furred chest to the little pillows of flesh that composed his abs. I forced my traitorous eyes to zoom back up to his and not drop, even for a second, to what he had going on below the waistband of his athletic shorts.

He stopped a foot away from me, a grin playing at the corners of his mouth. "I thought my girlfriend would have a bottle of water cracked open and ready for her hard-playing man."

My eyes narrowed.

His grin widened. "Fine. Come here and give me a hug, woman."

It registered that I had a can of spray paint in my hand. I took a half step back and held it up. "Keep your hot, sweaty body right there."

"Or what? You'll spray paint me?"

He'd taken another step closer, forcing me to take one back. "Don't push your luck, Brady."

"So you'll set a bad example for these kids and start an all-out paint fight just to avoid giving me a hug? Come on, baby," he said in a husky tone. "Give it to me."

"All-out paint fight? From what I see, *I'm* the one with the can of paint, not you, so you'd better just stop right there."

"You wouldn't dare."

Not a good thing to dare me—I've never been able to resist one. So I started to shake the can. "Okay, if we're playing truth or dare, I'll pick . . . dare."

Brady immediately backed up. "Lennox. I was joking. Having fun with this."

I stepped toward him. "And now *I'm* having fun with it."

Then he stopped and threw his arms open. "Okay, wild thing. If you're going to do it, make it count."

I pressed my finger on the sprayer head and aimed at his chest. I made one long neon green line down the right side, and then a shorter line above the waistband of his boxers.

His mouth dropped open and he stared at the beautiful *L* I'd painted on his chest.

But I didn't have time to bask in my derring-do.

Brady snatched the can from me. Keeping a tight grip on my wrist, he aimed the nozzle at himself and turned the *L* into a lopsided *B*. Then he wrapped his arms around me, plastering our chests together.

And the man was so damn strong, he'd picked me up off my feet and held me in place with no effort whatsoever.

I squirmed, intending to smear the paint all over him, and he laughed. I looked up at him, my glare ready to fry his retinas, but the happiness I saw shining in his eyes stole my breath away.

"I'll never doubt your ability to refuse a dare ever again, wild thing."

"Put me down."

"I will." He smirked. "As soon as the paint is dry. But while we're waiting, tell me what time I'm picking you up for our date tonight?"

"When did I agree to a date?"

"Last night at the bar. I saved your pretty neck, remember? I said I'd be in touch, but since we're both here and it's a Saturday night, I don't see any reason to wait."

"What if I have plans tonight?"

A fierce light entered his eyes. "Break them."

And I was done arguing just for the sake of arguing. I wanted to see if he was a lousy date, and there was only one way to find out. "Okay. One date."

"A first date," he corrected.

"If you two are done playing grab-ass, I could use some help," Kiley said behind me.

Brady set me down.

I smirked at the paint smeared on his upper torso. It'd be a bitch to get out of his chest hair. And if he asked me nicely, I might just help him remove it.

For the next two hours we worked on covering the graffiti. Again, Brady's demeanor was different than I expected. At work he'd always acted more blatantly self-assured than quietly confident. Here he was more laid-back than I'd ever seen him.

During our lunch break, Juice said, "Hey, Brady. Whatcha do for a job, man?"

"I'm an accountant."

I nearly choked on my water.

"No shit? I suck at math."

"I'm sure you don't," Brady said.

"Then why am I getting a D-minus in algebra?" Juice demanded.

"Are you doing the homework problems?"

"Nah, I don't get *how* to do 'em. And they're pointless anyway, 'cause ain't no one uses algebra in the real world." He tore into his bologna sandwich. "Why'd you say I don't suck at math? You some do-gooder who thinks I just oughta apply myself?"

Brady took a drink of water. "Math is like basketball— if you don't practice it, you won't get any better. That means doing the math homework every night. It's a cop-out when people say they suck at math. Numbers make sense. There's an order and a structure to them. If you add seven to four, you get eleven, every damn time. With English, answers are subjective. So yeah, I think most people make math harder than it has to be."

"Maybe you should prove that it's so damn easy by tutoring me," Juice challenged.

"Then prove to me you want to beat your math phobia."

"How?"

"Do your homework every night next week. Bring your completed assignments and your textbook the next time and I'll take a look at it all."

"What do you want for helpin' me?"

Brady looked at me, then at Juice. "Advice. See, I've got this hot blond girlfriend I want to take out and show off tonight. I've been out of the club scene for a few years, so where should I take her to impress her?"

"Flurry," Juice and Tonto said simultaneously. "That is a wicked fun club. Five dance levels. The sound system cost millions. Lots of neon and chicks dancing in cages. But it's freakin' hard to get in. There's always a line. They pick the hot babes first, then hot dudes. Some rich guy owns the club. I heard the VIP section is sick."

"How do you know all of that?" Kiley asked Juice.

"My cousin got in one night."

Everyone started asking Juice questions, as if he were a celebrity who'd actually gotten into the club, and he ate it up. I looked over at Brady. He seemed lost in thought.

"Looks like you'd better track down some slutty club wear for tonight," Kiley whispered.

I went to bars—and not even all that much anymore to be honest—not clubs. But I wouldn't waste brain cells worrying about what to wear. My more immediate concern was how I'd keep my hands, mouth and other body parts off my date.

When Brady's heated gaze met mine, my heart raced. We were combustible.

"All right. Let's get this stuff picked up and you can go on your merry ways," Kiley said to her charges. "I appreciate all of you coming today. We'll do it here again next week—weather permitting." She pointed at me and Brady. "Let's give a shout-out to Lennox and Brady for helping out today."

After loading everything in the SUV, the kids went off in different directions, all of them at least paired up so they weren't walking alone in this sketchy part of town. Over the past couple of hours I'd noticed groups of three or four guys wandering around the perimeter of the playground checking us out. They never approached us, so we must've looked nonthreatening. Or maybe too threatening, as a group.

Kiley looked around the empty parking lot. "Where'd you park, Brady?"

"At the Walker."

"That's five miles from here," I said.

"Better place to leave my car." He shrugged. "I needed to run today anyway."

He ran five miles and then played basketball for two hours? And he wasn't exhausted?

Obviously the man had great stamina.

Makes you wonder what kind of staying power he has during other physical activities, doesn't it?

"No," I said aloud.

Both Kiley and Brady stared at me.

"Sorry. Thinking about something else."

"Well, if I drop you off at your car, can you take Lennox

home?" Kiley asked Brady. "All these supplies belong to the center and I have to return them today."

What was she doing?

"Besides, you need to know where we live before your date tonight anyway."

"True." Brady smiled at me and drained his bottle of water. "A ride would be great."

I called shotgun like a fifteen-year-old boy.

Kiley was preoccupied on the drive, and I didn't press her to talk, because chances were she couldn't tell me anyway if it involved her kids.

Ten minutes after we left the park, we pulled into the parking lot. "Which car is yours?" she asked.

"The black BMW in the corner."

"Sweet ride."

"Thanks."

"Thank you for showing up today."

"Truly my pleasure, Kiley." Brady exited the car.

I started to get out, but Kiley put her hand on my thigh. "If Mr. Tall, Dark and Smolderingly Sexy doesn't demand you grab your stuff and start the date with him right away? Wear your leather skirt tonight."

"Why?"

"Because you are smokin' hot in that skirt and you'll have every man in that fancy club panting after you. Oh— and pair it with that shirt. The one with the chains. Girl, you look fine in that and I never see you wear it."

"Any suggestions on shoes?" I asked sarcastically.

"Patent leather spike-heeled pumps. And wear your hair up." She patted my leg. "I won't barge in tomorrow morning and demand details, just in case you're not alone."

"I'm not sleeping with him on the first date, Kiley. Geez." With that, I got out of the car.

I knocked on the nearly black window on the passenger side of Brady's car. The locking mechanism clicked and I slid inside.

The interior was gray and molded around me as if I'd strapped into a rocket ship. "Whoa."

"Like it?"

"It's . . . space-age. Does it go fast?"

He flashed me a boyish grin. "Oh, yeah. Scared myself the first time I floored it. But it hasn't stopped me from doing it again and again."

I laughed.

"What's your address?" he asked and started poking buttons on the center console.

I gave it to him and he punched it into the GPS.

We weren't talkative as we cruised along, and for the first time the silence between us was awkward.

"I was really surprised to see you this morning," he said.

"More surprised than when you saw me last night?"

Brady seemed at a loss for words. He muttered something.

"What did you say?"

"Juice said he sucks at math? I suck at this."

I frowned. "I'm not following you. You suck at what?"

His hands tightened on the steering wheel. "Making small talk."

"You did great with those kids today."

"I'm not talking about them. I'm talking about this." He gestured between us. "I won't force you to go on a date with me, Lennox, if you'd rather not. I've already had one woman—although calling her that is a bit of a stretch—ditch me middate. Granted, it was more of a favor than a date, but I fear that maybe you'll see this as an obligation, and that's almost worse."

I couldn't have said what made me happier: Brady admitting a previous date had ditched him or that he wasn't confident when it came to dating. Seeing that imperfection in Mr. Perfect . . . it made him even more perfect in my eyes. I set my hand on his forearm. "You're not an obligation."

"Good to know."

"Set the scene for tonight. Tell me how you see it playing out."

He blushed. Omigod he was so freakin' cute when he blushed. "I pick you up, and we'd have dinner at the Korean-French restaurant on Marquette. Then, if we're feeling energetic, we hit the club, we dance, we have a drink or two, we stay there for a while after we find the only quiet corner where we can talk, but don't close the place down. Then I take you home, you invite me in, we tear each other's clothes off and go at it right there on the staircase."

I swiveled around to gape at him.

Brady laughed. "Just seeing if you were paying attention."

"I am. But my mind got stuck on fusion food."

"Not your favorite?"

"I don't like my food mixed up."

"Guess I won't be making my famous tater tot casserole for you."

I laughed.

"Christ, you have a sexy laugh," Brady said. "That's how I first noticed you."

"What do you mean? Last week was the first time you've ever spoken to me."

He shot me a quick grin. "Exactly. But it wasn't the first time I noticed you. That was months ago. I wasn't sure which department you worked in when I saw you down the hallway from the break room. But you were with that redhead from your office and you were laughing. There was just something about your laugh . . ."

Brady seemed embarrassed again and I don't know why I rushed to reassure him. "I'm happy to hear you liked my laugh rather than you telling me I sounded like a snorting donkey or something and that's why you noticed me."

"Never." He pulled up in front of my house and put the car in park. "What time should I pick you up?"

I faced him and discovered he'd moved closer. So that gorgeous face with the vibrant blue eyes and full lips was right there. If I leaned back, he'd take it the wrong way. Heck, *I'd* take it the wrong way. More than anything, I wanted to angle forward and have a taste of him.

Fortunately, my head controlled the situation, not my mouth. "I have a list of things to do today that I've been putting off." Not a total lie. "And if you're serious about trying to get into that club, I'd rather not go dancing after eating a heavy meal."

"Good point. We'll break this up into two dates. Clubbing tonight, dinner another night. And never fear, dancing queen. I'll get us into the club."

No doubt a few phone calls from him and we'd be in. It'd be best to remember that the Lund family name wielded results. "Fine. Pick me up at nine?"

"Perfect." He smiled and his gaze dropped to my mouth. "Feel free to wear the lip ring," he murmured. "It might actually be sexier than your laugh."

Holy crap. When he turned on his sexual charisma, he cranked it to high.

Just to be ornery, I moved in and angled my head so I could rub that gold hoop across his bottom lip.

Brady inhaled sharply but he didn't move.

I said, "See you at nine," and got out of his car.

Ten

BRADY

had to work after I dropped Lennox off. I knew if I went home I'd obsess for hours about our upcoming date. Focusing on numbers would keep my mind off her.

Off that sexy fucking lip ring.

Off that sexy fucking laugh.

Off that sexy fucking tattoo.

Off that sexy fucking way she walked.

Everything about that woman hit the right notes for me, which made zero sense analytically since I'd never been attracted to a woman like her before.

I'd dated women at various points in my life—none I'd ever call girlfriends. The closest I'd come to a steady relationship was in college. I had a fling with the college adviser for my master's, who taught me so much more than economics. The rest of my encounters were one-night stands. Although I rarely took advantage of it, I knew if I went to a bar looking to get laid, I wouldn't go home alone.

But all that changed two years ago when I reached the rung on the ladder I'd spent my entire life climbing toward. And I'd been holding on so tightly, with both hands, because I feared it would all slip away.

I backed up all my data and shut down my computer. After I locked my office, I called Nolan.

He answered, "I know, I know. I'm so damn much fun that you're calling to ask if I want to hang out with you tonight too."

I punched the down button on the elevator. "I had enough of you last night."

"Dammit, Brady, I recognize that elevator ding. Are you at the office? Are you working? You're supposed to be—"

"I needed something that I'd left here," I interrupted with a lie instead of snapping at him and asking who the hell he was to tell *me* when I could and couldn't work. "And for future reference? I don't see the allure of strip clubs, so we can skip that next time."

"As if we couldn't tell when you were on your phone instead of admiring all that beautiful naked female flesh. Anyway, why are you calling me?"

"You bragged that you could get into any club in town."

"Yeah, so?"

"Prove it. I've got a date tonight and I want to take her to Flurry."

"A date? Already?"

"Shocking, isn't it?"

"Completely. But seriously . . . Flurry? That doesn't seem like your scene."

"It's probably not, but I won't know unless I give it a shot. So can you get me in?"

"Not only can I get you in. I can get you into the VIP section."

I stepped into the elevator and hit the button for the garage level. "Is it that much different?"

"You wouldn't be asking for access to Flurry if you weren't trying to impress this woman. VIP passes guarantee you'll get laid."

"Like I need your help with that. Just get me and a guest on the list, okay?"

"Done." He paused. "So what are you gonna wear tonight?"

"A loincloth. God, I don't know. I haven't thought about it."

Nolan laughed. "You should think about it. Don't show up looking like an accountant. Maybe I ought to come over and help you pick out an outfit."

"Piss. Off." I hung up and used the remote to open my car. Just as I climbed inside, my phone rang. I answered it without looking at the caller ID. "For the last time, I don't need your help picking out clothing."

"Well, I should hope not," my sister answered. "And I really don't want to know who you were talking to."

"Nolan."

"Ah. That explains it."

"So what's going on?"

"I know how much you love small talk"—she snorted—"so I'll cut to the chase. I need you to back out of going to Mom and Dad's tomorrow afternoon for the football game."

I nestled my head into the headrest. "Can I ask why?"

When Annika stayed quiet for about ten seconds, I waited to hear what excuse she'd fabricated off the cuff.

"It's a work-related issue. I dropped the ball big-time and I need tomorrow to fix it. And it's one of those things that if I don't get it handled, it'll steamroll, and I don't need to blow this."

"What project?"

"Secret shopper. And don't get mad. I know I was supposed to have all the data done last week; I just got sidetracked. You, of all people, should understand that work comes first, Brady."

"Nice one. I, of all people, do understand that work comes first, which means I suspect you didn't prioritize this project and that's why you're scrambling."

She sighed. "As project manager I know my opinion holds a lot of weight, so I can't very well admit I hadn't stepped foot in any of the restaurants. So now I'll spend ten hours tomorrow eating."

"I agree that your personal input is necessary since I'll be tasked with making the final financial decision about the restaurants' future."

"Thank you. You can see that I'm in a bind. So can you call Mom and Dad? They're used to you bailing out on family day. Then it won't be such a big deal if I back out."

That stung, but mostly because it was true. "Yes, I'll call them. But you do realize Walker will be pissed if he's the only one there?"

Annika laughed. "Right. Like Mom won't call him and ask if he's going to back out like you and I did, which gives him an excuse not to go either."

"You're right. See you at the track Monday, since you'll need to run off all of those sweets you have to eat tomorrow." I hung up before she let loose and cursed me with a barrage of names.

It'd be best to just get this over with. I dialed my mother's cell number, instead of going the chickenshit route and calling their house phone.

She picked up on the fourth ring. "My darling boy. You're just in time for dinner. Come over and you can tell me in person what's on your mind."

Mom felt it was her duty to feed me. But since she gave the cook weekends off, I couldn't guess what oddball Swedish "fusion" she would concoct and pass off as a home-cooked meal. "I'll take a rain check. I'm calling to let you know I'll have to miss family game day tomorrow."

Silence.

I hated the silent treatment.

"Because you are working," she said flatly.

"Working" sounded like *whore-king* and I bit back a laugh. "No, actually I have a date tonight and it might end up being a late one. Since the Vikings are playing the early game, I just wanted to err on the side of caution."

"Well. That is . . . promising. You should bring her for brunch. I'll cook."

"I'm not bringing her home after one date, Mom. Especially not after you were partially responsible for that fiasco with Siobhan."

"Maggie had her own agenda, of which I did not want to be a party with."

"A party to," I corrected without thinking.

"Whatever. So where did you meet this mystery date?"

I laughed. "Nice try. I have to go. I'll talk to you this week."

"You better. *Jag älskar dig.*"

"Love you too."

I put my car in gear and headed home.

———

'm always early. I ended up driving around the block four times before I pulled up in front of Lennox's house.

Lennox must've been anxious, because she opened the door immediately after I knocked.

Not that I could even say hello when I got my first look at her.

She wore a leather skirt the color of cabernet with a sleeveless black silk shirt that dipped low, and the fabric moved sinuously across her chest. Her lips were dark red, her eye makeup smoky, her blond hair half up/half down.

No trace remained of the Stepford secretary.

I was looking at the ultimate bad girl, prepped and ready for a wild night out.

My gaze met hers but I still couldn't speak.

"Hang on one second. I need to grab my purse."

When she spun around, I had to brace myself in the doorframe to keep from falling over. Her shirt was backless, except for thin silver chains that held the material on the front in strategic places. And she had more tattoos back there, with one that looked like a Celtic knot—a tramp stamp—above the low-hanging waistband of her skirt. And that ass. Although I was a mathematician, the perfection of her ass practically inspired me to write a sonnet where I described every beautiful curve and how my hands and mouth would feel worshipping every inch.

When she whirled around and caught me looking with a feral expression of lust, she smirked. "I take it my club attire meets with your approval, Mr. Lund."

"You are beyond stunning, Miss Greene."

"Thank you. You don't clean up too badly yourself." Then her gaze wandered over me, taking in the lightweight black cashmere V-neck sweater and gray jeans, ending at the black loafers. When her gaze met mine again, she didn't bother to bank the heat in her eyes. "Casual suits you."

"Thank you."

"But not as well as a suit suits you." She grinned and snagged a shiny black coat off the newel post.

"May I?" I said, and took it from her hands to help her put it on.

She murmured her thanks again and faced me. Those hazel eyes of hers were hotly assessing. "I feel the need to warn you that we won't be going at it on those stairs like you mentioned earlier today."

"Seems a shame, but I'll survive." We stepped outside and she locked the door. "Although I did cancel plans with my family tomorrow just in case you and I ended up naked, sated and lazing in bed together in the morning."

Lennox whirled around. "Tell me you're joking."

"Of course I'm joking. About the naked part. I did cancel family plans and I did blame it on our date. But I had an ulterior motive, covering for my sister, who wanted me to be the first one to back out."

"So she wouldn't feel guilty canceling after you did?"

"Exactly. Now I'll just have to deal with my brother Walker being pissed he'll be the lone Lund child in attendance." I opened her car door and closed it after she climbed in. Then I got in and hit start on the GPS.

"Is your family get-together a weekly thing?" she asked.

"During football season? Yes, when Jensen has away games. If he's home, then we're in the dome cheering him on. 'We' meaning the entire Lund family—cousins, uncles, aunts . . ."

When she reached down to set her purse on the floor, her hair brushed against my wrist and my fist clenched voluntarily.

"I'll bet there's a ton of pride in your family for Jensen making it to the pros and the Vikings in particular. Hometown boy makes good and all that."

"He's living his dream. It's been great to watch him play and improve over the years. But yes, our mother would still demand nightly family dinners if she had her way."

"I see pictures of your mother all over the place. I've seen her at LI a few times. She's very beautiful."

I smiled. "That she is. Drives my poor father crazy that Annika looks just like her. He would've preferred to lock her in her princess bedroom until she turned thirty because, in addition to looking like our mother, she has that same fire and stubbornness."

Lennox stretched out her legs. "Do you mind me asking about your family?"

"No. I wondered if you'd worked with any of them."

"I temped in Annika's department for three weeks. I admire her energy."

"When she said she needed to work tomorrow, I know she wasn't bullshitting me."

"You're close to her?"

"Yes. I'm close to Walker and Jensen too."

"Must be nice. I'm an only child. I'd say that I'm the only hell my mama ever raised, but I wouldn't be here if she wasn't a hell-raiser of the first order."

"Speaking of raising hell, have you been to Flurry?"

She shook her head.

"I hope it lives up to the hype."

Flurry was located in downtown Minneapolis. It wasn't a place that had valet parking, but the area did have a parking garage close by, which helped explain its popularity. Standing inside where it was warm while waiting for admission to a club was preferable to shivering outside in the cold Minnesota winter.

"Looks like it'll be a trek from the parking garage. Would you rather I dropped you off so you don't kill your feet in those sexy heels?"

"I'm capable of walking." Lennox looked at me. "You like the shoes?"

"Not as much as I like the leather skirt," I murmured.

She gave me a throaty laugh. "You, Brady Lund, aren't what I expected. By that I mean better than I'd hoped for."

"Same goes, Lennox Greene."

She exited the car before I could cross to her side to help her out.

This was where I'd get confused. Did I reach for her hand? Drape my arm over her shoulder? Slide my arm around her waist?

Then Lennox was right in my face. "Kiss me."

"Pardon?"

She pressed her palms on my chest and said, "Kiss me. You know you want to. The first time we kiss I don't want a thousand strangers looking on."

Like a total dumbass, I said, "I kissed you at the park today."

"That little peck on my neck you gave me for the benefit of the kids? Doesn't count."

Not exactly spontaneous, but that worked for me. Now I knew exactly what to do with my hands. I curled one around the nape of her neck and the other beneath her jaw. I brushed my lips over hers, starting at the right corner and moving to the left, then gliding back before parting her lips with my tongue and urging her to open her mouth for me.

The softest, sexiest sigh accompanied her surrender.

I dove into that succulent mouth, hungry for her taste, but forced myself to not devour her. A low rumble drifted out when I felt her lips clinging to mine as my tongue rubbed and stroked against hers.

When the intensity got to be too much, I held her head in place as I backed off, switching it up to soft kisses. The exchange of heated breath between us. I circled her lip ring with the tip of my tongue and gently tugged on it with my teeth. Fucking thing made me hard. I imagined that bit of metal scraping down my throat, across my chest and moving south toward my groin. I kissed her harder, needing her to feel exactly how much I desired her.

She trembled and pressed herself against me.

I knew if I didn't stop right then, I'd lose the ability to do so at all. I pressed a lingering kiss on both corners of her mouth and then the center. "You sure staircase sex isn't in the cards for tonight?"

She laughed softly. "Maybe I was too hasty earlier."

"You were waiting to see if I made an idiot of myself on the dance floor? Or if I kissed like a cold wet fish?"

Her eyes—full of heat and surprise—locked onto mine. "Some hot guys don't bother to learn how to kiss. I wasn't sure if you were that type."

I resisted the urge to pump my fist in victory that Lennox thought I fell into "hot guy" territory.

"So I'm glad you're not that type." She licked her lips as she stared at mine. "But just to make sure, I need another kiss."

"No."

She blinked at me. "What?"

I rested my hand at the base of her throat. My thumb pressed into the skin beneath her jawbone; my middle finger pressed the other side. I felt her pulse leap. I'd always been a passive guy when it came to taking the lead with women. But that was about to change with her. "You asked for one kiss. I gave it to you. The next kiss is mine to take. Whenever I want."

Her lips parted and she expelled a soft "Oh."

"Come on." I kept my hand in the small of her back as we walked to the entrance.

Normally doorways to the various businesses served by the skywalk system in downtown Minneapolis were nondescript. But this one had been created for maximum impact. The exterior was pure white and looked like a snow cave with gigantic icicles hanging above it. Two separate doors marked the entrances. Bouncers manned both doors and music thumped out. I eyed the long line that snaked down the corridor and directed Lennox to the smaller door on the left. A notice beside the door read:

VIP ACCESS ONLY

DON'T WASTE OUR TIME ASKING IF YOU'RE ON THE VIP LIST! ANY CLUBGOERS WHO ATTEMPT TO GAIN ADMISSION THROUGH THE VIP ACCESS WHO ARE NOT ON THE LIST WILL BE BANNED FROM THE CLUB. NO EXCEPTIONS! ASK IF YOU'RE ON THE LIST AT YOUR OWN PERIL!

"That's a serious warning," Lennox said.

"It must work because there's no one in line," I said, steering her toward the VIP entrance.

"Are you sure about this?" she asked.

"No. We'll see if Nolan followed through."

The bouncer—a thick wall of a man, massive enough to play on the Vikings offensive line—gave me a bored once-over. "Help you with something?" he asked gruffly.

"My name is on the list. Lund."

He raised his hand—the size of a baseball mitt—to fore-stall any additional conversation and spoke into his mouth-piece. Then he said, "Club manager will be out to verify."

Verify . . . what?

Lennox snagged my hand and tugged. "Move over here," she hissed in my ear. "Don't piss off the bouncer."

"How would I do that? I'm just standing here."

"Exactly. You're in his line of sight. Trust me, I've worked at enough clubs to know this stuff."

Just as I was about to ask where else she'd worked, a man in a sharp-looking black suit headed toward us. He thrust out his hand. "I'm Benjamin Larken, VIP coordinator for Flurry. And you are . . . ?"

I took his hand. "Brady Lund. My cousin Nolan called to let you know I'd be here tonight."

"Ah. Nolan. He's not one to give recommendations for the VIP section. I can see why he'd make an exception." He flashed a smile at Lennox, then looked at me. "Is your cousin still seeing Sela?"

"No idea. It's too hard to keep up with Nolan's stream of women."

The man looked at me suspiciously.

I reached into my back pocket and pulled out my wallet. "I imagine you need ID that proves who I am?" I pushed my driver's license out of the plastic sleeve and handed it over.

He scrutinized it. "You don't look anything like Nolan. Or his brother Ryan."

"Nolan doesn't have a brother named Ryan." I laughed and the VIP coordinator glanced up at me. "I understand you're just doing your job, attempting to trip me up with personal questions about my cousin, to see if I'm trying to sneak into the club with a bogus ID."

"Stranger things have happened." He handed back my ID. "So Ash is your . . . ?"

"Other cousin. I'm sure you've heard of my brother—Jensen Lund."

His eyes widened. "The Rocket is your brother?" He grinned. "Then why didn't you say so? We're happy to have you here, Mr. Lund. It's open seating in the VIP section. And if you decide to become a VIP member, come see me and I'll go over the details. Including guest passes. We'd love to see The Rocket here."

I just bet you would. I smiled. "Thank you." I put my hand on the small of Lennox's back and directed her inside what looked to be a short tunnel. Hip-hop blasted out.

Lennox stopped and spun to face me, her eyes searching. "Does that happen a lot?"

"Getting grilled when I attempt to enter a club? No. But not because I normally have automatic access due to my last name. I'm not the club type. Why?"

"Not that. People asking about your brother."

"Yes. People would use me to get connected to him—if I let that happen."

"Protective of him?"

"Someone has to be."

"And as the oldest the role falls to you?"

"Yes." I helped her off with her jacket and passed her coat to the coat check girl.

After we found a place to sit overlooking the lowest dance floor, the cocktail waitress stopped by to take our order.

Lennox looked over at the bar before she placed her order. "I'll have a lemon drop martini. And a glass of water."

"For you, sir?" the waitress cooed, moving in closer.

"What Leinenkugel do you have on tap?"

"Sunset Wheat and Red."

"Red is fine."

"Got it. Would you like to start a tab, Mr. . . . ?"

"No. I'll pay cash."

After she strolled away, Lennox leaned in. "Cash? Is that a finance-guy thing?"

I shrugged. "I'm not in the practice of handing my credit card over to someone I don't know in a place I've never been. So maybe that does qualify as a finance-guy thing."

"Smart move. Our waitress was a little put out that you didn't give her your name."

"Another reason to pay cash." I reached for her hand. "You used to work at Maxie's? How'd that come about?"

The question made her nervous. She tried to hide it. But ever since I'd placed the kiss on the side of her neck, I'd become obsessed with that graceful arch. So I noticed when her pulse jumped beneath that smooth white skin.

"Maxie is a friend of my mom's. She gave me a job when I came back here and decided to go to school."

"Nepotism at work."

She looked away. "Something like that. The weekend hours didn't conflict with my class schedule. The money was decent."

I ran my thumb across her knuckles. "Do you mind if I ask how old you are?"

"Twenty-eight. Why?"

"I would've guessed younger."

"I'm just glad you didn't guess older. God knows I feel it most days."

Silence stretched out between us.

Lennox focused on the dance floor and I focused on her. She was a delicate beauty, from the long arch of her neck to her angular jawline. Even my Nordic mother would envy her high cheekbones. Her nose turned up slightly at the end, giving her an aristocratic look. Her eyebrows were several shades darker than her blond hair, making her eyes the most prominent feature on her face.

She turned her head and those caramel-colored eyes bored into me. "Do I pass your inspection?"

"You know you do."

"Then why are you staring at me?"

"Because you're beautiful. You'd think I was a pervert if you caught me staring at you during working hours. And earlier today I didn't have much of a chance to look at your face since you had your back to the basketball court. But I did get a pretty good look at your ass."

"And?"

I lifted her hand to my mouth to kiss the center of her palm. "World-class, baby."

She laughed. "Is this a practiced charm, Mr. Lund?"

"No. Why? Does it seem as if I'm feeding you a line?"

"Honestly? No. But I'm still a little confused by all of this, if you want to know the truth." Her eyes searched mine. "You're not the kind of guy I usually date."

"How so? What makes me different?"

"First of all, you have a steady job. That's a plus."

"And?" I'd kept ahold of her hand and I brushed my mouth over the pulse point on her wrist.

"And we've established that you're *a* boss, but not *my* boss, yet it feels like I'm not supposed to be out with you."

"And?"

"And when you kissed me, I know if we were alone I

would have been naked in less than four seconds and you'd have your hands all over me . . . and then I wouldn't care less about your job or mine or anything else."

"More like *two* seconds before I'd have you stripped with my hands and mouth all over you," I half growled.

Lennox turned her head and touched her lips to the corner of my jaw. "Is it too truthful if I say I'm out of my league with you?"

"No, but you couldn't be more wrong. I like that you are hot, and sexy and wild. In fact, I want you to teach me how to cut loose and unleash my inner wild man."

"Seriously?"

"Yes. Remember earlier today when you said you'd heard I work seven days a week? It's true. But my family has intervened and is trying to get me to change that."

"Ah, so that's what last night at Maxie's was about. A Lund family intervention."

I snapped my mouth shut. Maybe this wasn't something I was supposed to admit.

The waitress returned, giving me a chance to regroup. She set down the drinks and said, "That'll be twenty-two dollars."

I pulled out my wallet and dropped thirty bucks on her tray. "Keep it."

"Thank you, sir." She took off.

Lennox sipped her martini. Even over the loud music I heard her soft, sexy groan of approval.

"Good?"

"It should be, for what you paid for it."

I shrugged and took a swig of my beer. I watched the action on the dance floor. Bodies gyrating to hip-hop really made me feel out of my element. It was doubtful that the dance classes my mother had inflicted on me would come in handy since stripper moves hadn't been part of the curriculum. Maybe I should've watched *Magic Mike*.

"Brady?"

"Yeah?" I said, still taking stock of what was happening on the dance floor.

"Do *you* want to change?"

My gaze snapped back to Lennox.

"Or are you just going along with your family's 'intervention' to keep them off your back?"

How had she picked up on that? I could've lied to her, but it felt wrong. "I probably need to change some things. I do work too much. I don't have much of a life. But what bugs me about the whole intervention thing is my family assumes I've got an inner wild man. What if I don't?"

"What if you do?" she countered.

"Then you're exactly the type of woman I need to help me set that inner wild man free."

"Sure, I'll do it. But I do have a couple of conditions."

"Name them."

"You have to meet me halfway. I don't know you well enough just to create a bucket list for you and enforce it."

This woman impressed the hell out of me. "Agreed."

"And your list can't only be sexual positions you haven't tried."

Watching her eyes, I sank my teeth into the fleshy skin at the base of her thumb. "That's one area where I don't need help getting wild, baby."

Her eyes darkened with heat as she casually sipped her martini. Then she asked, "Did we come here to dance? Or just to eye-fuck each other all night?"

Mr. Larken stopped by our table. "Mr. Lund. How is everything?"

"Good. I have a question. Does your DJ take requests?"

"For you? Of course."

"Do you have a pen?"

He passed it over and I moved the beer mug off the cocktail napkin. I wrote down my selection, folded a twenty inside the napkin and handed it to him.

"If he could play it in the next half hour, I'd appreciate it."

He nodded and backed away.

"Now, you want to get back to the eye-fucking? Or shall we return to the 'getting to know you' small talk that I suck at?"

"Small talk."

"Fine. What did you mean when you said you came back to the Twin Cities? When did you leave?"

Lennox tried to extricate her hand from mine, but I held on. "Anything you tell me stays between us. Anything," I emphasized.

She sipped her drink. "My home situation was a nightmare, so I dropped out of high school and went on the road with a rock band for a few years. Then I bounced around, Omaha, Kansas City, Quad Cities, other places. I mostly worked in bars and the food service industry. And when yet another sorority girl puked all over me, I'd had enough of that life. Once I found out the business practices and clerical support program had openings for nontraditional students, I applied to the vocational school here and got accepted into the two-year program. After I graduated, I had a hard time finding a job—as I told you before. Then I went to work for LI."

She'd lived a wilder life than I'd imagined—and I knew she'd just skimmed the surface. "Were you in the band?"

"No. My best friend Taylar's brother, Travis, was the lead guitarist and singer. She dated—and eventually married—the drummer. I got tired of chasing someone else's dream."

"You were involved with Travis?"

"Yeah. Travis was a great guy. Just not the guy for me." She gave me a wry smile. "What about you?"

"I never toured with a rock band, but I did kick my brother Walker's ass at the video game a bunch of times."

Lennox laughed. "That's not what I mean, smart-ass."

"My life has gone according to plan. I just want to spice it up."

"I imagine you've got a very sweet life."

"Most days. Doesn't mean it can't be improved upon." I glanced down and saw I'd finished most of my beer. Then I noticed Lennox had shoved her empty martini glass aside and was drinking water.

The waitress returned. "Another round?"

"I'm good for now. Lennox?"

"Same here."

The opening notes of my requested song started. I stood and held my hand out. "Come on. They're playing our song."

"You requested 'Smooth'?"

"It's a great tango tune."

She froze. "Brady. I don't know how to tango."

I brushed my lips over hers. "Tango is all about knowing how to move your body. And you had no problem doing that on top of the bar."

"But it's not the same thing as a formal dance."

"Follow my lead and trust me."

Eleven

LENNOX

Trust me.

I was having a mild panic attack.

First, in a case of nerves, I'd blurted out my misspent youth. Now I would look like an even bigger idiot because *of course* a classy man like him knew how to tango.

Every episode I'd ever watched of *Dancing with the Stars* zipped through my mind and not a single movement stuck.

Then we were on the dance floor and I was trapped.

Brady clasped my right hand in his left. He flattened his palm against my lower spine and scooted in so we were chest to chest. "All you need to do is move with me, Lennox. There's four beats. Slow, quick step, quick step, slow. Forward first, then back."

He rested the side of his jaw to my temple and urged me forward. I counted. Slow, quick, quick, slow. He turned us a quarter turn and again danced us forward and back.

By about the fifth time, I didn't need to count steps. The music and the dance steps made sense in a way I'd never put together before. We fell into a rhythm as if we'd been dancing together for years.

I surrendered to the sultry beat of the music and the sensuous way Brady moved his body. The cashmere was buttery soft beneath my palm on his shoulder. The scent of his cologne became more noticeable as his skin warmed from exertion.

When he stepped back and spun me out to the side and then back in, I didn't miss a single beat.

"See?" He breathed in my ear. "You're a natural. God, woman, the way you move . . . it's like making love to you fully clothed."

That might've been the single sexiest thing a man had ever said to me. And I knew he wasn't lying; I could gauge my effect on him every time our pelvises touched.

The next time he spun me, he stayed behind me, with both hands on my hips.

I mimicked his side-to-side motion, still with the slow, quick, quick, slow steps as our bodies touched. Yes, we were grinding on each other, but it was a classier way to do it.

"Put your arms above your head like you did on the bar top."

As soon as I did that, it changed the angle of my spine and shoulders.

His left hand traveled up the outside of my body from the bend in my waist, over my rib cage, the outer swell of my breast, and slowly across my outstretched arm until his fingers circled my wrists. His lips grazed the slope of my shoulder as he flattened his palm on my abdomen.

That's when he started making small circles with his

hips. His mouth migrated to my ear. "Bravo. We're in perfect sync."

I tipped my head to the side, wanting to feel the soft press of his lips. Or even the light graze of his teeth.

He growled in my ear. "Not going to let anyone see how you react when I bite the back of your neck. That's for me alone." He feathered a soft kiss over the shell of my ear. "You want that, don't you? Your hands braced against something solid as I'm coming at you hard and fast from behind. Teasing you. Touching you. Sinking my teeth right here"—he flicked his tongue over the magic spot—"holding on to you as you come undone."

I just about had an orgasm. Right there in the middle of the damn dance floor of the hottest club in town.

My head screamed for me to retreat.

I lowered my arms and spun into him, trying to put a respectable distance between us.

But Brady was having none of that. He brought me against his chest, in a modified version of how we'd started the dance.

Neither of us said anything.

I could feel his heart thundering against my ear. The cashmere was soft against my cheek.

And I knew I should've disentangled from his arms when the song ended, but I didn't. The next song was slow, and we swayed to the music until the deep, thudding bass of a Keisha song had us breaking apart.

But instead of taking me back to the table, Brady towed me around the corner that separated the lounge area from the VIP restrooms. He lowered his head, his focus entirely on my lips. "I'm taking that kiss now, Lennox."

The way he kissed me with restrained hunger had me

throwing caution to the wind. He wanted me wild? He'd have to make me that way. But I was beginning to understand the gentleman needed permission to step outside the boundaries he was used to.

I slid my hands up his chest and pushed him back.

He locked his hot gaze to mine and waited.

"Show me that wild man, Brady."

The gleam in his eyes made my entire body tingle. He crowded me against the wall. One hand fisted in my hair; the other gripped my hip. He shoved his knee between my thighs. He slammed his mouth down on mine the same time he pushed up so I was intimately pressed against his quad.

This kiss was volcanic.

Each hot stroke of his tongue sent a burst of liquid heat through me. Just when I thought he'd retreat, he retreated only far enough to take the kiss even deeper, so I felt his heat, his need, his overwhelming passion in every cell in my body. His grip on my hair kept my head right where he wanted it so he could plunder my mouth however he pleased. When I started to move my pelvis forward, trying to get more friction, his grip on my hip forced me to remain still. To let him set the pace.

My whole life I'd avoided men with this powerful, raw sexuality. I chose men I could control and bend to my will. Although I'd goaded Brady into showing me this side of him, I expected to be able to control my reaction to him.

Not so.

Not at all.

When he broke the seal of our lips and placed sucking kisses down the front of my throat, I tried to chase his mouth because I wasn't nearly done kissing him.

Brady just growled his displeasure and increased his hold on my hair.

I'd never been so turned on in my life.

He slid his hand up the outside of my torso to cup my breast. He squeezed gently and gooseflesh broke out as he swept his thumb over my hard nipple.

I let my head fall back against the wall in total surrender.

"That noise," he rasped in my ear. "I can't wait to hear that noise when you're naked."

"Brady—"

"Sweet Jesus, do I love the sexy, breathy way you say my name. Say it again," he demanded.

"Brady, please."

"Please what?"

"Stop. If you keep touching me like that and murmuring in my ear, I'm afraid I'll lose what little inhibitions I have left and I'll let you nail me right here, right now."

He smiled against my throat. "I'm good with that. Except I'd turn you around and hike up your skirt so I could nibble, bite and lick your neck while I pounded into you."

Then he caught my moan in a kiss. He'd slowed the heat between us to a simmer. But these soft-lipped, tender, sweet kisses were as addicting as the fiery ones.

Keeping his gaze on mine as he teased my mouth, he said, "As much as I want you to come home with me tonight, I won't pressure you. Especially if you've got things to do tomorrow, because I wouldn't let you out of my bed until we left for work Monday morning."

"Thoughtful of you to give me a choice."

"You made that choice when you agreed to help me crack open the door to the cage to see if it houses a wild beast, baby."

I buried my face in his neck, unsure what to say.

Brady released my hair and tenderly smoothed it back. "You want to have another drink and stick around and dance?"

"No. You got us into the hottest club in the Cities. You get props for that. We couldn't top that last dance and, frankly, I don't want to try."

"Me neither." He stepped back and ran a hand through his hair. "You ready to go?"

"I left my purse at the table. I'll grab it while you wait here."

He scowled. "I'll come with you."

I pointedly looked at the rather large bulge below his belt. "Maybe give yourself a few minutes to calm down."

"Fine. I'll meet you at the coat check."

The walk down the cold hallway would be good for him.

No one had messed with my purse in the VIP section. I'd just retrieved it and slipped the slim strap over my shoulder when a woman around my age approached me.

"You're here with Brady?" she demanded.

"Who?"

"Don't play stupid. He's not exactly inconspicuous."

I'd give her that. "Yes, I'm here with him. Why?"

She gestured to my clothing. "A slutty outfit like that won't get you into the hallowed halls of the Lund estate to meet his family. And that is the ultimate goal for a cheap woman like you, isn't it? You'll let him maul you in public so you can get your hands on his family's money and connections."

I gave her the same perusal she'd used on me. I could tell by the cut of her clothing it hadn't come off the rack at Dayton's. "Who are you?"

"I'm a Lund family friend."

With designs on Brady, no doubt. I could snap this toothpick-shaped brunette like a twig. "A Lund family friend or Brady's friend?"

She shrugged. "One and the same. I've known Brady a long time and you're not his type."

"Here's where you tell me you're his type?"

"Of course I am. Now that I get a close-up look at you after everyone watched you dry humping him on the dance floor, I see your temporary appeal. But Brady is slumming with you. He'll sow some oats, act wild and free, and when he tires of it he'll be back at the country club to find a proper woman who wouldn't embarrass him in front of his family and colleagues."

"It's sweet of you to show such concern. Who may I tell him is keeping such close tabs on him?"

"Persia."

"Like the country?" I said, and didn't bother hiding my snicker. "Please tell me you have a sister named India and another one named Holland."

She huffed, turned and strode off.

My amusement about the situation lessened the closer I got to the coat check. When I was in the moment with Brady—on the dance floor and then in the hallway—I hadn't considered people would be watching us. Maybe taking pictures or videos of us. And while Brady was one of the more low-key members of the Lund family, he was still part of that upper echelon of society. And because of that, he could get away with taking a walk on the wild side with a woman from the wrong side of the tracks. For him it would be a momentary indiscretion. But for me . . . it had the potential to affect my career. If the society reporter found out who I was, and where I worked, it wouldn't be the CFO in danger of losing his job—it'd be me.

The thought of my life story being splashed across the local newspapers nearly had me hyperventilating.

"Lennox?"

I jumped and whirled around to face my date. "You scared me."

"I said your name twice. Is everything all right?" Brady held out my coat and helped me into it.

"Yes. Thanks."

He slipped his hand into mine and led us out of the club.

The line behind the velvet rope had gotten longer. I ducked my head so most of my hair obscured my face. But I needn't have worried, because no one stopped us.

He opened the car door for me. After he climbed in, he said, "Am I just taking you home?"

"I think that'd be best. It's late."

"No problem. But you still owe me dinner."

"I'm sure we'll figure something out."

"That's not very reassuring."

"Sorry."

The sharp angles of his face were even more noticeable in the glow of the dashboard lights. I forced myself to look out the window rather than continue to stare at him.

We didn't speak or even hold hands on the drive back to my place.

He parked at the curb and cut the engine. "Did I say or do something wrong?"

"No. It just got intense. I thought we'd better cool things down." I reached for his hand. "I had a great time tonight, Brady."

"Me too. I'll walk you to the door."

Outside on the sidewalk I shivered and he draped his arm over my shoulder.

"So does 'great time' mean you think I have an inner wild man?"

"Yes."

"Will you help me draw him out?"

I sighed dramatically. "I *suppose* I can suffer groping sessions at hot nightclubs while I'm knocking back expensive drinks. Somehow I'll muddle through."

He chuckled. "You are a little trouper."

"What's next on your 'wild man' list? I draw the line at skydiving."

"I've already gone skydiving. Same for cliff jumping."

"Parasailing?"

"Yes."

"Base jumping?"

"No. But I was with Jensen when he did it. He's into all that extreme sports stuff."

"Heli-skiing?"

"Me? No. But I rode in the chopper and watched Jensen bail out."

I faced him. "Why did you ask me to help you? Sounds like you've already done all the really daring stuff." Maybe being with a woman like me was a daring move for him.

Brady framed my face in his hands. "Don't you get it? None of that was me. I want to find my own thing."

I could believe that. So I kissed him.

After we broke apart, he angled his head and swept his tongue over my lip ring. Then he grazed it with his teeth and tugged playfully. "Have a good day tomorrow and I'll see you Monday."

I wasn't sure if running into Brady at work on Monday would be awkward.

Mr. Lund, I mentally corrected.

When I reached my desk, Sydney whistled. "Is that a new outfit?"

"Actually, no. It's an old one I found in the back of my closet and I worried it might be out of style." I smoothed my hands over the slim-fitting moleskin skirt. The buckskin color paired well with the brown leather riding boots with a slight heel. The top was a deep pumpkin-colored, dolman sleeve sweater that fell to my hips. I'd cinched a belt, braided together with three hues of leather and three thin ropes in brown, dark green and burnt orange.

"Old doesn't matter when you wear it like that." She fanned herself. "We'll have to turn the heat down in here, because you are smoking in that outfit."

I loved Sydney's enthusiasm. "Thanks. I'm just going to put away my lunch."

"Hurry. The meeting starts in five minutes."

Instead of taking the elevator, I cut down the two flights of stairs to the fourth floor. No one was in the break room, so I quickly stuffed my lunch on the bottom shelf and made it back in time to pour myself a big cup of coffee.

Our department was comparatively small. Ten full-time office temps and Lola, our coordinator. On the days we didn't have temp assignments—which was rare, since a company with over fifteen hundred employees in one building meant someone was always out sick, on vacation or taking a personal day—we worked in the Personnel department. Anita Mohr, the head of Personnel, was a complete hag. She was old, set in her ways and had no reason to change, while constantly parroting to her bosses that change is necessary—and then never changing a damn thing. I suspected she was the reason LI didn't even have casual Fridays and still maintained a dress code.

Inside the conference room, I noticed the entire temp

staff, including Lola, in addition to two people I didn't recognize, as well as Anita.

Hooray.

Lola sat at the head of the table. She'd seen a lot of changes in the forty years she had worked as a secretary. She constantly reminded us that technology evolved but people skills were still the most important ones in our arsenal.

Anita took over the meeting. "None of you are in trouble, so relax," she said with a brittle smile. "These people are envoys from Finance and Operations. They're here to iron out a few wrinkles that have appeared. Or at least pinpoint the source of the wrinkles."

"Finance" kicked off my warning bells.

Don't be ridiculous. This has nothing to do with you. Or your weekend with Brady Lund.

"Renee and Zach are the oversight committee that will meet with each of you individually over the next two weeks at various times, so please cooperate with them in whatever manner they require."

No one looked around the room at anyone else. We all seemed to be looking at the conference table, hoping this wasn't a bad portent.

Screw this. If our jobs were on the line, we had a right to know. "Ms. Mohr?"

"Yes, Lennox?"

"Is this a performance review for the department? Or individual performance reviews?"

"Departmental review. It's been several years since this subdivision of Personnel has been subjected to the checks and balances the other departments are required to comply with yearly. When the oversight was discovered, I decided to rectify it at once."

The way she said "subdivision" sounded like "subpar."

Why couldn't I leave this alone? "Thank you for the clarification. Will we be accompanied to our temp jobs during the course of this review?"

I felt Sydney nudge my knee under the table.

"Yes."

"To all aspects of that job?"

"Of course. This seems to trouble you. But if you've got nothing to hide, then their presence shouldn't be an issue."

"I am only speaking for myself, that I have nothing to hide, but it's not me that I'm worried about. Sometimes we deal with personnel matters for other departments and those managers expect discretion and privacy, which allows them to be honest in their assessments. The same with legal matters that can contain sensitive information. I imagine having another person in the room judging us on how we perform our job won't give an accurate assessment of how we perform anyway, or where these wrinkles might be starting."

I could feel Anita's eyes burning into me, but I could also feel the silent gratitude from my coworkers that one of us had spoken up.

"Lennox has a valid point," Lola said. "Since this department is an arm of Personnel, the managers expect confidentiality. That's not to suggest that either of these two would talk out of turn, but many times my office staff are called in specifically because they've got no stake in interdepartmental politics."

"What are you suggesting, Lola?"

"That assessments be done after the fact. Say Lennox is asked to draft a letter for Mr. X. They don't need to be in Mr. X's office with her. She doesn't have to disclose to the oversight committee the nature of the correspondence, just that she did it and the amount of time it took her, and have the supervisor in that department sign off on it. That way we keep the privacy that Lund Industries has always strived to maintain for their employees."

I wanted to stand and clap for Lola's sarcastic response to this PC bullshit. Basically Anita wanted to justify looking at all our records. If word of that got out, none of the departments would request our services, meaning we wouldn't do some of the more delicate aspects of our job, which in turn would make it appear that we had fewer responsibilities than we actually did.

"Fine. We will discuss adjusting the parameters." Anita and her minions stood. "I wasn't expecting this much resistance, Lola."

Not until they were out of the room did Lola say, "Right. You were expecting us to roll over."

I laughed. But my laughter died when they all looked at me.

Lola cocked her head. "Thank you for speaking up, Lennox. For once I'm grateful that you're not the 'eyes forward, don't rock the boat' type of employee."

My cheeks heated. "I don't like bullies. And that's what this feels like. We know our worth. It isn't that I resent us having to prove it, but no one in Legal, Acquisitions or Finance would allow those parameters."

"True." Lola looked around the room. "No external gossip on this. If I'm taking a stand on the privacy side, I'd better not hear a whisper that this was discussed elsewhere. Understood?"

Nods of agreement around the room.

"Good. Individual schedules are in your in-box. If you need me, I'll be at the drugstore loading up on antacids and aspirin."

I'd been there one hour and it was already looking to be a very long week.

———

My heart raced when I saw Brady enter the employee break room on Wednesday just after noon. The man wore a suit like no other. His hair wasn't as styled as usual and I wondered if it was an incidental side effect from running his hand through it.

He scanned the room—I had the foolish hope he was looking for me. I hadn't seen him since Saturday night. When his gaze landed on me, his lips curled into a knowing smile before he grabbed something out of the industrial fridge. Then his cousin Ash strolled in and a collective silence filled the space.

Two Lund corporate officers breaking bread with the lowest-level employees?

Brady handed Ash a plastic container and they made their way to a table by the windows.

"That's odd, isn't it? The CFO has deigned to eat in here. Think the catering company quit? Or maybe just his personal chef?"

"He doesn't have a personal chef," I said without thinking. I felt Sydney staring at me.

"And you know that how?"

"Something about that came up when I was in his office last week," I said offhandedly.

Sydney speared a chunk of her salad. "Whatever happened with that project?"

"It's ongoing." I changed the subject.

And it worked for fifteen minutes . . . until Brady wandered over. He shoved his hands in his pockets and made a point of looking at Sydney first. Then me. "So how're things in the secretarial pool?"

I knew he said that to get a rise out of me. So I didn't disappoint him. "'Secretarial pool' is an antiquated term, Mr. Lund."

"As I'm aware, Miss Greene. But the term *floater* isn't appealing. What the office temps need is a cool moniker like the IT or HR departments have."

"Maybe HR should run a contest. The person who creates the cleverest name wins a paid day off from work."

"Excellent suggestion. I'll bring it up at our next staff meeting." Brady smiled at me and I got that funny tickle in my belly. "Perhaps even I'll submit something."

"Make sure you do it anonymously. We wouldn't want to end up with a stu—" Crap. I couldn't say that. "Stuck with a name HR chose as a winner only because the CFO suggested it and they felt pressured to choose your entry by default."

Brady raised that one eyebrow at me and my face heated. Not from embarrassment, but the last time he did that I ended up plastered body to body with him, my mouth fused to his.

Sydney, apparently oblivious to the sexual tension winging between us, leaned in to get his attention. "I, for one, would be happy if you submitted a suggestion, since that indicates upper-level management is aware of the necessity of our department."

Dammit, Syd. Don't go there.

Brady broke his gaze and focused on Sydney. "I realize I initially misunderstood the wide range of responsibilities the office temps undertake, but I assure you, I'm fully aware of the importance of the department now."

"Does Anita Mohr know that?"

"Pardon?"

"Are you *fully aware* that Ms. Mohr has mounted an

internal investigation of what we office temps 'do' on a daily basis? And each one of us has to report to the assigned two-person oversight committee every day?"

I watched as the mask that he wore as CFO slipped back into place. "Yes, it's standard procedure and that's all I can say." He smiled at Sydney. "But thank you for the reminder." Then Brady's gaze moved to me and pinned me in place. "Miss Greene. Please speak to my admin about scheduling a brief meeting at the end of the day today regarding that project we're working on."

"Of course, sir. I'll do it as soon as I finish my lunch."

"Thank you. Enjoy your day, ladies." After that, he walked off.

O ne benefit of being a floater was that even with the daily schedule changes, we spent the last half hour of our workday back in our department. Today, it allowed me time to gather my thoughts before dealing with the CFO.

None of my coworkers were back at their desks, since some departments at Lund worked from seven to four or from nine to six, not just the eight-to-five shift. I e-mailed Lola my report, gathered my things and headed up the nearly forty floors into the lion's den.

Jenna smiled at me warmly and indicated I should wait while she finished her phone conversation.

"Yes, sir. Mr. Lund will accept the invitation. Please forward all the information to me at the e-mail address that's listed on the letterhead and we'll coordinate his schedule from there. Thank you." Jenna touched her earpiece and used the stylus to scribble on her tablet. Then she looked up at me. "Lennox. I'll let Mr. Lund know you're here."

"Thank you."

I'd barely started to pace in the reception area—which was a misnomer, because this was his executive assistant's space; she was the second person one had to go through to get to the CFO—when Jenna said, "You're welcome to head on back."

I nodded, squared my shoulders and forced myself to keep my steps slow and steady. A set of gigantic double doors loomed in front of me. I palmed the handle, inhaled one deep, calming breath and opened the door.

Brady wasn't sitting behind his enormous desk in his oversized leather chair with his back to me. No, he was resting his behind on the front edge of the desk, directly in front of the chair he expected me to sit in.

I moved behind the chair, placed my hands on the top of it, putting the piece of furniture between us. "It's not five o'clock yet."

"And that concerns you . . . why?"

"I just need to clarify whether I'm here as your employee or your—?"

"You are not my direct employee, Lennox. You don't answer to me." The muscles in his jaw bunched as he clenched his teeth. "Is it so hard for you to admit we're involved?"

"Are we?"

He made a growling noise. "Come here."

I was such a sucker; that imperious tone did it for me in a bad way. I liked it when he showed me his commanding male side, which had driven him to become the youngest CFO in Lund Industries history.

Skirting the chair, I stood in front of him. My mouth had gone dry and I'd started to sweat just from the determined look in his eyes.

Brady's gaze never left mine. "You're off the clock." Then

his hands clamped onto my hips and he tugged me between his legs. Despite the advantage of my high heels, I didn't loom over him. But even if I had, he'd still retain control. He slid his hand away from my left hip, stopping between my hip bones. Then he made a leisurely pass up the center of my torso until he could curl his hand around the back of my neck. He pulled my head down and kissed the living shit out of me.

His mouth . . . God, the way the man used his tongue had me imagining where else he'd expertly tease, stroke and swirl it like that. He kissed me with urgency and a hunger that caught me off guard, because I'd assumed he'd be controlled even in passion.

I had never been happier to be proven wrong.

I sifted my fingers through his hair, loving the soft groan he made when my nails scored his scalp. I kissed him back with equal voracity. The heat from his body intensified the scent of his cologne. I couldn't take a breath without the warm scent of his skin filling my lungs. I swallowed and his taste permeated my mouth from my lips to the back of my tongue.

By the time Brady slowed the kiss, I was surprised to still be standing.

He nuzzled my cleavage, his breath coming hard and fast across my damp skin, his hands squeezing and releasing my hips. "Fuck, I want you. Earlier in the break room I imagined hauling you to your feet and kissing you so everyone would know that we are involved." He lightly bit my neck, sending a delicious shiver through me. "Intimately involved."

Part of me wanted to demand, *Then why didn't you?* But the smarter part prevailed and said, "Thank you for your restraint."

He pushed me back a step so he could stand and loom over me. "Since we're off the clock, I can admit I wasn't aware that Anita had mounted a full-scale investigation of your department. I'll add a disclaimer that rarely do department heads share that type of information with me."

"I figured that might be the case after that first meeting when you were surprised by the size and workload of our department."

Brady dropped his hands and sidestepped me to walk to the window. Several long moments passed before he spoke. "I'm trying to find a balance here, Lennox, between being pissed off that you didn't talk to me about this and being grateful that you didn't bring it up."

Say what?

"After lunch I did some checking. The oversight committee has marked off two weeks for a thorough"—was it my imagination or had he sneered that word?—"investigation of the office temps department. I understand why you'd prefer to keep our involvement out of the spotlight." He looked over his shoulder at me. "But fair warning. I don't give a damn. We're not keeping this in the closet. This weekend I'm introducing you to my family as my girlfriend."

"You are?"

"Yes. The Vikings have a home game and we've got a private box, so the whole family will be there."

A case of nerves hit me so hard that I felt dizzy and had to sit down. But I drew the line at dropping my head between my knees.

Then Brady was right there. His hand beneath my chin, tipping my head back. That too handsome face too close to mine. "Lennox, baby, why are you as white as a sheet?"

Because the thought of meeting your mother—who the

employees secretly refer to as the "Vicious Valkyrie"—
scares the life out of me. She'll never accept me—the girl
with the unwed mother and the roadie for a father, who ran
away from home at age sixteen and spent years running wild.

Yeah. I could just imagine the look on her face if I
showed up on Brady's arm as his date at one of those fancy
charity functions that the Lund family sponsors.

When he said, "Talk to me," I realized I hadn't responded
to his question.

"I'm a little freaked out, okay? And just because *you're*
used to moving in the upper echelon of Twin Cities society,
that doesn't mean I'd be comfortable with it. In the Lund
family private skybox I'd be rubbing elbows with the Lund
Industries CEO; your cousin Nolan, who's being groomed
as the next CEO; your cousin Ash, the COO; as well as your
siblings—Annika, the PR whiz, and Jensen, a football phe-
nomenon. Oh, and there's your cousin Jaxson, the hockey
star; your mom, who was a former model; your dad, who
heads up corporate relations; your other uncle, who is president of the board of directors. And your aunts, who are
responsible for several of the biggest charities and charity
events in the city." I paused to take a breath.

"You done?" Brady asked in a frosty tone.

"No. I don't even know what your brother Walker does,
but I'm sure it's equally amazing."

"He's a carpenter."

"I bet he's more than a carpenter. He probably owns a
construction business."

"Yes, but that's beside the point."

"It's not! You don't—"

He closed his mouth over mine and I lost all coherent
thought as he kissed me mindless. When he'd erased my

will to protest, he eased back only far enough to look into my eyes when he murmured, "That's what matters to me, Lennox. What anyone else thinks of you is immaterial, because I like you. Say you'll meet my family."

Stupid, sweet man. "Okay."

He grinned and kissed me again.

Two knocks sounded and the door opened behind us. I jumped.

Brady put his hand on my shoulder as if to keep me in place and pushed himself upright. "Yes, Jenna?"

"I'm leaving for the day, sir. Answering service is on and the doors will be locked behind me."

"Thank you. Have a good evening and I'll see you tomorrow." The door closed with a soft click.

I covered my face with my hands and groaned.

"What's wrong?"

"Seriously?" I looked at him. "You aren't the least bit bothered that she caught us making out?"

"She'll likely give me props tomorrow, since that's the first time I've been in this situation."

I wanted to believe him. But honestly, he was too good looking to me for it to be true. Wasn't he aware that most of the women who worked for Lund Industries swooned over him and were scared of him in equal measure?

Brady tugged me to my feet. "Besides, I told her that we're involved."

"You did?"

"Yes. I needed her to know that if you came up here or called, she was to let you in and put you through immediately." He brushed his mouth across mine. "Which didn't happen the past two days, much to my disappointment, forcing me to demand a meeting with you."

"That's probably the only way you'll get me up here, Mr. Lund."

"I'll remember that," he murmured, and gave me another barely there kiss.

"So I'll see you tomorrow."

"Count on it. Oh, and I expect we'll have dinner tomorrow night. After."

My brain immediately added *we have sex* to the word *after*. I ignored my body chiming in with a loud *Hooray!* and asked, "After what?"

"It's a surprise."

"Have I mentioned I hate surprises?"

"No." He feathered his lips down my jaw. "Remember when you said I had to meet you halfway? That I had to come up with some wild things I wanted to try on my own?"

"Yes."

"I came up with one." He sounded so proud of himself.

It made me happy that, even though his family had pushed this change thing on him, he'd started to embrace it on his own terms. "I can't wait to see what it is."

He kissed my forehead. "I still have work to catch up on. So I'll walk you to the door."

The next day after work I had a sense of déjà vu. Jenna greeted me, and I waited until she okayed me to enter the inner sanctum of the CFO's domain. I walked into Brady's office. "Okay, spill it, Lund. What's your secret wild adventure tonight?"

Brady grinned wickedly. "We're hitting a tattoo parlor. I'm bringing you with me to whisper all sorts of dirty distractions into my ear to take my mind off the pain."

I rolled my eyes at his usage of tattoo parlor. "I hope

you're not choosing something weird just to prove you're edgy."

"Define weird."

"Getting an actual brand."

His eyes widened. "Such as a hot branding iron seared onto my skin, like with livestock?"

"Yeah."

"I'll pass on that one."

"Good." I glanced down at his crotch. "I won't stick around if you choose to get a barber pole tattooed on your . . . well, pole."

"To be honest, I'm a little scared that you know about that kind of tat." He paused. "You've seen that?"

"No, I've seen a couple of different guys who had something similar done. It wasn't like I dated these dudes; they just felt the need to drop their pants and show me their ink. A friend of mine swore she dated a guy who had his lollipop inked like one of those rainbow-swirl suckers."

"Not touching that one. But rest assured, no dick tats. No branding. No piercing." His gaze dropped to my mouth. "Even though I have a new appreciation for them."

Of course he did. "Where did you decide to go?"

"Zorn."

"You mean Zorn's?"

"Yes. Zorn is doing the tat."

"Zorn himself?"

Brady frowned. "Why? Is there more than one Zorn?"

"No, that's what I'm saying. You're having *the* Zorn do your ink?"

"Yes. He did the design too."

That must've cost him a fortune. Then again, money wasn't an issue for Brady Lund.

He stroked my cheek. "I've wanted to do this for years,

Lennox. Being with you just provided the prompt that was already there."

"You're sure?"

"Positive."

"Then let's go."

Twelve

BRADY

"Remember," Lennox warned me, "the phrase 'tattoo parlor' is as antiquated as the phrase 'secretarial pool.'"

"Good to know."

"You've got the design?" she prompted.

I picked up her hand and kissed the inside of her wrist. "I think you're more nervous about this tattoo than I am."

She huffed out a breath. "Of course I am."

"Why?"

"I'm afraid this is an impulsive decision you'll regret."

"Do you regret any of your tats?"

"Just the one on my ass," she muttered.

"Are you trying to get me hard? Because imagining you naked does have that effect on me, Lennox."

She blushed. I loved seeing that rosy flush on her cheeks.

I opted to parallel park. I'd rather passersby gawked at

my car out in the open instead of leaving it to chance in a parking garage.

Lennox got out of the car before I could help her out.

Immediately two guys around my age stopped to check out my car. "Dude. Is that a Maybach?"

"Yes." I'd ordered it the year I was named CFO. I had to call it an investment to justify the expense, but it was cool as hell to drive such a rare car.

"What's it got in it?" the surfer-looking dude asked.

"V-twelve."

"Holy shit." Then he looked me over. "You a politician or something?"

"Actually, I'm a spy with British intelligence."

His red-rimmed eyes lit up. "Like James Bond?"

"Exactly." I slid an arm around Lennox's waist. "So if you'll excuse me, I don't want to be late for my appointment."

"No problem." As they strolled away, I heard him say, "The chick he's with could totally be a Bond girl."

"See? That's the ultimate evaluation of your hotness."

She sighed. "From two stoners." She stopped and got in my face. "How many cars do you own?"

"Several. Why? We're not going to get into an argument about the differences in our current financial situations, are we?"

"No." She started to say something but stopped herself. Then she threaded her fingers through mine and tugged me toward the front door of Zorn's.

The reception area looked like an upscale salon. Instead of pictures of hair, there were pictures of tattoos and designs. The receptionist sported a head of vibrant blue hair in addition to sleeves on both arms. She was pierced everywhere: lips, ears, nose—even her dimples were dotted with stars. I tried not to stare at the diamond-stud piercing below the hollow of her throat, but I couldn't help but wonder how one got pierced there.

Her gaze moved between me and Lennox. "Something I can help you with?"

"Brady Lund. I have an appointment with Zorn."

She finally smiled. "Lovely to meet you, Mr. Lund. I'm Tawny." She offered her hand.

When I shook it, I felt the cool press of metal since she had rings on every finger.

"Before we head back to Zorn's station, I want to go over the charges with you, so you don't suffer from sticker shock."

Then she went into a spiel about Zorn's qualifications, awards and all that crap that justified the six-thousand-dollar price tag for a custom image and for Zorn to tattoo me personally.

"Any questions?"

"None right now, thank you."

She placed her hand on my forearm and squeezed. "You'll have to ditch the suit jacket so I can gauge how tight your shirt is."

"Excuse me?" Lennox said.

"If your shirt is loose enough, you can leave it on," Tawny said to me, ignoring Lennox completely.

I shrugged out of my suit jacket and handed it to her, watching as she hung it up. I unbuttoned the shirt cuffs and rolled up the left side first to the bend in my elbow.

Tawny returned and ran her hand down the outside of my arm. "This fits you to perfection, but I'm afraid it might cut off blood flow, so it'll have to come off."

"Then I'll be the one to remove it." Lennox moved in so close our thighs brushed. Then she began to unbutton my shirt.

The act of her undressing me as her right put Tawny in her place and she backed off.

"How do you not roast every day?" she murmured when she saw that I wore a thin V-neck T-shirt beneath my dress shirt.

"I'm used to it."

She locked her gaze to mine and the lust in her eyes knocked me back a step. "You have so many outer layers, Brady. Is that intentional? What I'll find underneath is better than the outer wrapping?"

What a loaded question.

After she got all the buttons undone, she flattened her palms on my abdomen and floated her hands up my torso with deliberate provocation. When she squeezed my pecs and feathered her thumbs across my nipples, I released a low warning growl that had her gaze snapping back to mine.

"Not. Here," I said with a rough edge.

But my warning didn't deter her. She pressed her lips to my chest where the vee of my T-shirt ended. She slipped her fingers beneath the open collar on each side of my shoulders and pushed the dress shirt down my arms. After she'd removed my shirt, she held it out for Tawny to take, without looking away from me.

Such a sexy show of possession.

So I returned the favor. I brought my hand across the front of her throat and held her in place. I leaned in. "I think she gets it now, Lennox."

"What makes you think that was for her?"

I kissed her. Not with the passion she expected, but with tenderness.

"If you two are done marking your territory," a male voice said dryly, "there's a tattoo I'd like to get started on."

I glanced at the guy leaning on the doorjamb. He wasn't the bearded biker-looking dude I'd expected. He was taller than my six feet, two inches. His dark hair was parted in the center of his scalp and hung past his shoulders. He wore a YO, BITCH T-shirt and I smiled at the *Breaking Bad* reference.

He started toward me, his hand outstretched. "I'm Zorn."

"Brady Lund. I appreciate you fitting me in this week. I understand you're usually booked weeks in advance."

"Months, actually. But I had a client cancel due to a family emergency. And your design concept intrigued me."

Lennox offered her hand. "I'm Lennox, Brady's girlfriend."

Zorn's gaze moved over her. "Where are you inked, babe? Tramp stamp?"

"And this." She gave him her back and lifted her hair with one hand as she pulled her shirt down with the other.

"Nice. Who did that?"

"Pixie. She owns Pixie's Skin Pixels in Kansas City. Do you know her?"

"I haven't met her in person, but I've seen a few designs here and there." Zorn ran his fingers across the design and I clenched my jaw to keep from telling him to get his hands off her. "The ink needs refreshing. If you're not going back to Pixie to have her do it, that's a service we provide."

"Thanks. I noticed the one on my arm needs a touch-up too."

Zorn looked at me again. "Is she coming back with you?"

"Yes."

"Cool. Get something to drink, babe, 'cause this is gonna take a while."

The pain associated with getting a tattoo wasn't as bad as having to sit still in the chair for four hours.

Since the tat was on the inside of my left forearm, I had

the ability to adjust the chair from a sitting to a reclining position. For the first hour I sat upright and talked with Lennox about the "getting to know you" stuff we'd skipped. Then the next hour Zorn and I talked. He was an interesting guy. He'd put his art degree to good use in a field where he actually made a great living. Once he learned I was in finance, he picked my brain about investments. Some of my colleagues in the investment world played their strategies so close to the vest you'd think they were guarding the secrets of the universe. But I was more of the mind-set that all businesses needed professional advice from time to time and I was more than happy to pay it forward.

After Zorn took a quick break, he resumed inking the design and I dozed off during hour three. When I woke up, I heard the *buzz buzz buzz* of another tattoo machine and looked over to see Lennox in the chair next to mine. I lifted a brow at her.

"Just getting the ink refreshed. I figured since I'd be rubbing gel on you, you could return the favor."

"As long as you're here, maybe you oughta get the one on your ass touched up too."

"Brady!"

"Just trying to be helpful, baby."

Zorn laughed.

"You know, that is a great idea, *baby*," she said in that sexy tone that always got me hard—even when she was being sarcastic. "We'll stick around after Zorn is done with yours. I'm sure it won't bother you at all when you see Zorn's hands all over my bare butt. Because one ass pretty much looks like the next one, huh, Zorn?"

"Not even fucking close, babe," Zorn said. "Some asses are a joy to work on."

A joy? Oh, hell no. "I changed my mind. The tattoo on your butt is just fine the way it is."

Lennox smirked. "I thought you might say that."

Zorn laughed again. "Now you two play nice—you're blowing my concentration."

After he finished, he sent Tawny in with aftercare instructions and he disappeared into the back room.

And it was done.

The whole thing was a little anticlimactic, really.

I paid and put my shirt and suit jacket back on while I waited in the reception area for Lennox to finish up. With the aftercare booklet was a photocopy of Zorn's design with a color key for each section.

"Is that your tat?" Lennox asked, peering over my arm.

"Yes."

"What is it?"

"The Jensen family crest and the Lund corporate logo melded into one image. I sent Zorn the two images and he combined them into one design."

"Brady. That is really cool."

I pushed a flyaway hank of her hair behind her ear. "You approve?"

"Yes." She stood on tiptoe and kissed me. "It means something to you, so now I believe you won't have regrets." She smirked. "At least until your high-society family freaks that the prodigal son got a tattoo."

"I've got a plan for that." I kissed her nose. "Blame you."

"If that's the case, then I'm skipping the family deal this weekend."

I tugged her against me. "I was joking."

"So we're still on for dinner?"

"It's almost nine thirty."

"So?"

I happened to glance out the window and in the street-light's glow I saw it had started snowing. "The Maybach isn't good in this weather."

"Did you do this on purpose?"

"What? Make it snow?"

She rolled her eyes. "Take the fancy car, knowing the weather was going to turn. And then you'll be all like, 'Maybe you should just stay at my place tonight, Lennox.' Wink-wink, nudge-nudge."

"And that idea is appalling to you?"

"It's manipulative. You said you'd take me to dinner. Now you're trying to turn it into something else. So you know what? Forget it. I'll just take a cab home."

Lennox acted possessive in public, but when it came time for the two of us to spend time alone . . . she balked? That made no sense. And since the snow was coming down harder, I didn't have time to wait around while she waged an internal war with herself.

"If that's what you want," I said to her. "Thanks for coming along. I'll see you at the office." I popped the collar of my jacket and hustled outside to my car.

LENNOX

My arm had started to sting from my tattoo touch-up. At least that's what I'd told myself when I poured bourbon into my hot tea.

I'd needed a shot of alcohol to calm me down. I hadn't retreated from Brady because I was afraid of how the night would end. I'd retreated from Brady because I'd known *exactly* how it would end.

The entire scene had played out in my head on fast-forward. We'd arrive at his trendy apartment. We'd crack open a bottle of wine. We'd have the requisite amount of small talk before we'd start to make out. Things would get hot and heavy. We'd adjourn to his bedroom and slowly peel off each other's clothes. Then we'd make love. It would all be very . . . nice.

But I didn't want nice. I wanted his heat and passion. I wanted the man I'd tangoed with Saturday night.

So yes, I'd retreated—for Brady's own good.

Although Brady had stepped outside his comfort zone and into a tattoo shop, he'd micromanaged every detail beforehand. While I wasn't an advocate of showing up drunk and having some hack tattoo artist ink a lame Chinese symbol onto a random body part, I also knew he didn't understand spontaneity.

I wasn't sure if that was something I could teach him. Or, more to the point, if that was something he wanted to learn. He'd told me that all the crazy physical challenges he'd done with his brothers and his cousins hadn't been his thing. He wanted to find his own track, off the beaten path. I could take him only so far; he had to take that first step, and no way was I making it easy on him. He wanted to be wild? I wasn't falling into his bed when he didn't have another, better plan.

The front door opened. Clothing rustled and then Kiley appeared in the doorway, big chunks of snow covering her black hair. "Hey, girl. It's getting crappy out there."

"I know. I don't think my cabbie knew how to drive on snow."

"Why does it seem like all the cab companies in the Twin Cities are hiring Somalian immigrants? There's no snow in Somalia! Of course these guys don't have a clue how to drive on snow and ice." Her brown eyes narrowed. "Why did you take a cab home? Something wrong with your car?"

"No. I left it in the parking garage since Brady and I had plans after work."

Kiley placed her hands on her hips and cocked her head at me. "You telling me that man didn't drive you home after your damn date?"

"Simmer down, mama bear." I sipped my tea. "We spent time together, and when it started to snow, he was more concerned about getting his fancy car back home than he was about anything else. It rubbed me the wrong way. So I told him I'd take a cab."

"Lemme get a toddy and I'll be back to discuss this in detail."

There was one drawback to having a counselor as a room-mate: Everything was subject to an in-depth conversation. And this time, when I needed some advice, I couldn't tell her what was really going on without breaking Brady's confidence.

Kiley had slipped on a pair of flannel pajama pants and her slippers when she shuffled back into the living room with a mug of tea. "You know, this flowery shit ain't half bad with booze in it."

"How'd your meeting go tonight?"

She scowled. "No luck in finding a permanent venue. And with the weather like this, I can't continue to meet with the kids outside. So I won't need your help this Saturday. But I do have hopes that there will be good news at next week's meeting since we have three leads on other places."

"I'll help in whatever way I can."

"I appreciate that. Now recap the evening's events for me."

"There's nothing else to add. Wait, he did plan on taking me to dinner. But we got done late . . . and then he made that stupid comment about needing to get his car home because it wasn't made for snow or something like that."

"He was talking about that sweet Beemer he was driving on Saturday?"

"No. It was a different car."

"What kind of car?" she prompted.

"I don't know. I tune out when guys start talking car stuff." I thought back. "It's a . . . May something or other."

"A Maybach?"

"Yeah, that's it."

"Well, that makes sense he'd be freaking the hell out about getting that car inside."

"It's a car, Kiley."

"It's a car that costs upwards of a million dollars, Lennox," she chided.

I choked on my tea. "What?"

"Every Maybach is custom ordered and custom built. So if he took you out in that car, he was seriously trying to impress you."

"But that's the thing! I don't know cars, I don't care about them, and if Brady knew anything about me at all he'd know that wouldn't impress me." I exhaled. "And yeah, now I get why he wanted to get the million-dollar baby out of the elements, but I couldn't help but feel I'd already served my purpose to him. That's why I took a cab home."

Kiley ran her finger around the rim of her cup. "So if Brady would've said, 'Tough crap, get in the car and after I switch it out I'll take you home in something more weather appropriate and then I'm feeding you at my favorite restaurant' . . ."

"I would've done what he asked." I hated admitting that.

"Well, well. My roomie has a submissive streak."

"What? No! No way."

"You like it when Brady gets all bossy and decisive.

You're not mad about the car; you're mad he let you go without a fight."

Okay. Although I hadn't given Kiley all the details, she had gotten some things right.

I did like it when Brady took control. That was what had made me so hot for him Saturday night. He'd touched me, kissed me, even danced with me the way *he'd* wanted.

That had been powerful stuff.

"Lennox?"

I looked at Kiley. "I dislike it intensely when you're right."

She grinned. She despised the word "hate" and had stricken it from her vocabulary and banned the use of it in her house. "So send the man a text and see if he made it home all right."

"We didn't exchange numbers."

"Why not?"

"I don't know. I guess maybe he knows he can get ahold of me at work."

"Think he'll do that tomorrow?"

I shook my head. "I have a dental appointment, so I'm taking the entire day off as a personal day."

"Nice. They're predicting snow tomorrow and Saturday, but promise me you won't sit around and mope all weekend."

"I don't mope." I finished my tea. "Where will you be?"

"Since I don't have a place for my kids Saturday, I signed up for a seminar in St. Cloud. I leave in the morning and won't be back until Sunday night."

The prospect of a long weekend by myself didn't fill me with the usual elation.

Kiley stood. "My last bit of advice, roomie. Don't be stubborn. You knew going into this thing with Brady that he has the mind of a CFO, not a lothario. Work with him.

Be forgiving of his slipups. And bear in mind you're not perfect either."

The next afternoon I'd changed into sweatpants after returning from the dentist. I had my laptop out and I'd finished my weekly bookkeeping when two loud raps vibrated against the door.

Probably the UPS man.

I'd grab the package later.

Two more raps. Louder.

I set my computer aside and headed down the stairs. I flipped the locks and opened the door as far as the chain would allow. I started to say, "Just leave it," when I noticed it wasn't the UPS man.

Brady stood there, peering at me through the crack.

"Let me in."

"What are you doing here?"

"I'll tell you if you let me in. It's cold as balls out here."

I closed the door in his face and allowed myself a quick, happy grin before I resumed a blank expression and reopened the door.

He stomped the snow off his shoes on the outside mat before he came in. "I didn't see you at work today—"

"I had a dental appointment and I cleared it with my supervisor so it's not like I called in sick—"

Brady placed his mouth over mine. His lips were cold, as were his cheeks, but his tongue was warm. He kissed me for a good long time. When he eased back, my fingers were clutching the edges of his coat and I'd pressed myself against his body—for warmth, since we'd left the front door wide open.

I reached around him and slammed the door shut.

Then he kissed me again. "I didn't embellish this," he muttered against my mouth.

No, he hadn't. In fact, I think I hadn't given enough credit to how physically compatible we were.

"Why are you here?"

"I didn't like how things ended between us last night." He rested his forehead to mine. "Christ. I let you take a fucking cab home. I should've tossed you in my car and made you come with me."

"Yes, you should have."

"So that's why I'm not giving you a choice this time." He stepped back and tapped my ass. "Get packed. You'll want a bunch of cold-weather clothing. Pajamas. Anything else you'll need the next two nights."

"What are you talking about? I can't just leave."

"Why not? You have other plans for this weekend?"

"No, but—"

His thick fingers covered my lips. "You told me being impulsive was the key to getting wild. So the advice you gave me isn't the same advice you'd take yourself?"

Dammit.

"Ah. It's true." He paused and his eyes searched mine. "Were you dancing on the bar that night because you needed a reminder that *you* used to be spontaneous? Is that why you agreed to help me in my quest to find my wild side?"

I raised my chin. "Projecting much?"

He laughed. "Defensive much?"

"So if I decide to go on this crazy quest with you, where would we be going?"

"You ask too many questions. You're either in or you're out."

"If I say out . . . ?"

"Then I'd cluck like a chicken at you before I left for my

fun-filled weekend. But I'd be back on Sunday morning to pick you up for the football game."

"It'd almost be worth it to hear your imitation of a chicken."

Brady smiled. "Come on. Be daring."

"Fine. But this place we're going better have coffee. Because I'm not a nice person until I've had at least two cups of joe in the morning."

"I can promise you coffee. Now are you coming with me? Or am I going alone?"

"I'll come with you." I started up the stairs. "But fair warning—I'm a notoriously slow packer."

"I've got nothing but time to wait for you, baby."

Thirteen

LENNOX

Brady carried my duffel to the back of his Land Rover.
After he climbed in the driver's side, he said, "This
vehicle is a much better choice than the Maybach."

"You're a car guy."

"Unapologetically a car guy. The bottom half of my
warehouse is dedicated to my car collection."

"You live in a warehouse?"

"Yes, in the Old Mill District. You know where that is?"

"That's a cool part of town. One of the most recent areas
to get urban-renewal funds."

"Which was a good idea in theory, but it lacked exe-
cution."

His mind fascinated me. "How so?"

"Four of the six board members on the restoration committee board were Realtors. So they almost had the city
convinced to condemn the entire area rather than restore.

Then they could've put in housing units at least six stories
tall, on the river, with retail spaces between the residences
and little to no green space. Luckily, my brother Walker got
wind of it and got it stopped before the bulldozer moved in.
Times like that I'm grateful the Lund name carries so much
sway in this town."

"But you still ended up with a warehouse. Was that out
of gratitude or something?"

He shook his head. "We've owned that section since the
early days. Lund Logging was the first business my ances-
tors started. From there we moved into flour mills. Each
generation has added to the company. Or we've reduced the
sections that don't work to increase profitability. Two ware-
houses we owned had been abandoned for the past thirty
years." He tilted his head. "Sorry. You look ready to fall
asleep. This is probably all old news to you anyway."

"The basic info is common knowledge. But I've always
wondered what it was like for the descendants of a hugely
successful company. There's got to be pressure to at least
maintain the status quo."

"Or, worse, not to drive the company into the ground.
My grandfather had a taste of that during the grain wars,
when Common Grounds paid premium price to our grain
producers for them *not* to sell to us. Then the public blamed
the food shortage on us. Meanwhile, CG stealthily moved
in and took our market share. CG did that to another small
manufacturing company too, so in the end we both ended
up selling to CG. It forced us to change and adapt. Which
we did, but CG is still our biggest competitor." He smirked.
"In some areas. In other areas they can't touch us, because
they've been focused on one market for so long."

The traffic thinned as we headed north.

"Did you always know that you'd be involved in the company on some level?"

That question seemed to make him uncomfortable. But he answered before I could retract it. "Yes. Did I know in what area I'd have enough expertise or the desire to learn more to ensure a worthwhile contribution? Not at first. See, my dad doesn't have one of the company titles. He handles all the corporate accounts as well as the smaller supplier accounts. He's the go-to guy because he's tactful and efficient. He's a helluva salesman, but he never comes across as one. He's charm personified. I've never been like that. Even as a kid I was serious and studious." He sent me a sheepish smile. "Big surprise I was predictable and boring, huh?"

"I don't equate those behaviors with boring, Brady. I haven't been at LI a year, but I can see why people become career employees, which we both know is rare in this day and age. Part of that loyalty is because employees can see the Lund name is still prominent across all departments—and not just as figureheads. You and your family members are there day in, day out. If the owners are invested in the company's future, doesn't it make sense the employees would be invested too?"

"I guess."

"I've spent my life working in shitty conditions for shitty wages. Where the job I had could've been done by anyone, so there was no such thing as job security. Advancement meant moving up from working the graveyard shift. I wasn't kidding when I told you I love working at LI." Then I felt like a total tool. He probably thought I wanted something from him.

We were quiet for a long time after that.

Since it was dark out and I had no idea where we were going, I closed my eyes and tried to sleep.

A hand on my thigh startled me.

"We're almost there."

"Where?"

He turned off the main road onto a service road. The headlights flashed on billboards bragging about cabin rentals and year-round fishing excursions. We were in a heavily wooded area with no streetlights and no sign of civilization.

"Seriously, Brady. I'm a little freaked out by all this . . ." *Nothingness.* "What are we doing here?"

"Going to a cabin in the woods." He turned onto a paved road that wound through the trees. We reached a big gate that was surrounded by a huge fence. He rolled down the window and punched a code into the machine and the gate opened. He watched in the rearview mirror until it closed behind us. Then he looked at me. "What?"

"I knew you were too good to be true. Smart, gorgeous, sexy and single . . . I should've known better."

"What are you talking about?"

"You're a serial killer, aren't you? Picking me up and no one knows where I've gone. I haven't been able to get cell service and now you're driving into some secret compound with a security system surrounded by an electric fence."

He laughed. "You're funny."

But I wasn't trying to be funny. I was about to launch into the other oddities when we came around a corner and a glass-and-brick mansion rose up before us like a modern-day castle. Lights shone through the windows and we headed toward a curved portico that covered the front door. Not a speck of snow was on the driveway or the stone steps. "Holy shit."

WHAT YOU NEED 179

"Welcome to the Lund family's weekend getaway cabin in the Minnesota North Woods," he said dryly.

"Cabin? It's gigantic."

"Not really. Only about ten thousand square feet."

Only about ten thousand square feet. Now I couldn't tell if he was joking or not.

He parked and shut the car off. When he didn't move, I teased him. "Are you waiting for the butler to come out and direct the houseboy on which bedroom suite to put our luggage in?"

"No butler, but the caretakers, Bill and Mary, opened up the house, turned the heat up and stocked the refrigerator for us."

This time I knew he wasn't joking.

Brady got out of the car and opened the back end. He shouldered both bags while I stood there like a dumbass. "I can carry my own bag."

"I know. But that doesn't mean you're going to."

At the enormous double doors, at least ten feet high and probably hand carved by artisans, Brady punched in another code and a green light flashed.

He opened the door and stood aside so I could enter first.

I paused for a minute inside the entryway. I'd expected marble, crystal and gilded fixtures, but this place was decorated casually. Wood floors, warm tones on the walls. Plaid and corduroy-covered furniture. I'd wandered halfway down the hallway when I realized Brady wasn't directly behind me. I saw him leaning against the newel post, watching me with hooded eyes. I walked back and shoved my hands in my coat pockets. "Sorry to just take off like that."

"No worries." He erased the distance between us. "I'll take your coat."

"Thanks."

He helped me take it off and then his arms circled me. He placed a soft kiss on the side of my neck.

It occurred to me we were alone in a way we hadn't been before.

"Please don't tense up. I wasn't kidding when I said I wanted this to be a fun weekend for both of us. No pressure."

"So we're not sharing a bed?"

"No."

Disappointment rolled through me.

"Don't take that as I don't want you." He pressed his groin into my backside. "Just now I had an entire fantasy going about pinning you to the floor and fucking you until you can't walk. But we talked about this not only being about sex."

My horny side argued that so far it hadn't been about sex at all.

"I also knew that if I didn't leave the city, I would've been in the office working." His breath teased my ear. "This is one of my favorite places and I haven't been here in ages. I wanted to share this with you."

His earnestness caught me off guard, because I didn't expect it.

"Okay. Show me this monster house. And feel free to give me all the details you can remember, because I love hearing history." I had little history in my own life—most I tried to forget—so I wanted to believe in happy family vibes like generations of Lunds coming here for holidays and summer vacations.

Brady took my hand and started the tour. "A lot of cabins in Minnesota are by lakes. But since the Lund mansion is right on Lake Minnetonka, my grandfather wanted their cabin to be secluded in the woods."

The deep cadence of his voice soothed me as much as the comforting presence of his palm pressed against the small of my back.

BRADY

We'd ended up in the kitchen after the tour. I hoped that Mary had left some prepared meals in the fridge. If not, Lennox and I might starve.

As Lennox sat down, I pulled out two bottles of beer from the fridge and handed her one.

"So what's the plan for tonight?"

"What makes you think I've got a plan?"

"Because you're you." Lennox's gaze dropped to the bandage on my forearm. "Any problems with the tattoo?"

"It itches like crazy."

"Part of the healing process. Wait until the skin starts to peel. That's pretty gross."

Awkward silence lingered after that.

In a burst of inspiration, I said, "Truth or dare."

Lennox considered me a moment before she said, "Truth."

"When was your last relationship?"

"Four years ago."

"Why'd it end?"

"He wanted to get married and I kept saying no. So he slept with a coworker, to make me jealous or to make me see how perfect we were together. But all it did was make me mad. That's when I left Omaha and applied for school here." She swigged from her beer and said, "Truth or dare."

"Truth."

"The last person you had sex with."

"Tiffany somebody."

"A one-nighter with no last names, huh?"

"It was after my buddy's wedding. She was the bride's cousin. She didn't bother to learn my last name either. I think at one point when we were going at it she even called me Brody."

She laughed. "Ouch. I once had a guy call me Linux."

"Like the operating system?"

"Yeah. I didn't correct him because I was impressed he knew what Linux was." She shook her head. "There was a time when my criteria for a hook-up was dumb and pretty."

"How ironic—I had the same criteria at one time too."

"When did that change for you?"

"Who says it's changed?" I shot back.

"Ooh. Is my skin red after that burn?"

"No. Jesus. I didn't mean you. I meant that in general terms."

"Did you ever sleep with that Persia chick?"

That startled me. I hadn't seen her in years. "Where'd you hear her name?"

"She introduced herself to me at Flurry last weekend."

I tipped my bottle up and drank. "What stunning life insight did she share with you?" *And why didn't you mention it before tonight?*

"Just that I was a ho-bag who was not good enough for you. That you'd bang me and move on like you'd done with everyone else. And she had your parents' approval to be the future Mrs. Lund so she's waiting for you to get your fill of skanks before you settle down with a real classy woman like her."

I laughed. "No, I never slept with her. She'll be waiting a long time for that marriage proposal."

"Well, I didn't want her to continue to pine away for you,

so I told her you were lousy in bed anyway and she shouldn't waste her time."

"Seriously?"

She smirked. "You tell me. *Did* I tell her that?"

"No. But I'll bet your sweet ass that you got the best of her."

"*Ding ding ding.* Give the man a prize." She lifted her bottle and I touched it with mine. "Your turn."

"Truth or dare."

"Dare."

I figured she wouldn't be able to resist the dare for long. I patted the counter. "You sit up here and let me stand between your legs for the rest of the game."

"Easy peasy." She hopped up on the counter and widened her knees, making room for me.

I stepped in and ran my hand up her thigh. "You want to keep going?"

"Of course, since it's my turn. Truth or dare."

"Truth."

Lennox's gaze encompassed my face. "Tell me, in explicit detail, what would've happened between us if I'd gone home with you last night."

"I would've tried to keep my hands off you."

"Boring."

I leaned closer and placed my lips near her ear. "But I would've failed miserably." I inhaled the scent of her—warm skin and citrus. I wasn't sure if it was her lotion or her shampoo; I just knew it hit me like a damn drug.

She shuddered and made a low moan.

I continued to nuzzle her fragrant flesh. "And if I would've touched you, I would've failed both of us. Because as crazy as I am to have you naked and wild beneath me, I'd have put the brakes on, believing I needed to savor you rather than gorge on you. So our first time as lovers would've been . . . nice. Because I'm a considerate lover, Lennox." I brushed my lips over the shell of her ear. "I'd make sure you came at least once before I got inside you. And we would've been face-to-face in my big bed, me making love to you slowly, learning what you liked, whispering how good you felt, asking if what I was doing to you was okay." I buried my face in the curve of her neck. "Does that sound okay to you? Does that sound . . . *nice*?"

Lennox didn't respond.

"When I got home, I was glad you'd taken a cab and weren't there, waiting for me to seduce you properly."

"Brady."

I rubbed my mouth up and down the section of her throat next to her voice box. "So in the past twenty-four hours, I've had time to reflect. And know what I've come up with?"

"What?"

Then we were eye to eye, almost mouth to mouth. "Not a damn thing. When I fuck you, it won't be some lame-ass preplanned seduction. It'll happen in the heat of the moment. When I can't wait another second to know what it's like to be buried inside you."

She swallowed hard.

"Until then, I'm going to enjoy the hell out of building us up to that point."

"So I don't get a say in this?" She reached down and palmed my erection. "What if I said take me right here, right now on the kitchen counter? That'd be spontaneous."

"Would it? Or are you just goading me?"

"I'm goading you, definitely." She smirked and kept stroking me. "And you seem to like it."

"That part of me likes it and wishes you'd never stop. But thankfully my brain isn't in my boxers." I removed her hand

and clamped my hands on her ass, pulling her closer. "My turn. Truth or dare."

"Dare."

"I dare you to give sexual control to me."

Lennox blinked. "What?"

"You always call the shots when it comes to sex, don't you?"

"Of course."

I leaned forward and pressed my mouth below the hollow of her throat. "By letting that go, you can prove that *you're* spontaneous and not stuck in that rut of always having to be in control. Trust me to take care of you and give you what you need. On my time frame." I followed the ridge of her collarbone with my tongue. "I dare you, dancing queen."

"Does that mean no messing around at all?"

Christ, I loved the pouty way she said that, as if I was taking away her favorite treat. "That'll be up to me to decide, won't it?"

She moaned when my lips grazed the upper swell of her breast.

"Unbutton your blouse, Lennox, and let me at you." My heart hammered as I waited for her to play along or retreat.

Then her fingers were between us and she undid the buttons. One quick twist and the front clasp of her bra popped open. Watching my eyes, she pulled the fabric back on both sides, revealing her bare torso.

A low growl rumbled free and I had the overwhelming urge to sink my teeth into that abundant flesh and mark her as mine. She was beautifully feminine, all soft white curves and pale pink nipples. I opened my mouth over her right breast and sucked hard, feeling that sweet tip harden beneath my stroking tongue.

She made the sexiest noise and I wanted to keep doing

that over and over to see how many more times she'd sigh and moan with bliss.

But I backed off and looked up at her.

Lennox met my gaze. "I've never been able to resist a dare."

I grinned. "Good to know." I refastened her bra and redid her buttons, starting at the bottom. I placed a kiss below her belly button and worked my way up. I pulled her down until her mouth was level with mine. I said, "You are one sexy woman, Lennox Greene," before I swept a fleeting kiss across her mouth. "Now let's see what there is to eat."

Mary had left us a veritable feast: a pork roast with a side of sage and apple stuffing, a veggie medley of diced squash, corn and green beans, and homemade wheat rolls. We heated the food in unison as if we'd done it several times before, and afterward we cleaned the kitchen up. The domesticity wasn't familiar. The women I'd dated more than a few times had never cooked for me, nor I for them.

Lennox's arms circled my waist and she rested the side of her face on my shoulder blade. "What're you thinking about so hard?"

"That this should feel awkward, but it doesn't."

"I was thinking the same thing. Oh, and how much I'd love to have a personal chef preparing my meals."

"Me too."

"But you could have that. Not to point out the obvious, but it's not like money is an issue for you."

The way she'd said that wasn't snarky or judgy, just matter-of-fact. I faced her and she immediately stepped in, nestling her face against my chest. Lennox was a lot more openly affectionate than I'd ever imagined. "True. It's a multitude of issues."

"Such as?"

"Such as . . . do I let the chef plan every bite that goes into my mouth? Will it always be healthy? Will it always be good? If I'm paying a lot of money for food and it isn't what I'm in the mood for, isn't it a waste to throw it away? How am I supposed to know what I'm hungry for a week ahead of time?"

She smiled against my pec. "I can see you've thought this through."

"Not to mention my issue with having people in my place when I'm not there. Pawing through my kitchen and making a mess. Who wants to come home at ten at night to the lingering odor of cooked fish?"

"First of all, there wouldn't be an odor if you hired a good chef. Second of all, how many nights a week do you work until ten o'clock?"

"Too many."

Lennox looked up at me. "Has that changed with this quest you're on to change your life?"

"Let's see, last night this hot blonde dragged me out of my office right at five. But the nights before that . . . I think the earliest I made it home was nine."

"I imagine it's a gradual process. One hour earlier this week, maybe an hour and a half earlier next week. Within a few months you might get done in time to make yourself dinner in your kitchen."

I scowled. "I have no desire to learn how to cook."

"If you say because it's women's work, I'm punching you in the stomach."

"Such a violent streak." I kissed her scrunched-up nose. "But you'd have to beat my mother to the punch—*ha ha*—because she believed in gender equality when we were growing up. Annika had to learn how to run the lawn mower and where to put oil in her car, whereas Walker, Jens and I knew how to use a vacuum and we were well versed in scrubbing toilets."

"The Lund children, heirs to a billion-dollar fortune, had . . . chores?"

"As my mother pointed out, only half of our DNA came from privilege. The other half came from hardworking blue-collar Swedes. That's not to say *Mom* scrubbed her own toilets after she married Dad."

"I'm all-pro at all kinds of cleaning. Heck, I surpassed amateur status at an early age. You might say I was a cleaning savant."

I laughed. She had such a way with words.

"So now that the kitchen is cleaned up, what are we doing tonight?"

"A hike up to the summit. I haven't done it since I was a kid. There are no snow clouds and no moon, so we'll really be able to see the stars."

"A night hike. Uphill. In the dark. With snow on the ground. And temperatures in the low single digits?" She studied me as if that was the worst torture she could imagine.

"What? I know what you're thinking. But you're wrong. This suggestion does not border on serial killer behavior."

"No, but it definitely borders on sadism."

LENNOX

Go to sleep, go to sleep, go to sleep.

I should've been exhausted from the hike. It was hard for me to admit I'd had fun. Mostly it was fun to see Brady so relaxed. To see him smile. To hear him laugh. To watch his very fine denim-clad ass just a few feet away, bunching and flexing with each step he took.

To see the lust burning in his eyes every time he touched me.

When we returned to the cabin, I'd given him a hug and a quick kiss good night.

In the Rose Room, I stripped and crawled between the covers. The room was colder than I was used to, so I slipped on my flannel pajamas.

I stared at the ceiling for a while. Then the walls. I don't remember at what point that night I realized that the rose wallpaper looked like big splotches of blood.

Once my thoughts jumped on that train, there was no getting off. I spooked myself. Big-time. I swore I heard animals scratching at the window. When the hot-water heater kicked on with a *clank-clank-clank* that sounded exactly like a ghost's chains rattling, I threw back the covers and tore down the hallway to Brady's room.

Why were we on opposite ends of the hallway? To keep me out of the range of temptation?

I opened the door slightly and peeked in.

Of course he was snoring.

If he was that sound asleep, maybe he wouldn't notice until morning that I'd crawled in with him. I took a step closer and a floorboard beneath me creaked.

The snoring stopped. He sat up. The light shining through the crack in the bathroom door cast a sliver of light across his bare torso. "Lennox? What's wrong?"

"I think there's a bear trying to get into my room."

"A bear," he repeated.

"Yes, a bear. You told me there were bears up here, so you can't expect me not to"—*obsess*—"think about it."

"Since we're on the second floor, I'm pretty sure we're safe from bears," he said dryly. "Besides, I told you the bears were hibernating this time of year, so we wouldn't see any."

I guessed I missed that part of the conversation. "Oh."

"What's this really about?"

He said that . . . accusingly. As if I was pretending to be scared just so I could get into his bed.

Screw that. I *was* scared. I'd never slept in a cabin in the woods before, but god knows I'd seen my fair share of slasher movies detailing the horrible things that happened to people staying in a cabin in the woods—especially for the first time. My fear was not misplaced; however, my pride was much stronger than fear and I'd cower in my bed alone.

I spun around and booked it down the hallway. I heard a noise behind me and my flight response kicked in. I screamed but I didn't stop running until two bare muscular arms immobilized me.

"Christ, Lennox, it's just me."

My heart pounded so hard and so loud that it distorted his voice.

"You scream loud enough to wake the damn dead."

"Leave me alone." I hustled into the bedroom and slammed the door shut behind me. I dove onto the bed and scrambled beneath the covers.

The door opened. The bed dipped. A warm, hard body moved in behind me. "Baby, you're shaking like crazy." He paused. "You weren't pulling a prank. You really are scared."

Nice of you to notice and make fun. "Yes." I scooted closer to the edge of the bed.

"Come here."

"I'm fine. Go away."

He snaked his arm below my shoulder blades and hauled me against him.

Immediately my shudders lessened. I relaxed into him

even more when he pressed his lips into the back of my head and murmured something nonsensical and soothing.

After I'd calmed completely, he said, "Talk to me, Lennox."

"I don't know what to say. I'm not the outdoorsy type. Stuff in nature freaks me out."

"You don't like camping?"

"I've never been camping."

"Seriously?"

"I've never stayed in a cabin in the woods either—although this is several steps above the rustic cabins in horror movies. But still . . . it's unnerving to be in this big house out in the middle of nowhere."

"You grew up in Minnesota, right?"

"I grew up in the Twin Cities suburbs. On the weekends my mom's husband stayed inside and watched TV. So all the 'Land of 10,000 Lakes' and outdoor life that most Minnesotans love? I never experienced any of it."

"That makes me sad for you. During my growing-up years I spent more time outside than inside."

"But you had playmates in your brothers, sister and cousins. I had no one to play with. So I stayed in my room and read."

"I did that late at night when I was supposed to be sleeping."

"See? You've got a rebellious, wild side."

"I doubt that a twelve-year-old secretly poring over *Fortune* magazines under the bedcovers with a flashlight counts as adventurous," he said dryly.

I smiled. I could just see him, owl-eyed, hair sticking up everywhere, the financial magazines a different form of porn for a brainiac kid like him.

"So you didn't play sports?"

"No. We didn't go to church either. Sometimes I got to

go over to a friend's house, but it had to be a special occasion. My mom's husband didn't have any family around. Neither did my mom. I know I missed out on a lot. But when I was old enough to make my own choices, I didn't choose to do anything outside or sports related because I didn't like it."

"How could you know if you liked it if you never tried it?"

"I had real-life stuff to keep me occupied, Brady. By then I didn't have time for extracurricular activities because I had to get a job."

Let it go. Just let me stay warm and safe with you in the present and ignore my past.

"How old were you when you started working?"

"Fifteen. I wasn't pulling fries in a fast-food restaurant. And I didn't work for fun money to blow on nail polish, trashy magazines and candy."

Brady shifted and nestled his face in the curve of my neck. "Tell me all of it, Lennox. Even the things you don't think I'll understand."

So I spilled my guts to him—telling him every dark thing I'd left out before.

He was quiet for a long time after I'd finished speaking.

Of course he is. What did you expect? He's heir to a billion-dollar corporation. He was born with a silver spoon in his mouth and he still eats with it. Your situation is a foreign concept to him. When will you ever learn that honesty isn't always the best policy?

I hadn't realized I'd been holding my breath until he whispered, "Breathe," and spread his hand open over my chest to make sure I did.

I didn't feel as if a great weight had been lifted. I didn't feel a deeper connection to Brady. I just felt drained.

When he finally spoke, it wasn't what I'd expected. "We'll see if you have an affinity for the great outdoors tomorrow."

"More hiking?"

"No. With the fresh snow it'll be a perfect time to go cross-country skiing. And don't worry about equipment. The Lund cabin is fully equipped."

"Cross-country skiing . . . Is that the thing where we shoot guns too?"

He chuckled into my hair. "No. That's a biathlon."

"Sounds like more fun if we're armed." I tried to imagine myself on a pair of skis. I pictured myself falling over. A lot.

"You tensed up again. Why?"

"I'm just thinking that maybe you could go cross-country skiing and I could have a cup of hot chocolate waiting for you when you got back. I'm thinking maybe I'm more the 'hang out at the cabin and tend the fire' kind of a chick."

"No. I want you with me."

"Because I'll be so loud and clumsy that I'll scare off any wildlife that might attack us?"

Brady sighed.

I suspected he was trying not to laugh.

"Go to sleep, Lennox. We'll talk about it in the morning."

"You're sleeping here?"

"Yeah. I'm too comfy to move."

Such a lie. But it was sweet that he knew I didn't want to be alone. "Thank you."

"My pleasure."

I wasn't used to sharing a bed with someone. I worried I'd lie there for hours with no sleep in sight. But the rhythmic sound of Brady's exhales soon sent me floating off into slumber.

Fourteen

BRADY

I woke up alone.

In Lennox's room.

I rolled onto my back and stared at the ceiling, letting the sleep clear from my brain, thinking about last night.

Lennox's story had haunted me.

My childhood had been relatively normal. I fought and played with and defended my siblings and cousins. None of us were raised by nannies, although my mom did have her sister Britta live with us for a year after Jensen was born to help out. What I hadn't known at the time was that my father had largely been absent that year, due to the dissolution of various divisions of Lund and Sons as it was rebuilt into Lund Industries. After the grain wars, the government had stepped in and forced us, and our largest competitor, to divide our assets so there was no possibility of a merger between our companies so we could create a monopoly.

It'd been a stressful time in my parents' lives. Four children under the age of six, plus an uncertain financial future. What had been a life-changing time for them hadn't even been a blip on my radar. Kids are oblivious. Kids of wealthy parents even more so.

As the oldest kid in the family, my parents expected a lot from me. With no nanny, if my mother was busy, I was put in charge of keeping an eye on my siblings. I had to lead by example. I didn't mind, likely because it'd been such an innate part of me from such a young age that I didn't think about it and also because I always got to be in charge.

We lived in a gated community—both my uncles and their families had houses and guest quarters on the property—that we jokingly referred to as the Lund Compound in our later years. The year I'd turned ten, I started to notice things that I wasn't allowed to do, like ride my bike to a friend's house, or hang out at the community pool, or meet my school buddies at the baseball fields. We lived right on Lake Minnetonka, but I wasn't allowed to go down to the lake without adult supervision. The only place I could ride my bike was down our long driveway. I didn't understand why I couldn't walk to the local convenience store for candy. Why I couldn't have any of my friends over to my house without an itinerary decided weeks in advance.

I'd started to get resentful. So I tested the boundaries. I'd jump the fence and sneak to the lake. I'd walk around unsupervised. None of these excursions lasted long, but it was a rush, having freedom and secrets.

So I'd bragged to my friends that I could do whatever I wanted. They dared me to prove it. One day we made plans to meet and ride our bikes to the new BMX track. I'd set out while my mom was busy directing the gardener, the housekeepers and the kitchen staff. I rode my bike along the road, avoiding the freeway and commercial areas with traffic and people. I felt vindicated when I reached the meeting place on my own.

But after an hour I knew my friends were no-shows. Instead of returning home, I decided to ride to the BMX track by myself. After two hours of riding through the suburbs, I knew I was lost. Really lost.

Life was much harder in the days before cell phones. I'd seen pay phones, but I'd never needed to use one and I hadn't thought to bring money with me anyway. I knew better than to talk to strangers; what if I knocked on their door and asked to use the phone and they locked me in the basement? I was better off out in the open, where I might see something familiar that would lead me back home.

Although I pedaled like mad, it seemed I was going in circles. Lost, alone, hungry and scared, with no idea what to do next, I took a break at a school playground. While I sat on the swings and cried, some kids stole my bike.

After walking for hours, I was sunburned. I had blisters on my feet. I was covered in bug bites. Night was falling and I feared being murdered in my sleep, so I vowed to myself I wouldn't sleep.

Then I saw a police car. I ran to it, beating on the windows for the cop to open the door, and I was so relieved that I fainted.

When I came to, in an ambulance, my parents were there, both frantic and relieved. I'd never seen my dad cry, but right then he grabbed me and sobbed.

After I was discovered missing, my parents thought I'd been kidnapped. The cops had been looking for me all over town. Although I later learned they were sure I'd snuck off to go swimming and had drowned, and search and rescue had been notified they might have to dredge the lake.

The next morning my father took me into his office, so I knew I'd surpassed trouble and gone straight into big trouble.

He'd told me I'd never be an ordinary boy. That I had a bright future and I'd play an important part in the company that bore the family name, but I had to understand that responsibility came with a price. There were people who'd want to hurt me. There were people who'd try to persuade me to make bad decisions. There were people who'd use me. I had to assume that most people wanted something from me. So my search for freedom had resulted only in my seeing the entire cage—not just a small corner of it—far sooner than I would've liked.

"What are you thinking about so hard?" Lennox asked.

I lifted my head and saw her leaning in the doorway. "Just some childhood memories."

She sauntered over and perched on the edge of the bed. "Did those memories include a hyper but loveable dog named Sparky?"

"No. Why?"

"I always wanted a dog. Like Nana in *Peter Pan* or Shadow in *Homeward Bound* or even a Chihuahua like the Taco Bell dog." She plucked fuzz off the flannel sheet. "But my mom said no to pets. I couldn't even have a goldfish. So I love hearing about pets people had growing up."

"We had an Irish wolfhound for a couple of years. After Cuddles got cancer and died, Mom said no more pets because we were all so upset." I reached for her restless hand. "Did I snore too loud and chase you away last night?"

She looked at me. "Not at all. I went looking for a coffeemaker."

"Did you find one?"

"No—and, buddy, you promised."

"That I did." I threw the covers back. "Coffee first. Then we'll decide what we're doing today after we hit the skiing trails."

I t was strange to be in the kitchen at the cabin in my pajamas with a woman I barely knew.

"It's awkward, in the light of day, isn't it?"

I looked up at her, wondering if I'd voiced that thought out loud. "What?"

"This." She gestured between us. "We hiked in the dark last night. You came into my room after I was freaked out about the dark. Now, today, I'm wishing for gloom and snow." She sipped her coffee. "Or maybe it's awkward because I'm not who you wanted me to be."

My eyes narrowed on her. "Explain that."

"My wild days are in the past, Brady. After telling you about my crappy upbringing, it just reminded me that I don't want to go back to that girl who fucked and fought and got high and danced on the bar and had nothing going for her. I'm sad and embarrassed for the girl who believed ink and piercings would say to the world, 'Screw you, this is who I am, I'm unique, I don't conform,' when in reality I was just like everyone else having an identity crisis." She closed her eyes. "That was an eye-opener, the day I realized that in running away from my mother, I was just like her. That's when I stopped running and worked to have something different."

Her openness floored me. In my limited experience, people who'd remade themselves were reluctant to talk about their past, about who they'd been before.

Lennox is not this open with everyone, dumbass. She covers her tats and leaves out her piercings at the office because she wants to conform as much now as she did when she tried so hard to be nonconformist.

I crossed the room and framed her face in my hands. "Lennox. Look at me."

She lifted her long lashes.

"Thank you for talking to me."

At that, she offered me a smile.

That smile loosened the tight feeling inside me I'd been carrying around for years.

She sidestepped me. "Let's strap on the gear and get the skiing thing out of the way."

Lennox lasted longer than I'd predicted on the skiing trails.

I didn't make a single crack about bears. Nor did I point out all the different animal tracks. But then again, her fear last night had led to our sharing a bed. I couldn't remember the last time I'd spent the entire night with a woman and I knew it'd never been so easy as it was with her.

And torturous.

"Hey, dreamy mountain man," she shouted at me.

"What?"

"I've had enough of this nature shit. Let's get dressed and take the sled dogs into the village for supplies. We can practice yodeling on the way back."

"Yodeling. Seriously?"

"What? Your mom is from Sweden. They yodel there, right?"

I honestly had no idea.

"Besides, I want to test you on that 'stepping out of your comfort zone' promise."

"I already fulfilled that one this week." I tapped my forearm. "I got a tat, remember?"

"Lucky for you, then. This is gonna be a twofer."

stared up at the sign on the building. "You're kidding, right?"

"Nope. Come on, Mr. Lund—this will be fun. Let that creative side out."

"At Pottery to Paint? Lennox, look in the window. The average age in there is like . . . eight."

"Yay! I'll be above average for once."

"Let's go back to the bowling alley."

She rolled her eyes. "You only want to go back there so you can keep making cracks about the size of your blue balls."

I laughed.

"Maybe you'll get lucky and they'll have a paint-by-numbers option, since you claim that numbers make sense and you're scared of plain old creativity."

"I'm not scared." I brushed my lips over hers. "And, baby, I'm plenty creative when it counts."

"Prove it." She shoved me toward the door.

An hour later, we were still painting our coffee mugs. Evidently, that wasn't a big seller with the grade-school crowd.

"Pop quiz time," Lennox said.

I groaned.

"Oh, stop. You suck at small talk, so I'm throwing you a bone in the 'getting to know each other' portion of our endless date."

"Feel free to throw me a bone whenever you want."

She flicked paint at me.

"Fine. Small talk questionnaire. Go."

"Favorite movie."

"*Avatar.* Yours?"

"*Bridesmaids.*" Without looking up from painting, she said, "Monopoly or Scrabble?"

"Neither." I'd finished my mug and watched her concentration as she painted. Her tongue would dart out. Then she'd sink her teeth into her bottom lip. Sometimes she'd scrunch up her nose. Or she'd narrow her gaze until she was almost cross-eyed. She was so damn cute. Everything she did, she gave her all, which fascinated me. Because I was exactly the same way?

"That's cheating."

"No, I'm just not conforming. My favorite game is chess."

She lifted her eyes to mine. "I saw a chessboard at the cabin. I challenge you to a match tonight."

"Challenge accepted." Maybe I'd challenge her to a game of strip chess. "My turn. Favorite music."

"Rock. With some thrash metal thrown in. You?"

"Guess."

"Classical. With a preference for piano arrangements."

I leaned forward. "Classical? I'm not that much older than you."

"Ah, but you're that much *classier* than me, moneybags." She smirked. "Besides, I saw the piano at the cabin, so I'm assuming that, in addition to dance lessons, Mama Lund made you take piano lessons and you had to practice even on vacation."

"Only Annika lasted longer than a year with the lessons. Walker actually took wire cutters and snipped all the piano strings so he wouldn't have to play. Now guess again."

"Jazz fusion."

"Wrong."

"Blues."

"Wrong again."

"Show tunes."

"Piss. Off."

She laughed. "Okay. Obscure hipster coffeehouse emo crap only played on a recorder that was handcrafted in Peru?"

I shook my head.

"I give."

"Rock."

"Prove it." Lennox set down her paintbrush. "Best rock song ever recorded."

"Easy. AC/DC 'Back in Black.'"

She snorted. "Wrong. Guns N' Roses 'Welcome to the Jungle.'"

"I'd agree that's the third best song . . . after 'Back in Black' and 'Kashmir.'"

"'Kashmir' is overrated. 'Whole Lotta Love' is way better."

"Whatever. Where'd you learn to love rock music?"

"My mom. She mostly listened to eighties hair metal bands and seventies arena rock. What about you?"

"My parents. The first night they met my dad actually told my mom ABBA sucked and then forced her to listen to 'real' music."

"Do you ever listen to ABBA?"

"Not that I'll ever admit to."

"Hmm. We'll have to swap iPods. Our musical tastes are in tune."

Impulsively I curled my hand around the back of her neck and pulled her in for a kiss. "I'm 'Crazy on You.'"

"Back atcha, 'Magic Man.'"

I kissed her again.

The table of eight-year-olds next to us broke out in a chorus of "Eww! Gross!"

"That's our cue."

"I'm done anyway. It'll look better once it's been fired, but—*ta-da!* This is for you." Lennox turned the mug around. The lettering read, WHO'S THE BOSS?

What a sweet thing. "Thanks."

"You're welcome. Let me see yours."

"Not here, baby. Think of the children."

"Omigod, you are such a perv!" She clapped her paint-spattered hands on my cheeks and kissed me hard. "I like that about you so, so much."

We played chess. In front of a roaring fire. Sipping wine. With classical piano music playing in the background, because Lennox was a smart-ass that way.

She thought the whole thing was an attempt at seduction and warned me that our "first foray into fucking" wasn't going to be clichéd.

I don't think I'd ever laughed so much as I had with her.

But then sometimes I'd look at her and let her see in my eyes all the dirty, kinky things I planned to do to her when the time was right.

She went into the kitchen and rinsed the wineglasses.

I followed her, moving in behind her at the sink. I pulled her shirt down so I could kiss the back of her neck. I loved the sound she made when I put my mouth on her there. I loved to feel the gooseflesh beneath my lips. I loved to absorb her shudder of pleasure when I sank my teeth into the curve where her shoulder became the nape of her neck. "Lennox. I want you in my bed tonight."

"Is that a command?"

"No. It's a request. I liked sleeping with you last night. And that's all that'll happen tonight."

"You sure?"

"Yes. If I gave up the perfect opportunity to make love to you in front of a roaring fire on a snowy night in a cabin in the woods with wine and soft music . . . then I won't settle for a quick tumble."

"All right. But I do plan on sleeping naked to test your resolve."

"Naked? But what if there's a fire?"

Lennox sidestepped me and pointedly looked at my crotch. "There's already a hot spot in your pants, Brady. Maybe you'd better put it out before you come to bed."

Fifteen

LENNOX

It wasn't my idea of fun, getting up at six A.M. on a Sunday.
Especially not when I'd been enjoying having a warm male body spooning me. Then firm—yet soft—lips trailing down the nape of my neck and across my shoulders, while rough-tipped fingers lightly caressed my arm, my hip, the length of my thigh before moving in to stroke my belly and tease my breasts.

It was heaven.

It was hell.

A hell I'd willingly signed on for when I'd given control to Brady.

By the time he'd gotten me so worked up I was squirming against him, he softly kissed the curve of my jaw and retreated. "I'll shower down the hall." Then he vanished.

That'd been an hour ago and I was still . . . annoyed.

"You're grumbling, baby. What's going on?"

"I'm tired."

"Close your eyes. It's two and a half more hours until we reach the Cities."

"Aren't you tired?"

"No."

But I could tell he was restless. From nerves? Was he having second thoughts about introducing me to his family?

I'd assumed that because he was brilliant, sinfully good looking and rich, he'd never lack for female companionship. But I hadn't banked on Brady Lund, CFO, to be a little shy.

God. That shyness wrecked me.

I'd gone beyond nervous to meet his family, to petrified.

Hi, I'm Lennox Greene. Yes, I work for Lund Industries. No, you don't know my parents—heck, even I don't know who my father is.

"Lennox. I can feel your whole body twitching."

"Brady. Maybe this isn't such a good idea."

"What?"

"All of it!" I gestured to nothing and everything. "You and me. Me meeting your family. You taking me to a football game at the Metrodome and us sitting in the skybox. Maybe you should just run me home first. You can tell them I ate something that didn't agree with me. I just . . . don't think I can do this."

"Why not?" he asked calmly.

"Because I won't fit in. Because I'll probably say something stupid or be a smart-ass and embarrass you. Because it's too soon. We just started dating and no one in the company knows and this is how rumors get started."

Brady pulled the car onto the shoulder and parked. He scrubbed his hands over his face and I realized he hadn't shaved today. As sexy as that made him look, it wasn't something that should've escaped his notice.

Of course I blamed myself. His assorted family members—including the CEO and the COO—would take one look at his disheveled appearance and then aim their judging gazes on me, and believe we'd spent all weekend defiling the family homestead.

And then I would feel the need to overshare and let them know that, no, we hadn't spent every waking moment in bed—but then again . . . we had *slept* in the same bed both nights; we just hadn't gotten naked and sweaty in that bed—well, except we had slept naked . . .

Strong fingers curled around my jaw, forcing my attention to him.

"I've said your name like four times while you were in whatever freak-out zone you jumped into. So let me set you straight. It's not a rumor; we are together. If you're worried about losing your job, don't be. I can make it very clear that anyone who fucks with you fucks with me. My mother will likely be a serious pain in the ass, but understand it's only because I've never brought a woman to family day."

"Never?"

"Never. Ever." Those intense blue eyes seemed to look into my soul. "You might think I'm playing at this. That this is just a phase for me, trying to reform myself more than just who I am at work. But I promise you, Lennox, it is not a phase."

He'd just, in effect, told me that I was his girlfriend.

Holy balls.

I wasn't sure how to feel about that, because I'd never been in this position before, meeting a guy's family when his family mattered to him. But I had been used as fight fodder: *Hey, Dad, look at the tattooed bar skank I brought home for Sunday dinner. Pass the potatoes and the judgment, please.*

"You don't believe me."

"Yes, I believe you. I just have a hard time getting a grasp on the fact this is happening to me."

"It kills me to hear you say that, baby."

He stroked my cheek in such a sweetly loving gesture I felt the back of my eyes sting.

And somehow he knew I needed tenderness. So when Brady kissed me, I melted into him. I floated to that happy plane where the taste of him, the scent of him, the feel of our bodies touching was all I'd ever need.

He seemed reluctant to break our connection as he continued to gift me with soft smooches, little nibbles and the sweet sensation of his breath drifting across my sensitized lips. "Better?"

"Infinitely." I rubbed my fingertips over the stubble on his cheeks. "This is a good look on you."

"Drives me crazy. I want to scratch my face off."

"Maybe later today you can find a nice soft place to help you ease the itch."

"The insides of your thighs would make great scratching posts, now that you've mentioned it."

Heat raced down the center of my body as that image popped into my head.

He chuckled. "I'd better get us back on the road."

I took a little catnap while he drove and woke up refreshed. I grabbed my makeup bag and fixed my face, trying to find the balance between *cares too much* and *doesn't give a damn*. The Vikings jersey that I was required by Lund Law to wear covered the tattoos on the back of my neck, and the long-sleeved shirt I wore hid the bandage on my right arm.

So I slicked my hair into a ponytail and then tucked it under so it looked a little more finished. After I added pink lipstick, I glanced over to see Brady staring at me.

"What? Too much? Do I look like a tramp or something?"

"Not at all. You look amazing. I was just thinking I prefer how you looked first thing this morning, so sleepy and sexy in my arms. So naked." Then his gaze dropped to my mouth. "I was also thinking that lipstick is the exact same shade as your nipples."

"Is that right?" I unbuckled his seat belt and reached across the console to tug his jersey up.

"What are you doing?"

"Eyes on the road, Lund." I snaked my hand under his shirt, pushing it up, bunching the extra material in my other hand. When I had the right half of his upper torso exposed, I leaned over and ran my lips across his nipple, smearing lipstick on him.

Brady groaned and I warned him not to close his eyes, because he did jerk the steering wheel hard one time.

I tugged his jersey back into place and refastened his seat belt. Then I offered him a smile. "Now our nipples are the same color. Think of me when you get undressed tonight."

"Evil woman."

"You started it."

I reapplied my lipstick and then we were in the thick of Minneapolis traffic, which was surprisingly heavy for a Sunday morning. We joined the long line of cars headed to the Metrodome.

He cut across three lanes of traffic to the VIP/valet stand.

The guy manning the booth grinned when he saw Brady. "Mr. Lund! Glad you could make it today. Think that brother of yours will see any game time?"

"I sure hope so."

"Us too." He skirted the front end and opened my door. "Ma'am."

Then Brady was right there, draping a lanyard over my head. "This place is confusing on the upper levels. So if for some reason we get separated, all the information about where you are and which access point you need to use is on the back of this pass. Anyone in the stadium wearing a jacket like Eddie's can help you."

"Okay. But I'm pretty sure I'll be stuck to your side for the entire game."

He draped his arm over my shoulder and kissed my temple. "I won't complain about that."

We walked with the crowd up several ramps and then we cut around to a bank of elevators. Brady swiped his pass and up we went. We switched elevators one more time. An older guy stood sentinel-like in front of a curved hallway as we exited.

"Mr. Brady." He offered his hand. "It's good to see you today."

"You too, Bart. Although I'm sorry you got stuck with the rabble-rousers again."

"Your family are the only ones on this side today."

Brady frowned. "Where are the Abbotts? They don't miss games."

"Miss Martha is in the hospital again. So they're all watching the game from her room."

"That's a shame. I might sneak into their skybox and leave a note for Chuck."

"That'd be much appreciated, I'm sure." He patted Brady's hand. "You enjoy the game."

Then Bart leaned in to me and whispered, "Don't let 'em

scare you off, miss. But I ain't gonna lie. They're gunning for ya."

Awesome.

Brady had walked ahead and was waiting for me by the open door.

So I took a deep breath and stepped into the judge's chamber.

And just as I expected, the space went silent as I got the head-to-toe perusal from the twenty-plus people in the room.

Everyone else hung back and waited as one couple approached us.

Brady's parents didn't look old enough to have a thirty-two-year-old son. But as I watched them, I could pick out certain features that Brady had inherited from his dad: hair color, the size and build of his body, his smile. And from his mom: her Nordic eyes, her cheekbones and her mouth.

Brady kept his hand circled around my waist, even as he bent down and kissed his mother on both cheeks.

His dad clapped him on the shoulder. "Well, son, introduce us to your young lady."

"This is Lennox Greene. Lennox, this is my dad, Ward, and my mother, Selka."

I offered my hand. "I'm happy to meet you in person, Mr. Lund. I do see you storming the halls at LI occasionally."

His eyes narrowed. "You work for us?"

"Yes, sir. I'm in the office support department."

"IT?"

"No, I'm a floater."

"I am not familiar with this 'floating' term," his mother said.

"Like the secretarial pools back in the day, Mom. Lennox

fills in in any department where she's needed. So she has a wide range of skills and responsibilities."

I shot Brady a look. I didn't need him bragging like I was something special to his supermodel mom.

Selka took my hand. "I'm very pleased to meet you, Lennon."

"Lennox," I corrected.

"Ah. Right. Sorry."

Like hell you are.

"So you and my son met when you showed him your . . . office skills?"

Brady stiffened beside me. Then he laughed. "No, actually we met at the LCCO outreach program. Lennox's roommate heads up the county's program. I'd run into Lennox a few times before that at LI, but we both just happened to volunteer on that day."

Selka's eyes burned into me. "You have roommate?"

Her accent sounded part Scandinavian, part Russian. "Yes. We share a house."

"I had roommate once. Terrible person. She wore all my clothes."

"Fortunately, I don't have that problem with Kiley."

"Have you been married before?"

"No."

"Do you have children?"

"Mom," Brady said with exasperation. "Knock it off."

Selka patted Brady's cheek and said something in Swedish.

"No, Mrs. Lund, I don't have any children."

"You're lovely. You must be part Swede." She cocked her head. "My son is handsome, yes?"

"Jesus." Brady looked at his father for help.

But Ward Lund just held up his hands in surrender.

"Yes, Brady is very handsome. And he's smart. He can be very funny." I paused. "What surprised me most about him, though, was his kindness. He was great with the teenagers in the program the morning he volunteered. That's why I agreed to go out with him, despite our potential conflict of interest with the CFO dating a lower-level clerical employee."

I felt Selka studying me as Ward said, "We don't have rules about interpersonal relationships at LI. In fact, several of our employees met there and have been married for years."

"And just as many were divorced," Selka added.

Looked like I was scoring points with Mama Bear. *Not.*

"I'm happy you're here," Ward said. "I'm sure you at least know of the other members of the family, so we'll let you get on with the introductions, Brady."

Selka said nothing.

I didn't ask Brady's take on how I'd done with his mother once they'd walked away. He had no other experiences to judge it by. And men were often clueless about women stuff anyway.

Brady introduced me to his uncle Monte, who was president of the board of directors, and his wife, Priscilla. Next we moved on to his uncle Archer, CEO of LI. He was an imposing man and my hand shook as if I was meeting a rock star. Archer's wife, Edie, thought I was cute and asked me a bunch of questions about my position at LI, which calmed me a little because she knew Lola. She also knew Anita, and the way her nose wrinkled told me she didn't care for her either.

Annika was the biggest surprise. She hugged me. "Lennox! Look at you, dating my brother. Everyone thinks he's the big bad wolf so I'm glad to see someone got past his sharp teeth."

"Thanks for that analogy, sis."

"Did Lennox tell you I tried to hire her?"

I closed my eyes and willed her to stop talking.

"No, she forgot to mention it."

"Well, when May had her baby, Lennox was assigned to my department. She was so efficient and got us all caught up on a backlog of filing and she even cross-referenced all the information. It was amazing. So when May came back and saw all that Lennox had done, she knew she'd been busted for doing the absolute minimum and she requested a departmental change from Personnel as well as a job-share position to part-time."

Yes, I'd done my job so well that I'd cost a new mother her job. I still felt guilty about that.

"But when I tried to get Lennox to stay on as May's replacement, she declined. She said she was still too new to the company and wanted to remain in her current position for at least a year." Annika punched me in the arm—right on my recently re-inked tattoo. "Crazy loyal, huh?"

"What are you? A thirteen-year-old boy? Stop smacking my girlfriend, Nika."

"Shit. Sorry." Then she proceeded to rub really hard on the spot she'd just hit. "I'm just glad Brady finally showed he has good taste in women."

"Uh . . . thanks?"

Brady steered me away. Then he got right in my face. "Are you okay?"

"I'm fine. It just stings."

"Annika tends to forget sometimes that she's a girl. Blame it on three brothers and three older boy cousins."

I set my hand on his chest.

He took my other hand and kissed the inside of my wrist.

"Nice little PDA you've got going on, cuz."

"Fuck off, Nolan."

"Such language." He laughed. "And who is this lovely lady who is far too beautiful for the likes of you?"

Nolan Lund was as outrageously good looking as he was charming, which was why we'd nicknamed him "The Prince."

I offered my hand. "I'm Lennox Greene, Mr. Lund." I didn't remind him we'd met before. Being overlooked as part of the furniture was part of the gig as a temp worker.

He scrutinized me. "You look familiar."

"I work at LI." Maybe he'd seen me dancing on the bar—not that I'd offer up the prompt.

"I take it you're the one who accompanied Brady to Flurry last weekend?"

"Yes."

"And? How did you like it?"

Brady and I exchanged a look and my cheeks flushed as I remembered the sexy, sensual way he had moved against me on the dance floor. "It was fun."

When I looked up, Nolan had returned to his date—a skeletal redhead with a bored expression and Botoxed lips.

"Looks like you saved the best for last, bro." A gorgeous blond man, with the physique and beard of a lumberjack, stepped into my personal space. "I'm Walker. The black sheep of the family."

"Black sheep. Yeah, right," Brady scoffed.

"I'm Lennox." My face was starting to hurt from smiling so much. "Brady's told me a little about you, so it's nice to finally meet you."

"Well, sweetheart, you were a complete surprise to me. I had no idea Brady was dating someone." Walker's eyes, a frostier blue than Brady's, lit up. He sent Brady a *You dog* look. "That's where he saw you. Dancing on the bar."

"No, I'd met Lennox before that. At *work*," he emphasized.

"Whatever. I'm glad to see you here with him. Can I get you something to drink?"

"We were making our way to the bar, so I'll take care of her."

Walker grinned. "I'll just bet you will."

Lord have mercy, he has the biggest dimples I've ever seen.

"Stop sighing over my damn brother," Brady muttered.

"And I'm not even the hot one," Walker said, keeping that dimpled grin in place.

"I know. I've already got the hot one." I squeezed Brady's hand.

Brady murmured, "That comment would so get you laid if we were—"

"Kickoff in three minutes," Ward announced.

"Have a seat over there." Brady pointed to a corner where none of his family sat. "What would you like to drink?"

"Just a Coke."

"Really? Okay." He paused. "What about food?"

"I'm good for now."

I felt the watchful eyes as I slid onto a super-comfy lounge chair.

I'd never been much of a football fan, but I knew enough about it to keep my mouth shut and listen to those who did know what every play meant.

And this crowd was serious about football—as if the dozen LUND jerseys weren't hint enough.

When Brady didn't sit next to me, I turned to see him deep in conversation with his dad. By the way they were intently watching the field, I could tell they were discussing the game.

I took a second to check my phone since I hadn't bothered up in the North Woods. A missed call from Maxie. A text from Kiley to let me know she'd be back earlier tonight than she'd planned.

"Bored already?" Brady whispered in my ear.

"No. I thought maybe you'd ditched me."

"I just got the lowdown from my dad on why Ford isn't playing. That means Jensen will definitely get field time."

Brady spoke of these guys as if they were friends. I supposed in a way they were, since they were his brother's friends.

"It's a slim crowd here today."

"Is this all of your family?"

"No, my cousin Jaxson is a hockey player with the Chicago Blackhawks, so it's a travel day for him. My cousin Ash isn't here yet because he's helping his little sister Dallas. She won't be here since apparently she fell off the pyramid and screwed up her knee yesterday."

"Your cousin was in Egypt?"

He laughed. "No. She's a U of M cheerleader. Their pyramid crashed during the halftime show and she was on the top."

"Oh. Now I feel stupid about that too."

He grabbed my chin and gently forced me to look at him. "Don't ever say that." He kissed me hard. "Now watch the game."

I tried to focus. But my body seemed hyperaware of every movement Brady made. Of every deep grumble of disapproval. Of the ease with which football terms flew from his mouth.

Tight End.

Hard-line offense.

First down.

Roughing the passer.

Off sides.

Half the distance to the goal.

Repeat third down.

And my personal favorite: got stuffed.

I moved around during halftime. I knew Brady was itching to discuss the finer points of the first half with his family, so I wandered out of the skybox. Even Bart had bailed. I found an alcove between the two skyboxes where I could look down onto the field. The flexible dome roof made it windy at the top of this side, but I welcomed the air and breathed deeply for the first time in over an hour.

The third quarter started and I knew I should get back inside, but I needed a few more minutes of solitude. I kept an eye on the field and saw number 88 leap into the air to catch a pass. The Lund family broke out into a collective cheer so loud I bet Jensen had heard it. On the next down, once again Jensen caught the ball and he made it a few yards before he was tackled.

The next play had Jensen "The Rocket" Lund living up to his name. The quarterback was able to buy them enough time for Jensen to get way downfield at the ten-yard line. The pass the quarterback threw? A perfect spiral. Jensen caught it, hunkered down and didn't stop until he'd passed the goal line.

The stadium went nuts.

I felt that rush of adrenaline from sixty thousand rabid fans roll over me in a wave. Everything was so loud I couldn't hear how hard the Lunds were celebrating right next to me. I remained where I was, reluctant to interrupt their family celebration. Hearing them talk, I could tell this was the moment they'd been waiting for all season.

The kick was good and the Vikings were up by fourteen over Detroit.

Brady didn't track me down until there were only four minutes left of the third quarter. He was so solid and so warm when he moved in behind me and he was one of the few men I'd ever been with who made me feel petite. And when he put his arms around me I felt protected. I closed my eyes and savored the feeling.

"Did it get to be a little much in there for you?"

Sitting so close to you, having you touching me but not really touching me . . . hearing the deep rumble of your voice . . . it all mixed together to create a very potent cock-tail I couldn't sample.

"I needed some air."

He kissed the top of my head. "I hate to admit I didn't see when you left."

"No worries. I was out here when Jensen made his big play. Talk about exciting."

"It's what we've been waiting for, for two years since Jensen signed on with the team. He had one game-making play in the regular season his rookie year. But the team hasn't utilized him like they should. Jensen has wanted to play for the Vikings his entire life. But he knew if he didn't get enough time on the field this year he'd become a free agent."

"Brady."

"Yeah, baby?" he murmured behind my ear.

"Can I tell you something?"

"Anything."

"It is a huge turn-on to hear you talking football. The inflections in your voice, the passion, even those very ripe curses—it's like an auditory aphrodisiac for me."

"Lennox, I just went from freezing my balls off to completely hard in like five seconds."

I angled my head to nuzzle him. I let the tip of my tongue tickle the beard scruff beneath his chin. "*You* were getting to be too much for me, Brady. That's why I had to leave."

"And what do you think we should do about that?" He circled my wrists with his fingers and lifted my arms, placing my palms flat on the concrete walls on either side of me. Then he followed the undersides of my arms down to my chest. He squeezed and teased, his breath coming hot and fast in my ear. "Should I give you a personal play-by-play?"

"Of the football game?" I answered breathlessly.

"No, of what I'm going to do to you." He nipped my earlobe. "You've gotten a peek at the pregame plan, but this? This is the real deal. I'm going to keep after you until I get you to the goal line. How's that sound?"

"Like a challenge."

"I'm up for it."

My knees went a little weak when he urged, "Spread your legs."

But I managed to step out and give him room.

"That's a girl. Now listen up." He lowered one hand to my hip and used the other to continue to torment my breast. "We're starting fresh. It's first and ten. Tell me what that means."

"Ten moves until you score?"

"I hope not. You're primed, baby. I don't want to rush for the goal. It's too easy to fumble." He lifted the bottom of my jersey and slipped his hand beneath the silky fabric. He swept his thumb along the top of my jeans, making my belly quiver with every pass. "Do you know what it means when someone's buttoned up?"

How was I supposed to think when everything about him—sight, sound, scent, strength—surrounded me? "It means conservative?"

"Very good, Miss Greene. You were buttoned up from the moment I first met you. But it's a decoy play, isn't it?" He delicately licked behind my ear and my entire body shuddered. "Let's dispense with it." He gripped the denim between his thumb and forefinger and pulled until the steel button slipped through the hole. "Next let's move on to the zipper line offense. Which just means the most direct path with the least amount of resistance."

Zip. My jeans were undone.

He mumbled about an easy cover play when my panties were no barrier for him.

"He uses the side-to-side sweep, looking for that elusive opening."

My flesh went hot and tight. My heart thundered. I clenched my thighs.

"He's blocked."

"Sorry."

"Next pass, he spreads out."

Then my intimate skin was opened up with his tender fingers and I held my breath.

He said, "Lund goes deep," in that whiskey-rough voice.

I groaned when he plunged a finger inside me.

Once. Twice. Three times.

Brady scraped the scruff of his beard down the left side of my neck.

"He's searching, then he reaches out and finds that sweet spot." He stroked me with renewed determination. "He drives toward the finish. Pumping harder. Faster. Deeper."

"There. Right there."

"Tell me you trust me to get you over the goal line."

"Yes. Please. Just . . . don't stop." I was panting as if I'd actually run down the football field.

When that moment of release came, Brady's voice stayed in my ear. Telling me I was beautiful, telling me I blew his mind.

I slumped against him, letting my arms drop, deciding in that moment that if ceding control to him resulted in this? I never wanted it back.

"Lennox."

"Hmm?"

"Look at me."

When I glanced down, I expected to see my clothing askew, but he'd righted it. How hadn't I noticed?

Oh, right. He'd blanked my mind to everything except orgasmic bliss.

I turned toward him.

Brady framed my face in his hands and kissed me. It was urgent, desperate, reckless. I wanted to climb him like a goalpost and wrap myself around him so tightly every millimeter of our skin would touch.

He tore his mouth free but kept his hands in place. "I want more of you."

"You have all of me." I'd never said that to another man in my life and the fact I'd said it without conscious thought scared me a little.

"It's a big day for Jensen. He'll come looking for us when he's done with all the media stuff. I understand if you don't want to stick around, but please understand I don't have a choice."

"You want to be here anyway. As you should be."

"How pissed off would you be if I loaded your stuff into a car service and had it drop you off?"

"I wouldn't be pissed at all." *I'd be relieved.*

"Do you want to stay for the fourth quarter?"

"No. I'm sure traffic is ridiculous after the game, so I could get a jump on it if I left now."

"You're sure?"

"As long as you can come up with something plausible to tell your family on why I left without saying good-bye."

"I'll tell them you weren't feeling well but you didn't want me to miss out on the celebration."

I smiled. "I'm so damn thoughtful that way."

He laughed. "That you are." He pressed another lingering kiss to my forehead. "I can call the valet stand. Eddie will coordinate with the car service. And you don't have to pay or tip your driver. I want you to text me when you're home, okay?"

"Of course." I stood on my tiptoes and pecked him on the mouth. "Until tomorrow. Have fun."

Sixteen

BRADY

I couldn't sleep.

At five A.M., I gave up, threw on workout clothes and headed downstairs to my home gym.

Normally I crank the stereo while I'm on the treadmill, but I ran six miles in silence.

Except for the voices in my head that kept replaying the hot interlude with Lennox at the football stadium yesterday afternoon.

It blew my mind that I affected her that way. It really blew my mind that she'd told me that without artifice. It'd been a long damn time since I'd had that level of honesty from a woman. The more I got to know Lennox, the more I liked her.

The alarm to the side door buzzed and I stopped stretching to see who had shown up to work out this early. Both my brothers and Nolan and Ash had access to this space. I realized after putting in a state-of-the-art gym that it wasn't any fun working out by myself. So I invited them to use it whenever it fit their schedules. A couple of times we'd even had private kickboxing instruction and Jens had brought his personal trainers here when he couldn't get the time he needed with the Vikings trainers.

I mopped the sweat from my face, surprised to see Jensen strolling toward me. He'd topped out at six foot five his freshman year of college. He'd gone from a beanpole with a four-foot vertical jump, who could also run a twelve-second hundred-yard dash, to a beast that maintained his speed and agility after adding thirty pounds of muscle to his frame.

To say he was a big guy was putting it mildly.

But I still saw him as my baby brother. The funny kid in the family, prone to practical jokes. The kindhearted soul who picked up strays—both the four- and two-legged varieties. Even when he'd outgrown any need for my protection, I felt more protective of him than ever. Pro athletes were magnets for scam artists, gold diggers and shyster agents. Pro athletes who looked like Jens—he'd inherited Mom's model genes, angular Nordic features, glacial blue eyes and wavy blond hair—were an even bigger target.

"You're here early," I said, and he looked up, startled.

"I didn't hear the usual shitty music, so I didn't think you were up."

I shrugged. "I couldn't sleep."

"Yeah? Me neither."

"Too pumped after the amazing game yesterday?"

He flashed his crooked smile. "Partially."

"Let me guess. In your celebratory mood, you brought a girl back to your place last night, and she's still in your bed, so you bolted, hoping she'd get the hint and leave."

"Inviting her over seemed like a good idea at the time. But when I got up in the night to use the bathroom, I saw she'd brought a suitcase with her." He scraped his shoulder-length hair into a ponytail. "Fuck, B, I don't even know her last name. Why would she think it'd be more than just a one-off?"

"Did you—"

"Use a condom? Yeah. And when will that stop bein' the first thing you ask me? Christ. I'm twenty-six, not fifteen."

"I'll stop asking, Jens, when you stop picking up random chicks who think they'll win your love through blow jobs and kinky sex."

Jensen dropped onto the bench. "You're right. Man, I hate that you're always right. But it sucks being alone."

"Says the guy who's surrounded twenty-four/seven by teammates and trainers and coaches and the media."

"Not the same. I meant to say there's a difference between being lonely and alone."

"So get a dog."

"Smart-ass. Maybe I should just sell my apartment and move in with you. A single dude doesn't need this much space."

"I like my space. And you are a slob, bro. Isn't that why Drew moved out?"

He scowled. "Drew moved out because he's pussy-whipped. He bought Brianna an engagement ring and he's gonna propose on the Jumbotron at halftime during the Green Bay game. Original, huh? Besides, Drew has been off his game all season. If he doesn't get his shit together—" He stopped. Shook his head. "Enough football talk. I came here to get away from it." His eyes gleamed. "Let's spar."

"What kind of shape are you in?" Sometimes he was so banged up the day after a game that he spent hours alternating between hot and cold therapy.

"I'm good." He lifted his tank top. His ribs were dotted with bruises. "I get hurt worse during practices."

"Fine. Get your gear."

Jensen could outrun me, outcatch me, outlift me, but he rarely beat me in sparring. Except I wasn't up to sparring this early, so I'd work with him on technique rather than power.

Once we were in the ring, Jens held the practice mitts and I started to strike.

"So you seemed mopey at the after-party last night."

"Cover your face," I warned and threw a left-hand jab.

"Mom said you brought someone to the game."

I struck low and he blocked. "Yeah."

"Why didn't she come with you to the after-party? I would've liked to meet her."

"You will meet her. I believe she'd had enough of the Lund family after the cool reception she got from most of them yesterday."

"I don't know why you expected something different." He turned the mitt to block a forearm strike. "You never date anyone and the first woman you bring to a family deal is a coworker?"

I stopped and propped my gloves against my hips. "She's not a coworker."

"So you don't work on any projects with her at all?"

"It's one project."

Jensen grinned. "Then you *are* coworkers, bro."

I released a flurry of combinations that tired me out before I tired of pounding on my little brother.

He made the time-out sign.

I tore off my gloves and climbed out of the ring in search of my water bottle.

Jens sat beside me. "Tell me about her."

"Lennox is . . ." I chugged a mouthful of water. "She's smart. Got a bit of an attitude, which is how I initially noticed her. And she's hot. She's got this curvy body that's . . . amazing. We've been out a few times and she's funny. She's blunt. She's sexy as hell. She's lived on the wild side, but she's settled down since then." I liked her wild side, even though it killed me to hear why she became that way.

"Is she that wild between the sheets?"

"I imagine she will be." I felt Jens looking at me.

"What do you mean, you *imagine*? Are you saying you haven't hit that yet?"

"Nope."

"Is that by mutual decision? Or is she one of those 'number of dates' chicks?"

Confused by his phrasing, I looked at him. "'Number of dates'?"

"You know. The women who have set a minimum number of dates—three, five or even ten—before they'll consider getting naked with you."

I shook my head. "It's not that."

"Then what?"

"If anyone is holding back, it's me."

"Why?"

"I don't know." I let my head fall back against the wall. "Actually, I do know. Sex screws things up. I don't want to fuck this up, Jens. I really like her."

"Sounds like it."

When he didn't razz me or start offering lewd advice, I knew he was holding back. "Just spit out whatever you're thinking."

"Don't get pissed."

"Nothing good ever starts that way."

"I know. Look, both Nolan and Ash cornered me at the party yesterday. They think this Lennox chick might be playing you."

That floored me. "Why the hell would they say that? They don't know her."

"Evidently she's ambitious."

"You say that like it's a bad thing."

"It is, if her ambition is to hook up with one of the big bosses." Jensen fiddled with the cap on his water bottle. "Did Ash tell you that he's worked with her?"

"With Lennox? No."

Why hadn't Lennox mentioned it? And why hadn't she mentioned her time in Annika's department?

"What happened?"

"Ash didn't go into all the details beyond saying his admin complained to Personnel and Lennox's supervisor about her overstepping boundaries in her role as a clerical worker. Basically Nolan said the same thing." Jensen sighed. "I hate being the one to tell you this stuff. I don't even work at LI, so to me it all sounds like interdepartmental politics."

"Nolan's worked with her too? Then why did they both act like it was the first time they'd met?"

"Not Nolan personally, but Nolan's—"

"Let me guess—Nolan's admin has had run-ins with Lennox."

"Yeah. More than one time. She complained to Anita. Anyway, Anita suggested to Archer that the office temp concept had run its course."

And as per company protocol, Archer had requested an internal audit before making his recommendation.

Dammit. This was not what I needed to hear. Not because I believed Lennox had done anything wrong—but she had stirred up a hornet's nest. Rather than the queen bee going after Lennox, she targeted the entire temp staff. "Did Nolan and Ash ask you to talk to me?"

Jensen shook his head. "They specifically asked me not to talk to you. But it felt like that reverse psychology crap. Afterward, I decided it's much easier to get knocked on my ass all day long than to deal with the corporate bullshit."

At least I could laugh at that.

Two knocks sounded on my outer door, and then Jenna strolled in. "So I hear you came out to your family this weekend."

I looked up from my computer. "Did you get to yell at your husband first thing? Is that why you're in a good mood on a Monday morning?"

"And you're in a lousy mood, considering you took Miss Greene to the Lund family shrine yesterday."

"How'd you already know that? It's barely nine in the morning. And we haven't told anyone besides my family." As soon as the words left my mouth, I realized how stupid that statement was. "I assume Maggie is the culprit."

"No, sir, your mother is the culprit. Maggie is just the air horn that your mother chose to make the announcement."

"Please get me the bottle of Laphroaig out of the cabinet. I'll need something stronger than coffee to get me through the morning."

Jenna took the seat in front of my desk. "Skip the booze, unless you want 'drunk' added to the phrase 'in love' that's floating around about you now." She snickered.

"You have to pick more obscure pop culture references to slip into conversation, Jenna. Queen Bae was too easy."

"Shoot. Anyway, at least I got first crack at the melded name."

I lifted an eyebrow. "Maybe you've already hit the Laphroaig this morning, because you're not making any sense."

"Melded name. A new moniker. Like Brangelina. Or Kimye. I've dubbed you and Lennox . . . Brannox."

"You've got to be kidding me."

Jenna grinned. "Nope."

"Maybe I should work from home today."

"In all seriousness, I'm happy for you, Mr. Lund. I never would've put you and Lennox together, but you're a good fit."

"I hope she can withstand the scrutiny."

"She's no shrinking violet. She'll do fine."

And there was my opening. "Someone mentioned Lennox isn't well liked around here."

Jenna snorted. "You know I can't dig for dirt if you don't point me toward the right pile. Someone who?"

I told her everything Jensen had told me and it did feel like junior high gossip. But it bothered me and if there was something—or nothing—to it, then Jenna would suss out every detail.

Her light mood had turned somber. "This stays strictly between us, boss. Nolan's admin, Toni, is a snake. That's why I hope Archer doesn't retire too soon, because if Nolan takes over as CEO, Toni will have an immense amount of power. Ash's admin, Olivia, is loyal to Ash and only Ash. There's something hinky going on there but it's not against corporate rules. I'll see what I can find out."

"Thank you."

She stood. "In the meantime, I e-mailed the month-end reports you requested. You have meetings at two, three and four—I set the reminders on your daily calendar. The details for the separate agendas are in the zip files coded for each department. Since you'll forget to eat and work right up until your first meeting, I'll send for lunch."

"You are a goddess among admins, Jenna. Thank you. No interruptions this morning, at all, for any reason." I had hundreds of pages of financial documents to dissect and diagram. It required my full focus. "On second thought—"

"Reschedule your meetings."

Sometimes it scared me how quickly she anticipated my needs.

LENNOX

Lola pulled me into her office first thing Monday morning. That was a little frightening.

"Lennox. Are you involved in a personal relationship with Brady Lund?"

This was really not how I wanted to start my week. "Yes, I am. Why?"

She smiled. "Cracked the Ice Man. Bravo. I'll bet he's hot as fire under that stuffed shirt. But watch your step. LI is a different place for you now."

"Is it a different place for Brady?"

"No, honey, it's not. But he's at the top of the food chain and you are chum. The sharks will swim in closer and eat you alive."

I had to bite the inside of my cheek to keep from laughing. How long had Lola had this shark analogy speech prepared? Because she looked pretty excited that she got to use it.

Hey, how about you focus on the real meaning behind her words?

"If your relationship with him inhibits your ability to do your job, you come to me right away."

"Lola. My relationship with Brady won't affect how I do my job."

"I believe that. But it may affect how other employees interact with you while you're doing your job."

I wanted to point out that there were fifteen hundred LI employees in this building. I doubted anyone would know what was going on with the CFO and the lowly temp—to say nothing of caring enough to gossip about it.

"Lennox?"

I looked up at my boss. "Thanks for the warning."

"You're welcome. Today I'm sending you to main reception on the first floor. You're manning the call center."

Hooray, my least favorite job. *Thank you for calling Lund Industries. How may I direct your call?* Ninety-five percent of callers had no problems navigating the automated phone system. The other five percent, callers who wanted "to talk to a real, live human and not a damn machine" . . . those were the calls I'd get to deal with. All day.

My day was fully complete when I looked over and saw Renee sitting in the reception area monitoring me.

The situation felt like punishment.

I didn't think it was a coincidence I didn't see Brady all day.

The skies were gray, the streets were gray, my mood was black.

I wanted to slip into my pajamas, crawl in bed and pull the covers over my head, and hope tomorrow was better.

Kiley had counseling sessions on Monday nights, so I had the house to myself.

I was hungry but I hadn't been grocery shopping in ages,

so my choices were a) starve, b) eat Kiley's food, c) call for carryout.

Then I remembered I'd stashed a candy bar in the glove compartment. That would tide me over until I could grab a breakfast burrito in the morning.

I slipped on my coat and opened the door.

Brady froze as he reached the top step. "Hey. I was just about to ring the doorbell."

Hey? All I got was . . . *hey*? Where was my hug? Where was my kiss hello? Where was my *I missed you, baby*?

"Why?"

"Why what?"

"Why were you going to ring the doorbell? Because it doesn't look to me that you're too thrilled to be here."

His eyes narrowed. Then his gaze moved over me in my long coat, snow boots and keys in my hand. "And it looks to me like you're going somewhere."

I would not admit my pathetic plans to this man who thought I had a wild streak as wide as the Mississippi River. So I did what any self-respecting wild woman would do: I lied my ass off.

"I was just about to hit the gun range."

Brady laughed.

His laugh pissed me off. "I'd be careful—you're laughing at an armed woman who has had one shitshow of a day."

His smile slipped. "You're seriously going to the gun range? Right now?"

"Yes. Why?"

"I've had a shitshow of a day myself and I'd like to tag along."

Crap. This was exactly why I didn't lie. "Oh. I can't promise you range time, since you're not on the schedule, but if you don't mind just standing around watching me enjoying my bullet therapy, then it'd probably be okay." *Bullet therapy?* God. Next I'd be bragging about busting a cap in a paper target's ass.

"Sounds good." Then Brady moved in, lowered his head and fused his mouth to mine.

I leaned into him, grabbing on to his lapels, losing myself in his kiss.

He curled his hand over my cheek and pulled back. "I missed you today."

"Same."

"Let's go."

Time to stall. "Come inside for a minute. Right before you got here I realized I don't have a gun. I usually borrow Kiley's, but she has hers in her car, so I have to call the range and see what they've got for me to rent." I gave him a smacking kiss on the mouth and said, "Be right back," and ran upstairs.

Maxie had called me Saturday night but hadn't left a message, so I hoped she'd pick up.

The phone rang four times before she answered. "Damn, girl, I'm glad it wasn't an emergency with as long as it took you to return my call."

"I was at a cabin up in the North Woods with no cell service. Look, Maxie, I need a huge favor."

"What?"

"Does Pistol still work at that gun range?"

"Yeah. He's there tonight. Why?"

"I need range time tonight. And a handgun. And ammo."

"Need someone to aim and shoot for you too?" she said snottily.

"Hilarious."

"Lenni, what's going on?"

"It has to do with my job." Another lie. I was on a roll.

"I have to show I have some self-defense skills to get an additional monthly discount for my health insurance. And I just found out today that the option expires tomorrow."

"Those HMO bastards have too damn much power."

"I agree. But it isn't something I want to argue with. I just want to get signed off on it."

"Pistol mentioned he was closing tonight, so I'll call him and let him know you're on your way."

"Thank you, Maxie. So, so much."

"Any chance you can swing by the bar when you're done?"

"I can't, because my boss will be with me at the range. To, uh, make sure I'm not falsifying the claim. So could you ask Pistol to play it cool when he sees me?"

Maxie laughed. "Never a dull moment with you, Lenni. I miss your crazy ways. But, darlin' girl, you gotta make time for me, because we have to talk. Soon."

Just as I hung up I heard the stairs creak. Then Brady filled the doorframe. "Is everything all right?"

"Yes. They put me on hold but we're good to go."

His focus wasn't on me, but on the bed behind me. "So this is your room."

I waited for him to continue.

"Does the bed creak as loudly as the floors?" He started toward me.

"What?"

He loomed over me. "Your bed. Does it make noise?"

Totally flummoxed by his nearness and the intensity in his eyes, I just stared at him.

"Only one way to find out, isn't there?" He picked me up and tossed me onto the bed. Then he crawled over me on all fours until his knees were by my hips and his palms were above my head. "Touch me, Lennox. Put your hands on my shoulders."

I didn't think about it; I just did what he told me.

Brady's face was inches from mine. He rolled his body forward, without really moving anything but the mattress and the bed frame.

The bed frame creaked loudly, followed by a bang as the headboard hit the wall.

Another roll of his hips and the entire bed moved again. And again.

If it had been any other man, I might've laughed at the way he rocked above me in a parody of making love. But it wasn't funny; it was hot as hell.

Creak, creak, bang.

Creak, creak, bang.

Creak, creak, bang.

The only place we touched was where my hands gripped his shoulders. Our eyes were locked, our breath mingled.

But with the steady rhythm he built, I felt as if he was moving on me, in me.

"I'm the first man you've had in this bed."

"Yes."

Something feral—like triumph—flashed in his eyes. Then he buried his face in my neck and sighed.

He rolled off the bed and I scrambled upright, sitting on the opposite side, trying to find my sanity. We were both fully clothed. We hadn't done anything.

Yet . . . somehow we'd just been as intimate as if we had been naked.

This whole thing freaked me out. I was letting Brady call all the shots.

At the cabin this weekend.

At the football game.

Just now.

Enough.

I had to regain some ground. I had to do more than talk the talk about doing the unexpected; I had to walk the walk.

I whipped off my shirt and opened my top dresser drawer. Reaching behind me, I unhooked my bra.

"Lennox. What are you doing?"

I spun around to face him and his eyes went nowhere near my face for several long moments. "That bra digs into the underside of my breast when I'm shooting, so I'm changing into a sports bra. Why? It's not like you haven't seen my bare chest before." Feeling ornery, I cupped my breasts and caressed them. "Going braless is so much better. I wish I could get away with it all the time."

"Uhh."

I snagged a workout shirt with a built-in bra and pulled it over my head. I eyed his clothing. A snappy suit, of course. That's when I knew I couldn't share range time with him. Wielding a gun, he'd look all sexy and badass like James Bond, and my hormones could handle only so much in a day.

He said, "What's the plan?"

"You can follow me to the gun range."

"Why don't we ride together?"

"It'll be easier this way. If you get bored, you can leave."

His eyes glittered. "I doubt watching you waving a gun when you're not wearing a bra will be boring, baby."

"I guess we'll see, won't we?"

BRADY

I'd been hard since the moment Lennox wrapped her fingers around that cold metal.

She'd tested the weight and heft of three handguns before she'd chosen a Smith & Wesson 1911.

Her friend Pistol tried to load her clips, but she'd done it herself.

How many women did I know who could shove nine-millimeter bullets in a clip and hold a conversation about ever-changing HMO requirements?

Just one. And I couldn't take my eyes off her.

Lennox's first target looked like Swiss cheese.

Her second target had been markedly better.

She discussed groupings with Pistol before she set up her third target range.

I watched her from the gallery the entire time. Her shoulders were back, her arms slightly bent at the elbow. Her stance looked relaxed, but I knew it was a difficult position to hold for any length of time.

Bang, bang, bang, bang, bang.

Shell casings flew as she fired.

She dropped her head from side to side, stretching her muscles and giving me a glimpse of that sexy tattoo on her neck. I wanted to run my tongue over it, tasting her sweat. I'd rest my hands on her hips as she fired, feeling the power of the gun and the strength in her arms.

She turned and looked at me. The raw lust I witnessed in her gaze blew my mind.

Bang, bang, bang, bang, bang.

I had to squint, but I could just make out that she'd aimed high on the paper target at the shoulder.

More shrugging and twisting of her lush body as she readied herself.

Bang, bang, bang, bang, bang.

She ejected the clip, set the gun on the counter and reeled the target back to check out her handiwork. Then she turned to me and grinned, giving me two thumbs up, looking so damn cute in her oversized pink ear protectors that I couldn't stand it.

The second she walked off the range, I was on her. "That"—I pecked her on the mouth—"was"—another kiss—"so"—a longer smooch—"cool."

"Thanks. I had fun." She passed over her last paper target. "A souvenir for you."

"As a warning to tread lightly if I ever piss you off?"

"No. It's supposed to assure you that if we do run into bears on our next biathlon, I can fire away at Smokey and protect you."

"I'm so crazy about you, Lennox."

"Same here."

"What now?"

She cocked her head. "Do you trust me?"

"Yes. Unless you want to play William Tell, and then . . . hell no."

"Maybe next time. They do have an archery range here." She took my hand and led me out of the building. But instead of going to the parking lot, she towed me around the corner and pushed me against the bricks.

I touched her face reverently, because she touched me on so many levels.

She reached up and loosened my tie. "How many times did you run your hand through your hair? Because—no offense, but it is kind of out of control."

"I had month-end reports to do and they're always hell on my hairstyle."

Lennox unbuttoned my shirt as we spoke. Then she pressed kisses down the center of my chest. She opened her mouth over my left nipple and began to suck on it through my T-shirt. That felt so damn good it didn't register that she'd unzipped my pants until I felt cold air hit my boxers.

"What are you—?"

"I'm touching you, like you touched me yesterday." She

stroked my length over the fabric, and that was more erotic somehow than her bare hand.

She bit down on my nipple and I arched back with a soft groan.

I clenched my hands into fists at my sides, my knuckles scraping the rough bricks, in shock and awe at how this woman had known what I needed, when I hadn't known myself.

Soft lips moved down my jawline. She flicked her tongue over the pulse pounding in my throat, her hand sliding up and down as her thumb rubbed across the wet tip. Fast. Slow. Her grip perfectly tight, but perfectly tender.

"Don't hold back," she warned in a husky voice that made me harder yet.

This . . . interlude had caught me by surprise, and was such an epic turn-on, the way she knew just how to touch me—not only with her hand, but with the little nuzzles, the openmouthed kisses and hot breath across my damp skin— that I didn't have a prayer of holding back.

I whispered her name and tacked on a drawn-out "Yes" when she pulled me over the edge.

Her mouth was hungry on mine, sharing her breath with me, because I'd forgotten how to breathe.

When I finally came back down from that rocket ride into pleasure, I felt her smile against my throat.

She tucked me in, zipped me up and rebuttoned my shirt, while I was helpless to do anything but watch her ministrations.

"You okay?"

"Better than okay." I forced my fingers to unclench and I touched her cheek. "Are you okay?"

"Yes. Because now we're even."

"Lennox. Baby, I'm not keeping score."

"Neither am I. I wanted to touch you and I did." She turned her head and kissed the base of my palm. "I've let go with you once; you've let go with me once. Next time, I want all of you. I'll give you all of me."

I murmured, "We'll see," just to watch the fire flash in her eyes.

"Yes, maybe we will. Maybe I'll show up in your office wearing just a trench coat and a smile. Since we are officially out as a couple."

"Did you have a difficult day because of that?"

"No, but I was pretty isolated. We'll see how tomorrow goes." She opened her mouth. Closed it.

"What?"

"No PDA at work, okay? I don't want what's between us to cause more gossip than it already has." She leaned in and rested her cheek against my chest. "We're both private people. Let's not let anyone change that for us."

"Deal." I tilted her head back to get at her mouth. The kiss we shared was lazy and sweet and we were both reluctant for it to end.

Her shiver broke me out of the haze and I gently urged her back. "You're cold."

"A little."

"Any chance I can warm you up in my bed tonight?"

She shook her head. "Another night."

"That's why I wanted to see you."

"I'm not going to like this, am I?"

"Only if you care that I'm going to Atlanta for the week."

"The whole week?"

"Yes."

"But you'll be home on the weekend?"

"No."

Her face fell.

It probably made me a dick that I was a little happy in her disappointment because it mirrored mine. "Jaxson has a hockey game in Atlanta Friday night, and Jensen plays in Atlanta Sunday night. The whole family is flying down for both games. So I won't be back until Monday night."

"That sucks."

"I'll call you when I can this week, okay?"

"Okay. But it won't be the same."

"No. It won't."

Seventeen

LENNOX

ONE WEEK LATER . . .

Brady hadn't even been in the office all week and I was dealing with questions and comments about us.

"So you and Brady Lund, the big bad CFO."

"Did he ask you out when he learned firsthand how good you give . . . *dictation*?"

"I heard you two were doing it in the office supplies closet on the seventh floor."

I was wrong about the level of interest my relationship with the Lund CFO would garner—it seemed everyone who worked for LI felt the need to weigh in or ask whatever question popped into their heads, even a week after we'd been outed and it should have been old news. I wanted to bust heads, but I knew what Lola had been getting at: My every action was under way more scrutiny than it had been before.

But I still had a screaming headache by noon.

Sydney and I were eating lunch in the employee break room. She'd been the least surprised by the fact Brady and I were together.

"I knew that he had it bad for you from the moment he started stopping by our floor wanting to argue with you about everything."

I was picking through the salad I'd gotten on my way to work this morning. My head was throbbing so much my vision seemed fuzzy and my stomach was upset.

All the chatter in the area died and I knew Brady had walked in.

I hadn't seen him in a week. I should've tackled him and kissed his lips off. But I didn't move.

He didn't give any pretense that he'd come in here for any reason other than that he was looking for me. I felt his hand on my shoulder, but he addressed my coworker first. "Good afternoon, Sydney."

"Same to you, Mr. Lund."

"Lennox?"

I looked up at him. The man was so gorgeous he hurt my eyes.

Or maybe that was just the headache. I couldn't muster a smile. "Hey."

"After I've been gone a week, I get a 'Hey'?" His eyes searched mine. "You okay?"

"No, she's not okay," Sydney answered.

"I'm fine."

"She's got a really bad headache," Sydney said to Brady. "Lennox never complains, and god forbid she'd ever go home sick, but you can see she's in pain."

"Yes, I can see that." Brady crouched down. "Look at me."

I lifted my head and winced.

"Do you get migraines?"

"I never have before."

He curled his hand around the side of my face. "Christ, Lennox, your skin is clammy."

"I'm sure it'll pass."

"Have you taken anything for it?"

"No."

"I have some stuff that'll help." He stood. "Sydney, would you please dispose of Lennox's lunch for me?"

"Absolutely, sir."

"Come on. Let's get you fixed up." Brady pulled my chair back and helped me to my feet.

I was aware of every pair of eyes on us as he placed his hand at the small of my back and guided me out of the break room. I tried to keep my professional distance.

As soon as we were in the elevator, he said, "Come here," and wrapped me in his arms.

His hold on me tightened. I sighed and he kissed the top of my head.

I was vaguely aware of us entering his office suite. I felt so dizzy and nauseous that I stepped back, afraid I'd throw up on his expensive suit.

But I swayed and my vision went black the way it would right before passing out.

"Goddammit, Lennox," Brady barked and swept me into his arms. "You'd rather face-plant into the wall than let me help you?"

"You have more important things to do, Mr. CFO, than tend to me."

"Wrong."

We started to move, but I couldn't open my eyes to see where we were going.

"Jenna, see that we're not disturbed."

"Yes, sir."

"Call Lennox's supervisor and let her know she'll be out the rest of the day. Have someone bring her things up here."

"Of course. Is there anything else I can do?"

"No. I'll take care of her."

"Brady, you can't—" I tried to protest.

"Stop fighting me on this. I'll do whatever the hell I want."

A door slammed behind us.

I figured he'd set me on the couch in his office, so I was surprised when I opened my eyes to see us enter a room off the sitting area that I'd assumed was a private bathroom.

But it was a private bedroom.

With a bed.

An unmade bed.

Brady gently laid me down. As soon as the back of my neck met the cool pillow, I closed my eyes and sighed. I turned my head and the scent of Brady's cologne drifted up, so I knew he'd spent the night in here recently.

A rough-skinned hand circled my ankle and he wiggled my left shoe off my foot, then my right shoe.

The room went silent.

I tried to focus on my breathing, hoping that would chase away the stabbing pain in my head.

The mattress dipped.

I immediately tried to sit up.

But he pressed one hand on my shoulder and the other against my stomach, cautioning me, "Slowly."

As soon as I was upright, I noticed he held a glass of water and a bottle of pills. "What's that?"

"A miracle drug. It'll get rid of your headache. The only drawback is it will knock you out for a few hours. But you can stay here and I'll keep an eye on you." He shook out a pill and held it to my lips. "Open."

I couldn't look away from the tender concern in his eyes as I swallowed the medicine with a long drink of cold water.

"What is this place?" Half a dozen suits hung in the open closet space. There was also a rack of ties and several pairs of dress shoes lined up on a shelf next to workout wear and gear.

"It's supposed to be a dressing room. I got rid of the uncomfortable chaise in favor of an actual bed."

I smoothed my hand down the outside of his arm. "Brady, how often do you sleep in here?"

A muscle in his jaw ticced. "Too often."

"Did you sleep here after you got back from Atlanta?"

"Yes." He ran his knuckles across my jaw. "I knew if I went home I wouldn't be able to sleep, so I caught up on some work and crashed here about three A.M."

"You should be the one getting TLC, not me."

"I like that you know what this is." He swept his thumb across my bottom lip. "I like that you let me do this for you."

It seemed appropriate somehow when a fresh wave of pain nearly split my head in two that I realized I'd fallen for him. Four weeks ago, he was the beautiful, aloof CFO I admired from afar. Now, here I was in his private dressing room, with him tending to me with a loving touch that surprised both of us.

Brady pressed his lips to my forehead in a lingering kiss. "You'll want to be lying down when the medicine kicks in."

As soon as I'd gotten settled, he draped a cool cloth over my eyes and tucked the blanket around my feet. "I'll leave the door open. I'm right outside if you need anything."

---

woke up and my head was clear, completely free from pain.

The dressing room didn't have windows, so I didn't know what time it was. Before I sat up, I stretched out in this bed Brady regularly slept in. It caused a sharp ache in my chest to think of him in this tiny space alone and exhausted.

Once I was upright, I noticed he'd placed a can of Coke on the table with a note propped up in front of it that said DRINK ME in Brady's bold handwriting. I reached out and the can was still cold. I popped the top and chugged almost the entire thing. Within a few minutes, the fizzy sugar buzz pushed me one step closer to feeling human.

Off to the left of the dressing room was another door that did lead to a bathroom. A "Holy shit, the CFO has a nicer bathroom in his office than I have in my house" kind of bathroom. All marble, glass and chrome, with a walk-in shower, the toilet separated like a water closet, and a deep sink and vanity with a mirror that rose up at least twelve feet to the sloped ceiling.

I used the toilet, washed my hands and face, ran a comb through my hair and went looking for my man.

Brady was still at his desk. Papers were strewn everywhere. His dark hair nearly stood on end, he'd run his hands through it so many times.

But it wasn't his crazy, sexy hair or the pursed set to his full lips or even the hint of chest hair peeking out from his shirt where he'd loosened his silk tie. No, what snared my attention was that Brady Lund wore glasses.

Tortoiseshell glasses that made him look even more like a smart woman's wet dream—a geeky brainiac numbers man.

Glasses that made him look hotter than ever—I'd take Clark Kent in his suit and glasses over Superman any day.

Glasses that made me want to climb on top of him and test the bounce factor of that chair.

So I decided to go for it.

"It's not fair, you know," I said as I sauntered toward him.

He glanced up and gave me a head-to-toe inspection before the concern in his eyes melted into warmth. "You're feeling better."

"Yes, thanks to you." I walked behind the desk, grabbed on to the armrests of his fancy office chair and spun him around to face me.

He seemed curious about my invading his space, but he merely quirked his eyebrow in the way that made me want to lick him all over.

I whispered, "Ask me."

"Ask you what?"

"Ask me why I said it's not fair."

"What's not fair, Lennox?"

"This." I gestured to incorporate all of him. "You, being the sexiest man I've ever laid eyes on. You, being the smartest man I've ever met. I can even forgive you for covering up your smoking-hot body because no other man wears a suit as well as you do. No one."

He waited for me to continue, because he knew I wasn't done.

"But then I wake up, in your bed, after you cared for me so sweetly, and my skin smells like you, my hair smells like you and all I want *is* you. So I come out here and find you still wearing that suit that drives me wild. Not only that, you're wearing glasses."

Brady's hand immediately went up to his face as if he was surprised—or maybe embarrassed—that he'd been caught with them on.

I stayed his hand. "Huh-uh. Leave. Them. On."

"Why?"

"Because it makes you even more appealing to me, Mr. Lund. That is what tipped me over the edge."

His gaze zoomed to my cleavage so he didn't see it coming when I climbed on his lap. I kissed his mouth. Then his nose. Then I very carefully took off his glasses. "Tell me no if you don't want this."

His hands moved up my thighs and around my hips to cup my behind. Then he pulled me closer to his body. "You really think I'm going to say no?"

"I didn't want to assume."

He laughed softly.

I kissed him. And kept kissing him as he unbuttoned my blouse, as he unsnapped my bra, as he thrilled me with the greedy touch of his big hands on my breasts and my belly. He shimmied my skirt up my thighs and his fingers slipped between them. He groaned against my lips when he found me hot and wet. His groan turned into a growl when I reached down and squeezed his rigid shaft.

Brady kissed a path down my chest and latched onto my nipple. With his teeth.

That made me crazy.

He licked and sucked, bit and nibbled and had me ready to crawl out of my skin; all the while he kept up the maddening—and sometimes fleeting—strokes over my aching flesh.

The temperature in the room had increased by about a thousand degrees. We were both sweating, panting, straining, and it wasn't enough. I needed more.

Then Brady's hand was in my hair and he yanked my mouth back down to his. His kiss revealed the same desperation that was consuming me.

"Lennox—" He panted against my throat. "Turn around."

Wait. Was he—?

"Bend over the desk."

Oh. My. God. I almost came right then.

Brady Lund was really doing it. Giving in to passion. Not giving a damn about the proper way we *should* make love for the first time. Not giving a damn that I'd probably knock all of his important papers off the desk when he slammed into me on that first thrust. He wanted me fast, he wanted me hard and he wanted me *now.*

I scrambled off his lap so quickly I almost fell on my butt.

He steadied me, his eyes hot enough to scorch my skin. He jammed his hand into his pants pocket and pulled out his wallet. From that wallet he fished out a lone condom.

I said the first thing that popped into my head. "Just one?"

"I didn't want to assume." Then he gave me that nipple-tightening, panty-dropping grin.

And it was one of the sexiest things I'd ever witnessed, Brady holding that condom between his teeth as he undid his belt and dropped his trousers. He lifted that sexy brow, an unspoken question blazing in his blue eyes: *What are you waiting for?*

I turned around.

But before I could figure out what to do with my hands, or how far I was supposed to lean over, Brady's chest connected with my back. He nudged my hair aside with an openmouthed kiss as he peeled my blouse down to expose more skin. Then he placed my left hand on the edge of his desk, anchoring me there with his left hand.

He didn't tell me what to do; he just positioned me how he liked. Nudging my legs apart, sliding his right hand between my hip bones and canting my pelvis. I felt the tip of him press against me once, then twice, and gasped when all that smooth male hardness filled me.

His breath was hot against my neck as he started to move.

"Fucking sexy tattoos. Christ, woman, I want to sink my teeth into you."

"Do it. Do anything you want—just don't stop."

"Never."

We were both too far gone for this to last very long— that's what weeks of foreplay will do to you.

His soft kisses on the slope of my shoulder belied the near punishing rhythm he'd set.

A roaring in my ears had my entire body clenching in anticipation. Brady's terse "Give it to me" sent me soaring.

He followed me into that place where pleasure existed on a different plane—separate, yet together. Connected by more than just throbbing body parts.

That was the new aspect for me. Even as I silently swore I wouldn't make my usual move and retreat, I feared that he would.

"Lennox."

I turned my head and looked at him.

"Not done. Not even close."

I curled my arm back and sifted my fingers through his messy hair. "Me neither."

He held my hip as he eased out of me.

I didn't bother to pull my panties all the way up or my skirt down as I stepped away from the desk. The molten heat in his eyes indicated I wouldn't be wearing these clothes much longer anyway.

"Bed. Now," he growled.

"Wait. Do you have more condoms?"

The look on his face—now I knew the definition of crestfallen.

And it thrilled me that he didn't have condoms stashed in his dressing room.

I poked him in the chest. "Then it's a good thing I slipped a box in my purse this morning, isn't it?"

We did it in his bed. Twice.

We tried to be good in the shower, but the instant those clever hands of his were loaded with creamy soap and he started "washing" me, good clean fun was forgotten in favor of getting down and dirty. He hoisted me against the wall of the shower.

My mind went into a foggy free fall as he proved he was just as good vertically as he was horizontally.

After that we showered separately.

I was wrapped in a bedsheet when he emerged from the bathroom. Naked.

"Baby, that sheet won't protect you if I want you."

So cocky. "You've had me plenty."

"No such thing." I watched his tight little butt cheeks and the broad plane of his back as he rummaged in his drawer for clothing. "I needed something to sustain me for the rest of the week."

"Why?" I picked up my clothes and started to get dressed.

"I have to go to Chicago tomorrow. I'll be there through Friday night."

He was going to be gone again? "I realize I never asked if you travel a lot."

"More than I'd like to." He studied me. "I wish you could come."

"Doesn't Jenna go with you?"

"No. She made it clear from the beginning she won't travel. Not even now that her kids are older. She's on vacation starting tomorrow since I won't be in the office. Ash is going with me."

"I'm sure my boss would love it if I missed a few more days this week." I buttoned my blouse, happy to see it covered the hickey he'd left on the side of my breast. "The gossip mill would go crazy with the speculation that I'm using my relationship with you to get out of doing any real work."

"You think I wouldn't make you work in Chicago?" He smirked. "Taking notes for ten hours a day sound like fun?"

"Sounds better than answering phones for ten hours a day like I did yesterday."

"Next time I'll give you advance notice so your supervisor can clear your schedule."

"Deal. Besides, this is the last week that Lurch and Lurchette are shadowing us, so I want to make sure it's not perceived that I've screwed up."

I noticed his shoulders stiffen. Which was weird.

"How's that going?" he asked.

"Who knows? I suspect you'll know before any of the rest of us will. Why?"

He shrugged into his shirt. "Rumors and such."

"Any rumors I should be concerned about?"

"No. Just . . . there's been some interdepartmental grumbling about abuse of power. And confidentiality rules being broken."

"By the office temp staff? Unlikely."

"Come on, you're telling me you guys don't gossip?"

"Sure. We gossip about inappropriate office outfits and we talk about our lives, but we don't gossip about the jobs or people we're assigned to. Lola keeps a close eye on her staff and runs a tight-lipped ship."

"So if I ask if you've done work for, say, my dad . . . ?"

What was he getting at? "Depends. If he wants whatever tasks I'm doing for him kept confidential, then only Lola and I know. Lots of times when I'm working at my desk in the department, I'm doing work for another department, because they don't want my presence in that department. Sometimes I feel more like a private investigator than clerical support." I buttoned my skirt. "Are you asking specifics because of what Annika said?"

Brady tied his athletic shoes. "You mentioned you'd worked in her department, but that was it."

"That's all I'm allowed to say. And I don't do a job hoping to make another employee look bad. My only concern is doing the job to the best of *my* ability. When I first started at LI, I'll admit I was gung ho. Being the hardest worker isn't always appreciated."

He crossed the small space and kissed my nose. "I disagree. But I'm a workaholic, so I've got a skewed work ethic."

"You can't be all work and no play. So along those lines . . . you have to do something fun and wild while you're in the Windy City."

"Like what?"

"I'm not dictating what you do, just reminding you to do it. I'll expect a full report when you get back, Mr. Lund."

"Deal." He smoothed his hand over my hair. "I'll miss you. Tonight was—" Lust darkened his eyes. "Better than I've ever had, Lennox. Better than I've ever known it could be."

Now there was a compliment.

My phone started to buzz in my purse. Grateful for an excuse to break the intense moment, I dug out my cell. "Hey, Kiley. What's up?" She started babbling and I was afraid she'd had a run-in with her ex and she'd climbed in the bottom of a bottle. "Slow down. Start over." When I finally made sense of what she was saying, my heart hurt for her. "Look, I'm on my way home. Do you want me to bring you anything? You sure? Okay. See you in a bit." I hung up.

"What's going on?"

"Remember those kids we did the volunteer session with through LCCO? I don't know if you're aware that we met in the park that day because they had lost their normal meeting place. With the snow last week, they couldn't meet in the park. Kiley just found out one of her kids from that group got arrested. And she feels like she failed him because she hasn't found another place for them to meet. And with crappy weather being forecast for this weekend . . ."

"So they just need a place to let off steam and chill for a few hours?"

"I guess."

"I have a half court and a full gym at my place. They could hang out there for a few hours."

I stared at him. "Brady, while opening your home to them is"—*crazy talk*—"above and beyond, I hate to say it, but these kids are borderline delinquents."

"Which is why they need a safe place to go, right?"

"Yes, but you were trying to keep a low profile. Brady the accountant, not Brady the heir to a billion-dollar company with a million-dollar car and a multimillion-dollar house in the Old Mill District. You heard Juice that weekend, bragging about his cousin getting into Flurry. What if he does that? Brags to his cousin about the rich white dude with a soft spot for kids with issues? What if their thug friends show up at your place? What if they break in and rob you? What if they threaten you? God, what if they *hurt* you?"

"Lennox. Take a deep breath. First of all, they don't have to know it's me. You don't even have to tell Kiley I live there. Just let her know you've got a place lined up for this weekend through a friend of mine. Since it's a warehouse built into the back of a bluff, there's no way they could know what's on the level above them unless I take them up there. And, baby, I'm a Lund, so my security system is the best money can buy. Nobody is getting anywhere I don't want them to."

"You're serious? It's not just the afterglow of crazy hot sex talking?"

He grinned. "Maybe. But this volunteer project is special to me. I don't need to tell you why."

There was his sweetness again. "I'll talk to Kiley." I had a thousand things on my mind as I walked out of the dressing room. I was glad to see someone had fetched my coat and hung it up on the coatrack just inside Brady's office door.

"Forgetting something?" he said behind me.

I whirled around. "Security. I bet you have to let me out."

"Yes, I'll walk you out. But that's not what you're forgetting." He hauled me against him and made my knees weak and my head fuzzy with a reminder of how it had been between us, locked in passion. When he finished ravishing my mouth, he murmured, "Plan on staying with me Saturday after the kids leave."

Once again I hoped the week went by fast.

Eighteen

BRADY

The three-day trip to Chicago seemed to drag on for three weeks.

Ash and I spent all day Wednesday touring the facilities of the factory we were interested in acquiring. I managed to beg off from a dinner out with the corporate officers, but Ash happily went to represent LI. I needed to clear my head, so I left the Ritz-Carlton and headed down Michigan Avenue and actually wandered into a couple of shops. When I passed the perfume and jewelry stores, it occurred to me . . . Was I expected to bring my girlfriend a gift from my travels? Since I was new to all this, I wasn't sure. That set me on edge and everything I saw afterward looked cutesy or schmaltzy and that wasn't Lennox at all.

I ended up returning to the hotel, but stopped in the Harley-Davidson store on the same block. I looked at leather jackets, remembering how damn fine Lennox looked in leather pants and that microscopic leather miniskirt . . .

"Sir? May I help you tonight?"

I turned toward the saleswoman, who didn't look as if she belonged on Michigan Avenue, with her tats, piercings and chains, her abundantly curvy body squeezed into leather pants and a matching vest. She reminded me of Lennox. I smiled. "Yes. I'd appreciate your help."

I'd never been an impulse shopper. Until now.

Thursday, after a more in-depth tour of the factory, the owner finally opened up his books to me, but not until late in the afternoon. I'd planned to order room service and go over everything so I had a better idea of whether this acquisition would be beneficial to LI, or whether we needed to keep looking.

But again, the owners had made surprise plans for us—we'd all be attending a televised Thursday night football game at Soldier Field. They assumed—wrongly—that since a Lund played for the Vikings we'd be just as happy watching the Bears play. Ash and I exchanged a look. We both hated the Bears, almost as much as we hated the Green Bay Packers. But what could we do? I took several pictures during the game and of the skybox, tempted to send them to Lennox. Ash caught me and scowled. Apparently I was supposed to be listening to the majority owner, Bud, drone on and on about the Bears' "near perfect" season the year they won the Super Bowl.

Another late night meant no work got done. So the next morning, when I went to organize the papers I'd brought from my office—financial documents—the entire stack was missing. So was the thumb drive that contained that information.

What the ever-loving fuck?

I searched my briefcase and my suitcase but to no avail.

Then I remembered. I'd just . . . left the office Tuesday night. I hadn't packed my briefcase; I'd just grabbed my laptop case and played grab-ass with Lennox as we'd walked out. I'd left everything in my office. And without that information, I couldn't make heads or tails of the supply lists and manufacturing costs without a breakdown of revenue.

I never did shit like this. *Never.* Going into a meeting, any meeting, I was always the person who overprepared. Being underprepared was almost as bad and lazy as not being prepared at all.

For the first time in the two years since I'd become CFO, I had completely fucked up. And everyone would know it.

Shame burned me from the inside out.

Ash knocked on my door.

Rather than admit I'd dropped the ball, I decided that since the factory owners had basically stalled us the last two days, it was time to return the favor.

A t least Ash had his paperwork together.

When it came time for me to present my questions midafternoon, I crashed and burned.

Spectacularly.

After an hour passed and it was obvious I didn't know what the hell I was doing, Ash stepped in.

"While we'd hoped to wrap this up today, as you can see there are a few unforeseen issues that have come up in our findings that Brady and I need to discuss in depth before we can voice our concerns to you. So is it more convenient for all of you to meet back here first thing in the morning? Or shall I schedule a conference room at our hotel?"

I knew my cheeks, my neck and even the tops of my ears were blazing the same red as my tie.

The group conferred and Bud said, "We'll meet here. Nine A.M."

It was obvious none of them were too happy about it.

They had nothing on my cousin. He exploded as soon as we were in the limo with the privacy screen engaged.

"Brady. What. The. Fuck. Just. Happened?"

"I didn't have the information I needed."

"No. Shit." He glared at me. "We've been working on this for six weeks. You've had every bit of fucking information *you needed* since day one. If you hadn't had it, then we wouldn't have moved forward. So tell me. What the fuck?"

Time for the reckoning. "I left it all in my office."

Ash stared at me blankly. "Explain to me how that happened."

"I had hard copies with all my notes on my desk. I'd scanned most of it and had cataloged it on a thumb drive—which I also left there."

"Again, how'd you forget everything?"

Well, see, I had Lennox bent over my desk, and in the moment I was slamming into her, spreadsheets, thumb drives and P&Ls were the last thing on my mind.

His mouth tightened at my silence. "You've *got* to be kidding me. She distracted you that much? You blew off preparing for a major presentation because you were too busy getting blown by her?"

Not exactly, but the end result was the same.

"I'm all for you having a life outside of work, but this is inexcusable. You are supposed to separate work and pleasure, not bring pleasure into your damn work space. The office is not a place to fool around—it makes a fool of you. And now it's made a fool of me."

I resisted asking him whether he followed the no-fooling-around rule with his admin, since rumor was that she had excellent dictation skills. But this wasn't about him messing up; it was about me allowing myself to be distracted by Lennox and screwing up at work. "I know. It won't happen again."

Ash scowled. "See that it doesn't. I assume since you hadn't finished scanning everything that you didn't download any of it to the server?"

"No." What the hell had I been thinking? I'd just walked straight out of my office with Lennox that night after we'd had sex on my desk, in my bed and in my shower without any thought to my responsibilities.

"Then you'd better call your admin and have her download the data on the thumb drive to our secure server so you can at least access that."

Oh, this just kept getting better and better. "Jenna is on leave this week and next week, since I planned to be out of the office."

"Of course she is. And I suppose next you'll tell me why Jenna's secretary can't download the drive from there? Is she on vacation too?"

"No, but the thumb drive is locked up in my desk drawer and Jenna and I are the only ones with the key." A lie to save face. I'd left everything strewn across my office like a damn yard sale. That's how I dealt with sensitive financial information when I was getting laid? I just let it lie about? What the hell had happened to my brain? If this was what it meant to get a life, then I'd pass. I couldn't stand to lose part of myself that was worth something.

But it's not the only *thing about you that's worth something, remember?*

Ash picked up the phone to talk to the limo driver. "Change of plans. Take us to Midway." He paused. "No, I'll be going back to the hotel alone." Ash pointed at me after he hung up. "It's a damn good thing the LI plane was already here to take us back to the Cities."

My stomach churned and I thought I might be sick. "You're sending me home?"

"Just to get what you need for your portion of the presentation tomorrow. And I don't give a damn if you're up all freakin' night getting it done. You *will* be back on the top of your game tomorrow, Brady, if I have to pump your body full of caffeine and prop you up on the conference chair myself. Got it?"

"Yes."

I'd had a plan in place by the time the plane landed at the Minneapolis airport. The flight crew stuck around and filed a return flight plan while I hopped in a cab and headed to the office.

Now that I'd been given a second chance, I would comb through every bit of data and have the most complete findings in the history of the world to make up for my epic fuckup.

I hustled across the lobby, my mind on other things, when I heard my name. Any other time I'd be thrilled to run into Lennox since it happened so rarely, so of course we crossed paths the one time I didn't need to see her.

Her enormous grin spread across her beautiful face, her joy at seeing me evident. "Hey. I didn't think you were getting back until later tonight."

I glanced at the ornate clock in the lobby. It was just after six P.M. Good. That gave me plenty of time to get my shit together.

"Brady?"

"Look, I don't have much time. The cab is waiting for me."

She frowned. "Cab? I can give you a ride home."

"That's the thing. I'm not going home. I have to go back to Chicago."

"Tonight? Why?"

"Because I left all my presentation materials here. In my office. I just discovered it this morning and we had to postpone the meeting until tomorrow."

Her eyes were clouded with confusion. "How'd that happen?"

So maybe I acted harsher than I needed to, to get my point across. "Tuesday night? In my office? When I shoved everything off my desk so I could fuck you over it? Then we fucked in my shower and in my dressing room? And then I walked you out and locked the door behind me, forgetting about all the materials I had to take with me to Chicago the next damn day? Because I was too sex-addled to function like a CFO?"

Lennox gaped at me. "You're blaming me?"

"Yes." I blew out a breath. "That's not—"

"*My* goddamned fault, Mr. Lund, that *you're* so disorganized that you can't function like a CFO when you don't have Jenna or Patrice packing your briefcase for a business trip!"

I probably deserved that.

"And you sure as hell weren't complaining about being sex-addled after the first time, since we did it two more times."

"I was on some kind of sex high, Lennox, because I never act like that."

"Wasn't that the whole point? You needed to change your life and wanted to take a walk on the wild side? You did it—what, one time and now you can cross it off your 'wannabe wild man' list and move on?" She glared at me. "Because that's what this feels like."

"Because of my negligence, I have no idea whether LI would be making a huge mistake acquiring this company. And it is my job—and my job alone—to know that. Except I didn't do my due diligence last weekend because we were together at the cabin. And what I did accomplish, I left in a pile on the floor after we were together in my office."

Lennox took a step back and dammit if I didn't let her.

"So I'm going back to Chicago as soon as I have everything I forgot to try to salvage this mess tomorrow."

"Wait. Tomorrow Kiley and her kids are supposed to be coming to your place, remember?"

I'd completely forgotten about that. "Well, obviously we'll have to reschedule."

"Reschedule? This isn't a board meeting, Brady. These kids have no other place to go on a Saturday. You offered your space to them. Kiley was really counting on this. So were the kids." She released a bitter laugh. "I should've known you'd back out."

"That's not fair. It's one freakin' time, Lennox. That's it."

"No, it's the first time of what I expect would be many times and many disappointments."

When she backed away from me, I wanted so badly to grab onto her and make her understand. *This* was my real life. Not weekends at a cabin. Not weeknights at the gun range or getting a tattoo. I had to fly off at a moment's notice because five thousand people depended on me to make the right decisions. She couldn't possibly know what a huge load that was to bear.

"Don't worry—although I'm sure you won't; out of sight, out of mind, right? I'll tell Kiley that tomorrow is off."

"Tell her I'm sorry. Tell her I'll make it up to her next weekend." I paused. "But that won't work because I'm in Charlotte all next week."

"How about if we just forget it. All of it." Lennox turned and walked away.

Stop her.

A big part of me longed to run after her, but the louder voice in my head urged, *Let her go. This is for the best. Don't dwell on it. Get back to where you need to be.*

But as I returned to Chicago—and sat in my hotel room alone—I remembered that where I thought I needed to be was always so damn lonely.

"You were full of shit, weren't you?"

I faced my brother Walker and bit back a snarl. It'd been a grueling eight days on the road. Dealing with meeting after meeting until they all blurred together. One thing I did know: I'd been absolutely on top of my game.

Another thing I knew? I was completely unhappy, and for once it had nothing to do with my job performance.

"You ignoring me, asshole?"

I blinked at Walker. "No," I said evenly. "Just trying to figure out why you're hammering me today, and what I might've done."

"You've done nothing. You've learned nothing. You've changed nothing. That's why I'm pissed off."

"You're talking about—"

"The ritual. Yeah, we know you thought it was stupid, but you don't get it." The anger in his face softened to disappointment and that was ten times worse. "See, that night wasn't about doing shots and torching a piece of paper of your bad habits in the hopes you'd overcome them. It was about Ash, Nolan and me opening up about how worried we are about you, Brady."

I said nothing because I didn't know what to say. But I couldn't look away from the distress on my brother's face, even in the guise of watching the football game. The whole family had come to Charlotte to watch the Vikings play the Panthers for the Thursday night game. Hard to believe it'd been only a week ago that I'd suffered through the Bears game, not knowing how much my life would implode the following day.

It'd seemed like a lifetime ago.

A chorus of boos from my family rang out behind us. I'd paid little attention to the game since the Vikings offense had taken to the field for a total of five minutes in the first two quarters. But I knew that even if Jensen had been killing it out there, I'd still have felt . . . listless. I'd finished my last seminar and I just wanted to go home. But I was expected to stick around another day, since the Blackhawks were playing the Carolina Hurricanes in Raleigh the next night.

"Jesus, are you even listening to me?"

"Yeah, Walker, I'm listening."

"Look, I'll cut to the chase. Nolan, Jensen and I aren't firstborn Lund sons. We each do our own things and we don't feel the pressure of the Lund legacy. But we are aware of the pressure on you and Ash and even Jax—when he's done with the NHL—to run the company. We just didn't know who'd put it there. Because it sure as hell doesn't come from Dad, Uncle Monte or Uncle Archer. So I suspect with you it's entirely self-driven."

Some of it was, but not all. My gut churned when I was thrown back to the summer after I'd graduated from high school and first worked at LI. Everyone had thought it was so cool and generous of Grandpa Jackson Lund to step out of retirement to mentor me. It'd been the worst months of my life—yet he'd instilled in me the drive I needed to prove myself worthy of the Lund name and eventual leadership in the company, community and family.

He didn't drive you. The nasty old man browbeat you, berated you, convinced you that you'd never be good enough or smart enough to amount to anything. That the only reason you'd even have a job at LI was because of your last name. That, as evidenced by your mediocre grades, you didn't have the mental capability of running a company the size of LI. That you'd be just like your father—sliding by with charm instead of brains.

How had I forgotten that? Christ, how deep had I buried that shit? It hit me like a brick wall that I hadn't even been aware that proving my grandfather wrong had been my sole focus since I turned eighteen. A man who'd been dead for thirteen years.

"Brady?"

I glanced up at my brother.

Something on my face had him switching tactics. "Talk to me, bro. Honestly. What happened to you in the last week?"

As tempted as I was to lie to save face, I wanted to be beyond that. And it was obvious I was too far in denial about my ability to change things to do it by myself. So I didn't hold back.

After I finished unburdening myself, Walker got up and grabbed us each a beer. Then he said, "You screwed up."

"That's why I've thrown myself into this seminar."

Walker shook his head. "Was there ever any doubt in your mind you'd get back on track workwise?"

"Maybe at first."

"Dude. Be real. You jumped back in and focused on it until you fixed it."

"Yeah."

"You need to do the same thing with Lennox." He pointed his beer bottle at me. "But you don't have the first friggin' clue how to fix things with her, do you?"

I jammed my hand through my hair. Then I tossed a look over my shoulder, surprised that we hadn't been interrupted. "No. And why would she want anything to do with me after how I acted anyway? I was a dick to her. I blamed her, I let her and her roommate down, and I made it sound like I regretted being intimate with her, when it was the most outstanding sex I've ever had. She's different from any woman I've been with before."

When Walker studied me, I figured I'd given him too much information. I prepared myself to take a rash of shit, but that wasn't what he gave me.

"That day you brought Lennox to the game, I watched her very closely." He smirked when I growled at him. "Back off, beast. She is damn fine to look at, but what struck me, watching her, was that she kept watching you. As she did, she had such a starstruck look on her face. It might sound sappy as shit, but she just . . . lit up around you. And, bro, you were the same exact way around her. Everyone noticed it. You know why everyone noticed it?" He swigged his beer. "Because for the first time in a long time you looked really frickin' happy. It was a beautiful thing to see, man. I'm sure part of it was the rockin'-hot sex—"

"Wrong. Lennox and I hadn't slept together yet." I corrected his assumption.

Walker's jaw dropped. "So she acted all love-struck and shit just because she just likes you that much?"

"I guess."

"You guess." He set his elbows on the table. "You have a woman like that? Who's beautiful, smart and sexy, who gets you and likes you anyway—when you're not being an overthinking workaholic dickhead—you go after her with everything you have. *Everything*. You do not waste another day waiting around wondering if she'll forgive you. You do whatever it takes to make that happen. You get me?"

For the first time in a week, I actually had hope that I could fix this. "I get you. But since you've got way more experience groveling than I do, you'll have to help me out."

"I thought you'd never ask."

Nineteen

LENNOX

At first, I'd thought I had weathered the Brady storm pretty well.

Okay, the man had rolled over me like a hurricane and swamped me with emotions I hadn't been aware I was capable of feeling. I'd always been the one to end things. So to have him call it quits on our relationship and accuse me of distracting him from doing his job because I was too . . . wild?

I'd never experienced anger on that level.

Or hurt.

I let anger rule me the first few days. That's what I needed because Kiley had been so upset about disappointing her kids again. And since she has an outer shell of armor and a soft, squishy inner core, she used money from her personal account to take the kids to the Walker Art Center. She bought the deluxe art lover's package for the entire group, which included a personalized tour of every section of the gallery, lunch and a private art class where all the kids got to paint a small canvas.

So I'd made it twenty-four hours without crying. But I broke down completely when all twelve of Kiley's kids had handed over their paintings to her as a thank-you. They knew what it had cost her not to disappoint them again.

That's when I lost it. Three hundred bucks was a drop in the bucket of Brady Lund's financial world. But that money would put a huge dent in Kiley's monthly budget.

In a fit of anger I'd texted her Brady's number so she could send him the bill. Of course she wouldn't do that. Then she let me cry on her shoulder, allowing me to pretend I was upset only on her behalf, not because the superfine CFO had proven himself to be exactly what I'd feared: a man who pays lip service to changing, but when it came right down to it, he wouldn't. I didn't have the ego to believe the few steps he'd taken toward cutting loose had scared him because he'd liked it so much. No, I could accept I wasn't like the women he usually dated. He'd gotten a taste and it'd been satisfying enough he didn't need to go back for seconds.

"What are you having?" Kiley prompted me.

It was our usual Friday night at Sake Palace. Kiley had tried to back out, but I told her it was my treat since I didn't want to dwell on the misery I'd felt last week by sitting home alone on Friday night. "Is it boring if I say I'm having the usual?"

"A little. But you know what you like and there's no reason to change that if you're happy with it."

I peered over the menu. "You seem very Zen tonight, K. What gives?"

She laughed. "I'm just happy things work out the way they're supposed to sometimes. It gives me hope."

I splurged and ordered the rainbow roll for each of us, and my usual spider rolls, spicy tuna rolls and tempura rolls.

The food came fast and we ate in silence. I could hear the restaurant filling up behind us and the activity at the chef's station increased as the flurry of Japanese between the waitstaff got louder and faster.

Once our plates were cleared, we ordered green tea and let our meal settle.

My roommate seemed preoccupied. "You all right?"

"Fine. Just thinking."

"So tomorrow. You've got a solid plan for the group since it's supposed to be snowy and cold?"

Kiley stirred sugar into her hot tea. "Yes."

That's all she said. I leaned across the table. "You gonna share those plans with your number one volunteer?"

A smile curled her lips. "Nope. It's a surprise."

"I hate surprises."

She mumbled something like, "You're really gonna hate this," but I could've misunderstood since she'd spoken under her breath.

Kiley snagged her purse. "I'm going to the bathroom."

I waited for her to say something smart like, "Don't worry; I'll come back," since the last time we'd eaten there Brady's date had ditched him. But she'd avoided any mention of his name all week. She patted me on the shoulder as she passed by.

I set my elbows on the table and rested my head in my hands, closing my eyes.

A few minutes later, clothing rustled as Kiley brushed past me and slid into her seat.

I said, "Took you long enough," and lifted my head to look at her.

But it wasn't Kiley sitting across from me. It was Brady.

"It did take me seven very long days to figure out a way to apologize."

He looked . . . sort of crappy, which made me feel marginally better. "Where's Kiley?"

"She agreed to take off after dinner so you and I could talk." His hungry gaze encompassed my face. "You look beautiful as ever, Lennox."

I snorted. "I don't need your flattery, nor do I want it. Say whatever you've come to say, so I can accept your apology and we can both move on."

Brady took my hands in his. "I don't want to move on. I want to go back to the way things were."

Fat chance, bud.

"I'm here to apologize for how I acted. I'm sorry I was a condescending ass. I'm sorry I accused you of things that weren't your fault. I'm sorry you haven't heard from me in the last week—it's taken me this long to figure out how to apologize after my colossal fuckup. And I realized this was something I needed to do in person."

I waited as he spoke. Didn't petulantly jerk my hands away, but neither did I go all starry-eyed and blurt out my immediate and unconditional forgiveness. I guessed that's what I was waiting for. For Brady to slap on excuses for what he'd said.

But he didn't. He sat there gazing at me so longingly that I had to look away. He shifted his stance too and I caught a whiff of that druglike scent of his skin—warm musk and his cologne.

Retreat!

So I did. I removed my hands from his and grabbed my

teacup. That's when I noticed his knuckles were skinned up and scabbed over. "What happened to your hands?"

He shrugged. "I had a bad week, so I punched things."

"Did punching things make your week better?"

"No."

I hadn't granted my forgiveness. It wasn't a power thing that held me back, but Brady's implication that we could just pick up where we'd left off.

"I didn't know you liked sushi," he said. Then he sighed. "Dammit. That sounded lame, didn't it?"

"A little."

"I'm not a huge fan of sushi myself, so it's strange that I've been in this place twice in the past six weeks."

Here was my moment of truth.

My mouth made the decision before my head or heart weighed in. "I know."

Those blue eyes narrowed.

"See, I was here that night you came in with that jailbait-looking waif."

"That's actually a very apt description of her."

"I thought you were on a date with her."

His posture stiffened, as if to say, *Please leave it at that. Don't pry for more information.*

"But it didn't appear as if you were having a good time."

Brady shook his head. "It was bloody awful," he said with a hint of a brogue.

"Her accent was hard to place."

"Wait. You talked to her? When?"

Why couldn't I be a smooth liar? And now that I'd opened the door, I had to go all the way through it. "In the bathroom. Look. The truth is, I saw you and planned to stop at your table and say hello, if for no other reason than to see if you felt guilty for dating jailbait"—he snorted—"but I chickened out at the last second and went to the bathroom. That's where she—" I paused.

He got right in my face. "No editorializing. Tell me. All of it."

By the time I finished, Brady had dropped his forehead to the table as if contemplating beating his head into it.

I laughed softly.

He looked up at me. "It's not funny. But damn, do I love to hear you laugh. I've missed it . . . So the woman I'd been crushing on from the moment I saw her witnessed my humiliation that night and heard some choice bits, right from the horse's mouth, about what an uptight ice-cold wanker I am."

I'd sort of tuned out after his admission that he'd been crushing on me.

"That's great, Lennox. I'm actually blushing just thinking about it."

He was. His face was flushed and there was a look I'd seen in his eyes only once before: vulnerability.

Almost without thinking, I reached out and placed my hands on his cheeks.

He put his hands over mine and we locked eyes.

"Why did you agree to go out with me when you saw firsthand what a clumsy, clueless oaf I am when it comes to dating?"

"Because that's not what I saw."

He groaned. "It's worse, isn't it? You thought I was pathetic and you agreed to a date out of pity."

I leaned in closer. "Brady. Shut up. If you stop trying to analyze me, I'll tell you why I went out with you."

"Please. I'm dying here."

"First of all, you demanded the date. But if I hadn't

wanted to go, nothing would've gotten me in that car with you." I stroked my thumbs over his cheekbones. "So what if you suck at dating? You aren't a one-dimensional man. You excel at everything else. Do you really think I would've preferred if you were some asshole player? And you've never acted like an entitled dickhead around me. Well, except for last Friday."

Brady watched me with eyes filled with hope and that just did me in.

I was crazy about all the different sides of this man. He'd come here with an honest-to-god apology from the heart, no excuses. What more did I expect him to do? I closed the distance between us and pressed a soft kiss to his mouth. "I accept your apology."

He rested his forehead to mine. "Thank you."

We stayed like that for a few moments longer before we broke apart.

"I want to spend the night with you."

I raised an eyebrow.

That earned me a glorious grin. "Not like that, although I've heard makeup sex is hot." He picked up my hand and kissed my palm. "We can watch TV or something. Hell, I'd even watch paint dry as long as I get to do it with you."

There was that sliver of sweetness that made me go all gooey inside. "Okay. But my roommate will be home and she's probably still pissed enough at you to let fly. So fair warning."

"Kiley forgave me when I promised my place to her and the kids tomorrow with no chance of me backing out."

The little sneak. No wonder she'd hedged and claimed tomorrow's location was a surprise.

"And I reimbursed her for last weekend. Plus I gifted her

three more Saturdays at the Walker, so if she runs into this problem again, she's covered."

"You are so forgiven."

He laughed.

"I've missed that laugh too, Brady."

"Let's get out of here."

"I have to pay the check."

"Already taken care of."

I opted not to argue.

Outside in the chilly night, I started to wrap my scarf around my neck when Brady grabbed the end and tugged me against his body.

"My lovely Lennox." His mouth came down on mine. Not tenderly, not with gratitude or reverence, but with the hunger that quickened my blood and my heartbeat.

I'd missed kissing him like this. A little desperate. A little sloppy. A little impatient to sate the passion that flared between us.

"Come on," he whispered against my mouth after he broke the kiss. "Let's go to your place."

Later, as we were lying in my bed, after we'd watched a movie—*The Blind Side*, not my first choice, because, hello? sports movie—I finally asked him the question I'd been dying to.

"So everything turned out all right in Chicago? After you retrieved your missing materials?"

He spooned me, with his chin on the top of my head and his fingertips trailing up and down my arm. "Yes. The numbers were solid and we made them a decent offer. It'll take a few months to transition to our product line, but we aren't

WHAT YOU NEED   285

demanding they stop manufacturing for our competitor. Yet."

"I'm glad you didn't have any serious setbacks, Brady."

"Me too."

"After that you went to Charlotte."

He stilled his hand. "Checking up on me, were you?"

"No. Patrice took great pains the first two days to inform me of your whereabouts in the employee break room. For the rest of the week I ate at my desk."

"Smart move. I had meetings with a couple of financial institutions in Charlotte and then I led a seminar on family-business practices. Pretty boring, dry stuff, I imagine. Jens had a game last night, and luckily for the Lund family, Jax had a hockey game in Raleigh tonight, so they're all cheering him on."

"Why aren't you there?"

"Because I'm here. Apologizing and working on fixing things with you. Making it right for Kiley and her kids was more important to me than watching a puck flying across the ice."

"I'm glad you're here." I snuggled into him.

I thought he'd fallen asleep, but then he said, "I had to face the music with my family too, not just you." A long pause followed. "Remember I told you about the intervention my cousins and my brother staged that night at Maxie's?"

"Yes, I remember. That's why you wanted to prove you have a wild side."

"I wanted to get them off my back because it was annoying, humiliating and embarrassing to have them treating me like a child. So as they showed me they cared about me, I blew them off and followed my own agenda."

"Was I part of that agenda, Brady?"

"God, no. They made me promise to quit working so much. And yes, they encouraged me to find something out-side of work that let me enjoy my station in life. I found you."

I smiled in the darkness.

"Then I had the crisis with the Chicago project." He inhaled a deep breath. Exhaled against my hair. "I'd done a bang-up job convincing myself I couldn't have both you and my job."

He didn't have to tell me which one won out.

"I figured I'd blown it with you, so I expended all my energy into the job. That was a familiar place for me to retreat. And excel. Because, god knows, that's all that mat-tered. That I proved I'm worthy."

"Worthy of what?"

"It's more like worthy of who."

"Then who?"

Brady remained quiet for so long that I thought he wouldn't answer. And when he finally spoke, his voice was so soft I hardly heard him. "My grandfather."

I wondered if he'd had this helpless feeling as he'd waited for me to talk about my past. I wanted to soothe him before he even said a word, because I suspected he'd need it.

"I'd forgotten about it. Blocked it out, most likely because it—" His body tensed behind me. "If someone had asked me what drove me to earn multiple undergrad business de-grees as well as master's degrees, I'd likely have answered with something pat like I wanted to be an asset to LI. But the truth is, I did it because my grandfather was a nasty, arrogant old bastard who assured me I'd never amount to anything. Maybe it's a coping mechanism to block some-thing like that from memory, but when Walker cornered me, I had a flashback."

I couldn't remain silent. "To when? To what?"

"Grandpa Jack never pretended to be kindly and wise to his grandkids. Despite the fact he lived on the other side of the Lund Compound, we hardly ever saw him. He wasn't the kind of man to go to football or hockey games. Or dance recitals. So it surprised and—I'll be honest—excited me when he offered to mentor me at LI the summer before I started college.

"But from the get-go it was awful. He berated me from the time I got there until I left at night. I couldn't do anything right. I was stupid. Lazy. Ugly. I was lucky I had the last name Lund because I was too much of an idiot to survive outside the hallowed company walls and I'd never make enough money to support myself."

That feeling of numbness began to unfurl in my belly.

"He was beyond mean and he was crude. At first his favorite taunt was, 'The only reason a woman will want to get into your pants, Bratty, is to find your wallet.'"

"His nickname for you was Bratty?"

"One of the nicer ones. And maybe it makes me a whiner to say this, but I'd had a rough time of it at my high school and I transferred to an all-boys school my senior year. So he went off on a tangent about me liking dick so much I changed schools."

I listened. And seethed.

"I was barely eighteen. My entire life I'd heard what a shrewd businessman Jackson Lund was. From the office staff—none of whom had actually worked with my grandfather during his glory days, so they had no clue about the type of verbal vitriol he was capable of. So for the first month I threw up every day before I went to work. By the second month I just had that continual gnawing in my gut because I knew that my grandfather was right. I was stupid, lazy and unfocused. Ugly, too. I'd probably die a virgin. And I'd end up just like—" He shuddered.

I rolled until my cheek was pressed against his chest and wrapped my arms around him. "Like who, Brady?"

"Like my dad. Not only had Grandpa picked me apart until I was nothing but a shell, he went after my dad. Telling me every day that he was embarrassed that his son had no drive, no brain for business. He went on to brag that the only reason my father even had a position at LI was because he'd allowed it. My dad was a pitiful example of a man who slid by with the minimum amount of work. Then he'd demand, 'Is that what you're striving for? Is that your big life plan—to be like your old man?' So by the third month, I'd gotten mad. I swore I'd prove Jackson Lund wrong. I'd never be like my father. The fun guy. He set up corporate parties. He smoothed things over with clients. He wasn't out acquiring and making the big money. I made myself a promise that I'd be running the goddamned company before I turned thirty-five, making me the youngest corporate executive in LI history. When I went off to college, I took every business and finance class they offered."

"And you exceeded even your own expectations."

"Yeah. I guess. Even after my grandfather died, I didn't slow down. And that mean bastard didn't live long enough to see my success. Part of me is glad, because I know nothing I ever accomplished would've been good enough."

I kissed his chest over his heart, my own heart heavy with sadness. He'd been as much a victim as I had. Economic disparities didn't matter; harsh cruel words bounced off a solid surface regardless of whether it was in a mansion or a trailer. "Does anyone in your family know how cruel he was to you?"

Brady shook his head. "I was too embarrassed to tell

anyone because I was afraid they'd start to look at me differently. It would've killed me to have them see me like *he* saw me."

"I'm sorry you went through all that."

"Know what I'm the most sorry about? The skewed perception I had of my dad. He's a great man. Way more complex than what Grandpa claimed. Way more loving and kind."

I held on to him tightly.

"About an hour after I'd finished talking to Walker last night, my dad approached me. In his supportive, kind way he told me he was so proud of me and hated to see me struggling. And if there was anything he could do . . . his door was always open to me." Brady swallowed hard. "That's the kind of man I want to be, Lennox. And it has nothing to do with my position in the corporation."

"It sounds like you finally had the kind of moment of clarity that your brother and cousins were trying to force on you."

"Yeah."

"So you're all right?"

He tipped my head back and kissed me with the sweet surety that made my belly flip, my heart swell and my eyes sting. "I'm much better now. Because this time I'm positive this isn't a temporary fix for me."

"Good."

Twenty

BRADY

Lennox and I had decided she'd show up with Kiley and her charges, so no one would suspect it was actually my place. She'd be seeing it at the same time as everyone else. That made me more nervous than having a dozen teenagers roaming around. I hadn't been in a relationship before, so having my girlfriend stay over hadn't come up.

The outer buzzer sounded and I shut off the alarm system to this floor before I opened the door.

Excited teens poured in, eagerly zipping past me to check out the space. I smiled and made noncommittal noises, my eyes searching for her.

And there she was. My beautiful wild thing.

She moved into me first, wrapping her arms around me tightly and nestling her cheek into my chest. She didn't tell me she missed me; she didn't need to, because her actions spoke loud enough.

Although I couldn't kiss her the way I needed to, I couldn't not touch my lips to hers. She gave me a cheeky smile when I saw she'd worn her lip ring.

I held her hand as we joined the group.

"This place is beyond awesome—it's like a dream, man," DeMarius declared. "Who owns it?"

"And how do *you* know them?" Tonto asked.

"And why'd they let you use it?" Juice said.

They were all looking at me suspiciously. "I saved the guy who owns this place a lot of money in taxes. He lets me use it once in a while."

"The guy is an athlete, isn't he? With that half court I bet he's a Timberwolves player."

Juice shoved DeMarius. "Dude. A pro player would have a full court. I bet the guy plays for the Vikings."

"Nah. The place doesn't smell like broken dreams," Tonto said.

I had to laugh at that one. The rest of the kids hung back, letting the three guys lead.

Kiley stepped in. "You know the drill. I'm trying to get you to see that you get to choose the way you live. You see yourself living in a place like this? You gotta work for it. You aren't gonna earn it as a two-bit go-between for some crackhead dealer. You aren't gonna earn it picking fights and ending up in juvie. You aren't gonna earn it chopping cars, stealing cars or driving the getaway car. You guys feel me?"

The guys had their arms crossed over their chests, heads back, looking down on Kiley as if by listening to her they were doing her a big favor. I didn't know how she dealt with this shit day in and day out. If even one of these kids got out of their home life situation and went to college . . . would one in twelve be considered a success rate? Or a failure rate?

"Education is the key to earning your own way. College,

vocational training, the military—all ways you can step up and be more than you ever thought you could be, and that'll quiet down your friends and family who are telling you everything you can't do."

"*Shee-it.* My mama told me I got thug blood," DeMarius said. "She just don't say if it's from her side or the sperm donor's side. So I tell her, hell no, she ain't putting that on me."

"Good for you, DeMan!" Kiley said. "Anyone else wanna talk about family stuff that might've gone down since we last met?"

"Jonesie got arrested," Juice said.

"Yeah, I heard that. What'd he do?" Tonto asked.

"He got high and went to his mom's place to confront his stepdad. Took a swing at him and when his mom tried to stop him, she ended up in the line of fire. Jonesie hit her hard enough to break her jaw. The cops took him to juvie in St. Paul." Kiley sighed. "I talked to him. He doesn't remember anything. So yeah—so much for drugs taking the edge off. He's gonna do a long stint for this last stunt."

"It's not fair," the quiet blond boy said. "His stepdad should've been locked up. He's been beating on Jonesie forever."

"The court never takes the side of kids," Quay said, dropping his arm over his little sister's shoulder. "We gotta protect them the best we can."

"Sometimes your best ain't good enough," Juice said.

These kids had been through hell. They were still going through it. Rather than putting up with it, Lennox had left. I knew it had been a gutsy move, but I didn't know just how gutsy until now.

"Anyone else have anything to add?" Kiley asked.

Silence.

"All right, then. Let's move on. Since Brady is a numbers

guy, and some of you have problems with math, he has generously offered to do some tutoring."

Lennox squeezed my hand.

A couple of the kids hung back and looked around as if they'd entered an alien world and were about to be probed.

"And since I know not everyone likes sports, there's a table set up on the other side of the boxing ring with games like chess and checkers. Next to that we've thrown out some canvasses, and there are paints, markers and other supplies."

The Hispanic girl raised her hand.

"Yes, Maria?" Kiley asked.

"Where is the bathroom?"

"Back by the weight room. The only place that's off-limits is the boxing ring, so no boxing or MMA-type sparring, okay?" I said.

"What's upstairs?" Willa the tall redhead asked me.

"I have no idea."

"There's plenty to keep you all occupied down here, so don't go looking for trouble," Kiley warned.

I rubbed my hands together. "Who's ready to solve some equations?"

Two guys actually ran for the basketball court.

I laughed and pointed at Juice. "Did you bring your book and assignments?"

He looked embarrassed. "Yeah."

"How'd the last couple of weeks go?"

"Fail, fail and fail."

"Well, even the slightest improvement will be a forward step. Grab your stuff."

I slid my duffel bag over to the table I'd set up and reached inside for my glasses case. I tossed out a pad of graph paper, several mechanical pencils, erasers and two calculators—a basic one and a scientific model with graphing capabilities.

Juice yanked the chair out across from me. "What's all this shit? Man, I don't got the kinda money for that fancy-ass calculator. If that's what I need to pass the class, I'm screwed."

"I wasn't sure if you were in trigonometry or algebra."

"Algebra." He shoved his assignment at me. "I only did the first problem."

I recopied it and within four steps solved it. Then I put our papers side by side. "Tell me the difference."

"Yours is right and mine is wrong."

"Besides that."

Juice looked from paper to paper. "I don't know."

"Yes, you do. Follow each step. You have to show your work, Juice. I know teachers harp on that, but there's a reason they do. If you show your work and you don't get the right answer at the end, then you can go back through each step and see where you missed something." I tapped on the paper. "Next problem. Show your work this time. Remember, this isn't a race. There's no buzzer to beat. It's more about finesse than speed."

A startled look crossed his face, as if he hadn't expected that. "Okay."

I purposely took longer than usual to solve the equation. While I waited for Juice to finish the problem, I glanced over at Lennox and saw her watching me with heated eyes. She bit her lip—right over the damn lip ring she'd worn to taunt me. So I deliberately adjusted my glasses, knowing it'd make her crazy.

Her sexy sigh echoed to me across the vast concrete space.

I'd always taken pains to hide the fact I wore glasses. But Lennox being so hot for me when she saw me wearing them, and then seducing the hell out of me, had put a new spin on it. She had no idea how deeply her acceptance about everything about me had affected me. Being away from her these last few days had driven home the point I didn't ever want to be away from her. And what I felt for her was probably that elusive love thing.

"Brady."

I tore my gaze away from Lennox and focused on Juice. I passed my paper to him. "Check your answer against mine."

A pause, then, "Hey! I got it right."

"Why do you think that is?"

"Because I showed my work."

"Exactly. Keep going."

When I took my paper back and jotted down the next problem, I found Juice staring at me. "What?"

"You're not gonna go play ball or play grab-ass with Lennox?"

I raised an eyebrow at him. "You don't want me here doing homework with you?"

He blushed. "It's not that. It's just . . . teachers usually sit through one problem, then say I'm on my own."

"That doesn't make sense to me. If I help you with the first problem, that's no guarantee you'll grasp the concept for the second problem. I'm not going to do the work for you, but I won't abandon you either until you've got a better handle on it."

"Thanks."

The noise level increased as the kids relaxed enough to have fun. When Juice stayed with it, Tonto, Quay and De-Marius came over to see what he was doing. They returned to the court, but Quay got out his notebook and stayed. He did the same set of problems as Juice, and I had to withhold a chuckle when Juice reminded Quay to show his work.

Kiley provided food, and after lunch I played a game of horse with Willa and Needra. I tried not to obsessively track Lennox's movements, because I knew I'd have her moving under me soon enough.

The kids had exhausted all sources of entertainment by three o'clock, so Kiley started rounding them up. She'd managed to score transportation from the Outreach Center and the kids razzed each other about being stuck on the "short bus." They were so busy checking their phones—Kiley had enforced a no-phones rule during their activity time—that they didn't notice that Lennox hadn't gotten back on the bus with them.

I waited until the bus pulled away before I shut the door. I set the alarm system. I didn't want any interruptions.

Then I faced her.

"Brady."

"Lennox."

"What now?" she asked breathlessly.

"I've been obsessed with how this would play out when we were alone at my place."

She inched backward. "What did you come up with?"

"Taking you across the hood of the Maybach."

"I don't see any cars in here."

I stalked her. "I moved them out."

"What are your other ideas?"

"Boxing ring or the weight bench."

"Why?"

"Because they're the closest horizontal surfaces. Or maybe because they'll be softer on your back." I paused. "Or on your knees."

She swallowed hard. "Are those my only options?"

"Unless you've got other ideas."

"I do." She stopped moving.

"Name it."

Her chest rose and fell and the pulse jumped in her throat. "Your bed. I know you want to prove you're a wild man and I can't think of any place I'd rather be when you let loose."

Of course she said the perfect thing. I offered her my hand. When she sauntered closer, I held my other hand up to stop her. "This is as much skin-to-skin contact as I can deal with right now."

"So if I did this"—she fisted her hand in my shirt and pulled me toward her until we were mouth-to-mouth—"and then this"—she rubbed her hips against mine—"would that speed things up?"

I fastened my mouth to hers, plunging my tongue between her lips, cranking up the need to a near combustible level. When she turned her head to take a breath, I played with that lip ring with my teeth and tongue until she whimpered.

"No, baby," I whispered. "That just slowed things way down."

Clasping her hand, I led her up the steel stairs to the outer door. I punched in the code for my residence and, once inside, took her up the stairs instead of using the elevator.

I could feel her wide-eyed gaze on my back as I entered the code required to exit the stairwell and enter my loft. We stepped into a dark hallway and I turned right. I'd give her the full tour later—the only place she'd see right now was my bedroom.

I hadn't made my bed. My suitcase was open on the floor. The blinds were still drawn. Letting go of her hand, I picked up the bag from the drugstore with the box of condoms and tossed it on the nightstand. Then I saw her standing in the doorway.

"Come here."

The sassy woman put an extra sway in her hips as she crossed the room.

I ran the backs of my knuckles across her jaw and down her throat, between her breasts and over her belly. Then I slid my hand down and cupped her. "Take your clothes off for me, Lennox."

She didn't ask if I wanted it done fast or slow. She circled my wrists and flattened my palms on her breasts without saying a word.

I hissed in a breath at her hardened nipples stabbing into my palms as I sank my fingers into the soft flesh of her unencumbered breasts.

She kicked off her snow boots. Then she hooked her fingers in the sides of her yoga pants and peeled them down her legs to the floor.

No underwear gave me a peekaboo glimpse of the pale curls covering her sex before her flannel shirt fell forward.

"I've got it from here," I said, snaring her mouth in a teasing kiss as I unbuttoned her shirt. Once I had that done, I tossed it on the floor and lifted her camisole over her head. Then she was utterly, gloriously naked.

"Beautiful," I said, starting the kiss at her mouth right on that temptingly sexy lip ring. I kissed her and let my hands roam, mapping the dips and curves and sweetly feminine grooves of her body.

I'd started out wanting to devour her and ended up slowing things down so I could savor her.

Every inch.

Then I realized there was such a thing as too slow.

As I nuzzled her breasts, I grabbed her hips and settled her on the edge of the bed. I dropped to my knees and trailed my fingertips up and down the tops of her thighs.

Lennox made a soft groan when I planted kisses down the center of her body.

As my mouth connected with her skin, I watched her head fall back and she arched, automatically parting her thighs wider to accommodate me.

My heart raced when I breached that barrier of curls with my tongue and found the sweet flesh nestled inside. I'd intended to take this slow and explore. Build her up and up and up and then send her soaring.

But I was too greedy. The taste of her too intoxicating. The sounds of her pleasure too addictive that I became obsessed with hearing her cry out over and over.

Twice.

Before I'd had my fill of her—I'd started to suspect I never would—she tugged on my hair and pulled me away from my new favorite part of her.

"Brady."

I looked up.

"My turn." She pulled my T-shirt over my head. She tugged on the waistband of my athletic shorts until I stood.

In the next moment she'd dragged my shorts down to my ankles and slid her wet mouth over the entire length of me.

"Christ, Lennox. That's—" *Incredible, amazing, god, yes, use your teeth, baby.* My other head prevailed and I curled my hands around her face. "That's not what I want." I smiled and traced the fullness of her lips. "This time."

"What do you want?"

You. Looking at me like this. As often as possible.

And the weird thing about that silent proclamation was, it didn't feel weird. It felt right.

"Scoot up into the middle of the bed and I'll show you."

As I started to follow her across the mattress, I realized I still had my shoes on. I stepped out of them and reached for the box of condoms.

Lennox wore a sexy smirk as she watched me roll on protection.

"What?"

"I can't believe I'm here with you. It feels a little surreal."

"For me too." I crawled over the top of her, making sure as much of our skin touched as possible—her softness to my hardness. "So how about if I make us both feel good."

I started to move inside her and she closed her eyes. I stopped. "Lennox."

She slowly opened her eyes and the raw emotion I saw there went straight to the heart of me.

"Don't hide that from me, baby. If being with me brings that beautiful light to your eyes, I want to see it. I need to see it."

"Brady . . ."

"Let me in. Move with me. See how you move me."

Lennox twined her arms around my neck and wrapped her legs around my hips.

I rested my forehead to hers, breathing her air, watching her eyes as I slid home.

"That feels amazing," she whispered against my lips.

"That it does."

"Is this time going to be slow and sweet?"

"Yes." I smiled and bit down on her lip ring. "Until it gets wild."

———

Lennox had her head on my shoulder and she was playing with my chest hair.

We'd fallen asleep but then the little nymph had woken me up with her mouth. So I was feeling very loose. Relaxed. And like the luckiest guy on the planet.

"Tell me what you did in Chicago and Charlotte besides attend meetings."

I wondered if this would be Lennox's thing—grilling me after every trip. I liked it. It gave me a sense of peace. "Like what?"

"Like . . . did you eat a Chicago dog?"

"No."

"Did you eat Carolina barbecue?"

"I might have—I was too preoccupied both times to remember the food."

Lennox got quiet.

I swept her hair back from her face. "I did do something a little . . . impulsive in Chicago."

"Tell me!"

"I bought a motorcycle."

She raised her head and looked at me. "You're serious."

"Yes."

"I'll bet it's a Beemer, isn't it?"

"No, baby, it's a hog." I chuckled. "Harley-Davidson all the way. It's the newest model. They'll deliver it to the dealership here in the spring."

"You. Bought. A. Bike."

"And I'll probably get one of those badass leather jackets. Leather chaps. Biker boots. I'll put my wallet on a chain and attach it to a loop and shove it in the back pocket of my Levi's. You might get off work next summer and see me waiting for you, resting against the bike, in my leathers, sunglasses on, face unshaven, smoking a cigar. If you saw me like that, would you let me take you for a ride?"

Lennox rolled on top of me. "I'm thinking you could take me for a ride right now."

I laughed. "So me being a biker dude does it for you?"

"Brady. You do it for me in a bad way."

"Does it scare you that I've admitted I'm thinking long term with you?"

Her body stiffened. She stared at me for several silent moments. "No, it doesn't scare me." She paused. "And that terrifies me."

My eyes searched hers. "Why?"

"We haven't been together long. And neither of us has been in a long-term relationship."

"Do you want to slow down?"

She shook her head. "But I don't want to go any faster than this right now either."

I banked my disappointment.

She noticed it and kissed me. "I see your confusion. I feel the same way, so I can't explain it. I've never felt like this. I shouldn't trust it. But I do. I trust you."

"That's all I need to know, Lennox."

She stretched out on her belly with a sigh. "I love this big bed."

"I love having you in it." I swept the hair from her shoulder and let my knuckles follow the birds tattooed down the back of her neck. She'd told me they were starlings, not blackbirds, which had intrigued me enough to do a little research. "Did you know a flock of starlings in flight is called a 'murmuration'?"

"Yes, I did know that. Have you seen the footage of them? It's an aerial ballet as they shift and move as one, as if they're of a single mind instead of thousands."

I kissed the bird right below her hairline. "What do starlings mean to you, Lennox?"

"Adaptability," she said softly. "Starlings exist all over the world, but they're unique to where they live. They're monogamous—most pairs mate for life, which I found highly romantic at age eighteen when I got the tattoo. They're mimics, which goes back to their adaptability. And they're not sexually dimorphic, which means the males and the females have the same color of plumage. I saw a special on them when I was a kid and the images stuck with me."

I brushed my mouth across the next tat, strangely touched by her practical and yet oddly sentimental reasoning, mostly because it fit who she was so perfectly. "And yet you have the tattoos in a place where you can't see them and enjoy them." I traced the largest one with the tip of my tongue. "So perhaps enjoying them and admiring them should be my job." I nipped the nape of her neck and was rewarded with a deep body shudder. "You know how seriously I take my job. So relax, because this will take a while."

Twenty-one

LENNOX

Usually, whenever I have a bad day, I get the urge to ask the universe what else could go wrong? Bad idea today. Bad, bad idea.

It wasn't even a Monday.

When I arrived at work thirty minutes late, I got stuck with phone duty again, but this time at the security desk on the first floor. Working in the main reception area meant everything was amplified. Shoes clicking and squeaking across the tile. The constant *ding-ding* from the bank of elevators. Conversations were loud and carried up the set of escalators to the second floor.

So far it wasn't noon and I'd already had ten people yell at me.

One woman spilled her coffee on the reception desk and chewed *me* out for it because I'd asked to see her ID.

When I called upstairs to talk to Sydney to see if I'd

somehow pissed Lola off, Sydney told me that Lola had been in meetings all morning.

For lunch I grabbed a quick bite at the deli around the corner and checked my messages to see if Brady had tried to get in touch with me.

Nothing.

But two missed calls from Maxie.

That wasn't like her. I ducked around the concrete pillar and called her.

She picked up on the second ring. "Lenni? I'm sorry. It's not my fault. We got to drinking and—"

"Whoa. Slow down. What's not your fault?"

"Lisa is on her way to your office."

I froze. "My mother is here?"

"That's why I've been trying to get ahold of you. She told me two weeks ago she was coming, but she didn't know when and she needed a place to stay since you wouldn't let her crash with you."

"When did she get here?"

"Friday night."

At least she hadn't ruined my weekend.

Not nice, Lennox.

"Did she come with Billy Ray?"

"No. She said she might be done with him. Anyway, she had a crazy Friday night. She got totally hammered. Then she did the same thing Saturday and Sunday nights."

I closed my eyes. "Not fun for you, Maxie."

"When she's shitfaced she acts like the Lisa I used to know. So, ah, I sorta told her some stuff I shouldn't have. And I'm sorry, Lenni."

"Stop calling me Lenni—my name is Lennox." I inhaled but couldn't manage a deep exhale as I was dangerously close to hyperventilating. "What stuff did you tell her?" It couldn't have been too bad, because I hadn't confided in Maxie for a long time—not since before I'd taken the job with LI.

"Remember that night you were in and danced on the bar? I asked if you knew the guy who'd caught you, since one of the guys he was with is a semiregular."

"Who?"

"He's a hot blond with a beard and is built like a lumber-jack. He comes in a couple of times a month. I found out his name is Walker Lund."

I felt the blood drain from my face.

"And I knew you were lying to me, Lenni—Lennox—about knowing the slick-looking dude who'd caught you after you'd biffed it off the bar. So the next time Walker came in, I chatted him up. He told me all about you being involved with his brother, who is one of the head honchos over at Lund Industries. Guy in charge of all the money. That's a big deal. And damn, girl, I was proud for you getting you a piece of that, porking the boss."

"I'm not porking the boss. Brady is not my boss. And Jesus, Maxie, no one says 'porking' anymore."

"There it is, that bitchy 'I'm better than everyone' atti-tude."

Don't take the bait. It was obvious she'd been hanging around with Lisa since she channeled her way of speaking.

"I'm sure you have to get back to work, but I might've told your mom about you landing a rich one. Then late this morning when I got up, she was already high and making plans to see you at work. Her exact words were 'make that ungrateful little bitch notice me.'"

I could feel my throat tighten, my eyes pulse and my lungs shrink from the impending panic attack.

"I just wanted to warn you."

"She hasn't been here."

"I hate to hope she got sidetracked looking for another score."

"What'd she take?"

"Pretty sure it was oxy. Pistol said she was asking around for some."

"Maxie, if she shows up here and causes a scene when she's freakin' high—"

"Call me and I'll deal with it," she pleaded. "Don't call the cops. Please. We both know your mom doesn't do well in jail."

"I can't promise—"

"You have to. I know you have issues with her, but if you call me I'll make sure she leaves you alone."

I recognized it as an empty promise. Neither one of us could control Lisa Greene Hamline Gruber Dunwoody and only Maxie had cared enough to try.

"Lennox. Please."

"Fine. If she shows up here—if she's not already in jail because she went looking for drugs—I'll call you."

"Thank you. And I'm sorry. I just really—"

I hung up. I stood. I paced. I cursed. Tears threatened but I choked them back as I always did.

Maybe it'd been karma that, of all the days my mother had decided to visit, I'd been right there on the main floor, ready to greet her.

She didn't show up until three.

At first, I didn't recognize her, because I expected to see a strung-out junkie. But she looked better than the last time I'd seen her. Although her overly bright eyes and the way she continually sniffed let me know she was still high.

I hung back and watched her interact with the security guard.

WHAT YOU NEED   309

"May I help you, ma'am?" he asked.

"I'm here to see my daughter."

"Does she work in this building?"

"Yes. Would I be here if she didn't?" she snapped.

"Did she arrange for a guest pass?"

"No. This is a surprise visit. Just call her. She's secretary to the president of the company or something."

"Mom?"

She whirled around. Her eyes narrowed. "Lennox? What are you doing down here?"

"Working."

A couple of seconds passed and then she laughed. "What a little liar you are, telling everyone you've got some impressive job and you answer phones at the security desk." She sneered. "God. To think I ever was the smallest bit proud of you."

Frank, the security guard, looked at me with pity. It would take one word from me and she'd be escorted from the building. I gave him a slight head shake. I'd handle this the same way I always did when it came to my mother: the hard way.

"So it's just another lie that you're fucking one of the big money bosses?"

My face flamed. "Are you trying to embarrass me?"

"Well, you tried to embarrass me, by making me ask for a person that doesn't even exist—my successful daughter."

"Hey, hey, now. I'ma ask you to refrain from such language or I'll escort you out."

"Frank, I'm taking a break. I'll be back in ten."

"Take your time."

I started to steer her toward the big windows by the front door.

"Or maybe he's the big boss you're fu—"

I stopped and got in her face. "Shut your mouth or I will have him call the cops. Because you are quite obviously high." I glanced at her big purse. "Wonder what they'd find if they searched you."

"You'd love to do that, wouldn't you?"

I didn't answer. I just stormed over to the corner and waited for her to follow. "Why are you here?"

"I told you I was coming to visit."

"Why? You don't even like me."

She notched her chin up. "You're my daughter. I don't have to like you to love you."

"Did you pick up that gem on one of those crappy day-time TV shows you're addicted to?"

"So? It's true."

"If Maxie hadn't told you that I was doing some rich guy, you wouldn't have shown up here today. You thought if you tried to embarrass me, I'd give you money to go away, didn't you?"

And there was the nasty glare. "You're a pretty girl, but I can see you haven't learned to curb that nasty tongue. No wonder you haven't got a man to marry you."

"Because having a man is your definition of success?"

"Better that than pretending answering phones is some kind of glamorous 'career,'" she said with a sneer. "I don't understand you, Lennox."

I forced myself to loosen my fists. "You've never under-stood me. So why don't you just go? Don't pretend you came here to see me. You fled to Minnesota to make Billy Ray jealous. I'm sure you've already called him and bragged about Maxie begging to hire you, and how much money you're making in tips because you're still so hot. Telling him how many guys hit on you. It's some kind of test for him to see if he hauls ass up to Minnesota to get his woman back. In the meantime, you're partying your ass off like it's 1985."

"You think you're so smart. I shoulda listened to Adam and smacked—"

"Ladies. Is there a problem here?"

Brady. God. I needed to hear his voice, but I didn't want him here for this. I didn't want my mom to know that I'd fallen for this sweet, sexy, warm, funny and loving man. The fact he had money didn't matter to me, but all my mother would ever see when she looked at him was dollar signs. Let her think I was too bitchy to "catch" a man. Let her think I had delusions of grandeur about my job. It'd always been easier for her to believe a lie than see the truth.

"Miss Greene?"

"No, Mr. Lund, there's no problem. I was just giving her directions and she's about to leave."

"Frank said—"

"I'm sorry I left my post. I'm going back there right now."

My mother gave me a disgusted once-over, wiped her nose on the sleeve of her coat and said, "You're pathetic." Then she walked away.

Breathe.

"Lennox."

"Give me a moment."

He moved in behind me, there if I needed him.

But I could control this. I'd been doing it for years.

I watched her until she got into a cab.

Please be gone, out of my life for good.

I flinched when Brady put his hands on my arms.

That didn't deter him. "Who was that?"

"No one."

"Lennox, who—?"

"I told you. She's no one to me."

He sighed into my hair.

Despite my emotional state, I loved these little pockets of sweetness he gave me. I didn't even mind that we were in the lobby, where any of my coworkers could see us together.

"Come upstairs with me."

"I can't. I'm on phone duty for another hour and a half."

"Someone else can take over."

I faced him and tried to put myself back together. "While I'm happy you want to be my loving, protective man, right now I need to keep up a false front. I can't afford to fall apart."

"And it's too much to ask me to hold you together? That's what I'm supposed to do, dammit. That's what I *want* to do."

"Later. Okay?"

He retreated and ran his hand through his hair. "Okay. But you'd better be on your way up to my office at five oh one."

I got a text from Brady fifteen minutes before five saying that he'd be on an overseas conference call that would last a while and I shouldn't wait around for him.

He didn't mention me going to his place to wait, so I was at loose ends. I'd been prepared to lean on him, tell him why my mother had shown up today, but now he was occupied. I could ask Sydney if she wanted to grab a drink . . . but then I remembered she'd said earlier that she had a date tonight.

I'd decided to go home when I saw Brady's sister, Annika, leaving the building. I called out her name.

She turned around, her eyes searching the crowd until she saw me. She smiled. I hadn't noticed before that she and Brady had the same smile. "Hey. What are you doing down here?"

"Subbing for the desk clerk."

She whistled. "Who'd you piss off to score that crap job?"

"No idea. Are you done for the day?"

"Yep. I was debating on whether to head for the gym or the bar."

"I could use a drink or twenty, if you don't mind me tagging along with you to the bar."

"Thank god. I always feel pathetic drinking alone."

"People act like you're just sitting there, waiting for guys to hit on you."

Annika nodded. "Let's avoid the usual places around here. There's a piano bar six blocks over, if you don't mind walking."

"I could use the fresh air."

"Cool."

We didn't talk while we walked, but it wasn't weird.

Or it wasn't until we were seated in a corner with our two-for-one drinks, away from the hipster happy hour crowd, and I caught Annika studying me.

I'd never played the shrinking violet very well. It occurred to me that maybe Annika didn't know that. I'd been quiet and efficient when I was assigned to her department. At the Lund family thing, I'd been more watchful than talkative. So she probably didn't know what to think of me and maybe that put us on even ground.

"Let's get the personal stuff out of the way first."

"Shoot."

Annika leaned in. "I like you. I like you with my brother. He's been all business for so long I'm happy to see he's having a life. You get him, don't you?"

"You mean, do I call him on his shit? Yes. I see the man beneath the power suits and the haughty attitude and the math brain. But it's only because he's chosen to show me the sweet, sexy and kinky sides. I appreciate how rare that is for him."

Her eyes widened. "Kinky? Umm, TMI, Lennox. He's my brother."

I grinned. "Just seeing if you're paying attention."

"Jerk."

"I'm glad you like me. Your mother . . . not so much."

"She's playing a part. She'll get tired of it, trust me." Annika slurped down her drink. Then I watched a change come over her. The same kind of *Let's get to business* expression Brady had.

Uh. Oh.

"You've been in the office temp department for almost a year. Is that where you're the happiest? Because it's something different every day?"

"That's part of the appeal. Why?"

"Where do you see yourself in five years?"

Why did people in positions of power ask this question? Was it supposed to prove loyalty? "I see myself on a houseboat in the Philippines cooking empanadas and fried plantains."

Annika laughed. "Points for creativity. Maybe you should be applying to Marketing instead of PR."

"Applying?" My heart jumped into my throat. "This is a job interview?"

"I told you I wanted you on my team, Lennox. You've had almost eight months of floating to other departments. And tell me, did you feel overqualified to sit at a desk in reception and answer phones? Did you feel like your potential was being wasted?"

I squirmed.

"Truth."

"Yes."

"Good. That's what I want to hear. Look, I have no doubt that you could run the clerical support program when Lola decides to retire. The money would be good. It wouldn't be a huge challenge. There's nothing wrong with wanting that type of job."

"But?"

"But PR is faster paced. We have more autonomy. That's not to say we don't have rules—we do; it's just no one knows them."

I laughed.

"Let's cut to the chase. There will be an opening in PR in three weeks. Are you interested?"

"You want honesty? Here it is. I'm not interested in the creative side. I like order. I like lists. I like checking things off my list. I like checking to see if others have checked things off their lists. I like to work with other employees, not clients. I can't sell anything to save my life."

Annika stared at me and I thought I'd blown it.

Until she said, "I have a crazy girl crush on you right now, Lennox Greene." She laughed. "You are exactly what my department needs. That's why I was vague on the details of what the job entails, because I wondered if you wanted to be on the creative side. Now that I know you are more the math brain type like Brady, I want you to come to work for me. You'll be challenged—you'll be the queen of lists in Post-it note creative chaos. And the money is rockin'."

She gave me a starting salary amount that dropped my jaw.

"Now your turn for truth, Annika Lund. Is that number because I'm involved with your brother?"

"That's industry standard salary for one year's experience." She sipped her second drink. "Look it up."

"I will."

"I understand you'll probably want time to think it over, but don't take too long, because the job gets listed on Tuesday. And before you ask, yes, I have full hiring and firing authority, and it is not a requirement for me to post the job opening. I can hire and promote at will." She grinned. "It's good to be me."

I drained my drink. "You know what? I don't need time to think about this. I'd be delighted to work for you, Annika."

She clapped her hands. "You won't regret this. And you know you'll fit right in."

I'd loved working in PR, and I would've snapped that job up except for the fact I'd wanted more experience and a more solid employment record. Now that I had that . . . look out. I glanced up at her. "Will it bother you if people in the company assume that I got the job because I'm involved with Brady?"

"Nope."

"What if things go south between me and your brother?"

Annika rolled her eyes. "I'm hiring you, not him. I wouldn't put it past him to do some dumbass thing to test your commitment to him, because he is a man, but it won't be intentional. Just do me a favor—don't tell him I hired you until you officially give notice."

"Sure. Should I give notice tomorrow?"

"Yes." Annika held up her glass. "To you making my work life easier."

I touched my glass to hers. "Sounds like a plan."

"Now. Tell me every little thing about you, Lennox."

That's when I burst into tears.

Twenty-two

BRADY

I didn't have time for this bullshit personnel meeting. I had fifty other irons in the fire, and trying to get everything done in forty hours—okay, maybe fifty hours—a week instead of eighty hours had proved to be a serious challenge. Jenna had picked up some of the slack and had delegated her basic secretarial duties to Patrice. When Patrice heard I had a girlfriend, she'd stopped being moon-eyed over me and actually began to do her job.

Before I walked into the sixteenth-floor conference room, Jenna took me aside. "I just heard about this."

"What? This meeting? Join the club."

"No, the topic of this meeting. There haven't been any whispers about it from my usual sources, which should've set off my alarm bells."

"Whatever. I need to get this over with."

"Brady."

I froze. And turned around slowly. My admin never called me by my first name.

"You have to know this so you don't go in there blind." She grabbed the sleeve of my suit and dragged me around the corner. "Anita has a problem with the temp department. That's why she ordered a thorough investigation."

"I know. The oversight committee ended the investigation last week. I'm still waiting on the results."

"The results are in. I just heard that from—never mind. The point is, they gave the results and their recommendation to Ash, not you."

"Why?" I asked, even though I knew exactly why.

"Because you're involved with Lennox. According to my source, Anita believes you can't be impartial about the department when your girlfriend's employment is at stake. So she requested the COO look at the report with a recommendation before it goes to Finance."

"Which means Anita is recommending dissolving that department."

"I would assume so." She blew out a frustrated breath. "Okay, that's a lie. I know that's what she's already done because she bragged about it to Lola."

"You're kidding me."

Jenna shook her head. "Lola has been talking to me for the last few weeks. As head of Personnel, Anita has access to all of the classified information regarding annual reviews and employee reprimands. Some of the documents that the temps have delivered to Lola have been mysteriously lost after Lola logs them. And it's not a coincidence that the ones that are missing are from the admins that Anita is tight with."

"Who else knows about this?"

"I guess Lennox figured it out. When she brought up the

missing paperwork with Ash, he referred her back to his admin. His admin threw a fit about a lowly temp overstepping her bounds and Anita was going to fire Lennox outright, but Lola intervened. Since then, Lola has been giving Lennox lower-level clerical jobs until her annual review. Then her position is somewhat safer."

"How did this get so fucked, Jenna?"

"Your girl is too smart and too much of a go-getter—that's what this company needs, but instead of being promoted for it, she's been held back, and that pisses me off." Her eyes glittered. "This bullshit has gone on long enough. I don't know what immunity Anita has through your uncle, but I'd like to think the CEO wouldn't stand behind a woman like that who's freely allowed to carry out corporate sabotage."

"Can you get me proof of any of this?"

She ran her hand through her hair. "Yes. Lola swears she documented everything. There are two immediate problems, though."

"Which are?"

"First, the meeting is happening now and I'll need time to sort through everything so you have all the documentation at your disposal. You can't take this on without it. Second, your impartiality will be questioned since you're involved with her."

"Sounds like this began months ago, before Lennox and I started dating. So it won't be an issue—I won't allow it to be." Renee and Zach from my department walked by and I gave them a head nod before I lowered my voice. "I authorize overtime for you and Lola and anyone else you trust to get all the data compiled. I don't care if it takes us all night."

"Us?"

I lifted an eyebrow at her. "Did you forget that a large portion of my job is finding and reporting discrepancies?"

She laughed. "Yes, I guess I did."

"Batten down the hatches—it's about to get rough."

I straightened my tie and grabbed the file folder from Jenna's hands. "Make sure IT knows that no computer security changes are to be authorized for the next forty-eight hours. I don't need Anita getting wind of this and blocking access. If anyone questions the order, tell them it has to do with a financial matter you're not at liberty to disclose."

She rolled her eyes while offering me a tight smile. "This ain't my first rodeo, boss."

I strolled into the conference room and made a mental note of everyone who was there. Anita and her secretary. Ash, his admin and her secretary. Nolan's admin. Renee. Zach. Gaby from HR. I didn't see Lola. I smiled, knew it looked strained and didn't care.

"While I'm not entirely certain what this meeting pertains to, and as my department received the memo a full day later than the other departments"—I looked at Anita—"your color-coding system gets a big fail for that, by the way—I can assume this is not an emergency. Since I do have a real crisis under way with one of the banks we deal with in China, this meeting will be postponed until eleven o'clock tomorrow. Any additional questions can be directed to my admin in the morning."

I walked out.

LENNOX

'd come in thirty minutes early to talk to Lola and give her my two weeks' notice.

Her office door was closed. As were her blinds.

Unusual.

Unsure what to do, I took a seat in the hallway and tried to keep my nervous fidgeting to a minimum. I checked my phone for the fifth time—no messages, no missed calls from Brady. He didn't seem the type to cut off all communication when he was upset. Then again, hadn't I done that to him? Cut him off when he'd just wanted to offer me comfort?

I closed my eyes. To further complicate matters, after four cocktails the whole mess with my mother had poured out to Annika. I'd cried like a freakin' little girl in front of the woman who would be my boss.

The defensive voice inside me retorted that I needed to talk to someone, and better her than to lay the burden at Brady's feet. Annika had been so warm and understanding. She'd mentioned issues with her own mother, but then she brushed them aside as trivial when compared with what I'd dealt with. It hadn't occurred to me that Brady might be upset that I'd spoken to his sister about my troubles rather than to him.

I watched the time tick away until fifteen minutes had passed.

Then the door opened. I stood and Jenna, Brady's admin, hustled out and rushed past me without a word.

Why was Jenna down here talking to Lola?

Not my business. I smoothed the wrinkles from my skirt and approached the partially opened door, knocking twice.

The barked "Enter" should've been my first indication that all wasn't well. The instant Lola saw me, her scowl deepened. "Lennox. What is it?"

I've come to tell you I received a great opportunity for advancement within Lund Industries. I'll be assuming the position of office manager for the PR department in two weeks. I've enjoyed working with you.

But of course that wasn't what I said. I blurted out, "I'm quitting."

"Shut the damn door."

I did as she asked and then lowered into the chair in front of her desk, which sat a good foot below her throne.

"You're quitting. And of all the days you decide to tell me . . . of course you choose today."

It didn't make any sense to me, since I'd just been offered the job last night. "Yes. That's company policy—"

"Oh, stuff the company policy and procedure. That's what this whole mess is about."

"Umm . . . pardon?"

She scrutinized me. "Did you have advance knowledge of this?"

I didn't know how to answer.

"Did Mr. Lund give you a heads-up last night to offer your resignation so you didn't get caught in the net and go down with the rest of us?"

"Lola. I didn't see Brady last night. I have no idea what you're talking about."

"Sure you don't. And to think that your questions about procedure and protocol are what started all this. Well, that chaps my ass, girl. Big-time."

I wondered if I was witnessing some kind of psychotic break when she shook her finger at me and warned, "Don't you breathe a word of this to anyone. Got it?"

"Absolutely. We are talking about me giving notice, right?"

She looked at me and laughed. "Yeah, that's all we're talking about." She pointed at the door. "Get to work. You're still on main-floor reception the rest of this week."

Great. "Thank you."

She muttered something and spun her chair away from me.

Well, that hadn't gone as I would've liked. But at least I'd gotten it out of the way.

And I was actually happy to be away from the craziness on the sixth floor for the day.

I didn't eat lunch in the break room. I found a lunch counter on the other side of the tower that catered to lone diners, with single seats and no booths. Otherwise I would have been too tempted to tell Sydney my news. While I trusted her, I suspected she'd be upset I was leaving and essentially moving up before she did. Then again, Syd hadn't struck me as the ambitious type—not that there was anything wrong with staying in one place and doing a job you enjoyed.

That brought my mind back to my conversation with Brady Saturday night.

I had been sprawled facedown on his big bed, my body limp and sated after Brady had proven to me for the third time how much he'd missed me while he'd been traveling. His fingers were trailing up and down my spine, and he'd stop every once in a while and feather his lips over my tattoos.

"You have the most beautiful skin."

"Why do you say that?"

"Because it's true. It's pale, almost translucent. No freckles or sunspots. No scars."

"I've been called a vampire a time or two. But I've never been a sun lover. Not for any reason besides until recently I'd always worked until late at night and slept away most of the day. Cocktail waitressing is the ultimate SPF 100."

"I can't believe with how smart you are, and how hard you work, that you weren't offered managerial positions."

"Oh, I was. But I turned them down."

"Why?"

"Because I had more freedom just clocking in, taking care of my customers and clocking out at the end of the shift.

I looked at the managers and felt sorry for the poor bastards. Scheduling nightmares, staff that doesn't show up for their shifts, or they show up high. Then they also had to deal with jerky customers and complaints. Plus doing all the ordering."

"Sounds like you really thought that through."

I rolled over to face him. "I saw a lot in ten years. I mean, technically, I wasn't old enough to be serving drinks, but I had an ID that said I was. So by the time I turned twenty-one for real? I'd been a cocktail waitress for five years."

"None of your bosses ever said, 'Hey, you don't look older than seventeen, girlie'?"

"At first. But after I'd worked a few nights, they didn't care." I ran my fingers through the dark hair on his chest. "So I'm also living proof that a work ethic isn't inherited. My mother is lazy."

"Then I'd say your work ethic was learned from what not to do, which can be just as powerful a motivator, Lennox. Sometimes even more so." He bent his head and traced the tattoo on my biceps with his tongue, sending gooseflesh rippling across my neck.

"I don't mean to sound like a recruitment poster, but why not do your job better than you thought you could? Where's the satisfaction in being average? No matter where I worked, I took the job seriously. If I saw someone doing something wrong, I called them out on it. And if not them, at least the supervisor, and that puts me back to exactly why I didn't try for a managerial position. I'd have to deal with someone like me."

Brady chuckled against the curve of my breast.

"That tickles."

"Mmm. Not sorry." Then he looked at me. "So I shouldn't be worried that you're gunning for my job at LI?"

"Don't be ridiculous. The best I can hope for is an office manager position. Doing what Lola does."

"Or what Jenna does?"

"God, no. Because then I'd have to deal with you or someone like you."

His eyes glittered when he lightly bit down on my nipple. "Hey!"

"Sorry. I'll kiss it and make it better, baby."

And he did.

I shook myself out of the memory because I could sit here all damn day and moon over how thoroughly my man had seen to my needs all weekend.

I pulled out my phone and texted him: *I miss you. Can we talk?*

Less than thirty seconds later he replied: *Sorry. Swamped. I'll text you later.*

At least I'd gotten a response.

I made it through another day of answering phones. Just two days left this week. It made me wonder what crappy jobs I'd get my last week in the floating pool.

I returned to the sixth floor and the place was like a graveyard. Spooky. After I finished the report, I remembered I didn't have to do that anymore since the audit was done.

On impulse I took the elevator to the forty-fourth floor.

Jenna wasn't at her post, so I wandered down the hall. The door to Brady's office was propped open, which was also spooky.

Brady's angry voice drifted out. "What else did she screw up?"

"I'm trying to find it."

"Christ, how did this happen? It's not like filing office documents is rocket science."

A sick feeling took root in the pit of my stomach.

"Why wasn't she supervised?" he demanded.

"They have some autonomy, sir."

It'd taken me a moment, but then I recognized the voice as Lola's.

What was Lola doing in Brady's office?

"I don't care who signed off on her. She doesn't get to move to a different department without answering to me."

Holy crap. Had Lola approached Brady because I'd given my two weeks' notice?

I saw Brady throw a folder on the desk. "I should've seen this coming."

"Sir, with all due respect, you couldn't have known."

"Everyone has talked about how ambitious she is. She was even invited to Lund family functions."

My heart stopped.

"She thinks just because we—" He made a snarling sound. "I'll fire her ass myself. And I'll make sure she's unhireable everywhere else in the Cities."

Oh. God. I clapped my hand over my mouth.

"Lennox."

I faced the sharp-toned whisperer.

Jenna said, "You can't be here."

I wanted to demand an explanation for why I didn't have a say in this—I'd done nothing wrong except take what was offered to me.

"Go."

I left.

Afterward I didn't remember much of the drive home except for sitting in the driveway and watching the snow fall in big puffy flakes until I couldn't see out the windows and I began to get cold.

Kiley had company—a man, by the sounds of it. So I quietly crept up the stairs and into my room. I lay on the bed fully clothed in my outerwear and stared at the ceiling, absolutely numb.

Eventually I overheated in my hat, mittens, wool coat, scarf and snow boots. I needed to cool off and shut down the endless loop of questions circling my brain.

I shed every piece of clothing and crawled between the sheets naked. I slipped in my earbuds and cranked my MP3 to hearing-damage levels.

But it worked. I fell asleep and I didn't dream.

The next morning I woke up to the "We're Not Gonna Take It" anthem by Twisted Sister.

It was exactly the kick in the ass I needed.

Furious, I got dressed, drove to work and stormed into Lund Industries with all the swagger I could muster. I took off my coat and turned around.

Sydney, Penny, Belinda and Margie gaped at me.

"What? You've never seen tattoos?"

"Uh, we've never seen them on you, Lennox."

"Yeah, well, I got tired of wearing itchy sweaters all the time to cover them up."

"The lip ring is cool," Penny said. Then she confessed, "I've been debating on getting my nipples pierced."

With the tight shirts she wore . . . that was not a good plan.

I said, "I had mine done and let them close up. It was more annoying than I thought it'd be."

"Good to know. Thanks."

I glanced over at Lola's closed door. "Is she in there?"

"She was. I got a peek at it before she ran out. Her office looked like someone ransacked it." Penny wrinkled her nose. "She'd better not expect one of us to file all of it."

It's not like filing office documents is rocket science.

I hated hearing that sentiment echoing in my head, especially when that was so unlike the Brady I knew and loved.

Sydney poked the tattoo on my arm. "I'm happy you're not hiding these anymore. They're much more mainstream." She cocked her head at me. "I heard that Brady got a tattoo. Rumor is he got a shark bursting out of where his heart would be. Is there any truth to that?"

"I'll never tell."

"I know you're working on the main floor today, but please come upstairs and have lunch with me."

"You've got it."

And I held my head high as I went to the reception area to answer the damn phones.

I'd taken one bite of my soup when she walked in wearing a gorgeous fur coat that brushed her ankles. Her gaze swept the room in that haughty demeanor few women could pull off—but of course she did.

Then Selka Lund looked right at me. And started toward me.

I sat up straighter. I wasn't a bootlicker and she could just deal with that.

She stopped just short of the table. "Lennox. A moment of your time, please."

"I was just having lunch with my friend—"

"It's fine," Sydney said. "Go ahead. I'll catch up with you later."

Pushing my chair back, I grabbed my lunch combo and headed to the back of the room.

She followed and sat across from me. "I haven't been in here for ages."

I wasn't in the mood for small talk. "Mrs. Lund. Why are you here?"

"I was too hasty in judgment of you."

Not the same thing as an apology. "Okay. And . . . ?"

"And two things I'd like to talk about today. First thing. I hear your roommate, this Kiley, is very special social worker, yah?"

"Yes. She's a wonderful person. She is appreciative of the caliber of the volunteers LCCO sends to help out."

"Of course she is. We strive for best." She leaned in and her long hair, almost the same color as mine, brushed the table. "Brady said their regular meeting place had been changed."

"Closed down completely. So Kiley has been getting creative in finding places for them to go on Saturdays. But she's afraid the kids will stop coming, especially now since it's the start of winter and she's running out of options. Why do you ask?"

"Why didn't she ask LCCO for help?"

"She did. LCCO sent Brady as a volunteer."

"No. Help in finding a permanent space. We have many buildings at our disposal. Tell Kiley to call this number." She reached in her pocket and pulled out a business card. "We will get her fixed up in a place at no charge."

I barely kept my jaw from dropping—or from whipping out my phone and texting Kiley right then. "She'll be thrilled. Thank you so much, Mrs. Lund."

"Second thing. You and my son."

I bristled automatically.

"You like him."

"Yes." *Very much but I'm pretty sure that's a moot point.*

"When we first meet, I thought you were like Loki—the trickster. Telling me what a mother wants to hear about her child." At my blank look, she said, "You talked about Brady being so kind. That is not how he is viewed. It surprised me equally that you saw it in him as it did that he showed that part of himself to you."

How was I supposed to respond to that?

"Annika spoke to me about you." She sighed. "She and I are what you call . . . Polaroid opposites."

"Polar opposites?"

"Yes, that. Anyway, my daughter and I fight. Hard. But it's never mean. And it doesn't mean we don't love each other fiercely, like tigers."

I held my breath, afraid where this was going.

"Annika . . . told me about your mother and all the horrible things she said." Then I watched as Selka Lund's eyes filled with tears. "I am broken up for you. I don't understand how love for a child could ever be soured. It's been bitter for you, yes?"

"Yes."

"And yet, you're not bitter person."

I shook my head. "Some days I am. Annika caught me on one of those days."

Selka reached for my hand. "What you said to my daughter had her calling me in tears. She thanked me for loving her and for not being cruel to her. She shouldn't have to thank me because that is a mother's job. To love without conditioners."

"Conditions," I corrected.

She waved aside my correction. "And after hearing that, I realized why kindness is important to you. Why you picked that word above all others to describe Brady. Because you haven't had much kindness in your life, have you?"

My eyes welled up because I'd wanted this from her, and I was getting it only now that things were over between me and Brady.

"My son, he will be good for you. And I see that you are good for him. He opens his home and his heart to you."

"Mrs. Lund, as much as I want that, I'm afraid that Brady and I are done." At her blank look, I said, "We're over. Finished."

"Why in the hell would you think that, Lennox?" Brady said behind me.

Twenty-three

BRADY

Lennox stared at me as if she was seeing a ghost. "Brady? What are you doing here?"

"I work here." I glanced over at my mother. "The better question is what are *you* doing here, Mom?"

"Visiting my daughter and I ran over Lennox."

"Ran into," I corrected.

"Yah, whatever." She waved her hand. "We were—"

"Finished," I said, running my hand down Lennox's bare arm. Why'd she pick today to let her tats show? And she'd worn her lip piercing. I made a low noise. For some reason I felt possessive of that damn piercing and didn't want anyone—especially other men—to see how sexy she looked with it. "Lennox, I need to speak with you privately."

Panic flashed on her face.

Why on earth was she scared of me? I reached for her hand.

She stood, but she tugged her hand free. "I'm a big girl. I don't need hand-holding for this."

That was a strange thing for her to say and so I stuck close behind her as we left the break room. But instead of heading for the bank of elevators, she cut down a side hallway and walked through the open door of a conference room. "What are we doing in here?"

Lennox spun around and took two steps back from me. "I don't particularly want to do the walk of shame through your suite of offices, in front of your admin and her secretary, and then have to do it again on my own floor. Just get it out of the way so I can get my shit packed up and get out of here."

I moved in close enough to smell her breath.

"Omigod, you've *got* to be kidding me! You think I've been drinking?"

"You are acting irrationally."

"Under the circumstances, who would blame me? Maybe it would've been easier if you'd done this over the phone."

"Done what?"

She tossed up her hands. "Fired me!"

"Why would I fire you?" I searched her eyes for some answers to her behavior. "I'm not your boss."

Confusion darkened her gaze. "But . . . I heard you. Yesterday afternoon. I came up to talk to you and you were ranting in your office about me and how I was misleading and ambitious and you planned to fire me yourself."

"Why would you assume I was talking about you?"

"Because Lola was in your office, Brady. She *is* my boss. And since I gave her my notice yesterday—"

"Whoa. What do you mean, you gave her your notice yesterday? You're quitting LI?"

Lennox appeared even more confused. "Lola didn't tell you?"

"Lola was in my office pertaining to another matter. I purposely asked her to keep you out of the things she and I discussed, unless it was relevant to our fact-finding mission. Now tell me why're quitting LI?"

She paced forward. Stopped. Turned around. "I'm not quitting LI. I'm resigning my position in the temp department because Annika offered me a better position in PR."

Although I wish I'd heard the news under better circumstances, I couldn't help but smile. "Lennox, that is awesome. Congratulations. You will thrive there."

"Thanks. So I'm not fired?"

"Not that I'm aware of."

"Then who is? Because when I heard, 'I don't care who signed off on her. She doesn't get to move to a different department without answering to me,' it sure sounded like it could've been me. And then you went on to indicate that she wouldn't get immunity or sympathy because we're—" She frowned. "You didn't actually finish that train of thought. Then you mentioned, 'She's been to Lund family functions,' which I also took to mean me because I went to the football game."

Where had my admin been while Lennox was listening at the door?

She answered my question next as if she'd read my mind. "Then Jenna showed up and told me I shouldn't be there. So I left and spent all night and this morning waiting for the summons to get the ax."

"First off, even if I was your boss and there was an issue with your job performance, is my reputation as a ruthless bastard so cemented that even after being intimately involved with me, you believe I wouldn't have given you a chance to tell your side of the story?"

"I . . . don't know."

"That's bullshit, Lennox. You do too know."

"You were so angry, Brady. I've never heard you speak like that. It scared me. It made me think that I didn't know you like I thought I did."

"Wrong. You know me better than anyone has in a long time. And after I've continually reassured you throughout our relationship that nothing that happens between us personally will affect your job, you still doubt me."

She closed her eyes. "I doubt *me*. And once those doubts creep in, or they're pointed out, I cannot get them out of my head."

"So that's why you're showing off your ink today? Because you figured you didn't have anything else to lose since you thought you were getting fired?"

Her eyes flew open. "I hate that you read me so well."

"You're the only one I can do that with." I slowly erased the distance between us. "I'm sorry you had a rough night." I kissed the top of her head. "I know it's not a good excuse, but I had a very tight deadline. We worked until two A.M. and then I sent Jenna and Lola home. I had phone conferences this morning and a meeting at—"

She briefly put her fingers over my mouth. "You don't have to explain or justify your schedule to me, CFO Lund. You are a very busy, very important man to LI."

"Just to LI?"

"No." She looked me square in the eyes so I could see everything in hers. "You're very important to me."

I pressed my forehead to hers. "Lennox. Please tell me you know that we're not finished. That you understand there wasn't even a chance of us being over."

"I'd hoped. But things don't usually go the way I want. I tried to prepare myself."

"For what?" *Please don't say the worst.*

"For what came next." She disentangled from me and stepped away. "I've had two days of pure crap, thinking I'd lost my job, and probably my boyfriend, plus the added bonus of dealing with my mother."

Her mother? Then it clicked. "Wait. The woman I saw you with that day downstairs—?"

"Yes, that was her."

"I'm so sorry. I didn't know, or I would have—"

"I didn't *want* you to know, Brady—that's why I acted like you were my boss, not my—"

Anger flared through me at her inability to say the word, but I forced it down. "If I had known, then I would have had the right to be there for you as your *boyfriend*. But instead you didn't tell me a damn thing."

"You texted me that you were busy. I've never been the type to unburden myself where I'm not wanted."

"That's what you think? That I don't want you?"

Lennox briefly closed her eyes. "Can we please not do this here?"

"Tell me why your mother came to see you."

"She showed up for a multitude of reasons." Her jaw tightened. "The only one regarding me was that she'd 'heard' I was involved with a man who was well-off and she wanted to see for herself." Her eyes narrowed on mine. "You want to know how she 'heard' that? Your brother Walker got chatty with Maxie at the bar. He filled Maxie in—Maxie, who is my mother's best friend—and she reported to my mother the good fortune that I'd landed myself a guy with cash to spare."

What the hell was wrong with Walker that he talked

about private family stuff to a stranger in a random bar? *That's beside the point, isn't it? Get back to her.* "What else did your mother say to you?"

"It doesn't matter. I talked to Annika about it and that helped."

"Annika? You could talk to her about it but not me?"

"I tried to talk to you, but you were busy."

"Bullshit. I would've dropped everything to be there for you."

"How was I supposed to know that?"

My eyes took on a glint I didn't bother to hide. "That's the point I'm trying to make. You *wouldn't* know that because you keep an emotional distance from me—and not because I'm an owner in the company you work for. Do you know how deep that slices me, Lennox? Hearing that you were hurting and you didn't think I was important enough to share that with?"

Those beautiful eyes widened, as if that was the first time she'd considered it. "I'm sorry."

"So am I."

Her phone buzzed and she pulled it out to check the time. "My lunch break is over."

"I don't give a damn. Take the afternoon off. We're not done here."

Her tone was as snappish as her eyes. "I may be changing departments, but that doesn't change how I work. And if you don't know that about me—"

I smashed my mouth to hers and hauled her close, my fingers circling the smooth skin of her strong biceps. I kissed her with hunger and finesse, with possession. My body reminding hers how well I knew it. Reminding her how good it was between us.

Lennox melted into me. Giving me the sweet fire she

always did. Making me want to get on my knees and thank the universe for bringing her into my life. Making me want to stand on the top of the tallest structure and proclaim my devotion to her. How could she imagine that there'd ever be anyone else for me?

Show her, dumbass. Don't tell her.

I released her mouth with just as much confidence as I'd taken it. "You're right. Let's not do this here. Come over tonight."

"When?"

"Seven. Unless you want to come upstairs when you're done and ride home with me."

"I'll drive over. I need to talk to Kiley first."

"About you not getting fired?"

She looked away. "I wasn't eager to tell the woman who counts on rent from me that I was about to be out of a job."

I tipped her chin back toward me. "Hopefully she'll figure out you're headed to my place for hot makeup sex as you're racing out the door with an overnight bag."

"Brady. Don't push."

"I'm the pushy type, baby. You know that about me, so you've got to expect I'm not going to sit back and wait when it's been days since we've been alone together." I brushed my mouth across hers. "Days since I kissed you." Another teasing kiss. "Days since I touched you."

Her eyes heated.

Good.

"I said I'd come over. But first I need to relay information to Kiley from your mom."

"My mom?" That was scary.

Lennox smirked. "It worries you, what your mom and I talked about?"

"No," I lied.

Her phone beeped again. "I've gotta go."

I kissed her again. "See you at seven."

I wasn't surprised that my uncle Monte, my dad, Ash, Nolan and I were called into Uncle Archer's private conference room. I was surprised to be the last one to arrive, however.

"Brady. Have a seat."

"Thanks."

"What the hell happened in the Personnel department today?" Uncle Archer zeroed in on me with his *I don't have time for bullshit* CEO stare.

"Bluntly? Anita Mohr has had way too much power for too long. Blatant disregard of company protocols. Leveling verbal threats at other employees. Misdirection. Extreme nepotism." I felt both Ash and Nolan studying me. "This time she's beyond your protection, sir."

"My protection?" He truly seemed shocked. "Why would you say that?"

"Anita has made no bones about telling anyone who disagrees with her that she has the ear of the CEO and isn't afraid to use it."

"Who'd believe that?"

"Everyone, sir. She makes them believe it. And maybe it's a scare tactic, but it works."

"For example?"

I filled him in on the HR complaints, the missing performance reviews and the bogus investigation after discrepancies were discovered. I didn't mention Lennox or Nolan's admin or Ash's admin's part. After the morning meeting they'd assured me they'd deal with the fallout. Ash had slipped into quiet anger mode and I could tell he hadn't slipped back out of it yet several hours later.

Archer nodded. "Thank you. How did all of this come to your attention? I've never heard of you getting mixed up in personnel matters, Brady."

"After I became CFO, Anita was my admin for a few weeks until Jenna got up to speed. She's used that to her advantage too. She overstepped her bounds, claiming she had the power to fire two of my junior staff members from Finance if they refused to run oversight in her investigation. Now she's trying to permanently move them from their respective departments. I wouldn't have heard anything about this, including the audit, except for the fact I'm dating Lennox Greene and, as you know, she works in the temp department, which was under investigation."

"Lennox spoke to you about a departmental audit?" Uncle Monte asked me with an edge.

"No, sir. Her coworker mentioned it to me. And that's a moot point, because knowing that a department is undergoing an audit is not a confidential matter. Normally I see only the end recommendation as far as the potential financial impact. I kept an eye on the process this time, initially because I was ignorant about the duties of that subdepartment. After Lennox and I became involved, I continued to get updates—but not from Lennox. I was blindsided by Anita's recommendation to eliminate that department entirely. I conducted my own investigation and found contrary evidence."

"So these incidents have nothing to do with you protecting your relationship with Lennox?"

"My relationship with Lennox has not affected my decision in any way and that will continue since Lennox will be working for Annika in PR starting next week."

Ash and Nolan exchanged a look that wasn't lost on me.

Archer sighed. "I hate this shit. Hate it. We place qualified people in these positions so we don't have to deal with this inconsequential crap that has no bearing on what we do in running the company. Fire Anita. Immediately."

I was about to open my mouth to argue, but my father beat me to it.

"I hate to disagree with you, Archer, but if Anita buried evidence of her wrongdoing within the company, what's to keep her from wreaking havoc with our competitors? If we fire her, she'll go to them and we'll have lost any ability for damage control."

Smart man, my father.

Archer looked at me, then at Ash, because this was Ash's area of expertise. "Ash?"

His voice was so low and so deadly we all strained to hear him. "I've thought about this. I've thought about little else since this came to light. If we fire Anita, I expect she'll take us to court even though she knows she'll lose. But she has nothing to lose because of union rules. She will continue to collect a paycheck during litigation, no matter how long it drags out. We won't dick around with her pension because we've never been that kind of a company. But we obviously cannot fire her or leave her in her present position." He smiled nastily. "That leaves us no choice but to reassign her to the Duluth office."

Silence.

Nolan laughed first. "Absolutely brilliant. If I remember correctly, the last contract we came to terms with the union provided for mobility within the company with no penalties— the employee's position change could be management led or employee requested. But if the employee refused the managerial decision and resigned their position, they give up any right to future litigation, and they're prevented from working for a competitor for a year."

"She can put whatever spin she likes on it. She's only—what, two years from retirement? If she quits and has to sit out a year, no company will hire her. Sad fact of life."

"You're certain she'll take the job?" Archer said to Ash.

"Relatively. If she does, she won't have autonomy. She'll answer to Zosia."

A collective groan sounded.

Our cousin Zosia Lund defined hard-ass—and she wasn't even thirty. She and her brother, Zeke, had come to us a decade ago when their father had put their fishing and shipping company in Duluth close to bankruptcy. We'd bailed them out and brought them under the Lund Industries banner. They'd rebuilt the business and were back up to one hundred employees. I wished I could see the look on Anita's face when she took in all five foot nothing of our Ojibwe and Norwegian cousin. Answering to a woman three decades her junior, and dealing with personnel in what amounted to a glorified fishing shack, would be the worst sort of punishment for Anita.

"Well, I, for one, am happy to see how well all of you have handled this matter," Archer said. "Any other issues I—we—should be aware of?"

Nolan, Ash and I each answered, "No."

"Good. We're adjourned."

No reason to stick around. I'd made it past the first set of doors when I heard, "Brady. Hold up."

I faced my father. "Hey."

"Got a moment?"

"Sure. What's up?"

He leaned against the hallway wall. "Is it serious between you and Lennox?"

Dad excelled in throwing me off balance. "What did Mom tell you?"

He laughed. "She told me to ask you that, and if you hedged, then I had my answer."

I shoved my hands in my suit pockets. "Is this where you tell me to take a step back? Because Lennox and I haven't been together long, so I can't know if we'll go the distance?"

"No, son, this is where I tell you that there is no standard operating procedure where love is concerned. There's no timetable. No charts and graphs to help you navigate."

"And you're telling me this . . . why?"

"Because this is one time when your smarts won't help you." He reached out and poked my chest. "Listen to what this is telling you. Your heart isn't as fickle as your dick. Your heart won't let logic dictate like your brain will. So trust in this. How you feel about her. How you feel when you're with her. But most importantly how you'd feel if you didn't have her in your life every day."

He was right. Part of me hated that he was right, because I now was at a loss for what to do next. Blow off our plans, run down to her office and declare myself?

"Son?"

"Your advice isn't helping me, Dad."

"It's not advice."

"Then what is it?"

"A warning. I know you. You overthink things. I see the wheels spinning and you're already wondering if the next step you plan to take is the right one. Be smart, be quick, but don't be hasty." He clapped me on the shoulder. "Keep your mother in the loop and she won't be forced to meddle."

I laughed.

My father grinned at me. "God, I couldn't even say that with a straight face. Good luck."

———

discovered I couldn't just sit in my loft and wait for her.

Since she defined punctual, I assumed she'd leave twenty-five minutes early, so I parked the SUV at the curb in front of her place and got out, resting against the passenger door.

My exhales created clouds of white in the cold night air. I shivered in my long coat. I hadn't bothered to go home to change. I'd just shown up.

I was so antsy I was about to crawl out of my fucking skin.

The door opened and my beautiful Lennox stepped onto the concrete stoop.

I was happy to see the duffel bag slung over her shoulder. She hadn't noticed me, as she was intent on finding solid footing on the icy sidewalk. I must've made a noise, because she looked up at me.

"Brady? What—?"

I met her in the middle of the sidewalk. "I couldn't wait."

"For what? Dinner? If you're that hungry, why don't we stop somewhere—"

I framed her face in my hands, which were cold enough on her warm skin to make her gasp. "This isn't about food."

We stared at each other.

"Truth or dare, Lennox Greene."

"Truth."

"I'm falling in love with you." I kissed her and absorbed the warmth of her mouth with mine.

"And if I would've said dare?" she whispered against my lips.

"I would've dared you to tell me how you feel about me."

I kissed her. Breathed her in. "About this." Another press of my mouth to hers. "About us." I looked into her eyes and saw everything I needed. But I wanted the words too. "Your turn."

"Truth or dare, Brady Lund."

"Truth."

"I've been half in love with you since the first time I realized your outer sharkskin protects a kind heart and your adaptability is as impressive as your sexy suits."

Such sweet honesty. "I liked the glimpses of the wild you, Lennox. But that's not all I see when I look at you."

"What do you see?"

"Beauty. Loyalty. A sharp mind. An honest heart. You're exactly what I need."

We smiled at each other for a long moment.

"Let's go before we freeze to death or before this gets too sappy."

"Agreed. You are feeding me, right?"

I slipped the duffel bag from her shoulder, and as I was straightening back up, Lennox scooped up a handful of snow and shoved it down my shirt.

"Act of war, baby. Remember, you asked for this."

I tackled her. Pinned her in the snow. Kissed her. Tried to make a double snow angel with me on top of her.

Things got a little out of hand before I buried my cold face into the crook of her neck.

"Brady! Stop! That's cold."

"Mmm. I've got some killer ideas on how we can warm up."

Twenty-four

LENNOX

FOUR MONTHS LATER . . .

"Don't take too long in there," Brady yelled to me from the bedroom. "I'm anxious to see the surprise you've got planned for me. I'm hoping it involves sexy lingerie and whipped cream."

I rolled my eyes and shut the bathroom door. After I stripped, I started to worry that my surprise was lame and would be a serious letdown for him. And that would suck because our weekend had been perfect so far.

Perfect.

Brady Lund, Mr. Freakin' Perfect, turned out to be the most perfect boyfriend ever.

I don't know why that surprised me. The man excelled at everything.

In the months we'd been dating, he'd put as much effort into our relationship as he did into his career.

It was humbling.

It was exciting.

It was life-changing.

But since Brady was the ultimate boyfriend, that meant he was always two steps ahead of me. Due to his newfound spontaneity, I was having a harder time coming up with a way to surprise him because he always thought of something way cooler first.

To mark our "anniversary," Brady had taken me back to the Lund cabin in the North Woods. In addition to forcing me to learn how to snowshoe, he'd taken me ice fishing. Then we'd attended the local Winter Festival, complete with ice-carving and snowman-making contests, an "ice wine" tasting and ending with a dance beneath the starry winter sky. The night had been magical even before we'd returned to the cabin, and he made slow, sweet, passionate love to me in front of a roaring fire. He'd even earned points for moving the bearskin rug out of the way beforehand.

As we'd returned to the Cities this afternoon, I suggested we visit his parents. Since the Vikings hadn't made the playoffs, we hadn't been spending every Sunday with his family—not that I minded hanging out with the Lunds because they were the most loving and welcoming people I'd ever been around—and I suspected Brady missed that family time. Once Selka had us in her sights, she whipped up a batch of her famous Swedish hot chocolate—who knew that vodka and chocolate mixed together would be so tasty? Then Walker, Annika and Jensen showed up, and we stayed longer than we'd planned.

At first I worried it'd be awkward working for Annika when I was involved with her brother, but so far we'd hadn't encountered any issues. I loved my new job. It challenged me, and Brady had to pry me away from my desk most nights instead of the other way around.

After we left the Lund stronghold, I asked Brady to drop me off at my house. He'd ignored me and driven straight to his place, hence his eagerness to get me into his bed.

I could admit I had gotten used to waking up with him. I'd gotten used to us inhabiting the same space when the workday ended and when the weekend began. Since I'd made such a big deal about taking things slowly, now I was having a devil of a time figuring out how to tell him I was ready to speed things up.

Two raps sounded on the door, and I jumped.

"Lennox? Baby, you all right? You've been in there a while."

"I've been in here two minutes, horndog."

He howled on the other side of the door.

Crazy man. "I'll be right there."

"Hurry. I miss you."

His sweetness killed me. Would I ever get used to the way he loved me with everything he had?

No. But now that I knew that type of forever love existed, I'd never take it for granted. I'd do everything to give that same heady feeling back to him every chance I had.

So quit stalling.

I dug out the shirt I'd stashed beneath the stack of towels. I debated whether to put it on. Would Brady think it was weird? Or stupid?

Only one way to find out.

I slipped the polo shirt on over my head, smoothed my flyaway hair and exited the bathroom.

Brady sat on the edge of the bed. When he saw me, his gaze skimmed over my bare legs and the boy-short panties to focus on the shirt I wore. "Where did you get that shirt?"

"I . . . uh . . . stole it from your closet two weeks ago when you were downstairs working out."

"What did you do to it?"

"Personalized it."

"When?"

"Last Saturday at the LCCO Outreach Center, when you were in Detroit. The craft that day was embellishing a shirt. I'm not the arty type, so I put my own spin on it."

"Want to explain why you put *your* spin on *my* shirt?" He eyed the glued-on decals warily. "Do you expect me to wear that?"

"No! This is mine." My next words came out in a rush. "Look, everyone in your family is always wearing Lund jerseys for various sports and LCCO shirts for charities, and LI shirts for corporate events, which is great and all. But I wanted you to know I'm the leader of the special team called 'Team Brady.'" I waited for him to smile at my football reference. When he didn't, I carried on.

"So I made my own version of a jersey and ironed on all these decals to represent you." I was particularly proud of the pi symbol I'd found, so I started there. "You're a numbers guy, so this is part of you. You're educated, so I added three diplomas. You have killer moves on the dance floor, so I found this one"—I pointed to a decal of a couple dancing—"although I couldn't find a tango image specifically. Since through your work at LCCO you've recently discovered you're a great teacher"—I smoothed my hand over the stack of books and the calculator below my left breast—"this also shows who you are now. I didn't have luck finding decals for cross-country skiing, but I did find this"—I spun around to show him the line of stick figures on my back—"to represent what a connected brother, son and cousin you are." I smirked at him over my shoulder. "The other thing you do so well would require pornographic stickers, so I skipped that one." He hadn't said anything, so I kept going. "The car represents your hobby of collecting cars—again, trying to find a Maybach decal was impossible." I pointed to the motorcycle at the small of my back. "A Harley, for when you're a badass biker dude in a few months." I spun around. "The heart because you're the most loving man I've ever met. The tattoo is for your boldness. The open hand is for your kindness." I paused.

He hadn't uttered a word.

"Say something."

"Why aren't the initials 'CFO' on the back of the shirt, below my name like numbers on an athletic jersey?" he demanded.

"Because this isn't about sports. You were convinced you were one-dimensional. This proves you're not. It's to show you that you're so much more than one thing. I've also left blank spaces for you to add new things that define you. And no matter what you choose to do in the future, I'll be right there with you."

Then he was off the bed and in front of me.

"You hate it, don't you?"

"No. I love it." Brady's hands framed my face, his eyes fierce. "I love you, Lennox. I'm just . . ." His eyes searched mine. "You really see all that when you look at me, don't you?"

"Yes."

He crushed me against his chest.

I held on.

"I know the next thing I want you to add on this personalized 'Team Brady' jersey," he murmured in my ear.

"What's that?"

"A key."

I leaned back and looked into his eyes, my heart racing. "What's the key symbolize?"

"This one is literal." Brady grinned and kissed my nose. "Move in with me, Lennox. I could point out that you're here most nights anyway, but the truth is you belong here with me. Let's make it official."

A thrill shot through me. "You're sure?"

"Never been more certain of anything in my life."

The love, hope and excitement I saw shining in his eyes quelled the last of my doubts.

"All right. But we've gotta set up some rules . . . Eep!" I found myself in the middle of the bed with my new roomie on top of me. "Brady!"

"You look damn good in that 'Team Brady' jersey, but it'll look way better on the floor."

Turns out, he was right about that.

Once he'd unleashed the wild man inside him, there was no putting him back in the cage.

And I wouldn't have it any other way.

Because no matter what anyone else called him—CFO, genius, shark, dork or beast—I could call him the only thing that mattered.

Mine.

DON'T MISS LORELEI JAMES'S

Wrapped and Strapped

WHICH IS AVAILABLE NOW.
CONTINUE READING FOR A PREVIEW.

Harlow Pratt panicked when she saw her sister Tierney's name on her caller ID. She answered with, "*Please* tell me you didn't go into labor a month early."

"No, that's not why I'm calling." Tierney paused. "You know Dad is here visiting. He had a heart attack."

"What? When?"

"This morning. We got him to the hospital in Rawlins right away and they opted to have him flown to the cardiac unit at Denver General."

"Is he all right?"

"He's having emergency heart bypass surgery now."

In shock, Harlow lowered herself into the closest chair. "How do you know what's going on?"

"There's a nurse who's keeping me updated because I can't travel this late in my pregnancy—"

"Don't feel guilty, T." Harlow grabbed a pen and a notepad from the nightstand. "Give me the nurse's name and extension number."

Tierney rattled off more info than necessary, but that was her way.

"Got it. Now stop pacing and put your feet up. I imagine Renner is fit to be tied." Tierney's husband's behavior defined tyrannical since Tierney had been prescribed bed rest for the last month of her pregnancy. Sometimes she needed a reminder that she had to limit her activity.

"You have no idea," Tierney whispered. "He made Hugh drive Dad and meet the ambulance halfway to town because he refused to leave me alone with Isabelle. He worried the stress would put me into labor the second he wasn't around."

"It's a valid concern." Harlow ignored the way her stomach jumped at the mere mention of the man's name.

"Where are you?"

"Still in LA." By the heavy pause, she knew what her sister was about to ask.

"Someone needs to be with Dad, Harlow. I hate to ask you to drop everything and fly to Denver—"

"But it can't be helped." Her snarky side pointed out that her father wouldn't think she was doing "real" work anyway. "I'll book a flight as soon as possible."

"Thank you. After the helicopter left Rawlins, Hugh took it upon himself to drive to Denver, which is above and beyond."

No, that was total brownnose behavior—a typical Hugh response because he'd do anything for Renner, his boss.

"And he's agreed to stay at the hospital until you get there."

Oh, *hell* no. "As soon as I have my flight info, you can call Renner's foreman and let him know I'm on my way, so there's no need for him to stick around." Did that sound harsh? Harlow didn't care. She could not deal with her father and Hugh Pritchett both on the same damn day.

"I know we've both had issues with Dad, but he was really scared," Tierney said. "I've never seen him like that. It actually scared me."

Harlow closed her eyes. "He's less of an ass to you since you're the vessel bringing forth the long-awaited grandson."

"That's not it. But Dad and I have reached a place where he can live with my life choices."

"I'm not holding my breath that'll ever happen with me."

"Your passion for what you do, Harlow—he doesn't discount it, even when he doesn't understand it," Tierney assured her.

That much was true. When her passion for service trapped her in a nightmare situation last year, he'd done everything in his power to get her out of it. She did owe him for that.

"Leaving at a moment's notice won't be an issue?" Tierney prompted.

"Not since I'm here on sabbatical."

"Do you think you'll get to Denver tonight?"

When her admission didn't register with her sister, Harlow decided to keep any explanations about recent career developments in her life to herself. "Flights leave LAX every couple of hours. You'll need to let the hospital staff know I'm on my way."

"No problem."

"Look, I'll probably be in the air when he gets out of surgery, so promise me that if the worst happens"—she knocked on the wooden window frame to ward off bad luck—"you won't tell me over text or through voice mail."

"I'd never do that."

Harlow breathed a sigh of relief. "Good."

"Love you, sis."

"Love you too."

Two hours later, Harlow had scored the last standby seat on a flight to Denver.

After boarding the plane and taking her seat—next to the bathroom in the last row—she slipped on her noise-canceling headphones and closed her eyes, hoping Michael Bublé's smooth vocals would soothe her ragged thoughts. Or better yet, lull her to sleep.

But her mind had other ideas. Like reminding her of the first time she'd seen one gruff cowboy named Hugh Pritchett.

Dammit. She did not want to think about him or that summer. But her brain had already rewound the clock and the memories rushed back . . .

THREE YEARS EARLIER . . .

WELCOME TO MUDDY GAP, WYOMING. POPULATION . . . Harlow squinted at the sign. Looked like someone had shot out the number of residents. That didn't bode well.

But with her arrival the population was one more than yesterday. Maybe they'd get a new sign.

She drove through the impressive entrance to the Split Rock Ranch and Resort and parked her Prius in the nearly empty lot. She climbed out, stunned by the pocket of beauty surrounding the Western resort. After traveling through miles of prairie and farmland en route from Chicago, she'd hit the High Plains desert and the near desolate Wyoming landscape. This wasn't what she'd expected.

The massive building ahead of her was gorgeous and yet didn't detract from the view. Her sister tore out the front door and down the stairs, practically throwing herself at Harlow.

"I'm so happy you're here," Tierney said on a choked sob. "I've missed you so much."

"Samesies. And stop crying or I'll start calling you Teary Tierney instead of Tenacious Tierney."

Tierney stepped back and wiped her eyes. "Sorry. A year is too long for us not to see each other. Promise me that won't happen again."

"I promise," Harlow said offhandedly as she was busy staring at her big sister's big belly. "How's baby Tenor?"

"We're fine." She grinned and smoothed her palms over her baby bump. "I love your nickname for the womb dweller."

"I seriously hope you're considering my suggestions for baby names."

"Jackie Jackson or Jack Jackson? Not happening."

Harlow stuck her tongue out. "Spoilsport. Tierney, this place is amazing." She rubbed her hands together. "I'm betting my digs are equally awesome. I can't wait to see them."

"Now?"

"Yeah. Why not?"

"Don't you want to see where you'll be working first?"

"No. I drove straight through, so I'm seriously close to going comatose."

Tierney's gaze sharpened. "You didn't stop at all?"

"Just for gas and more energy drinks." Harlow squeezed Tierney's hand and felt her anxiety lessening a little.

"Good thing I didn't plan a big 'Welcome to Wyoming' meal for you later tonight."

"Very lucky for me, since you're a horrible cook."

"I'm better than I used to be."

Harlow raised both eyebrows.

"Okay, fine, Renner does most of the cooking."

"Where is my handsome brother-in-law?"

"With the foreman down at the barn." Tierney pointed to Harlow's car. "Got room for me to ride along so I can show you the fastest way to get to the cabin?"

"Yep. I travel light, as you know."

They climbed in the car and Tierney had her drive by the row of trailers that made up the employee quarters. After dwelling in a tent for six months, Harlow would've been fine living there. But Tierney had insisted her baby sister move into the small cabin that she and Renner had recently vacated, since they'd moved into their new family-sized house.

She followed Tierney up the river-rock-paved sidewalk and checked out the landscaping. Very minimalist—but not due to Tierney's black thumb. She'd learned water was scarce around here. Since she had experience utilizing native flora and fauna on some of the projects she'd worked on, she approved the resort's choice to incorporate native plants, grasses and rock. Not only was it better ecologically; it showcased the uniqueness of the vegetation rather than using sod to cover up the natural beauty.

Harlow followed her sister into the cabin. The cozy space was all Tierney: elegant without being fussy. A compact kitchen. An open living area.

Tierney pointed to a closed door. "The bedroom and bathroom are through there."

"This place is perfect, T." She hugged her sister from behind. "Thank you for letting me stay here, but you didn't have to leave the furniture. I would've been fine with a camp cot and a beanbag chair."

Tierney sniffed like she didn't believe her. "We bought all new furnishings for the new house. Baby-friendly stuff.

I doubt that glass coffee table could withstand a toddler smacking toys onto it."

"True."

"Lots of happy memories in this house," Tierney said softly.

"No wild parties to taint those memories, I promise."

"I'll never forget the look on Dad's face when he walked in on you and ten of your friends from the homeless shelter doing karaoke."

"He's never had much of a sense of humor, has he?" Harlow paused. "Things are better?"

"Some." Tierney sighed. "He's been checking in on me a couple of times a week since I told him we were pregnant."

"Really?"

"I know it's hard to believe. Part of me wants to tell him it's too late to take on a fatherly role in my life when he couldn't be bothered when I *needed* a father."

Harlow said nothing. Her relationship with their father had been much different—although not better by any stretch. Gene Pratt hadn't had the same expectations for Harlow that he had for his brainiac daughter, Tierney.

"After all the shit Dad pulled when the resort was getting off the ground, Renner has every reason not to want to have anything to do with him. But he claims the biggest reason he won't cut him out of our life is because of me. And surprisingly, Dad respects that Renner is a bigger man than he is."

"You're so lucky. Not only does Renner worship you—he stands up for you."

"And my baby daddy is also one hot cowboy who fills out a pair of Wranglers to perfection."

"Also true. Too bad he doesn't have any brothers."

"Come on. Let's walk down to the barn so you can say hello to him before you sack out."

The steep incline had Harlow gripping Tierney's arm in case her pregnant sister lost her footing.

No surprise that Renner met them at the bottom of the hill, his assessing gaze on his wife. "Darlin', maybe you oughten be comin' down the hill in your condition."

"I'm fine. Harlow had a death grip on me."

"I'd never let anything happen to her," Harlow assured him.

Renner's gaze finally moved from Tierney over to Harlow. His quick half smile didn't reach his piercing blue eyes. "Good to see you, Harlow."

They'd met only four times and Harlow had gotten the impression that Renner didn't care for her. "You too, Renner." Harlow was about to say something else when her gaze was drawn to the big man exiting the barn.

He ambled toward them, his cream-colored cowboy hat angled down, keeping his face in shadow. His arms hung by his sides as his booted feet kicked up dust. He stopped beside Renner and finally looked up.

Her stomach cartwheeled. With his rawboned facial features and penetrating brown eyes, this guy epitomized a steely-eyed gunslinger from the Wild West.

But his gaze didn't remain on Harlow long. After a quick once-over his focus returned to Tierney. The hard line of his mouth softened. "You ain't supposed to be hoofing it down here. That's why Renner got you a damn golf cart."

Tierney scowled. "Stop treating me like I'm a delicate flower. Both of you. I would've had to walk all the way back *up* the hill to get the golf cart, since we drove down to the cabin."

Renner looked at Harlow. "Did you get settled in okay?"

"Not yet. At least I know where I'm going now." Her gaze returned to the man standing beside Renner. The lower half of his face was covered in dark blondish red scruff that stretched down his long neck. When she glanced back up at his eyes, the man was flat-out scowling at her. "Is there a reason you're glaring at me?"

"You've got pink goddamn hair."

"So?"

"So you look like you stuck your head in a cotton candy machine."

"Ooh. Nice one. Not very original, though. Next time try to work in a Pepto-Bismol pink reference instead."

"If you didn't want people lookin' at you, then you oughten dye your hair that wacky color."

She ignored his comment and looked at Renner. "And who is this charming redneck-cum-hairstylist?"

"Hugh Pritchett. He's the livestock manager and my right-hand man." Renner lifted his chin to Hugh. "This is my sister-in-law, Harlow Pratt. She'll be workin' at the Split Rock this summer."

Just then another guy exited the barn. He stopped, grinned at her and hustled up the hill. When he reached her, he thrust out his hand. "You must be Harlow. Tierney's told me all about you. I'm Tobin Hale. I do all the crap jobs around here that no one else wants to do."

"It's nice to meet you, Tobin."

He squinted at her and smiled. "The Mud Lilies are gonna love you with that wild-ass hair."

"What are the Mud Lilies?"

"It's a group of the best ladies you'll ever meet." Tobin dropped his voice to a whisper. "They're all retired and widowed, but that don't stop them from bein' the biggest troublemakers in the county."

"I can't wait to meet them."

"Unless you're meeting up with them tonight, they ain't gonna see your pink hair. No offense, Harlow, but that's gotta go if you're working here," Renner said.

Good thing she'd planned for that. "I assume you want the piercings out too?"

"I'd have her leave in the nose ring, Ren," Hugh drawled. "That way if she gets outta line, you can attach a chain to it and use it as a come-along."

Harlow's mouth dropped open. "Was that supposed to be funny?"

He shrugged those broad shoulders.

Tobin stepped between them. "Ignore Hugh. His ex-wife got his sense of humor in the divorce settlement." He looked over at Renner. "I know the boss will want his wife to put her feet up, so I'll show you around the rest of the place."

Flirting was second nature to her; she thought nothing of smiling up at Tobin as she threaded her arm through his. Such a cutie with that glorious grin, not to mention the devilish twinkle in his eyes. "Lead on."

"My pleasure."

She glanced over her shoulder at her sister—the only one of the trio who showed any amusement. "See you later."

"We've got a nine A.M. meeting to go over job expectations," Renner said.

"I'll be there with bells on."